ICARUS FLYING

The Tragical Story of Christopher Marlowe

Liam Maguire resides on the edge of London, having lived on the edge of many things, including politics, religion, penury, prison, wholesome health and marriage.

Previous publications include the novel The Wicked Stepchildren (an Ormond book), The Satie Suite (poetry), short stories, plays, critiques and other literary artefacts.

ORMOND BOOKS IN PRINT
The Wicked Stepchildren

ORMOND BOOKS IN PREPARATION
The Marinated Man
The Purification

ICARUS FLYING
The Tragical Story of Christopher Marlowe

LIAM MAGUIRE

ORMOND BOOKS

Published by ORMOND BOOKS 1993
9 Lower Morden Lane, Morden Park, Surrey SM4 4SE

Copyright © 1993 Liam Maguire

All rights reserved

ISBN 0 9520081 1 4

Printed and bound by Intype, London

This book is sold subject to the condition that
it shall not, by way of trade or otherwise, be
lent, resold, hired out, or otherwise be
circulated without the publisher's prior
consent in any form of binding or cover other
than that in which it is published and without
a similar condition including this condition
being imposed on the subsequent purchaser.

Cut is the branch that might have grown full straight,
And burned is Apollo's laurel bough,
That sometime grew within this learned man.

Christopher Marlowe: Doctor Faustus.

Destiny never defames itself but when she lets an excellent poet die.

Thomas Nashe: The Unfortunate Traveller.

Neat Marlowe, bathed in Thespian springs,
Had in him those brave translunary things
That the first poets had: his raptures were
All air and fire, which made his verses clear;
For that fine madness still he did retain
Which rightly should possess a poet's brain.

Michael Drayton: To Henry Reynolds, of Poets and Poesy.

Chapter one

"I AM Christopher Marlowe. Do you need proof? I am not dead."

The young woman on the pallet moaned and plucked at the shredded edge of the blanket. His sudden declaration seemed to have frightened her.

"Forgive me, Helen." The evening sun shone through the slit window on to her face and tinted the dead-white skin with a pale red hue. "See, see where Christ's blood streams in the firmament." He shivered. "Oh God, am I going mad? Spare me, sweet Yesu, in your infinite mercy, that final humiliation."

The young woman moaned again. "I burn! I thirst!"

"I'll fetch some water. I once lodged in this hovel." Though his limbs were constrained by a mesh of pain, he staggered across the room, pulled back the drape in the doorway and returned with a leather bucket. "There's very little left." He knelt by the pallet and dipped a corner of the blanket into the pail. "One drop – but half a drop is the measure of God's mercy." He pressed the damp cloth against her lips. The woman's body shook with tremors, her fingers clutched the covering and she turned her face to the wall. "Am I so repulsive then?" he asked.

A church bell rang out a slow peal, the doorway drapes quivered and from below a voice called, "Marlowe. Kit Marlowe."

"Who calls my name? What foul beast rises out of the depths of this desolation?" He choked and a violent fit of coughing racked him for nearly a minute. "Will this phlegm strangle me? Is this the threatened divine retribution? Marlowe, the maker of mighty lines, his mouth stopped by a surfeit of mucus, unable to speak his own epilogue, his epitaph unwritten." He looked sharply at the drapes and, though it cost him a rasping agony in his throat, shouted, "Hear me, then, whoever you are. I, Christopher Marlowe, deny your God, your devil, your heaven, your hell. I don't believe."

He waited a few seconds for a reply to his defiance but the only sound was his own harsh breathing. He turned Helen's head towards him and gently closed her eyes. "I won't ask you to look at my face, as pox-scarred as the weathered stone of Saint Paul's. You saw me in my smooth skin. You weren't at fault. The sin was mine. Mea culpa, mea culpa. The tavern whores called me a pretty boy then. Has the pestilence swept them into the grave-pits too? So many have gone. Greene, Watson, Manwood, Walsingham. If I had a rosary, I could tell a bead for every one." He rose and stumbled back to his crouching position in the corner.

The sun's beam had vanished and the dull light of dusk filled the room with shadows. The church bell rang out again.

"O, it strikes, it strikes! Now, body, turn to air, or Lucifer will bear thee quick to hell." The drape was pulled to one side and a figure stood in the doorway. "Let this hour be but a year, a month, a week, a natural day. Repent? And save my soul? I am damned. Where shall I begin? When I was a mewling baby in my mother's arms? Cursed be the parents that engendered me. Or when I ran, an eager schoolboy, through Canterbury's dark passages, a pilgrim for learning, to my wooden bench in King's School? Or my Cambridge years? A poor scholar, with precious few coins for bread and beer but richly glutted with learning's golden gifts."

He looked over to where the young woman lay. The watcher in the doorway withdrew and the drape trembled.

"Adders and serpents, let me breathe a while. Ugly hell, gape not. O, usurious fate, have I not repaid my pledge in full? Helen, Helen, your lips suck forth my soul: see, where it flies! You're not Helen. But Helen was a harlot too. Burn, burn the topless towers of Ilium. Listen to my story."

When he spoke again, his voice was reduced to a whisper.

"In the year of the Armada, the Spaniards marched upon the deep and laid the bones of their demented ambitions upon the rocks of our hostile shores. Were my ambitions so demented? To be no more than my own man, neither master nor servitor. To fashion Icarus's waxen wings and fly beyond ignorance and superstition."

Now his voice was like the breath of Death.

"I am Christopher Marlowe. I am not – yet – dead."

Chapter two

One September evening in 1588, a woman stood in her kitchen and sharpened a carving knife on the flat surface of the iron range. She was Catherine Marlowe, mother of the poet and scholar Christopher Marlowe and wife to John Marlowe, master shoemaker and freeman of the city of Canterbury. Without turning, she ordered the kitchen drudge to fetch the water and added the dire threat that if a drop was slopped on the flags the child would have a taste of a hard hand across her clod-head.

When the wispy creature trotted out with the wooden pail, Catherine unhooked a plucked fowl from the wall, slapped it down on the trestle table and chopped off the claws and head. "She'd be as bad as the rest of them, given a morsel of a chance."

The last remark was addressed to Mary May, a widow of mature years who had been in their service for so long that she was but a short breath from being one of the family.

"The ditch-leavings of vagrants are the worse for taking advantage," said Mary. "They'd think nothing of curling their toes under your oven and eating you out of house and home."

"She won't be warming her arse by my fire much longer," Catherine replied.

She separated the innards, threw the waste into a slop-bucket, rinsed the remainder in a basin of salted water, put the gizzard and neck into a stew pot and cut the liver and heart into tiny bits.

"Here am I, a city freeman's wife, toiling and moiling in my own kitchen like any slavey and if it wasn't for you, Mary May, I'd only have that miserable chit, half-deaf and wholly daft, to give me a hand's turn. As for those three lazy lumps upstairs, the less said the better."

She broke two eggs into a basin, added the chopped meat, several handfuls of flour and breadcrumbs, a pinch of salt, a dash of pepper, a sprinkling of herbs, a grated onion, slivers of a crab apple and a cup of water.

"Much promising and little pence is our lot," she continued as she stirred the mixture with a wooden spoon. "While others of little worth and less credit can eat from silver plates and pewter mugs, we must make do with earthenware."

Mary rolled out dough on another table, cut it into circles and laid the round slabs on a flour-dusted metal plate. "And what about your Kit now?" she asked. "With his high degree of education, he's sure to make his mark in the world. Imagine that now, the son of a shoe-maker strutting with the best and the most powerful."

This was a sly dig at her employer's pretensions and a salve to her own envy.

Catherine started to ladle the mixture into the chicken's belly and Mary, offering to hold the fowl's 'merry thought', placed her hand on its breast. When the carcass was stuffed and sewn up, Catherine smeared a pat of butter between its legs and carried it over to the oven in a shallow pot. The women placed their preparations on the shelves, the bread on top and the bird on the bottom, and then relaxed for a few seconds.

"As for Kit," said Catherine, "he's getting beyond himself with his high-faluting nonsense and the reams of rigmarole he's forever scribbling all night."

"I've heard that too much book-learning can give you a turn for the worse," said Mary.

"And when the humour's on him to preach, he dares to tell me, his own mother, it's not a goodly thing to whip that dribble-puss slut when she's unruly. Would you credit that?"

Mary nodded her head wisely. "Yesu only knows what the end of all these new-fangled ideas will be."

Catherine folded her arms over her bosom. "I said to him, I said, my house is my domain and if I must suffer fly-blows and ditch-leavings I'll treat them as I see fit. I tell you, they don't value Christian charity. A swift switch across the bare arse is as good as a sermon any Sunday."

"And did he have an answer to that?"

"Did he, indeed. With all his vulgar Latin, I stopped his mouth when I called upon the holy word of God as laid down in the Bible. There are them, the children of Canaan, who'll be the slaves of slaves and they'll be the hewers of wood and the drawers of water. Who are you to be judge of another's servants?"

"No truer word could be said," agreed Mary. "I recall my husband, God rest his soul – "

"Did you hear that ruckus?" Catherine swept across the floor, gave the drudge – who had just staggered in with the full pail of water – a clout in passing and charged out of the kitchen.

The bellowing came from Catherine's two younger daughters Dorothy and Ann, who were standing on a coffer in the upstairs room and jostling each other to have a better view through the lattice window. The third and eldest daughter Margaret was sitting by the dole cupboard with an embroidery frame on her lap. She pricked her finger and swore. "God's blast on this poor light and you, too, Kit Marlowe, for your deafness." She raised her head to call out but at that moment her brother appeared in the doorway. "There you are at long last. There's a lad out front asking for you."

Christopher had the skinniest frame in the family. He was such a sickly-pale contrast to his burly, strapping sisters that a stranger might imagine he had been born and bred between the pages of a book rather than sired by a Canterbury tradesman and borne by a sturdy Dover woman who numbered pirates and smugglers among her fishermen forbears.

At that moment the window-watchers, spluttering with laughter at the sight of a codpiece apparently stuffed with straw, tumbled off their perch as Catherine dashed in. "What's this hullabaloo?" She lashed the two girls with a wet dish cloth and their giggles turned to cries for mercy as they scrambled to their feet and cowered in a corner. Catherine gave the pair a final swipe and turned to Margaret. "And who's that half-pint lout leaning against our post?"

"He's asking for our Kit. I'll call him up if you wish."

"You'll do no such thing," snapped Catherine. "I'll not have every Canterbury patch-arsed loon traipsing through my house, dung-stinking scruffs from the Shambles. Bad enough with your father's drunken cronies banging on the door. Go down, Kit, and see what he wants. Mind you, when the likes of him call again he calls at the back door not the front."

The gangling youth slouching by the door jamb and picking his nose wore an assortment of filthy and tattered clothes that included, to Christopher's surprise, a King's School jacket.

"I know your coat but not your face," said Christopher.

The tumult of the narrow street was not conducive to polite conversation. Carts, drays and wains trundled on the cobbles, pedlars, beggars and bawdy-baskets importuned every passer-by with whining and wheedling cries while yapping dogs, a herd of grunting pigs, cackling fowl in wicker baskets and the mournful mooing of udder-filled cows added their tunes to the medley. The vesper chimes of St Mary Bredman's church carried the whiff of the High Street fish market through the hubbub.

The youth glowered. "Are you Kit Marlowe?"

"Are you familiar with Caesar, Sallust, Livy?"

"Never heard of them. I'm looking for Kit Marlowe."

"You're no King's scholar," Christopher said. "Where did you thieve that?" He made to grab the coat but the boy dodged him and took up a truculent stand two feet away.

"Keep your paws off me. If you're Marlowe, say so. If not, go piss up your mother's apron."

"I'm Kit Marlowe. What's it to you?"

"Nothing to me. You're to be at the George Tavern within the hour without fail."

"Why should I be?" Christopher roughly shook the devalued King's School jacket.

"Lay off, lay off and I'll tell you," whined the messenger. "Two men said so. I never saw them before. One's a fat-arse with a purple nose and the other's a scraggy tough from London. Lard-belly said to remind you about Rheims, I think, and your visit to Paris." He glanced across the street. "God's blast, they're over there waiting for you."

Christopher turned to look but a lumbering wagon obscured the view. The youth squirmed free, promised an early return visit with his numerous brothers and ran off. When the wagon passed, Christopher saw none there that he knew or cared to know.

That evening a victory celebration was being held in the George Tavern by The Two Hundred, the local militia. It was their fourth such indulgence since news of the Armada's scattering had reached the town.

A master cooper sang their marching song in a deep baritone and at the conclusion of each stanza, the assembly roared the chorus: –

'Then answer we one and all,/ Fear not, O Glorious Queen:/ The Bowmen of Canterbury/ Will guard our island green.'

Pots of ale followed in a more conclusive procession than the line of Spanish galleons in the English Channel.

At the far end of the tavern, two men stared glumly at the cup-sodden bravadoes. While the cooper was detailing the much-vaunted courage of The Two Hundred in the fourteenth stanza, the portlier man of the pair beckoned to the potboy.

"Has Marlowe come yet?" he asked.

"Marlowe come yet?" wheezed the toothless one. "He's been here from the first breaching of the barrel and he'll be here till the last drop through the bung hole. Didn't I tell so when you asked before? He's over there."

"Devil take him, I can't see Kit Marlowe among those windbags," said Richard Baines. His podgy jowls gave him the look of an angry toad, his piggy eyes squinted and his purple nose, a relic from a rat bite suffered in Rheims Gaol, seemed to glow.

"We did wrong," grumbled his pug-faced companion Richard Chomley, "not to grab him when the boy drew him out of the house."

"What, in full sight and sound of the whole street? Are you mad?"

"No less mad than sitting here listening to them bladderskites. We're ordered to take Marlowe to Scadbury House one way or the other and we'll – "

The anthem came to a thunderous close and the revellers began to disperse. The potboy was talking to a stooped man and they both looked over to where Baines and Chomley were sitting.

"Marlowe's gone out to the back," the waiting pair were told, "and he'll be with you presently. There'll be a right flood and enough piss in the barrels to keep the bleachers happy for a month or so."

Baines was puzzled. "Was that Marlowe?"

The ancient was aghast that anyone should doubt his word. "My eyes are not so scurvy-blasted that I don't know Marlowe. If you won't take my word for it, ask Master Capal and Master Portall. And now I'd be obliged if you'd pay the reckoning."

"Toss him some coins, Chomley," said Baines.

"You toss-pot, you pay him. I've nothing in my poke till I go to Essex for what I'm owed."

"Essex, is it, Chomley? Do we speak of the salt marshes of Essex or the unsalted march of the Earl of Essex, sly Dick?"

Chomley grimaced and was about to reply but Baines signalled him to be quiet and muttered, "Let's hear what these old codgers have to say."

With that remarkable ability of skinny vessels to hold vast quantities of liquid, the two tradesmen Capal and Portall had stood their ground with replenished pots.

Portall was talking. "And who on earth would have those scolds and common swearers? If it ever came to a match, devil a bit they'd have in their dowry chests with most of their substance gone on law-suits."

"True, true, I've heard it said myself they haven't three brass farthings to rub together and it's not only law-suits that's wasted their fortune. Goodman Marlowe is more attentive to the business of others than to his own trade. He says he's a freeman of Canterbury, as important as you like. As if stirring another's fire bakes bread for your own table."

"And what about his son Kit?"

"Him!" Capal snorted. "After all Marlowe's braggart talk, that young tearaway has more time for wandering players and other vagabonds than seeking a place of honour. Not that honour would sit easy on that lad, from the tales I've heard. Consorting with enemies of our faith and kingdom, I've been told, and nearly losing his place in Cambridge. Nothing was ever proved but there's no smoke without fire."

The reappearance of their erstwhile comrade, still fumbling with the draw-strings of his breeches, brought the gossip to an end. They gave him a fulsome welcome and expressed a desire to walk part of the way home with him, but he, with a nod towards Chomley and Baines, replied that he had very important business to discuss. With a nudge, a wink and a hearty backslap, the tradesmen went home to their wives.

A barely smothered belch rippled through Marlowe's lips as he leaned heavily on the table. "Gentlemen, how may I be of service to you?"

"I fear there's an error here." Baines adopted the smooth tone normally used for overbearing officials of limited authority and intellect. "We asked the potboy if Marlowe had arrived but the old fool, who has as much sense in his head as teeth in his mouth, mistook or misheard our question and accosted you."

"Hold your horses there, hold your horses. I'm Marlowe, John Marlowe, master shoemaker and freeman of the city of Canterbury. If you have business with Marlowe, I'm your man. Speak on." He staggered and slumped down on the seat.

"I'll be brief – " Baines began.

"Life itself is brief," said John Marlowe loudly and emitted a lugubrious sigh. "For what is life but a sparrow flying in one window of an empty church and out the other. These very words I said to me own son and heir, Kit Marlowe."

"Kit Marlowe is your son? Was he a scholar of Cambridge?"

"And a very good scholar at that and let no conniver, distractor or detractor tell you differently. Mind you, with all his learning, he doesn't know his upper from his lower. By St Crispin, we're enjoined to sew the heel well-hemmed or we'll go hell for leather and hang as high as Haman."

"We wanted to speak to your son Kit."

"Why didn't you say so before now instead of all this fiddle-faddle nonsense about sparrows and – and – never heard such tomfoolery in all my blessed life." He glared at them in a bleary-eyed attempt to focus on their faces. "Why are you waiting in this piss-hole for Kit? Respectable people knock on our door instead of skulking among these whoresons and – " The befuddled man struggled to his feet and swayed.

Chomley growled with impatience but Baines overlaid his feelings with the mantle of polite speech. "We'll do as you suggest and ask Kit out for a midnight stroll."

"You can't do that," said John Marlowe, smirking inanely. "The curfew will put a stop to your gallop. And don't have high hopes of meeting with him tomorrow. At least, not here in Canterbury, my fine buckoes. At cock crow, he's off, bag and baggage, to London." He slowly turned from them. "Must leave you, gentlemen, pleasure to have met you – " He stumbled out of the tavern, singing The Bowmen of Canterbury like a lilting dirge.

Robin Poley, gentleman, adventurer and paid agent to the Secretary of State, sat on a creaky chair in an upstairs room of an inn outside the West Gate of Canterbury and glared with disdain at the two men standing in front of him. His narrow face, dark eyes, overlong nose and sallow skin confirmed, for many, the rumour of Spanish blood in his veins.

"Fools, dolts, buffoons."

"We did our best," Baines pleaded. "What more could we have done?"

"You could hardly have done less," raged Poley, "and if ever I have another occasion for a similar task I'll send a raw stable lad, a simple horse-minder, rather than two donkeys. I ordered you to persuade Christopher Marlowe to present himself at Scadbury House and to express our willingness to accompany him on the journey to Chislehurst. But you couldn't even tempt him to share a drink with you in a nearby tavern. He's never been known to say no to a pot of ale."

In a fit of the sullens, Chomley muttered, "For my part it matters little if Marlowe goes to Scadbury House today, tomorrow or next week."

"For my part, you matter little today, tomorrow or next week," snapped Poley.

"I've always given good service for my pay, though that matter puts little in my purse."

"Your purse never hangs empty, though you may hang fully for your two-fold services."

Chomley scowled at Baines. "You weren't slow to tittle-tattle. I protest, when I said Essex – "

"Enough of this." Poley stood up. "You protest like a rumpled maid, but what else should a spy do but listen, learn and inform? Go to that red Welsh fox if you like. I won't retain you further in my service." He held out a coin to the rejected hireling. "Take this in quittance and be thankful to God's infinite mercy your quittance pay is not of another coin. It will be if our paths cross again."

Chomley hesitated as if to say more but took the coin and stomped out of the room. Outside he cursed his big mouth and Baines and then, after looking up and down the hall, put his ear to a crack in the door.

"We won't leave it to chance to discover when the Marlowes rise from their sweaty beds," said Poley decisively. "Perch yourself on a nag and wait till you see first light in their house. Then return to me and we'll ride out to greet our dear friend on the London Road."

"What about the curfew?"

"You're on state business. I'll give you a warrant to that effect."

When Christopher came downstairs for a bite to eat and a drink, Dorothy and Ann, under the strident supervision of Catherine, were folding linen sheets by the dole cupboard. Margaret pushed past him, holding aloft a trident pricket candleholder with white wax candles stuck on the points.

"Three virgins," he said, "untouched by passion's flame. I reckon they cost a pretty penny."

"Less than it does to keep you intact," Margaret retorted. She lifted her skirt to her knees, threw one leg over the form and sat down.

"Meg, Meg, if I've told you once, I've told you a thousand times," scolded Catherine, "maidens don't sit astride a bench as if they're louts riding a mare. Where's the virtue in your wits?"

Margaret pouted. "My wits sit in my head and my virtue lies alone in my bed. Who's taken my embroidery?"

Dorothy dropped the frame on the table. "You'll lose your wits before you part with your maidenhead with your cock-a-hoop virtue."

"And which is the cock and which is the hoop?" Ann asked. "I've never yet seen a mare practising to ride a lout."

"Shut up and put your backs into your labours." Catherine hustled the younger girls round the room. "Was there ever a mother so cursed with such harridans? This house is more like a cockpit than a roost of pullets." A loud rat-tat-tat shook the front door. "Yesu, who could be calling at this hour? Dorothy, stir your buttocks and see who's disturbing the night. And you, Ann, go fetch your father. He's the worse for wear from his carousing and he's sitting beyond, clucking like a broody hen."

Dorothy stopped in the doorway. "If we're all fowls of a contrary nature, what about Kit?"

"He's our prize capon," Ann sneered as she spurted out of the room.

"Her tongue is sharp enough to cut a measure of cloth for her shroud," Catherine muttered.

The two girls returned in their usual bustling hurry.

"Who was it then?" Catherine asked.

Dorothy shrugged her shoulders. "I never laid eyes on him before. By the shape of him, I'd say he's a roaring ruffian. Father is having a word with the tow-head."

As if called forth from a tomb, John Marlowe shambled in and slumped down at the head of the table. His jowls sagged, his eyelids drooped and his hands hung down between his knees like the giant claws of a dead crow.

The feminine tumult did not abate with his entrance. The first to receive his ill-focussed glare was Margaret. "What have we here? A bawling bawdy-basket ready to roar her trade all over the town with her sluttish shift trailing in the dung? As if I hadn't enough trouble without these shrews. Where's them other baggages?" Ann and Dorothy sat down at the table and Catherine poured out wine. "Wine? Is it high day or holy day?"

"It's Kit's last day and night," his wife replied, "before he traipses off to London to live among strangers." She hesitated. "And what about your caller? What was his business?" On more than one occasion an enraged creditor had come banging at their door with angry words and loud threats and shaming her in front of the neighbours.

"He came about Kit." John scowled at Christopher. "There you are and where have you been hiding the whole living day, leaving me to answer all the daft questions? When's your Kit going to settle down? Has he obtained a good position now he's crammed with Cambridge learning? And to cap it all, I've had them two rogues bothering me in The George with their blabbering on about sparrows in empty churches and them asking if you'd care for a midnight stroll in the cloisters."

"Who were they?" Christopher asked with contrived casualness.

"How the devil would I know? One was a man with more pork than port to his belly – mind you, he had a fine turn to his speech – and the other was no more than a thick-tongued rough from the alleys. Nice companions, I must say, for a scholar. 'Tell Kit Marlowe,' said that alley-rough at the door, 'to take care on the London road tomorrow.' "

"You're not in any trouble, are you, Kit?" asked his mother anxiously.

"No more trouble than it costs to keep body and soul together," he replied lightly. "I know the pair. They're just lads, one-time chamber mates of mine from Cambridge with more of a gut for beer than a stomach for learning. No doubt they're vext I didn't spend the day drinking."

For all her aggressiveness, Catherine was easily satisfied. With a baleful glance at her husband, she remarked that she wished others would give the alehouse a miss when there was work waiting on the bench.

John ignored her sideways swipe and snorted. "They're hairy lads if I ever saw any. As for the cut of the fat lad, I'd say he was shaped by Satan and there's the touch of the Papist priest behind that onion nose."

Christopher was startled by his father's acuteness. He knew Baines only too well. A low, conniving informer, a one-time ordained priest, Baines had been a spy in the pay of the Secretary of State, Walsingham. But then he himself was hardly in a position to cast stones in that direction.

Mary May brought in food and the girls helped themselves to wine. They became more pot-valiant by the minute while their father prated on about the way times were changing for the worse.

Christopher brooded upon the brief visit. Was it a warning or a threat? Either way, he resolved to keep his sword on hand for tomorrow's journey.

Chapter three

"Kit, Kit, if you must go away today, for God's sake be up and about. The wagon's here and there's food on the table."

Christopher groaned and shivered. "What hour is it?" he asked. A ball of acid rolled in the pit of his stomach.

"A fine hour for foxes and a bad hour for sots," Catherine retorted. "You look poorly." She bent over to look into his barely opened eyes. "And is it any wonder, with you and your windbag-father up half the night, prattling like a pair of gossips and guzzling my best Rhenish wine. I wouldn't mind so much but I'd laid it aside for the benefit of respectable callers. Not that we welcome many of them nowadays." She stood in the doorway and for a second allowed her features to carry a glance of maternal concern. "I've packed your linen neat and clean and put a plump cooked chicken in with the victuals. God only knows, you'd gallivant off to London in rags and tatters and be famished into the bargain if I hadn't my health and strength."

When she had gone, he flung off the blanket and dashed downstairs to the backyard to empty his bladder. Sighing with relief, he had a final shake and then sloshed rainwater on his face. Just then he heard the clop-clop of a horse and saw a cloaked rider passing by the gate. "I'm not the only clown venturing out this dank morning," he thought.

True to her word, Catherine had prepared a massive breakfast. "Mind you eat every scrap," she said. "It'll do you the world of good."

Ann lurched into the room, her long nightdress crumpled round her body and her hair bushed on her head like a wild furze. "God's nail, what's the hour?" A hearty yawn revealed a full set of brown teeth. St George's church bell chimed out three strokes. "By the blood of all the martyrs, is it that early? With your unholy ructions and stomping and shouting, I thought the last trump had sounded."

"Back to your bed," Catherine ordered. "Have you no shame, showing yourself like that in front of your brother?"

The girl scratched her thighs and sat down. "There's not a halfpenny's worth he'd see with this attire and what matters if he did and him my brother. Besides, I don't think Kit has much inclination for womanly flesh." She grabbed a fistful of meat from his plate and stuffed it into her mouth. Between hard swallowing and chewing, she asked, "And why are we roused before the cock's awake?"

"You know well enough, you slummock. Kit's off to London this day."

"Ah yes, our mallard is away to waddle in the London sludge and leave the Canterbury muck to the ducklings."

Mary May bustled in. "Your pardon, Mistress Marlowe, but Jem the Carter fears he'll miss the convoy on the road. And another thing, he's proving hard in the head in the matter of the drudge and swears he'll pay no more than two pence."

"He does, does he? Then I'll swear on a different Bible he'll take what I give him." Catherine swept out of the room, followed closely by Mary May.

Ann gave vent to a melodramatic sigh. "I wish it was me and not the skivvy off to London. What does she know of grand living, I ask you? She's the living spit of a tinker's ditch-leavings. If it was me, I'd wash my hands and face every day and sprinkle my bodice with rose water and then you'd hear fine gentlemen say, 'Who's the maid with the milk-cream skin and raven hair?' and I'd give them such a look as much as to say, 'My favours are beyond your paltry gifts.' " She sighed again and sopped up the gravy from his plate with a lump of bread. "But I'm spoken for, bad cest to the day, and I'll be a tavern-keeper's wife up to my elbows in sour ale, toss-pots and mewling babies."

She pulled back her sleeve and shoved a muscular arm under Christopher's nose.

"Is this not a delicate hand with the grace and beauty of a lady-in-waiting?" The same 'delicate' hand gripped his wrist. "Take me with you, Kit, take me with you," she demanded fiercely. "I'll wash your clothes and have food ready on your table every day. By God's oath, Kit, I promise I'll never be a hindrance to you.

Oh, if I were a man, I'd wear breeches and bucklers and board ship for the Americays but I'm not and there's no disguising it. By Yesu, I'd sell my soul to old Beelzebub if he'd magic me to them new-found-lands. Will you take me with you, Kit?"

Her brother found her intensity oppressive. He pulled his arm free and stood up.

"Don't covenant your soul for fripperies. There's more treasures to be had than you could find in the Americays, if only you had the spirit to seek them out."

"Where are they?" Her eyes dilated and shone with a spark of greed.

"In books."

Her bright expression dulled with chagrin. "Books, Kit Marlowe? And have your ranting rhymes and your rampaging shepherds striving to be kings brought you riches? Has your limping Tamburlaine filled your purse or even your belly?" She stuffed another morsel of his food into her mouth and dismissed him with an imperious flick of her hand. "Clear off to the sewers of London and take the slavey with you, for all I care. There's so little flesh on her bones that she'd be mistaken for a lad, and I reckon that's more to your liking."

Jem the Carter's ugly, grime-encrusted face was like a ball of crackled leather; and his bulk was enlarged by layers of sackcloth and shoddy coats tied round his waist with a tarred rope. He and Catherine had just finished haggling when Christopher entered and, judging by his moroseness, he had the worst of the bargain.

"I'm stealing bread from my children's mouths," Jem grumbled. He reached within his many folds for his purse, laid the coins on the table and then went over to a far corner where the child-servant stood shivering in her sparse rags. "Come on then, you worthless whelp," he said and, grabbing the diminutive body by the shoulder, hauled her out to the wagon.

"Where is he taking the chit?" Christopher asked.

"To London, the same as you," Catherine replied, "but not, I pray to God, to the same fortune. That hardneck will sell her to a household where they're in need of a drudge and can afford the cost of keeping her in bread and board."

"It's not fitting to sell a Christian as if she were one of Hawkins' blackamoors."

"As God's my witness, I'm no slaver," retorted Catherine. "I paid good money for that sickly, whining bag of bones at the quarter market and had little return for my precious coins from that day to this."

She ushered him out to the waiting wagon. Jem flicked his whip and shouted, "Let's be going or we'll never catch the convoy."

Suddenly Catherine grasped her son and hugged him to her breasts. "God go with you every step of the way, and with his divine help and mercy, you'll soon make a name for yourself. You're my only son and my only hope."

Lulled by the jogging trot of the horses, the steady rhythm of the creaking wheels and the drone of the carter's voice, Christopher drifted in a doze. The gist of Jem's rambling story was his self-vaunted superiority, both verbal and physical, in a recent conflict with a butcher and a baker. He was prone to interrupt his narration with, "And what do you think he did then, eh? Go on, have a guess. Well, let me tell you, no whoreson crosses Jem the Carter for nothing." Suddenly he reined in the horses, nudged his passenger and said, "Hell's blazes, do you hear what I'm hearing?"

Christopher, shaken into wakefulness, at first heard only the irate muttering of disturbed rooks. Then, as Jem slapped the reins and lashed the animal's flanks with the whip, he became aware of galloping horses coming up from behind.

The wagon lurched forward and the thongs sang and cracked in the air. "Giddap, giddap," Jem shouted. "May Satan's spit scorch their tails. The devil take them Chatham cheaters and Boughton bullies and the whole swarm of rogues and robbers hereabout. I said we should have made an early shift and caught the convoy."

Above the clattering of the cart and the thud of hooves came the shouts of the pursuers. "Ho, there. Stop. Stop."

"I'll stop for nobody," growled Jem. "Mother of God, we'll be stripped of every stitch."

The lead rider galloped past the wagon, pulled up about twenty yards ahead and turned his horse across the path. Jem tugged hard on the reins and, once again, the wagon came to a halt.

"Why didn't you stop?" the rider asked.

"Begging your pardon, sir, we meant no discourtesy to you," said Jem with mock humility. "We've a sick child aboard and we were anxious to find a leech. Come see for yourself, sir, if you doubt my word." He then whispered to Christopher. "There's a cudgel by my feet. When he comes near, lay it across him and I'll drive on the nags."

The first rider did not move but the second horseman approached from the rear and peered into the wagon. "God's truth, there's a whimpering child here."

"Take care not to come too near," said Jem craftily. "We fear she has a contagion."

"And I fear you're a liar," said the man as he grasped the side.

Christopher swung the cudgel and smashed it down near the man's hand. "Then fear this," he said, "and the next blow will make a fearful crack on your thick skull."

The first rider chortled. "Isn't that Kit Marlowe?"

Christopher felt a warning tingle and reached for his sword. "I am Kit Marlowe. What's it to you?"

"How soon you forget old friends, Kit."

Jem did not understand the drift, still thinking of the riders as robbers. "Sirs, we've only boxes and bags of oddments belonging to poor people of the parish who've lost house and home because they couldn't pay their taxes. Nothing of any worth to gentlemen like you. Now if you hurry on ahead, you'll come to wagons groaning with silver and pewter."

"Take your baggage of rags and tatters away with you with all God's speed," said the first rider. "We don't care about them or you. Our concern is with Kit Marlowe."

"And my concern is to bid you farewell and continue my journey," said Christopher. He drew his sword. "If you choose to think differently, I'll take pleasure in pricking your conceit."

"Yesu protect us, let's not be having sword play," pleaded Jem. "I'm a poor man with a houseful of children and I've no stomach for blood-letting."

"Marlowe had less of a stomach for blood-letting when the

Spaniards rode high on the seas," said the second rider. "Where was he then? Hiding behind his mother's apron, I warrant."

"Close your mouth, Baines." The first rider dismounted. "And you, Kit, put away your blade." As he approached, Christopher recognised the dark face and pointed beard. "Have I ever given you cause for quarrel, Kit?"

"Not yet, but setting your cur to bark at my heels could be enough. What do you want from me, Robin Poley?"

"A few private words, Kit. Why don't you step down and we'll confer a few feet from the wagon."

Poley took his arm in a friendly manner and they strolled a few paces along the verge.

"When did we last meet, Kit? Was it in Paris, Rheims, Cambridge? No, no, now I remember. It was when your drama of great rant and rhyme – Tamburlaine, scourge of God, if I recall correctly – was performed in old Burbage's Shoreditch playhouse for the edification of idle apprentices and Moorgate whores."

Baines had ridden up to the wagon and was talking to Jem.

"You know more about Moorgate whores than I, Robin." It was an unkindly reminder of Poley's seduction of a cutler's wife, and the friendly grasp on his arm became a tight pinch. "But surely we've not suddenly met in a muddy lane to exchange pleasant memories?"

"Indeed not. There is one who has a high regard for you and is most anxious about your present state of health and mind."

"Giddap, giddap." The carter's whip cracked, the horses jerked up their heads and the wagon began to trundle down the road. Angry and desperate, Christopher broke his captor's grip to run after the wagon. Baines' mount suddenly blocked his path. "Out of my way, traitor," Christopher shouted. He was grappled from behind, swung around, flung across a ditch and, as he stumbled, pushed against a tree. He turned, fumbling for his sword, and faced Poley's blade held two inches from his throat.

"I warn you, Marlowe, if you value your life, never shout traitor in my hearing." The man's thin face was as sharp as an executioner's axe.

"You delay me with pretence of friendship, then, acting the

roughneck, hold me captive while my books, papers and belongings vanish. What name would you give to that betrayal?"

"Shouldn't we have a close look at those books and papers before they go too far?" Baines asked.

"We'll have none of your prying here, Baines," Poley lowered his sword and stepped back. "And now, Marlowe, if you had the sense and courtesy to show yourself when first asked and not skulk behind your parents' barred door, we could have acted more temperately. We have been commissioned to bear you to Scadbury House by one – need I state his name?" Poley remounted. "It is nothing to me whether I deliver you hale and hearty to the Walsinghams or report, with great sorrow, that your poor bruised body was found foully murdered by the side of the highway.

"Ride behind me till we come to a farmhouse a mile along the road where we have a spare horse for your carriage," he added curtly. "As for your belongings, the carter has been instructed to stow them in your London lodgings. Hurry up." He held out his hand to Christopher. "We've a long journey ahead."

They rode about half a mile in the same direction as the wagon and then turned off left towards the farmhouse. Daylight emerging through the trees cast shadows across the road and a homeward-bound fox hurried across their path with its teeth firmly clasped on the neck of a still-warm goose.

Chapter four

Poley made sure to avoid the London Road and seemed to know every by-way and cart track in the area. In the early afternoon they stopped for a short while at Bluebell Hill to water the horses and eat and drink a modest meal at a nearby tavern. Then they forded a shallow stretch of the River Medway, crossed the Pilgrim's Way and trotted on apace till they were near St Paul's Cray and in sight of Chislehurst. Not a single word was exchanged during the journey. An hour before dusk they entered Scadbury House through the rear grounds. Christopher's captors ushered him up a narrow, winding stairway to a small, bare room. "Rest here, Marlowe," said Poley, "and Thomas Walsingham will be with you presently." When the pair left him – closing the door behind them and turning a key on the outside – Christopher was sure the fat man sniggered.

Christopher's mount had been a gentle old plough-horse but he was no rider. His legs, rump and spine ached. For the first few minutes he paced up and down, in part to exercise his stiff limbs and in part to exorcise his anger and frustration; but then, overcome by weariness of both flesh and spirit, he sat by the crenulated window and stared morosely through the slit. He saw only the circling rooks but he heard the tumult of carriages, horses and shouting.

The key turned and the door opened slowly. "Thomas, why am I – " Christopher began. An ancient lackey shuffled in and laid a pot of ale and a platter of bread and cheese on the table. "Listen, fellow, tell your master, Thomas Walsingham, that I won't – " The old servant stared at him and then shuffled out in the same lop-sided manner. "Hold hard, there." Christopher strode after the disappearing man but when he reached the door, it was slammed against him and the key turned again.

He ignored the food and sat by the window. When the door opened some time later, he did not bother to turn round.

"You haven't eaten, Kit," Poley said. "Have you lost your appetite?"

"I've no appetite for you or your yapping ball of lard."

"Come, Kit, no harsh words. We're only doing our duty."

"And what duty is that?"

Baines replied. "To snare Papist weasels and conniving traitors."

"You poisonous spoiled-priest, how dare you – "

"Pay no heed to that blabbering fool, Kit," Poley said quickly, shutting the door on his henchman.

"It seems to me, Poley, you take marvellous umbrage when the word 'traitor' is dropped near your feet but your dogsbody is allowed to scatter it in all directions."

"The man is a windbag and likes nothing better than to sniff his own fart." Poley sat on the edge of the table, one foot on the floor and the other dangling. "Are we not both men of letters and learning, nurtured in the halls of Cambridge?" he said smoothly. "Surely we should debate in a civil manner on diverse matters."

"A dialogue not too dissimilar to that of Socrates in the garden of Academus. And tell me, does that chalice" – Christopher pointed towards the ale-pot – "contain a measure of hemlock or stale Burton beer?"

"Ever the university wit, Marlowe, but I do hope for your sake, if others question you – "

"Question me? Is this a confessional chamber and you the ordained inquisitor? Where are the thumbscrews and the rack?"

"Quiet, Marlowe, quiet." Poley spoke in low, urgent tones and glanced nervously at the door. "We could be of great help to each other and this I promise you, whatever is said between us shall go no further than these four walls. Tell me, are you at one with the true faith?"

"What an extraordinary man you are, Poley. Do you really imagine I'd confess an allegiance to the Romish Pope and other sworn enemies of our Queen? Didn't you have a bellyful of such conspiracies when you fooled young Babington with your bad faith and sent the fatuous idiot to the gallows? Maybe you regret your sly part in separating Mary's Papist head from the crown of England."

"Rather, it was a harlot's body that was separated from her arrogance." Poley stood up and sucked in his breath. "As for your insolence, Marlowe, in your perversity you've wilfully misunderstood my drift. Perhaps it's to my advantage that you continue to wallow in your sins of ignorance."

"I hold that there is no greater sin than ignorance."

"That's your conceit, Marlowe, but for now I'll give you a warning."

"A warning? Am I to suffer the plague because I've neglected a bouquet of rue?"

"No, Marlowe, your rue will be of a different bouquet. Stinging nettles and belladonna will be the least of your posy. There are many who say – " He cursed at the sound of loud voices outside. "God's blast, he's here."

The door was flung open and Thomas Walsingham strode into the room. "I did not expect you to be here, Poley," he said sharply, "nor did I expect to find a fat lout standing guard at the entrance."

Walsingham moved with the exquisite concentration of one considering his next step in a courtly dance, and his bejewelled hands were in a continuous flutter. These affectations disguised a shrewd and devious person whose undeclared ambition was to be as powerful a man as his uncle Sir Francis Walsingham, Secretary of State.

"We do not need jailers to keep our guests captive. Our warm welcome and generous hospitality is sufficient." He turned a cherubic smile on Christopher. "And their reward to us, dear Kit, is the pleasure of their company."

Christopher was not prepared to sing a new song to this change of tune. "It says little for your welcome when the pleasure of your guest's company is obtained at the point of your hirelings' swords." Poley scowled. "And, indeed, it says even less for your generous hospitality when your guest is caged in this room with alehouse fare for his meat, as if he were an absconding debtor."

"But, my dear Kit," Walsingham cried, "it was not my wish nor my intention – "

Poley muttered, "The Marlowes are no strangers to debtors' cells or rough bread for their supper."

"Hold your tongue, Poley," Walsingham snapped. "You're over-keen to meddle – "

"And question your prisoner," Christopher added mischievously."

"I warned you, Marlowe." Poley gripped his sword hilt. "Be prepared to mumble your Jesuitical prayers of penance – " He stepped forward, but Walsingham languidly intervened.

"Back away, Poley. You won't draw your sword or harm a guest in my house."

"Your guest? Your house?" Poley's rancour pushed him over the edge of insubordination. "You've inherited the Walsingham pride but you've not inherited the Walsingham estate nor their power. Your brother still lives, and he is host to this gathering. As for your so-called guest, you're welcome to him if it's your desire to embrace a dabbler in heresy."

"So I'm a heretic now," said Christopher calmly. "Was that the thrust of your interrogation, Poley?"

Poley and Walsingham faced each other, nose to nose, like a pair of fighting cocks.

"You are impertinent, Poley. By what right did you take upon yourself the office of inquisitor?"

"By the same right you took upon yourself to issue a warrant for Marlowe's apprehension. None of us are above the law unless the Walsinghams presume to be the law."

"It is you that presumes, Poley. You presume on my patience and you presume on our protection. You were to give Kit my invitation to Scadbury and guard him on the dangerous roads. Take care, presumptuous Poley, that your insolence does not become too tartaric for our taste. We may have to put you to one side."

Poley's sallow cheeks paled and his eyes glittered but he made no reply. The cock-pit bout was finished and he retreated with feathers ruffled and spurs unbloodied.

For his part, Thomas was pleased with his easy victory over an intellectual superior who was one step removed from a servant. The smile of a cherubim returned to replace the petulant frown. "Dear Kit, we must make amends for the indignities you've suffered. The fault lay with the messenger and not the message."

"Why was I brought here?"

"To join in our revels. We have raised the rafters of heaven with our thanksgiving for our deliverance from the tyrannical Spaniards, as all good Christians should. We are now gathering our many friends – and success breeds friends like midges on a hot summer evening – to celebrate our famous victory in a more profane manner. But before you join our feast, you and I have various matters to consider. We need something more refreshing than this" – he waved his hand towards the ale and cheese – "drover's fare. I'll have a servant sent up with a jeroboam of our best Spanish wine."

Sullen Poley, as if to make amends for his imprudent remarks, offered the services of Baines.

"No, that's not possible. I ordered him to the stables to see to some fresh horses. The three you rode from Canterbury were quite blown. You may have to ride out again tonight. Do you think he understood? He did not impress me as one who would take to simple orders. Though, from what I've heard, he has gone as far as to take Holy Orders. Do you usually employ one-time Papist priests to give absolution to your spying?" Poley grimaced and seemed as if about to retort. "I dare say you know him better than most and it's never healthy to question closely those who drain our cess-pits. Follow him down, Robin, and see to our wine. Ask for two goblets."

"Two goblets? Why not three?"

"And who would be the third? The Holy Ghost? Kit Marlowe and I have various matters to consider and I've no desire to share our discourse with others. Go to it, Robin."

Poley hesitated as if intending to refuse this mental task. "Thomas Walsingham, you know full well that I – "

Walsingham cut him short. "Robin Poley, I know full well we pay your wages. Do as I command."

At this belated show of authority, the enraged agent turned on his heels and marched out. At the bottom of the stairs, Baines hurried up to him. "What's afoot?" he asked. Poley growled. "The devil's cleft. Keep a weather-eye on our dear friend Marlowe and any of his comrades who come within your sight. He must not know he's favoured with your vigil. I am to receive first report.

I'll have none of your craven letters sent to the Privy Council for the sake of your own advancement."

Walsingham tip-toed over to the door and flung it open. "He's not here. How disappointing. I expected friend Poley to linger for a while by the keyhole but – "

"You owe me an explanation."

"Yes, dear Kit, I do owe you an explanation and I'll repay the debt with accrued interest. Was it only last summer when all factional squabbles, all religious strife, were laid to one side and we were united as never before in our kingdom? In those hot July days, we discovered something to strengthen our sinews and our resolve. We discovered that we were a nation of Englishmen."

He paused and sighed. "But today, Kit, in this urgent age of change, one-time friends are envious foes, boon companions are suspect and we watch each other, every minute, every hour, for a sign, a gesture, an imprudent word to mark the boundary of loyalty and the signposts to our own advantages. The old are no wiser and their palsied hands are weak on the reins, while the young champ on the bit and paw the ground."

"What's this to me?" Christopher asked. "I've no interest in your politics. I had played my part, not with honour but for honourable reasons, when I was at Cambridge. Now I prefer a different stage for my new role."

"Are you so innocent as to imagine the drama finished when the actors strip off their regal clothes? Even a jocular remark in a tavern is noted and reported; embellished, as it flies from mouth to mouth, with subtle tints to suit the teller's colours. I have heard from one who was told by a second who had it as gospel truth from a third that you, Kit Marlowe, spoke fondly of the Roman rituals."

"One day it's Marlowe the atheist, the next he's an heretic, then he's a Papist," Christopher exclaimed. "Will it be Marlowe the Muslim man tomorrow?"

"Hear me out. There were rumours – and rumours – like mushrooms, breed better in the dark – that Marlowe had renounced the world and retreated to his cell to contemplate like a reborn Saint Anthony."

Christopher laughed. "Saint Christopher of Canterbury, the famed anchorite."

"But isn't it true you went into hiding? From whom, from what?"

A spider had completed her web in the window arch and scuttled back to the nook to await her next victim. Christopher gently touched the gossamer to see if she would run out on a fool's errand but the dark lady stayed calm in her retreat.

"If you do not care to answer my question – " Walsingham came over and sat opposite Christopher. "Perhaps you think it not worthy. You cannot deny, Kit, that scholars have a marvellous affinity with the intricate lacework of disputations and that the insidious arguments of the Jesuits have seduced many wayward students, as we know to our cost, from Cambridge and Oxford, into their mesh at Douai, Rheims and Rome." He paused as if waiting for a reply. None came. "Did you visit Rheims, Kit?"

"This is known to Sir Francis. I disturbed my studies to go on a mission at his behest. Come to the point, Thomas. You've been hinting all kinds of things. I want to know whether this is an idle conversation between friends or a prelude to the Star Chamber."

"Take it, Kit, as a conversation between friends but not idle in intent. Others intend less amity. This was why I had you brought here, and for a short while sequestered in this small room. Kit, answer me truthfully and I'll see no harm comes to your person, are you a secret Roman Catholic?"

"God's nails, Thomas, was all this huffing, puffing and blowing merely to discover whether Marlowe genuflected to the East or the West? If you must know – "

The door was pushed open and the wizened lackey entered with two goblets and a flagon of wine.

"Have no fear about speaking in front of Jack," Walsingham said suavely. "He spent ten years captive on a Spanish galley and has neither speech nor hearing." When the old man hobbled out with the spurned food, Walsingham poured drinks. "We'll be pleasured steep in this Spanish wine and drink to their eternal damnation. They pulled out Jack's tongue for speaking heresy according to their lights but we are free to debate within the limits of our conscience. Kit, can you prove you are not a Catholic?"

"Can I prove I'm not a witch? A heretic? A heathen? Only that which is can be proved in the test and then only if it can be measured by sight, sound or touch."

"You cannot see, touch or hear God."

"Neither can I hear, see or touch the air but if I stopped my mouth and nose I would choke for the lack of the gas."

"There is a test of more certainty. Prove you are not a Papist by professing the contrary."

"And what is contrary to a Papist? A Protestant? No, by my faith, they are different sides of the Janus coin. Each prates prayers to an all-forgiving God, thumps their craws, preaches infinite mercy and then sends unfortunate wretches to hell with sword, fire and gallows."

"Stop, Kit, stop. If your auditor were another, rather than me, with less discretion – " Walsingham left the threat unsaid. "But to the point. What could be more contrary to a Papist than the taking of a sworn oath which would bring the anathema of the church down upon one's head?"

"Am I expected to swear allegiance to bright Lucifer?"

"If that's your wish, but it's not my desire to be party to such a blasphemy. Have you heard of a sodality, known to the commonality as the School of Night?"

"In passing, yes. I have also heard of the Society of Jesus."

Walsingham was not a man adept in the art of irony and he stared at Christopher for a whole second before continuing. "Putting that aside, Kit, tell me about the School of Night."

"One said it is a cabal of dabbling dodderers who by alchemical refluxes and distillations seek out forbidden knowledge. As far as I'm concerned, all knowledge should be biddable. A second said it was a coven of Satanic followers dancing stark naked by the light of the full moon. That should be a sight for sore eyes. A third told me it was a fraternity who sought to further learning by discourse in small rooms. Why discourse in small rooms when the streets are crowded with ignoramuses?"

"Your third informant was nearer the mark. Our sodality, call it what you will, contains men of power, men of wisdom and men of wealth, and it is our purpose, by means of debate, experiment and adventures of discovery, to enrich and strengthen our kingdom under our glorious Queen, so that it becomes a wonder to behold and the envy of all other nations."

"A laudable aim worthy of every good and true Englishman."

Once again Walsingham missed the irony. He became quite excited. "Dear Kit, I am so happy that you and I are of the same mind. I intend to nominate you as candidate for our brotherhood. But – " he now turned solemn. "Be aware, by swearing our stern and dreadful oath of fidelity to the fraternity you'll abjure all allegiance to the Roman Church. It is, as I said, a test to the contrary."

"As adjure is contrary to abjure. But Thomas, I did say I have no wish to be part of any faction. What if I fail to conjure the will to swear your oath?"

"It shall be confirmation to some of the tales of your suspected Papist preferences and will deprive you of our protection if the Privy Council seek to question you."

Christopher lost no time in coming to a decision. "When will I be inducted?"

"After our revels and our feast, our lodge assembles to consider possible novices. Let's make an end of the wine."

Chapter five

The feast was well on its way when Christopher was ushered to his seat at the long table. The noise of the pot-valiant crowd nearly drowned the madrigals and canzonets played in the gallery. Thomas Morley, the recently appointed organist to St Giles Cripplegate, frowned down upon the revellers. Garish jugglers capered in the middle of the great hall while several lean and shaggy hounds snuffled at their feet for tit-bits.

Christopher felt as uncouth and as clumsy as Jem the Carter among the ebullient gallants.

His two neighbours lobbed jokes and acerbic comments at each other over his head. When one spattered his left cheek with a wet witticism, Christopher angrily protested. "Sir, my ear isn't a trumpet for your babble."

The offender looked at him haughtily. "If our conversation is beyond you, take your proper place among the draggletails and kitchen scullions. Their rude speech would surely be more to your rank taste." Christopher was lost for a reply. "What? Are you dumbstruck? Shame on Christopher Marlowe. You don't merit your fame for mighty lines if you're sluggish with a sharp retort."

"You know me?"

"I've been led to believe you're Marlowe. What brilliant talk we'd have, I thought, but I fear I was mistaken. There's more chat from a jay."

"Since you chatter like a jay, dress like a peacock and squawk like a parrot, I'll take wing —" Christopher half-rose from the seat, "and leave you to ruffle your feathers with the other fowls."

The man laughed. "Throw away your wrath. I wanted to end your dour silence." Not wishing to appear churlish, Christopher sat down again. "Let's be familiar and make a festival of our meeting. I am Nicholas Skeres, disreputable son of a London merchant tailor; the obverse of you, a highly reputable son of a master shoemaker. And that rapscallion by your right haunch, who's now guzzling the mutton as if it were the lamb of God, he is Ingram Frizer."

Frizer wiped the grease from his mouth with his sleeve and asked, "Are you returning to London, Marlowe?"

"I had hopes to be in London tonight but Thomas Walsingham persuaded me to stay for the feast."

Skeres laughed again. "When they wish, the Walsinghams can be most persuasive."

"When I was last in London I visited the Shoreditch playhouse," said Frizer, "to take in whatever diversions those ranting actors had devised. I swear, if I gathered one flea I gathered a thousand." He brushed his lace-frill with simulated disgust. "There was such a concourse of bawdy-baskets, scruffy rowdies, idle apprentices and moth-eaten scholars, I could scarce hear Ned Alleyn prate his rousing rigamarole and, God knows, he bawls enough to turn the ships in Greenwich Reaches."

"What was the drama?" Christopher asked.

"Oh, a middling play of a mad shepherd and his goat, concocted, I believe, by one Thomas Kyd."

"There I differ," said Skeres. "That goat was no Kyd who led the flock to slaughter, but Marlowe here who caused the Scythian wool to fly."

Frizer stood up, holding aloft the bone he had been chawing, and began to orate in the manner of a third-rate actor.

"And ever still, from ragged-arsed groundlings to silk and satin nobles, came a tumult of riotous cries in dreadful fury for the scourge of God, crazed, impious Tambulaine the Great, in all his terrible lust for unbridled power; so given fearful voice in Christopher Marlowe's sculptured verse, hewn, as it were, from ravished Rome's abandoned Latin stones."

Christopher joined in the mocking applause for this histrionic foray. He ate like a starveling.

Fire-eaters and tumblers took to the floor and the musicians and singers strove harder to be heard. Mounds of beef, mutton, veal, capons, salmon, trout, swans, sparrows and larks and heaps of salted, peppered and buttered cabbage and carrots were demolished and disappeared in the space of ten madrigals. After the meat came the puddings and men and women of all ranks scooped the steaming balls of suet embedded with raisins and apples into their maws with hands and spoons; only pausing in their labours to wash down the mouthfuls with draughts of ale and wine. Hardly had the final lump disappeared than the servants hurried in with trays of tarts, conserves and jellies. The last was greeted with cried of admiration for the cooks' cunningly shaped images of birds, flowers and beasts. There was only one awkward moment when a dish of white and tangerine jellies were placed on the top table.

These were the colours of the Earl of Essex, the Walsinghams' deadly rival in the jostling for power. Sir Francis' daughter saved the day and the cook's neck by taking the dish for herself and announcing that, "Though she was but a woman she had the belly of a king." A few laughed at this allusion but others preferred to rid the world of the remaining confections.

When the platters were finally licked clean, the trestle tables removed and the oak tables covered with carpets, the bloated diners wandered from group to group. The privies were in constant use, but such was the stench that the more fastidious made use of the vegetable garden.

Returning from a second visit to the cabbage patch, Christopher was startled by a small explosion coming from a recess. Peering into the gloom, he saw a matronly dame bedecked in taffeta and silk and weighed down with jewels and beads. She was sobbing and farting and her two similarly-proportioned companions were holding her arms and making clucking, consoling noises.

"What is the matter, dear lady?" he asked.

Her jowls wobbled as she raised her face but then, presuming an inferior rank from his simple clothes, her thin lips snapped shut and her friends swung their bottoms round like a pair of heavy curtains.

"There's nothing to be done for her." Poley had silently approached. "Unless you have a mind to cuddle the widow's withered withers." He smirked at his bad pun as he linked arms with Christopher and they both strolled away. "The old mare, a distant cousin of the Walsingham stable, trotted here with her hobbled sire but he dipped his nose too deep in the trough and now awaits the knacker's men. May his soul rest in peace as, with bad debts, mortgages and ill-written wills, his estate now surely lies in pieces."

When they re-entered the great hall, Lady Frances was dancing a lively 'la volta' with Ingram Frizer. It was a rigorous gallivant that allowed certain familiarities in public which would never be tolerated in private. The onlookers were loud in their praises for the leaps, twists and showy footwork of the panting pair. When several couples took to the floor for the next dance, misleadingly called 'sink-a-pace', Poley manoeuvred Christopher to a far corner.

"Look, how they disport and stuff their craws without a thought for the unfortunate sailors who faced our enemies and now crawl through the streets of Ramsgate begging for a crust." Poley scowled as the music began to a burst of applause. "Oh ye of little faith. But yesterday they cringed, whimpered and supplicated deliverance and now they hop and hulloo like devils freed for the nonce from the flames of hell. I tell you, Marlowe, they fear more for their earthly estate than their immortal souls. Any why? Because they have, through the agency of false and perverted doctrines, elevated their worldly realms to be of the Elect and so elect to be God's chosen people, as it was with the wandering Israelites."

Christopher had little patience for sectarian arguments and less for preachers and their sermons.

"To me, the Jews were foolish to listen to that conjuror, Moses," he said, "and to follow him for forty years in the desert when the journey could have been undertaken in less than a year. Let whosoever desires it be elected in their place and God give them good speed on their travels."

Poley's glower vanished. "Remember, Marlowe, that fat, farting dame wallowing in tears for her blown and departed husband? I think it was the raisin pudding that aided his exit."

"And how exquisite was the aroma from her obsequies' censer."

"Let us pray our last farewell smells sweeter. Her late lord and master, in his youth, was called for the priesthood and to that purpose thumbed through his Latin grammar. When King Harry divorced the monks from their possessions, our good man forsook his adeum qui latificat to wed his present widow and with her marriage portion bought a parcel of sanctified soil. Then, when humble people, mean in property but great in faith, perished in Queen Mary's Smithfield fires, he once more bent a reverend knee to mumble ave maria. But when our glorious Queen ascended the throne a good Protestant he became and cried, 'God save Queen Bess' with all the other elderly cowards, slyboots, place-hunters and men of indifferent faith. Old men are a burden and I pray we'll need no more than a raisin pudding down their gullets to clear them from our path."

"Age is more of a burden to their rheumatic limbs than our supple backs and we shouldn't begrudge them their final sweetmeats." Christopher had hoped this offhand remark would end the conversation, but Poley had more to say.

"You do know, Marlowe, that Sir Francis is rumoured to be ill and Leicester has been vanquished by malaria? The Praetorian guard is falling like a forest of rotted trees. Who will take their place, I ask you? Young Essex? Young Walsingham? That dwarfish young Burghley? Is our governance to slip from the hands of old men into the paws of midgets?'

Christopher could guess why he was being plied with these questions by this insinuating creature. The question for him now was how to escape from the man without appearing to be offensive. The opportunity came when Skeres and Frizer, standing at the edge of the crowd, looked in his direction. They started to cross the floor.

"Why are you lurking in this secluded nook?' shouted Skeres.

"Perhaps they're dark conspirators," said Frizer, "hatching dragons' eggs in this shaded plot."

Frizer amiably suggested they go and listen to Lady Frances at the virginal. "She puts a good deal of spirit into Master Morley's music."

"It's only fitting," added Skeres. "She so murders the harmony its own spirit has long since departed."

Halfway across the hall, Frizer stopped and slapped his forehead. "Forgive me, Robin, I have a message for you and only now remembered it. Your man – what's the pork-fat's name? – Baines has made your horses ready."

"But I have no cause to leave. Not yet." The mask of jollity was replaced by a scowl of suspicion.

"There are important letters to be taken to Seething Lane."

"And Marlowe? Is he to come with us?"

"Heaven forbid. Did you not take a lot of trouble to fetch him here? Surely it would be a sin to let him depart at such short notice. No, he stays with us for this night at least."

The trio continued across the hall, leaving an impotently fuming Poley. When Christopher stopped by the virginal, Frizer tugged at his sleeve. "We have a different rendezvous beyond, Kit," he said firmly.

They walked down a narrow passageway towards a heavy brocade curtain which Skeres pulled aside. He opened a concealed door and ushered Christopher into a small room. The sole item of furniture in the chamber was a plain table upon which lay a long white cloth with fringed tassels. Another door faced them.

Frizer gestured for Christopher to stand by the table while he and Skeres moved to the other side. All signs of bland frivolity had vanished.

Frizer spoke in a stern, measured manner. "Christopher Marlowe, hear this. Your name has been set down as a suitable candidate for our sodality, the true name of which, in all its awful significance, will be revealed to you when you have served your novitiate."

He rapped once on the table. An answering double knock came from the second door. A Judas hatch was opened and an unseen person asked, "Is the candidate within?" "He is within this outer sanctum," Skeres replied. "Prepare him then for we are ready and waiting."

"Christopher Marlowe," began Frizer in the same weighty manner as before, "know you that we, Nicholas Skeres and Ingram Frizer, after due representation from a third party, have agreed to sponsor your candidature to our sacred sodality. You are an esteemed scholar whose loyalty to our Queen, our kingdom and our faith has been put to the test and proven strong and steadfast. All this being well and according to our will, it has been ordained that upon this day and upon this hour, the Question should be put to you. Will you, Christopher Marlowe, sign with your blood the covenant of our sodality and swear to hold our secrets, come what may? Take heed, by so swearing, you abjure allegiance, overt or covert, to any religion, cult, sect or political body whose intent lies in contradiction to the true governance of our kingdom."

Christopher had not expected this solemnity so soon after the revels. He winced at the thought of signing with his blood.

"I am prepared to swear," he replied with equal pomposity, "if nothing I am asked to say or do is contrary to my Christian belief."

It was a pious platitude that would have been treated with derision by those who knew him well; but the pair opposite betrayed not a flicker of amusement. Skeres knocked three times on the door and called out, "The Question has been put to the candidate and he is most willing."

The door opened and Thomas Walsingham entered. A dark blue gown, embellished with five pointed stars, Greek and Hebrew letters and mingled triangles and circles, covered his body from neck to feet. A conical hat of the same hue crowned his head and he carried a six-foot oak stave in his right hand. It was difficult to recognise the effete young man in this theatrical garb.

"Know you, Christopher Marlowe, that I am Warder-Elect of this concourse,' Walsingham began. Christopher was irresistibly reminded of stilted actors at the Shoreditch playhouses.

"There is a divinity in revealed truths and the sacred purpose of each and every one, though we be in our own person but a single candle, is to illume the Stygian darkness that encompasses man's stumbling journey on the narrow path of earthly bondage towards life eternal and his salvation. As the lodestone, by its ineffable force, directs the mariner across uncharted seas, so we, within the circumspection of our sodality, shall direct the traffic of our kingdom towards the rich wares to be discovered in those new-found lands of truth and knowledge." 'Would there be the beating of tabors and the sounding of a sennet to herald the opening scene?' Christopher wondered. Instead of drums rolling, Walsingham banged his stave four times on the floor. Frizer lifted up the candlestick and pointed to the triangle embroidered in the middle of the stole. Christopher dimly remembered the symbol from his King's School days but then he had never been very good at mathematics.

"Here begins the first revelation of our mysteries," Frizer pronounced. "As each line touches each line making one in perfection, so does God Almighty, great architect of the universe, design the final perfection of our state. Each side is proportioned to numbers fundamental, these being three, which is the Holy Trinity, four for the true gospels and the elements of fire, water, air and earth and five, the number of the first five books, the Pentateuch. The sum of their numbers is twelve for the disciples and the number of month is each year."

Frizer handed Christopher a candlestick and Skeres draped the stole round the candidate's neck. "Repeat after me," said Nicholas. "Audi. Vide. Tace. Here are your instructions. We will presently depart from this outer chamber to the inner sanctum. You will walk a straight path forward with your eyes fixed on the countenance of our parfait lord. To such questions put to you, you will answer thus, 'This I swear to hold fast.' If, in your heart of hearts, you cannot respond, then, in all conscience, you must declare, 'No, to this I shall not swear'. If this be so, you will be given leave to quit our company but, remember, you are bound by oath to keep these things secret. Upon the conclusion of the catechism you will confirm the articles of your indenture in the manner prescribed. Thus you will become a novice in the lower rank of our sodality, one who will ascend from the bottom level by diligence and purity of intent."

Walsingham thundered five times with his stave and beckoned to Christopher to walk with him through the open door to the next room.

A long strip of carpet, divided into twelve squares displaying each a zodiacal sign and flanked by six man-size candle-holders to the left and right, made a narrow lane down the nave. At the far end a large, carved chair draped with purple cloth stood upon a low dais. Enthroned on this seat was Sir Francis Walsingham.

Whatever doubts Christopher had about the induction ceremony and the sodality itself were now dispelled. Surely the Secretary of State, this old and eminent man, would not lend his august presence to foolishness or a gallimaufry of antique rituals and fantasies?

The emaciated frame of the elder statesman was smothered in a pelerine of many colours and a tall, peaked cap sat above his cadaverous face. The wavering light and the soft shadows thrown by the several candles failed to hide his weariness. Over the years he had dealt with squabbling factions, never-ending intrigues, external dangers to the state, internal threats of subversion and, above all, the whims and passions of a sometimes stubborn, sometimes gracious but always scheming and parsimonious Queen. Now, like a salmon in the still pool of the upper reaches, he was nearly spent.

With Thomas Walsingham by his side, Christopher walked the full length of the nave and, at a muttered command, knelt on the edge of the carpet.

"Who comes forward?" Sir Francis asked. His voice quavered and his raised hand trembled.

Thomas Walsingham announced: "We supplicate the admittance of Christopher Marlowe, one-time scholar of Cambridge, Master of Arts, poet of renown and faithful servant of proven loyalty to her glorious Majesty, to our ancient and honourable fraternity."

"Who supports this supplication?"

"I, Ingram Frizer."

"I, Nicholas Skeres."

"Prepare the neophyte according to our Catechism."

Thomas Walsingham produced a parchment scroll from his cloak and, after a preliminary cough and a good squint at the text, read out the first passage.

"What should a wise man do in a corrupt world? He should hoist his hem from the gutters. walk on high ground, cleave to his books, give tongue to truth, a lie to slander and forever keep faith with his brothers in grace and honour." He lowered the scroll and asked Christopher. "What say you to this tenet?"

From his lowly position the tutored respondent replied, "This I swear to hold fast."

Walsingham concluded the reading by rolling up the scroll and declaring loudly, "So be it."

Suddenly the tenor of the ritual changed to brutal menace. The candlestick was snatched from Christopher's hand, his head was roughly pulled back by the hair, his arms were pinioned from behind and Frizer stood over him with an Italian dagger pricking the now terrified poet's forehead.

Had he been ensnared by heretical folly? With the irrational observation of one in danger of quitting his earthly domain, Christopher noted every detail of the sinister features: the broken nose, the nostril-hairs, the scar on the right cheek, the spittle on the lips and the oily sweat above the brow. "Pray, if I should see the face of God," he silently said to himself, "it is not in the image of this man."

"Within the shell of your skull," began Frizer, "all chickling plans are hatched. If your Saturn children should run rampage against our sodality let this knife bleed the juice from that fertile yoke."

The dagger point was now an inch from Christopher's eyes.

"If these blessed orbs should reflect evil or look upon our sodality with contempt and scorn, let this knife blight the bloom of their irises."

The sharp edge was pressed against his throat. "If, through here, poisonous slander should spew out against our sodality, let these strings be severed and its shaking reed be sliced to less than a shaving on a carpenter's floor."

The blade was jabbed against his chest. "If the canker of hatred and envy for our brothers should rot this apple, let it be torn out, trodden under foot and thrown on the hell-fires of damnation."

The episode ended as suddenly as it had begun. Christopher was released and helped to his feet. A square parchment was thrust into his hands and he was ordered to read the document. Dazed and bewildered as he was, the Latin script seemed to leap and defy understanding.

"Will you sign our covenant with your blood?" he was asked.

"I will," he said shakily.

"Then give your hand to it." Christopher held out his right hand, Frizer turned the palm upwards, nicked the thumb pad and pressed the wound on the parchment. "Now say these words. With my blood I do sign this compact." In a very low tone, he repeated the phrase. "There is one more step to take but before you cross the threshold, heed the chorus of our assembly."

It was only then that Christopher became fully aware of the

number of men sitting either side of the nave. On his right voices cried, "Homo fuge" (Fly O man) and from the left came the question, "Whither shall he fly?"

Skeres rolled back Christopher's left sleeve.

From the right came the chorus, "O man, lay aside that covenant. Read the scriptures." The left side responded with, "Go forward, o man, and discover where all nature's treasures are contained."

Frizer pressed the dagger into Christopher's right hand. "Cut, then, the flesh of your bared limb and thus, by the flow of your heart's blood, let your worth be tested." Christopher hesitated. "Be resolved. Do it," Skeres muttered. "You have come so far."

Christopher grimaced and scratched the point across his skin. When the droplets of blood oozed out, Sir Francis rose and announced, "Consummatum est." (It is finished). The assembly echoed him.

Thomas Walsingham beat the floor seven times with his stave. "Take heed, one and all. By the sacred rites of our ancient order and the Solomonic antecedence of our mysteries, Christopher Marlowe is, by blood bond and covenant, a brother within our sodality. As he is so elect, therefore let you elect to offer him succour and aid in time of need, comfort when he is distraught, meat when he is hungry, as he, by this binding contract, shall do likewise to any one of you when need is most driven."

Frizer held up Christopher's right hand and showed the wounded thumb to the assembly. "By this mark shall you know him. Now greet our elected brother and welcome him within the ranks of our fraternity."

A concerted shout of, "Sat cito, si sat bene" (soon enough done, if well enough done) rang out and the new recruit was surrounded by well-wishers. He knew some by sight, such as Sir Roger Manwood, a stern and harsh Justice and a fellow Canterburian. The majority were complete strangers to him. He looked round for Sir Francis but the chair on the dais was empty and he caught a glimpse of the fur-fringed robe disappearing through a door.

As the crowd dispersed, blank-faced servants hurried in to roll up the carpet and return the chamber to its normal state as the private chapel of the Walsinghams.

Chapter six

London was a confusing tangle of sordid alleys, filthy lanes and narrow muddy streets, a place where the grand houses of the rich and powerful sat cheek by jowl with overcrowded tenements. It was a city into which poured landless labourers escaping rural poverty, foreign refugees flying from religious persecution, merchants, adventurers, chancers and, of late, a growing band of poets and scholars.

Though this was Christopher's second visit – his drama Tamburlaine The Great had been produced the previous year at The Theatre in Shoreditch – he had not learned to tolerate the noisome squalor and clamour. His close friend Thomas Watson, a fellow scholar and poet seven years his senior, had taken him under his wing, found him cheap lodging near Bishopsgate and introduced him to London's literary clique: a jealous lot who did not take kindly to strangers.

One day in November, returning from the bookstalls in St Paul's, they were attempting to carry on a civilised conversation through the hurly-burly of Cheapside – Christopher said that London was a short step to Inferno and Watson asserted that it was the upper level of Purgatory – when their passage was obstructed by a drunken mariner. As the friends tried to pass the swaying man, he stumbled and sprawled across three squatting beggars.

The mendicants consisted of a one-legged, toothless ancient in the ragged red coat of a London soldier, a blind black-clad crone and a sturdy lout who appeared to have no arms. The trio loudly abused the fallen man, belabouring him with fists and feet, while he bellowed back at them.

Christopher was anxious to put a distance between himself and the fray but Watson had a fondness for rough jokes.

The commotion attracted a gang of cut-purses who ran up to snatch valuables from the spectators. One sent Christopher tumbling down on top of the struggling bodies. Fingers clawed at his belt, the crone dug her nails into his thigh and a stinking cloth was thrown over his head. He tore off the smothering rag, distributed hearty blows left and right and was pulled to his feet by Tom. "Let's get away," shouted the sailor, who had suddenly sobered up, and the three of them broke through the scuffling mob to run as fast as they could down Cheapside towards Cornhill. "This way. This way," their new-found friend called out and Tom and Christopher followed him through a warren of passages until they found themselves in a backyard.

"You've led us into a blind trap," said Watson. "We're like rats in a pit."

"Don't you worry, me old mates. I promise you they'll never catch us here."

"I couldn't run another inch," Christopher said between gasps. "I hope you promise better than you brawl."

The mariner banged on a door. "We're safe as houses with Kate Quick. She'll see us alright."

Water spattered the refugees and, looking up, they saw the head and shoulders of a woman leaning out of an upstairs window. "Hey, you trugging doxy," the mariner yelled. "May your scabby dugs drop with the French marbles if you wet us with your piss again." The woman laughed and shouted, "That'll learn you, Jack Marlin."

She disappeared and reappeared two seconds later, a big-boned, strapping young woman, to stand four-square in the doorway. "Up to your tricks, are you, expecting me to give shelter to you and your street-scourings? Where were you last night? With your Hoxton whore, no doubt. You'll get what you deserve one fine day, Marlin, and I won't be slow to dance a jig on your grave."

The noise of many voices could be heard approaching. Marlin pushed past her, followed closely by Watson and Christopher, slammed the door fast and shot the bolts. Kate pushed her unwelcome guests down the hall. "Up them stairs with you and for Christ's sake keep quiet." As they groped their way to an upstairs room, the door shook with blows and men called out, "Open up. Open up. This is the law." Christopher went to look out of the window. "Away from there, you fool," a girl whispered harshly from somewhere in the gloom. "Do you want us to be whipped behind the cart?"

Down below, Kate had opened the Judas window and was heatedly asking, "Is it the law to barge round the arse of a respectable woman's house and break down her only guard against looting layabouts?" The men in the yard swore she was protecting three ruffians who had beaten up and robbed unfortunate cripples down Cheapside. She swore in return that no such men had crossed her threshold, adding that if they were ready to risk a contagion they could search the room where a sick woman lay.

The runaways had become used to the dull light and now saw that the fourth person in the room was a young girl, naked except for a thin shift. She shivered with both cold and fear. "You've no need to didder and dodder with us," said Marlin blithely. "We mean you no harm."

Kate clumped up the stairs. "They're gone and, for all I care, their day's sport is spoiled. As for you, Marlin, you'll be the ruination of me yet. Now, out of here, you lot. I've a customer coming and I won't damage my business for your sake." She looked out of the window. "Christ's wounds, he's here and waiting. It's a wonder he didn't take fright with all the hullaballoo." She pushed them downstairs into a recess. "Stay here till I'm clear and don't open your gobs."

They could hear her greet the caller with placatory and deferential phrases. "Ah, you don't know where you are nowadays with rufflers and roaring-boys roving as free as you like, as I was saying to another gentleman yesterday. Where is the law, I ask you. This way now, sir. Up here. She's a nice girl, from good Kentish stock, clean and neat, not one of them common fillocks you'd find traipsing the docks, and she's very religious into the bargain. When you're finished, I'll be glad to offer you a drink in the tavern. Eleanor will show you the way. I'll take the reckoning now, sir. Ah, God bless and keep you, sir."

She collected the trio from their hiding hole and they followed her like a string of ducklings through another door, across an alley and into the rear of The Gilded Lily.

"He was a right pig, he was, with his squinty eyes and his grunting. Not a patch on the gentry we've had at one time but,

God help us, in these hard days we have to take what comes. And the devil take them straight-backs and craw-thumpers trying to close us down. We'll starve before the year's out. Then what'll happen to us. We'll be Winchester geese, we'll be, and a right plucking that'll be." She called to the drawer to prepare pots of ale and directed the men to a table. "Nobody'll bother you here. I don't want to know your troubles. I've enough vexations of my own as it is."

The Gilded Lily had never been a fashionable place. Its glum clientele were apparently blind and deaf too. Only one man found them interesting.

A pug-faced character sitting near the street door, his manner and bearing marked him out as a leader.

"I must butter up Kate," said Marlin. "I fear I'm out of favour." When the so-called sailor crossed the floor, Tom and Christopher turned out their pockets to pay for the drink.

"Save those few coins you received for your books at St Paul's," said Watson. "I've had an advance from Walsingham."

"Surely you're not in the pay of – "

"I'm not one to spoil my hands with spying work. Young Thomas Walsingham has commissioned me to write a trifle." He looked round the tavern. "I don't care for this rogue's den and even less for our brawling companion. He's no more a sailor than I'm a musician."

"You could hardly be any worse than that pair."

Christopher nodded towards a scrawny woman who keened a doeful ballad and an old blind man who was as thin and worn as the fiddle he scraped. The theme of their lugubrious song was the plaint of a rejected lover and its refrain, 'O willow, willow. Sing, O the green willow shall be my garland' seemed to be the body and soul of every stanza.

"Willow, willy, waily, will she ever whist her wailing," Christopher said mockingly.

"And what's wrong with our song?" Kate stood over him threateningly.

"Why, Kate, lover-girl, our friend only means to – " Marlin tried to fondle her rump but she slapped his hand away.

"Shut your mouth almighty, Jack lad, I didn't ask you. I asked the pretty boy you've dragged in here like a scalded cat."

"I've heard better tunes cawed from a sour apple tree," retorted Christopher.

"You'd better fly back there and crow on your own dung heap. I don't keep a roost for cock-eyed cackling cheats."

The pug-faced man muttered to his cronies and, as they slunk out, he came over to Christopher's table. "Shame on you, Kate," he said. "Bawling out a young gentleman and a Cambridge scholar to boot for the sake of an idle jest."

"Oh, it's you, sly Dick," she said. "And how was I to know the pretty boy is a gentleman?" She was only slightly mollified. "You should do well in London, for drunk or sober Cambridge men always look after their own. Gentleman or not, I won't have any capering in my tavern, no matter what cloth you sport." She flounced off to the far end of the tavern.

Marlin, a big grin on his ugly face, greeted the new arrival. "Dick Chomley, you old rogue. Come and sit with us." Dick pretended extreme reluctance and then coyly sat down.

The seaman called for another round of drinks, and, for Chomley's benefit, launched into a heightened account of the Cheapside affray, adding a few extra bodies and casting himself in a major role.

Christopher was impatient to be gone. He was not easy in this den and even more uncomfortable in the company of the ominous Chomley.

"I wonder, Kit Marlowe," said Chomley, "that you and Tom Watson should choose this place and this company for your entertainment. Surely flocking to The Mermaid is a better place to preen your feathers?"

"Circumstances invited us here, not choice," Christopher replied coldly. "You've heard of our adventures from Marlin."

"Him! Jack is a born bragging liar and I'd doubt his words if he were to tell me rainwater fed rivers or" – Chomley paused and lowered his voice – "or he told me as a gospel truth that one Marlowe was a Walsingham agent."

"Are you by chance the Walsingham spy? Sir Francis is hard

done by if he has to recruit from whorehouses and thieves' taverns."

"I once did some small services for the noble lord, as you have done, but I'm not in his pay now. Are you?"

"What I am and what I was is none of your business." Christopher turned to his friend, but Watson seemed enthralled by Marlin's tales and showed no inclination to leave.

Chomley grabbed Christopher's right hand and turned the palm upwards. "So you are one of them. I'm no clodhopper. I know that scar and what it signifies. Pretend what you like, I'll believe differently."

"Then we'll choose to differ in our beliefs and go our different ways."

"Seeing is believing, isn't that a tenet of your faith? By my faith, I believe you're entangled with a band of political schemers. That so-called sodality, the School of Connivers, is hanging on a thin thread. When it breaks, and old Walsingham's death will surely snap it quick, they'll hang by a stronger thread."

"I'm a playwright, not a political plaything," said Christopher stiffly, feeling curiously impotent.

"Will that be taken into account when your precious sodality is thrown into the bear-pit to be savaged by the Privy Council's hounds? Listen, Marlowe, let's leave this rat hole and converse, you and I, in a quiet and private chamber. Think only of your own advancement. I've had occasion to warn you of danger in the recent past."

"We've never met before."

"I warn you now there's danger in the near future."

Before Christopher could reply, a commotion broke out at the rear. Kate Quick was attempting to slap a portly man around the head as they both bawled dire threats at each other. Behind them, cowering and weeping, was the girl the three had met in the upstairs room when they were hiding from the avenging mob.

Chomley swore. "It's that rancid tub of lard."

Christopher rose. "It's Baines. I have a score to settle with him and by God's death I'll quit that debt now."

Chomley also rose and laid a restraining hand on Christopher's arm. "And so have I, but this is not the place. Let Kate deal with him and we'll leave before – "

Marlin, as self-elected protector of the tavern's hostess, staggered to his feet, bellowed, lurched forward and ruined his gallant effort by crashing over a seat. Baines used the diversion to escape from Kate but his way was barred by Christopher.

"Hold hard, Baines. Words were said on a Kentish road one damp morning – "

Baines growled, "You're in my road now." He crouched and with a vicious head-butt to the chest, sent Christopher flying. The delay was enough for Kate. She leaped on Baines and, with flailing arms, struck him across cropped pate and shoulders.

"You sow's arse. You won't beat my girls," she panted. "You grunter's cheat. You lazard spit. You jake's turd." Marlin broke through the circle of onlookers. "I'll take care of him, Kate," he shouted, but she turned her anger on him. "You, with your louts and rowdies, barging in and causing me no end of trouble. Out of here, you arse-over-heels sailor and take your pretty boy and this swine with you." She gripped Baines' shoulder with one hand and clutched Christopher's nape by the other.

"Let me go, woman," squealed Baines. "I'll harass you and your whores and your thieves from this stalling ken before the week's over."

The assembled rogues, ruffians and layabouts turned baleful eyes on the sweating man and hands clawed at him. Suddenly the hunters became the hunted as cudgel-wielding men charged in from the street and the turmoil became an uproar. "It's a raid. It's a raid." In the confusion, Watson disappeared under a table, Marlin wrestled with a sheriff's man and the rest scattered like terrified rats in a pit. Baines turned on Christopher and clutched him by the throat. "You scribbling scut. Speak those words again then," he snarled.

Chomley reappeared out of the melee and punched the fat man on the nose. "Get away, Marlowe. The animal seeks to kill you."

"I'll kill him first."

Baines stumbled forward, blood trickling down his chin. Once more he tried to grapple with Christopher but his antagonist drew a dagger and drove it into the man's side. A gasp bubbled through the podgy lips and the portly figure rolled over a table.

"Run, Kit, run. You've killed him for sure." Chomley grasped Christopher's arm. "Come with me. I'll hide you."

Chapter seven

Chomley conducted Christopher to the top floor of a Thames Street tenement. "You'll be safe enough here," he said. "The house is cluttered with foreigners and herself is the only one with a word of English." Herself was a thin, slatternly woman with an aged face who was at all times surrounded by a swarm of semi-naked children. "Give me some coins for her and she'll make up your meals."

Christopher's cell-like room had one low three-legged stool and a rag-covered pallet. Daylight came through a slit window set high in the west wall and a long piece of cloth draped in the entrance was the poor substitute for a wooden door.

When Chomley left, after assuring his guest he would return soon with news, Christopher sat on the stool, contemplated his immediate past, his present residence in this hovel and cursed his own rash ill-temper. "When I'm freed from this stupidity, I'll never draw a blade again in any quarrel, no matter how I'm provoked," he vowed to himself.

An hour later, urged by a different agitation, he pulled back the curtain and was met by the unblinking stares of the woman and her retinue of infants. 'Where's the -?" A child sniffled, the baby squalled and the woman turned her head towards another drape at the opposite end of the landing. When he had emptied his bladder into the stinking piss-bucket, he returned and asked the woman for a drink. She shook the squalling baby, clouted the sniffling one on the ear and nodded towards a pail of water at the top of the stairs. An hour afterwards she brought him a bowl of thin soup and a lump of stale bread but said not a word.

He lay down on the hard pallet, listless and dispirited, and in a short while fell into an uneasy sleep. "Kit. Kit Marlowe," a voice called and a light shone into his now-opened eyes.

"You're awake to the world then, are you?" Chomley sat on the stool and laid the candle on the floor. "You slept so well, I thought for a moment I had a corpse on my hands." He seemed to be on edge, restless, nervous, head twitching from side to side like a foraging thrush. "You can see Durham House's roofs from the window if you stand on the stool. Sir Walter Ralegh's London home. Some say he's in league with the devil, others say he's a heretic but I say he's riding for a fall. You'll do yourself no good, Marlowe, if you seek his friendship."

"I've little chance of coddling anybody's friendship while I'm hidden here. Tell me, Chomley, why are you risking your neck by giving shelter to a murderer?"

"I have my reasons and they're good ones. But to the sticking point. I know people who know people who say, 'Tell Marlowe to keep his head low till arrangements are made in proper quarters'. And what are them proper quarters, you may ask? In short, Essex. The Earl, Robert Devereux himself. Have him as a friend and you're made for life. Not like that mouth-almighty Ralegh, the so-called great sea-farer. Him! He couldn't cross the Thames in a bum-boat without spewing up his Sunday dinner to poison the trouts."

"What's Essex to me?"

"What's your liberty to you? There's a man's blood on your hands, the streets are swarming with catchpoles searching for you and every nook and cranny is being rooted out by ruffians in the employ of them you've offended. Your yesterday friends of Scadbury House and your night-swearing sodality of brotherly love have turned against you now you've killed a Walsingham agent. They say you've changed your coat to another colour as they did when bully Baines and I were sent to fetch you from Canterbury."

Christopher now remembered the description given by the youth in the purloined King's School jacket.

Chomley stood up and stretched his arms. "As I was saying, Kit, the Earl of Essex is your best hope and I'd advise you to remain hidden till he returns to these shores."

"And when will that be?"

"Patience, Kit. In a day or two but not more than a week, I promise you, I'll bring better news. Say the word, and I'll fetch papers and books from your lodgings and not even oblige you for a simple thanks."

When his protector had left, Christopher gave vent to his rage. "Why should I stew in this sty and wait for that fine-plumaged cock to fly home to his own dunghill?" he shouted at the bare walls. He felt oppressively weary but was unable to regain the blessed relief of sleep. In time, he expected, he could become used to the Purgatorial noises, smells and smoke of the tenement; but the rats – one of which tried to nibble his ear – and the hordes of fleas, lice and blood-sucking bugs were another matter.

Just before dawn the house went quiet as if all the inhabitants were collectively holding their breath. The drape was jerked to one side and a thickset man poked Christopher in the ribs with a stave. "On your feet," he ordered. A second man held a lantern. "He's not Sly Dick. I'd know him anywhere and that skinny scut's not him. Let's be off before it's light. We'll catch him the next time." They left as suddenly as they had arrived.

"Who were those men? What did they want?" The woman put his daily ration of soup and bread on the stool but made no reply. Late that evening she finally spoke. "God blind me, but what about us?" she yelled as she and the children followed Chomley into the small room. "I'd sooner bed with a jake-farmer as have gallow's meat like you pawing me night and morn." Chomley roughly hustled the woman out and threatened to clout her good and proper if she didn't stow her cackling. The children howled a discordant chorus to her parting imprecation. "By God's bleeding wounds, Chomley, I pray you'll swing and I won't be your Magdalene at the foot of the gibbet."

The abused man muttered, "I'll shut up that Wapping mort once and for all with a mighty kicking to her trugging arse." He dropped a cloth-bound bundle by the pallet and sat down on the stool. "Heard you had visitors." Christopher could almost smell the other's fear. "Them two bully boys barging in at such an unholy hour, that's what's upset her, being disposed to fancies and frights. And wasn't it rare luck for you that they had no image of your features. Now, if somebody was to describe – "

"They mentioned you. You're their quarry."

"Me? Why should they hound me?"

"Then if I was the badger they hunted, it's better I leave this burrow before the dogs return to dig me out."

"Wait, Kit. Chance I was mistaken. It's them Flemings the catchpoles sought." Chomley nodded, grinned and winked as if struck by a brilliant idea. "They mentioned me, you say? That's it then, isn't it. Out of the goodness of my heart and with no thought of profit, I've given shelter to them who've fled from tyranny in their own land and have little in their purses to pay their way. Foreigners are supposed to have a licence and our two bullies were rooting out the crafty ones who've no permit. Mind you, give room to a handful and you end up with a houseful and before the week's out they're swarming all over the place. To walk down Cripplegate is to hear nothing but their gabble. You'd never think this was an English city." He undid the bundle and took out a candle. "I've brought you a half-dozen of these. No one can deny that I have an open hand with my gifts. I'll fetch a glimmer from the woman."

The bundle also contained papers, quills and an ink jar. Christopher's pulse quickened as he stroked the smooth sheets. Chomley's return was only welcome for the light he carried.

"About this murder, Marlowe."

Christopher chilled with the remembrance. "The birds of the air will tell of murders past," he replied.

"And the sparrows in the streets will have a word or two to say as well and if those catchpoles were after you, you'd be clapt in Newgate prison. Neither your Walsingham cronies nor your swearing sodality would lift a finger to help you. As for my master, Essex, why should he bend to pick up a fallen straw if you scorn his aid?"

"Was it offered? You play the usurer with your help."

"Then for your credit, I'll give you good counsel. Nothing is for nothing."

"Ex nihilo nihil fit."

"Don't befuddle me with your Dutch fustian. I have my learning and I'll cap your head with a blacker cap. Stipendum peccati mors est. The wages of sin is death. I, too, went to Cambridge."

"So did the butcher when he wanted fat Fen cattle for his counter."

"Listen to me, if the pig you pricked squeals, 'Marlowe, Marlowe' – "

"If he squeals? Isn't he dead?"

"If he squealed 'Marlowe', then surely Marlowe must hang. He is – was – a Walsingham man and when you strike one of them, you've attacked them all. There's only one man strong enough, and he's growing stronger by the hour, who could protect you."

"You're Essex's hireling. What do you want from me?"

"What would you like from Essex? Your freedom? Advancement? There'll be no limit to our power when he returns: riding up from Tilbury on his white charger and with one hand embracing his true, loyal friends and with the other brushing aside the old codgers, procrastinators and connivers." Chomley's enthusiasm for his chosen messianic leader seemed to have banished his state of fear. "Think hard on it, Marlowe." He stood up and looked down at the papers. "I'll leave you to your writing. What great drama are you preparing?"

"Didn't you look at them when you brought them from my lodgings?"

"I don't pry, though others did come to inspect your belongings. I had a hard time convincing the old crone who guarded your trunk that I meant you no harm. I only looked at the top page where you had written – what was it now? – The Malta-Jew."

"Then you know as much as I," said Christopher flippantly.

For the following seven days and nights, his only visitor was the woman bringing in the daily ration of soup and bread; a diet that varied only inasmuch as the soup was progressively thinner and the bread harder. In this opportune solitude he wrote and rewrote his drama with hardly an hour's snatch of sleep to interrupt his labours. He became oblivious to the rats scampering among the rafters, his aching limbs and his hunger. He lived not in the reality of this squalid tenement but in the imagined Malta of his scheming Jew.

Late on the seventh night, when he was down to his final candle stump, he was startled by a sudden half-smothered cough. "Yesu, Dick," he shouted, "must you creep – "

Chomley spoke in a near-whisper. "I don't want her to know I'm here. You've heard how she creates. She's my wife, well, not exactly my wife, not in one sense of the word but then in another – "

Chomley had brought a small leather bottle of acidic wine. Try as he might, Christopher was unable to fight off the weariness now paralysing his limbs. The candle's flame sputtered in the grease, darkness prevailed and the long-rejected sleep closed his mind.

"Come on, you. Out!" somebody shouted. A candle-lantern was held an inch from his opening eyes, a hand grabbed him by the scruff of his neck, another pincered him under his arm and he was hauled from the room to be slammed upright against the landing wall. He recognised the pair who had called a week ago. The woman and her clutter were huddled at the far end.

"I've told you before, he's not Sly Dick," one man said.

"So you say, but where is he?"

"Ask this one. Perhaps he belongs to their rabble."

"Are you a Peculiar?"

"A peculiar what? I'm Christopher Marlowe of no peculiar affinity. For God's sake let me gather up my papers. When you disturbed my sleep, your splay-feet trampled the sheets."

"It's an odd place to scatter written matter, I must say," grumbled one as he pulled back the drape and lowered the lantern. When Christopher crouched down, he glimpsed a pair of feet under the pallet rags. "I'm ready." He stood up. "Let's be gone."

"Who did you say you are?"

"God's nails, man, I've said I'm Christopher Marlowe. Haven't you heard my name before now? Poet and playwright?" Their heavy heads lolled from side to side and he could not resist a boast. "Haven't you seen Tamburlaine The Great performed by the Lord Admiral's Men at The Theatre down by Shoreditch?"

"Tamburlaine? I've heard of him. A famous fighting bear from Africay."

"Give me a roaring bear-baiting any day. I've no time for them prating dramas of wind and water."

"Do you have a warrant for my arrest?"

"Why should we?"

"Because I killed one Richard Baines in a brawl at The Gilded Lily."

"That's your problem. We've heard of no such killing and we've no warrant to that effect. You must have been cup-sodden to go brawling in the The Gilded Lily. Poet and playwright, indeed. More likely you're a runaway servant wasting his master's money on whores and bastard ale."

Having had high hopes of landing a pike instead of netting a penk, the men were sulky and enraged. In their chagrin, they turned on the woman and shook her with such violence the baby slipped from her grasp onto the floor. "Where's the whoreson, you trugging mort," they bawled, but she refused to be intimidated into a reply. Defeated and disgusted, they pushed her over the squalling infant and went their disgruntled way down the stairs.

"I know you two," she yelled after them. "You, Jem Scabarse, you jerkman, and you, Bill Blowhard and your bawdy wife. She keeps a vaulting house, doesn't she?" A toddler lifted his vest and peed down the well on top of the departing lawmen.

For the first time that week, Christopher felt an affinity with the woman. Not only had they been mauled and abused by the self-same rogues but they had also been cheated by the same scoundrel, the lying Chomley. Suddenly he remembered the feet.

"Light. I want light." He grabbed the only source of illumination, a metal cup filled with tallow. Picking his way through the nest of scrabbling children, he returned to his room and pulled back the top cloth from the pile of rags.

A sweaty face, made twice as ugly with fear, was revealed. "Get up, Chomley, or I'll prick you as good if not better than Baines."

Chomley's terror-struck grimace changed to a gargoyle grin. "Kit. Dear Kit. May all the saints be praised, Have they gone?" He scrambled to his feet. "They're hard men and not fit to hold office, but not too hard for Dick Chomley to give them the benefit of my fists. Oh yes, I'm a right rouster when I'm – "

The woman stood in the doorway and compared Chomley and Christopher, along with their friends, parents and antecedents, to the turgid contents of mephitic sewers. At the end of her diatribe, she snatched the lamp and left the men in darkness.

"Lucidus Ordo," Chomley extracted from his Latin ragbag. "And God said let there be light and there was light and it was good. The bitch said let there be pitch black and there was pitch black and the bitch stank."

"We lack light but let's not want for lucidity." Christopher stuffed the papers into his jerkin. "You lied when you said I killed Baines, you lied when you said I was wanted for murder. You stuck me in this sty. Those pugs were after you but she and I bore the brunt of their blows while you crouched in here."

"And will you be avenged by running to the law and informing against me?"

"I'm not one of your profession."

"And what did you profess in your Cambridge days, Marlowe, with your tales from Rheims? And who's to say you don't indulge in tittle-tattles to this day?"

"You're a liar and prevaricator, Chomley, and I'd rather rot in a Fleet ditch than suffer the embrace of your friendship. As for your proud Earl of Essex – "

"You've a clever and quick tongue, Marlowe, for lashing those without your privileged education. I've done my best by you. As it is written, there was a cry, a clamouring cry, fetch me the fox, the little fox, and that fox was you, Marlowe. You've shown your teeth and bitten their hound and they sought your brush for their pennant." The voice rose and took on the declamatory tones of a street ranter. "And I hid you within my covert while the dogs sniffed my lair, thirsting to lap my blood from the stones and hungering to feast on my peculiar flesh – "

"Peculiar! Scabarse and Blowhard spoke of the Peculiars. Who are they?"

A heavy sigh escaped the man. "Who cares for the children of Hagar, they who came out of Egypt and dwell among us? Who blesses the name of Ishmael? Who but thieves, vagabonds, mummers, jugglers and all those cast out from hearth and home and condemned to wander the face of the earth. Our divine mother is Mary, Mary Magdalene, the most holy and passionate of harlots, she to whom the risen Lord revealed his wounds and who nestled his head to her breasts when he wearied. It is she who is peculiar to our callings and it is she who'll be in the van of our hordes, as was Joan the French Maid, bright as a pillar of fire in her scarlet array. She is the harlot of our faith and she'll sound the trumpet for the first day of the first month of the first year of that thousand years of turmoil, slaughter, rapine, destruction, as foretold and revealed by St John the Divine, when the earth shall crack and the four horsemen ride out."

Christopher drew back the drape. "And what about your famous Earl of Essex? Will he be among you then, prancing on his white charger?"

"It is written. Don't go, Kit. They await you at every corner."

Christopher groped his way downstairs and stumbled out of the tenement. He ran down passages and alleys and stopped a hundred times whenever a lurking shadow emerged from a slit in a wall or the shelter of a doorway. The night was damp and cold and a brooding cloud hung over the city.

Chapter eight

Will Shakeshaft was a stout, sturdy man with a red blustering beard and hair to match. His immediate mission in life was to confront one whom he asserted had stolen his good name and thus deprived him of useful employment.

"Oh dear, o dear. What trials, what troubles, what tribulations are strewn across our paths," he said to his companions as the three hurried along Bishopsgate Street. "As if we hadn't enough botheration without them straightbacks – no offence to your wife, Tom – with their ranting and ravings closing every playhouse in the city and beyond. They say Satan carouses freely in the playhouses but I say, close the playhouses and Satan will wander freely on every highway and byway and roast his toes at every man's fire."

Will was also smarting from the caustic comments of Tom Watson's wife Anne when he had called while the family's main meal was being laid on the table. She was a religious woman of puritanical inclinations, genuflecting in the direction of the more austere Catholic beliefs. Her every remark was a monitory sermon. "Those who earn their meat by lewd and impious prating in the company of stinkards," she had said, "can and will sup with the devil."

Tom Watson had only smiled at his wife's thrust and now seemed to be turning a deaf ear to his companion's complaints. Perhaps he was too preoccupied with his own thoughts. More than a week had passed since the infamous Gilded Lily affray and Christopher Marlowe was still missing.

The third member of the group was Will Warner, a fellow writer the same age as Watson. He had achieved a middling fame for a rather long poem, due more to its patriotic fervour than its alliterative and tedious style. He was a small, pensive man whose mild manner suggested a lifelong struggle for self-effacement. In company he made a point of gently enquiring after the welfare of others and was always prepared to listen to the cause and consequences of various emotional disorders. There were some people who did not trust Warner.

"Tell me, my friend, why are you so angry with the world?" he asked Shakeshaft.

The unemployed actor needed little prompting to launch into a rambling tale full of bombast, rhetorics and extensive quotes from ancient prologues and interludes. The bare bones of his story was this: he had been in Lord Houghton's Company, but since the noble gentleman died, the group had disbanded and Shakeshaft had little opportunity to exercise his histrionic talents. Then he was invited by Ned Alleyn to fill the place left vacant in the Earl of Worcester's company by the murder of Will Knell in Stratford. Imagine his dismay and anger when he arrived in the city and discovered that Ned Alleyn had mistakenly taken on another actor whose name was similar to Shakeshaft. "A Wiltshire loon, a horseminder, a butcher's boy and a bankrupt glover's son," was how the deposed actor described the usurper.

The trio stepped through an opening off Hog Lane known as The Hole-in-the-Wall and found themselves on the edge of a crowd, in the midst of which were two combatants. One was a thin, ferret-faced man shivering with rage and the other a plump, stolid, almost phlegmatic person of about sixty. "Rogue, horse-thief, ruffler's cur, tinker's spit," ferret-face yelled out a litany of derogations, "and – and cack-handed carpenter." The last epithet made the stolid man flinch.

"Braggart Burbage is up to his tricks again," said Watson. "It's said he never pays a bad debt and never owes a good one." The thin man was accusing the stout man of stealing the widow's mite, cheating on the takings and holding back the players' share of the gallery. Burbage was a model of cool nonchalance. "Have I really done all that, Peter Street? How inconsiderate of me." He looked round the crowd. "Have you ever heard such lies and slander in one day?" he asked with a contrived air of innocence. Just then he spotted the three friends.

"Tom, come here and speak up for me. You know me as the only begetter of The Theatre and Curtain playhouses. I've brought many dramas comical and tragical for the pleasure of London's commonality, all for a penny a pinch. Step forward into the arena, Watson, pronounce in my favour and rout this scallywag."

Watson's cheeks blazed with embarrassment. The 'scallywag' was convinced that his antagonist had summoned rowdies to his assistance and thought to strike a final blow before making a rapid retreat. He leaped up, gave Burbage's nose a vicious twist and then ran helter-skelter across the fields towards Moorgate.

Burbage miraculously maintained his dignity. "You did me a favour there, Watson," he said affably. "Our hopping flea Peter Street – though he's a Peter of a different street, being a Dutchman – fancies himself a supreme craftsman, carpenter and builder, and has traipsed all the way over from Southwark to lay siege to my good nature for some trifle he swears I owe him." Grasping Watson's arm, Burbage led the small procession of four across what were once the pastures and vegetable gardens of a priory. Suddenly he stopped and spread out his arms in an expansive gesture. "Look, my friends, there is my life, my spirit, my joyous pride, my playhouse, The Theatre."

Shakeshaft, country bumpkin that he was, stood with mouth agape at the sight of the very first building since the Romans left London to be constructed for the production of plays.

From one angle, it had the appearance of a large barn with several doors cut into its side. From another angle, it was revealed as a structure with an almost circular shape. Men and boys dressed in garish costumes were coming in and out of the doors.

"Is there to be a drama today?" Shakeshaft asked.

"Today and tomorrow and every other day except holy days when our thoughts turn to praises of the Lord. Today, our wondrous, magnificent drama – " Burbage was a spendthrift with extravagant praises " – is written for us by that incomparable scribe, Thomas Kyd. It's called The Spanish Tragedy. Never since those walls resounded with the immortal verses of Tamburlaine The Great has there been such fire, such fury, such furious fiery passions. If dear Kit Marlowe were with us at this hour, he too would sing a paean of praise for – "

"You've heard news of Marlowe?" Watson asked.

Burbage scowled. "He owes me a play, but what else is new?"

"Kit Marlowe hasn't been seen for over a week. He is lost. That's why we're here."

"And I've come to reclaim my name," said Shakeshaft.

"Reclaim your name?" asked Burbage. "Have you lost it?"

"It was stolen."

"Stolen? Here is both a comedy and a tragedy in the making, for one has mislaid his name and the other his friend. Each can be replaced and, I imagine, by a better."

"There's none better than Marlowe," Watson said.

"True, while Marlowe lived there was none better."

"Is he dead?" Warner and Watson exclaimed together.

"The answer to that is, until he appears among the living he is dead to us all." Burbage turned to Shakeshaft. "And tell me, nameless one, were you cup-sodden to the roots of your red beard or were you lolling in the rank arms of a Bankside whore when your inheritance was filched?"

"But what about Marlowe?" Watson insisted. "Have you news? Could he have gone back to Canterbury?"

"Hardly," said Burbage importantly. "His own sister has been here asking for him. She's in the playhouse."

Watson and Warner picked their way across the muddy field. Inside The Theatre, rehearsals had stopped while actors stood facing the proscenium and gazed at a roaring man haranguing a tow-headed youth. The man wore a long, flowing cloak, a multi-coloured robe that reached down to his feet and a glittering crown on his head. The youth's gawky body was smothered in the voluminous attire of a noble lady.

"You're a stummerer and a stammerer, a Bishopsgate punk, a mangler of words, a lasher of lines," the man was shouting. "Repeat, repeat, repeat for me. Who are you supposed to be?"

"I'm the belly imperial," the youth blurted out.

The roaring man threw his crown on the floor, stamped his foot and declaimed, "We've called for players in the semblance of knights, warriors, grandiose nobles from the court of Portingale, beautiful maidens and distressed mothers – but what are we offered? Buffoons, clowns, trick-of-the-loop men, callow youths, Hog Lane grunters and squealers who outdo Finsbury Field's windmills with their arm-waving. Get rid of them all. Come, Kyd, prepare another play fit enough for the groundlings to wet their breeches with unrestrained laughter. They may have their drama but not Edward Alleyn."

As if on cue, his loyal supporters called out, "But Ned Alleyn is the heart of the drama."

Slightly appeased, Alleyn relented. "This once then. Speak the words as they are written." There was a sigh of relief as the rehearsal continued.

"Where's Thomas Kyd," Alleyn shouted. Kyd's dull, plain clothes made him foolishly conspicuous. He looked ill-fed, ill at ease and ill-tempered. "Ah, there you are, Thomas," Alleyn said grandly when the petulant writer approached the stage. "We have a handful of phrases and middling lines whose crudeness, in my reckoning, is unworthy of your talent, in tune only for the clod-ears of our country cousins. They fail to come trippingly off the tongue."

"What phrases? What lines?" snapped Kyd. Alleyn flicked through the prompt-copy and squinted at the script as if afflicted with sore eyes. While actor and author went into an argumentative huddle, the bystanders held their breath. It had all the makings of more doom and disaster on the day's performance.

"Master Kyd, Master Alleyn, if you'd bear with me." A bit-player clad in the uniform of a Spanish soldier approached them. "While I wait off-stage for my small part, I could amend passages that are the cause of contention."

"Who's this intrusive fellow?" Warner asked.

"A bumptious bumpkin," a nearby actor replied. "From Stratford or thereabouts, a well-whipped but unhung poacher from what I've heard, by the name of Shakebag or some such outlandish name."

Shakeshaft, grabbing a clown's clapper stick, leaped on the stage and began to whack the mock-soldier on the head and shoulders. Everyone else gaped at this impromptu scene while Alleyn and two others grappled with the tumultuous man and his victim escaped out of the building.

Riots in playhouses had a disagreeable way of turning nasty and both Warner and Watson also made a hasty exeunt; but Burbage had preceded them and was now standing some distance away, talking to the battered bit-player. A third person, a bulky, roughly-clad man, stood nearby.

"You had promised, James, that you'd speak in my favour," the discomfited actor was saying.

There was an impatient tinge in the evasive reply. "I'm only the owner and I lease the playhouse to whatever company wishes to perform there. I can't tell them how to compose their troupe. My son Richard is more acquainted with the commissioning of dramas. I'll have a word with him." The actor's face puckered as he trudged back to the playhouse. Burbage turned to Watson and Warner. "It would have done my heart good if your blazing-bearded companion had really slaughtered that pestering Warwickshire churl. I've a good mind to dub your fiery friend Will Slaughter. How does it sound to your ears? Surely he'll welcome a new name, his old one being soiled like a virgin's breached maidenhead. And now, Thomas Watson, there is no news of Christopher Marlowe." He grinned at their bafflement. "Where lie the bones of Christopher Marlowe?"

"Put flesh on the riddle," said Watson.

"This is the skin, sinew and marrow of the question. Are the bones of Christopher Marlowe lingering in a pesthouse or mouldering in the common grave reserved for destitute vagrants? Or are they resting on Newgate's rancid straw? His dear sister, having spoken to all and sundry, is now preparing her mourning weeds and her woeful journey back to Canterbury. This sackbag by my side is her knight of the road, one Jem the Carter."

Watson was unable to contain his irritation and turned to Jem. "Will you take us to her lodgings?"

The two were hard put to keep pace with the carter as he strode towards Bishopsgate and Gracechurch Street. He stopped near St Helen's, told the panting couple to wait and disappeared into a house. Within a minute the carter re-emerged and crossed the road into an inn. The pair meekly followed him and saw the oaf pleading with a buxom girl.

"Hold your horses, Jem. You won't harry me. I'd like to stay a bit longer in this God-forsaken city." She looked with scorn at Warner and Watson. "What sort of shrivelled cocks have we here?"

"Your brother's friends, or so they say."

"Fine example they are. They've got as much spine as a crushed snail in a thrush's gob," said Margaret, ever the truculent hayseed.

"We have also been seeking Kit." Watson, ever the gentleman, was polite and courteous.

"There's some who say he's gone to meet his maker," said Warner, "and we're ready to share your grief – "

Margaret put her hands on her hips. "Only if his maker was Belzebub himself, and a short visit at that. Hark at our wandering boy over there." She pointed to where a slim figure was reciting a ribald poem to a boisterous crowd of drunks.

"Kit! Kit Marlowe," Watson shouted.

"Who calls my cursed name upon this crowded field?" Christopher swayed and slowly turned to face his friends.

"By God's grace – " began Watson. "Or Satan's licence," added Warner. "Marlowe's returned from the portals of hell."

Chapter nine

Margaret folded linen into her basket, straightened up and looked round the room. "I can't say I'm sorry to leave this place."

The hubbub from the adjoining room died down as one voice began to dominate.

"Will you listen to our Kit, blathering away nineteen to the dozen for all he's worth." She spoke with a mixture of family pride and sibling disdain. "There's no holding him since he's returned from wherever he was. Even as a child his mouth was buttoned when he wanted to keep himself to himself. And talking of children, how are yours faring? Is the little boy's cough any better?"

"As the good Lord said, suffer little children to come unto us," Anne Watson replied.

"And suffer they will in this foul and filthy city. There's not a morsel of green underfoot till you're beyond the walls and then it's mud, mire and dog-shit every step of the way. How can you breathe with the fumes and the sea-coal smoke?"

Anne sighed. "I do fear – " She glanced at the other woman. "Won't you stay? Your brother needs a woman's hand about the place."

"Whether I like it or not, I'm honour-bound to be home in Canterbury for our sister Ann's wedding. She's marrying into a good family, tavern-keepers by trade but highly respected. You'd think he'd make the effort to come with me to wish her well."

"Is your sister much older than you?" A polite question but the wrong one.

Margaret's lips tightened and she slumped the clothes in the basket with scant ceremony. "She's the youngest of three girls," she replied testily, "and I'm the first-born living. We've nothing in our dowry chests but bond notes and promises and we've small choice in taking whoever comes."

An old woman peeped around the door. "There's another of

them men calling for Marlowe," she croaked. Margaret was well used to dealing with her father's creditors. "I can't say as how he's here or not," she replied. "Who's this one then?"

The crone disappeared and a stout man stood in the doorway. It was James Burbage in search of Marlowe.

Margaret was not intimidated by this imperious and pompous person. "Aren't you the old codger I met the other day in that big cowshed over by Sewer Ditch?" Burbage frowned at the woman's impertinence and stared fixedly at the ceiling. She waved towards the second door. "Kit's in there, prating a rigmarole drama of his to a parcel of roustabouts who've nothing better to do with their time. Now I've finished my packing I've a mind to listen while I'm waiting for Jem the Carter. What about you, Mistress Watson?"

"I'll have nothing to do with ungodly and impious play-acting," was the prim reply. "Such flauntings are an abomination to the Lord."

"God's forgiveness on this goose then as she joins the ganders."

"Whist, woman," Burbage admonished her.

"Whist, yourself, big arse, and shift your haunches."

She found it difficult to follow the drama about a scheming Jew called Barabas. She said as much to her immediate neighbour but he pretended not to have heard her.

And yet she was fascinated by the way Christopher impersonated the characters. First he spoke in a high-pitched voice – surely a noble lady – next he adopted a grandiloquent style – certainly a lord of some sort – and then he would be as gruff as a soldier. Each change of tone and timbre was accompanied by a subtle gesture. He crouched, twisted his mouth into a grimace and stretched out his left hand so that it looked like a claw. The grating voice intoned, "No, no: I drank of poppy and cold mandrake juice and being asleep, belike they thought me dead."

Margaret nudged Burbage. "It's good for babies with the colic or a troublesome tooth. Mark you, a hot cinder in water is better for the wind. They belch all the more for that."

Christopher continued. " – Against this trench (again it was the harsh voice and clutching claw) the rock is hollow, and of purpose digg'd to make a passage for the running stream and common channels of the city."

"I know the place well," Margaret informed the assembly. One hissed at her to be quiet. "I won't be silenced by the likes of you," she said, nettled by the fellow's temerity. "Why shouldn't I know that hollow rock and running stream when it's next nigh to the Holy Cross Church where the river Stour runs by in Canterbury. That's where I was born and bred so I should know."

At that point Christopher, pleading a dry throat, called a temporary halt to the reading. Burbage bore down on him. "You owe me a play, Kit Marlowe," he said with a touch of truculence.

"I remember a paltry advance that didn't do credit to a day's hunger."

"But penny for penny and talent for talent," Burbage blustered on, "payment is due on the interest and charity has its price. You must deliver your promise."

"O my ducats, my Christian ducats," Christopher mocked. "Rather had I, a Jew, be hated thus, than pitied in Christian charity. And are we not all Jews? Wasn't the man of Nazareth a Hebrew, as were his disciples? If we are Christians we are also, by doctrine and creed, Jews."

To stop an acrimonious debate before it started, Watson called out, "Come, Kit, you've wetted your whistle. Now blow for us the final tune."

"What about the play you've promised?" Burbage was hanging on like a terrier clutching a baited bear's neck."

"Must you harass me on all sides?" Christopher held up the sheaves of paper. "I have it here. The Play. The Play."

He began to read, "Now vail your pride, you captive Christians and kneel for mercy to your conquering foe – " His audience grew quieter, feeding on every word, and only raised a murmur when the scheming Barabas fell into his own trap and died in the boiling cauldron. Even Burbage, made phlegmatic from decades of stage dramas, was moved to exclaim, "A winner, dear Kit, a veritable winner."

After the protracted and fulsome farewells, only Watson remained. He looked thoughtfully at his elusive friend. "Some said you'd been to the gates of hell and the polt-footed porter there refused you entry. Others said he gave you remission for many years to come, while some asserted that Marlowe was short of the coin to pay the infernal boatman."

Anne stood in the doorway, a pale rebuke.

Watson smiled bleakly. "We'll talk more about this when we meet again."

"I need to speak to Meg before she returns to Canterbury," Christopher said. But by then his sister was sitting beside the carter on his rumbling wagon as they passed through Southwark on the first leg of their journey home. "She's gone," Anne said and allowed herself a smug smile of satisfaction. "And you are alone."

Chapter ten

Christopher's latest play, The Malta Jew, was indeed a veritable winner. Not only was it performed for five days in the first week at The Theatre but it roused such interest among all classes that the Company gambled on producing it again less than a month afterwards. The gamble paid off and gallants flaunting their ostrich-plumed hats, tradesmen reeking of their callings, flat-capped apprentices chewing hazelnuts and women of every rank returned to revel in the just retribution visited upon the crafty Barabas the Jew, the venial Papist monks and the infidel Turks by the ultimate glorious triumph of noble Christians. What God-fearing, Protestant Englishman would not exult?

Retribution was the theme of the times and many asserted that while the bare ribs of the Spanish ships still littered the shores, revenge should be exacted against the audacious invaders and their putative allies at home and abroad. There were unconfirmed rumours of a counter-Armada being fitted out at Plymouth to be led by Drake with the blessing – though not the money – of the Queen, designed to take the war to Spain's back door through Portugal.

Christopher was not warmed by this bellicose fever. On the contrary, he despaired of otherwise rational men who turned from the finer points of civilised debate to the saw-tooth edge of possible carnage, looting, destruction and desolation.

He found no refuge from all this within the ranks of the sodality, that fraternity with its self-proclaimed dedication to truth and learning. When he grudgingly attended a meeting held in a room above a Bread Street tavern, some men were more concerned with court politics than philosophy. The rest drooled over a book by one Richard Fields, which detailed in every gory particular the massacre of 800 Spanish soldiers and sailors on the west coast of Ireland by bands of wild Irish tribesmen.

Will Warner, a fellow-member, took Christopher to one side.

"I've been commissioned to speak to you, Kit, on certain matters affecting our sodality. I would have welcomed an earlier opportunity but you were nowhere to be found."

According to the cringing Warner, the first matter to perturb the sodality was the Gilded Lady affray. Christopher had, some said, endangered the honour of the fraternity by indulging in an unseemly brawl in a disreputable Cornhill whorehouse and compounded his offence by an unprovoked and murderous assault on an innocent passer-by.

"Innocent passer-by?" exclaimed Christopher loudly. "That fat, one-time priest and poisoner of wells was no innocent and I was provoked beyond endurance."

Warner glanced anxiously at inquisitive listeners. "Let us be temperate in our speech, Kit. We are not protesting from the playhouse stage. The man is known to us and neither his nor your innocence is proven by hearsay. Happily for him, the knife intended for his guts merely pierced his jacket's paddings."

The second charge laid against Christopher was that he had prepared heretical writings. The evidence was slight, a scrap of paper covered with fragmented scribblings. The lines which had alarmed the sodality were, "There is no sin but ignorance" and "Religion is but a childish toy". Warner could not say how the paper had come into their possession but hinted that when Christopher had disappeared his belongings had been searched by a hireling obtaining access by gulling the landlady.

Christopher seethed with indignation. "If the connivers, schemers and scandal-mongers of this so-called brotherhood had taken the trouble to attend the recent performance of The Malta-Jew at the Theatre playhouse they would have heard those very lines pronounced in the prologue by an actor in the guise of ill-famed Machiavelli."

He stormed from the meeting-place, vowing never to attend a similar conclave again. For the next few days he shunned all company, avoided the taverns where his fellow-writers congregated and took a perverse delight in his solitary state.

One day, while browsing through the bookstalls of St Paul's, he discovered a well-thumbed Latin copy of Thomas More's Utopia with a map of that equitable island state glued inside the cover. He had heard that Sir Thomas had drawn the contours of this happy land in the shape of a place once known as Badric's Island. Christopher resolved to venture beyond the bend of the river to discover for himself whether such a society of humanity, reason and learning still existed.

He went through Ludgate towards Fleet and the curving road to Charing village and Westminster. To the far right St Giles' steeple rose above the trees and houses and from the left came the acrid smoke and distant noises of Alsatia, the notorious area of Whitefriars where outcasts and debtors lived in numerous hovels. A yelping dog ran through the undergrowth to snap at the heels of the grazing cattle, an old woman bent double under a load of sticks hobbled across his path and a procession of ragged-arsed children, snivelling and shivering, trailed towards the church for their daily dole of bread and soup.

In Old Palace Yard he bought bread and cheese from a stall near the pillory. A middle-aged man, by his clothes either a tanner or a shoemaker, was tied to the post; his right ear nailed to the wood and the red-raw letters "SS" burned into his left cheek. "He's one of them seditious scribblers,' the stall-holder explained helpfully.

It was not wise to linger. Pickpockets and cut-purses mingled with the pilgrims and country gentlemen up for Parliament. When the law officers stirred themselves, which was not very often, they did not waste time considering whether a dawdling stranger was an innocent traveller or a wandering miscreant.

Christopher did not stop walking till he was out of Westminster and by the river bank. He had hoped to find a wherry here but all he could see was the shattered hulk of a boat half-submerged in the brown slurry and swirling, shrieking scavenger birds flying and squabbling over a floating mass of offal discharged from the near-by slaughterhouse. Holding his breath and nose, he hurried by the stinking detritus and followed a winding path by the water's edge. A mist rolled down the river, nudged the banks and peopled the trees and bushes with wavering wraiths.

After thirty minutes or so he came to a fallen tree and took the opportunity to rest and eat. "Shall I go on?" His former enthusiasm was now dampened by the watery vapours, and he began to question the validity of his quest. His thoughts were disturbed by a splashing sound and, peering into the haze, he saw a boat sliding through the water towards him. The hull scraped against the shallow's gravel and the oarsman, a grey-bearded man swaddled in layers of clothes, asked, "Do you wish to cross?"

"Is it better or worse than where I am now?"

"You be the judge of that when we arrive."

"Then I'll go with you."

"First I must be paid. No soul may be taken to the other side unless he meets the reckoning. Pay me two base coins big enough to cover your eyes."

Neither spoke till they were half-way between the banks.

"We are going up-stream."

"The tide is on the turn. We must pull crooked to make a straight line."

The strength and power of the boatman, as he dug the oars into the rippling water, belied his ancient, creased face. He did not pause for breath nor speak another word and his eyes, though directed towards Christopher, had the unblinking unseeing gaze of a blind man. For a while the obscuring mist brushed against them with clammy tendrils and then it suddenly parted as if a curtain had been drawn aside. They were in clear sight of an arch consisting of two fluted pillars and a granite lintel standing high on a earthen mound. A stone stairway led down to the river.

"What is this place?" Christopher asked.

The boatman shipped the oars and allowed the vessel to drift towards the steps. "Have you abandoned hope, young man? Are you seeking refuge?"

"I'm searching for the kingdom on earth where men live in harmony with each other and nature."

"God guide you then, young man. Go through the gate beyond. It is the beginning."

Christopher clambered out of the boat and as it floated from the shore, the old man cupped his hand over his mouth and shouted, "I'll be here when you return."

The lower slabs were slippery with green slime but the upper ones were dry and covered with fine ash. The mound itself was a rubble heap, the remains of a building which, by the evidence of blackened wood stumps and stained bricks, had been destroyed by fire. There were scattered signs of recent encampments. Rags, bones and broken pots were strewn everywhere and in the still-warm ashes of a fire-site, Christopher discovered the charred fragments of books. Kicking through the itinerants' litter, he found many scraps of paper, half-burned wood and leather covers.

"A library has been put to the flames. Have the Goths and Vandals of our city slums paid a visit? Even the barbaric crime of Theophilus before Alexandria wasn't equal to Christendom's savage outrages against learning," he muttered.

The view of the hinterland from the mound was uninspiring and uninviting. The dull-brown landscape of scrub and bushes seemed to stretch for miles with only a few scattered trees, gaunt and stripped of foliage, to break the tedious flatness. Further on the ground sloped upwards and in the far distance, on the height of the rise, the outlines of a monastery or castle could be dimly seen.

Christopher decided to make it his immediate destination. But the path disappeared and soon he was struggling through a tangle of undergrowth and shoulder-high brambles, his face slashed by thorns and his feet sinking into slushy mud. Panic rose within him. He could wander for days in this desolation until, weak with hunger and thirst, he collapsed and became a feast for foxes. If only he could hear another human voice. As if in answer to his heartfelt wish, a child called out somewhere ahead of him.

With renewed energy, he pushed on and eventually came to the beginning of the slope where, to his surprise, the earth was covered with lavender.

He had hoped to lay here for a while but hardly had he flattened the pungent herbs than he was distracted by snuffling and grunting. A herd of pigs, their aroma preceding them, came trotting towards him from the bushes. He scrambled to his feet to let them pass but, to his horror, the leading hog raised a most terrifying porcine squeal and the swines' shambling gait turned into a charging run. The child's voice called out again and the herd swerved aside to continue their progress into the bushes. "I'll risk their fury," he thought, "and speak to their guardian, be it man, woman, child or Behemoth itself." Their trail was marked with droppings and soon he came to a circle of about a dozen beehive-shaped mud-and-stick huts.

When he walked into the centre, snarling curs appeared as if from nowhere and stood around him as they worked up the courage to attack. The dogs were closely followed by people crawling out of what he thought were sties. The children were naked and the adults so encrusted with grime that only the matted beards distinguished the males from the females. Muttering and growling, they surrounded him and then clawed at his hair and clothes. His knees weakened and his gorge rose when he received the full savour of their stench.

Suddenly there came shouts and the pig people cowered back under a barrage of blows from cudgels administered by a party of four men. "Find your own swill by the riverbank. He's ours."

With their assortment of belts, sticks, swords and pistols, Christopher's rescuers were the kind of desperadoes that any lone traveler would dread to meet. "We've been keeping an eye on you since you landed at the wizard's house," a big, black-bearded man with a single gold earring said. "You mean the ruined building with the arch?" Blackbeard turned to clout an incautious pigman on the head. "Yes, the very place. You'll come with us."

The collective courage of the pig-people evaporated when another man fired a pistol at them. Some ran into their sty-hutches while the rest scattered across the lavender fields. A mangy cur, wounded by the shot, sprawled in the dirt, whimpering and whining.

"That'll be their meal tonight," said Blackbeard. "Though you would have been tastier. They'd eat anybody or anything. Seen the children, did you? Not many, counting the number. When they've too many mouths to fill, they fill their mouths with their boiled sucklings. Mostly the girls. The flesh is softer."

Christopher puffed and panted as they trudged along an even steeper path and it seemed to him they had marched for miles before a halt was called and the group looked down on a village in a hollow. There were only two brick houses, and they were derelict. The rest of the dwellings were huts, lean-to sheds and wattle-and-stick hives similar to the pig-peoples' sties. At the sight of a vast gathering dressed in grey habits, Christopher thought he had come upon an excluded religious sect. Then the villagers swarmed towards the men and he saw the raddled skin, the noseless faces and the raw stumps that should have ended in a hand or a foot. The lepers cried out, "For Christ's sake, alms, food, for mercy sake, help us."

"Hurry, hurry, give them what we've brought," urged Blackbeard. After throwing down hunks of bread and meat, they marched off in great haste.

It was near dusk when the party reached the top of the rise and the large building. It had ben a place of monastic seclusion before bluff King Hal had scattered its clerical dwellers far and wide, take the gold and silver for his own depleted coffers and sold off the remaining effects to his close friends. The present inhabitants of the ruined edifice were neither chaste nor celibate.

Groups of men and women were gathered round several fires and cooking pots, drinking and singing bawdy songs. Blackbeard conducted Christopher into the roofless chapel. "Don't move from here and I'll fetch you victuals presently," he said.

Christopher shooed several clucking hens from the altar dais, stretched out and began to doze off. "Here y'are then, as I promised." Blackbeard had returned. Christopher sat up, blinked his eyes, and in the prevailing gloom made out the shapes of half a dozen people. "Isn't that Dick Chomley? And Jack Marlin?" he asked but none replied. A scrawny woman laid a flagon of wine, a piece of dark bread and a hunk of red roasted meat by his side. "And you? What's your name?" She stepped back and all the shadowy figures vanished. Only Blackbeard remained.

The wine, though tartaric, was tolerable but the bread, a poor man's loaf of rye and beans, was harder to swallow. Christopher was reluctant to try the meat- was it horse, donkey or baited bull? – but rather than offend his host he sank his teeth into the tough flesh. It was not human. That would have had the consistency of pork.

"I should warn you," said Blackbeard softly, "we're the nameless ones."

"But I'm not. I am Christopher Marlowe, poet and scholar, and I'm known the length and breadth of Cheapside for my plays. What is this place?"

"See with your own eyes. A haven for outcasts, the wreckage of mankind, the havoc and harvest of hell, the end of the world. And you, master poet and scholar, what brought you to us?"

"Years ago a great man wrote of a wondrous kingdom where none is better or worse than his neighbour, ignorance was a sin and learning a virtue."

Blackbeard stood up and scratched his crotch. "Learning means nothing to me. It bakes no bread and doesn't fill my children's bellies. As for your fancy kingdom where none is better or worse than another, seek no further. We who are condemned by birth and fortune to be the sweepings and the scourings of the land are marked out to be the lowest of the low and none here are better or worse for that. Mind you, if you've a stomach for it, there's none more equal among themselves than the swine-herders wallowing in their pig-shit. And what of the God-forsaken lepers? Haven't they a great commonality in their misery? They're the outcasts of outcasts and many of them were once known for their beauty, nobility and learning. Rich or poor, it's to that unholy hollow they come to rot and die and the only difference between one and the other is the lack of a leg, a hand or a nose." From somewhere in the cloisters a bell tinkled. "It's the hour for our evening service. Find yourself a hole or corner till it's over."

The murmuring of many voices came closer and a man, cowled and robed like a friar, led a procession of men, women and children up the nave of the chapel. Tar-torches were stuck in holders on the walls and the congregation quietened as the robed man mounted the altar dais and turned to face the assembly.

The torches cast more shadows than light. Was that old scrawny man The Gilded Lily's blind fiddler? And the burly man leaning against a pillar? Was he not the drunken, dry-land sailor Marlin? And the man on the dais? The face was obscured by the cowl but the voice was the voice of Dick Chomley.

"Brothers and Sister," the false friar began. "The day of the gathering approaches and the signs of our peculiar calling shall redden the skies when the morning of our blood dawn breaks. Let us now, this night, honour and praise our blessed lady, Mary Magdalene, for the peace she had brought among us and her promises to us on the fulfillment of the seventh book's prophecies. Glory be to Mary, whore of God."

"Glory be to Mary, whore of God," the congregation responded.

"In our trials and tribulations she will intercede for us with her beloved Lord. Did he not lay his head on her lap when he was weary? Did she not clasp him to her breasts when he was in need? For the Lord was a man. Naked and unashamed he appeared to her when he had risen from the tomb and he knew her. He said unto her, 'Your children are my children. They shall be numbered among the humble, the rejected, the poor and the dispossessed and they shall inherit the earth.' And he said unto her, 'I give you a sign.' And he laid his hand on her heart whereupon a token of blood from his pierced hand stained her breast. Glory be to Mary, whore of God."

"Glory be to Mary, whore of God."

"And they who have become bloated upon the flesh of the people shall know the wrath of the risen One. There will be fire and pestilence and weeping and lamentations in every house. Then will the children of Mary, whore of God, and the sons of Ishmael descend from the wilderness, like hungry wolves upon the fold, and wander through the stricken streets, finding no door bolted, no gate barred. The hounds, for want of their masters' whip, will be meek to our commands. Brothers and Sisters, on that wondrous day, the children of Mary, whore of God, and the sons of Ishmael shall be garbed in satin and silks – how often, I ask you, had those poor bodies been stripped naked for the lash? – and they shall adorn themselves with golden ropes of pearls – how often, I ask you, had iron chains galled their flesh – and they shall gorge themselves from divers laden tables and see the cheeks of Lazarus fatten. Brothers and Sisters, let us pray."

As of one voice, the assembly chanted, "Hail Mary, Whore of God, blessed is the fruit of thy harlotry and keep us free from scourge, flesh-rot and the pox. Our will be done. Amen."

The preacher raised his arms. "Brothers and Sisters, before we disperse. There is a stranger among us. Do we accept him or send him away?"

"Is he a cut-purse? A house-breaker? A horse-stealer? A dice-cheater? Has he been flogged? Branded? Sentenced to be hung?

Is he a forger of coins? A beggar? A vagabond? A juggler? A strolling player?"

"He's a poet?"

"A poet!" Some laughed, some jeered and many cried, "Send him away. We don't need poets." Chattering like a conference of starlings, the crowd left the chapel. The cowled man spoke briefly to Blackbeard before following them.

"You've found favour, young man, if not acceptance," said Blackbeard. "It's our practice to send unwanted strangers into the dead of night to find their own path home but I've been asked to find lodgings in the convent for you and guide you to the river in the morning. Come with me." He took down a torch and led the way through the rear of the chapel, along several covered passages, down a narrow stairway and into a stone chamber that smelled strongly of must and mildew.

Blackbeard shouted, "We've a guest for you, reverend mother." An elderly nun carrying a horn lantern appeared in the doorway. "Reverend mother, by the grace of God and your peculiar vocation to the shrine of our blessed Mary, we pray you give this stranger shelter for the night and food in the morning. He'll be no trouble at all and will go in the morning." As the nun turned to leave, Blackbeard told Christopher to follow her.

They went down a narrow, low-ceilinged passageway that was flanked on each side by small cubicles. Christopher read out the names inscribed on the lintels. "Sugar Loaf, Elephant, Vine, Beerpot, Castle, Gun, Cardinal's Cap," he intoned. "Why are these monastical cells named after Bankside brothels?" he asked.

"Because they're our sacred places," replied the elderly nun. "Choose where you'll lie. You'll find them clean and wholesome with fresh straw and hard-washed blankets."

In keeping with the religious nature of this catacomb, Christopher choose the Cardinal's Cap. It seemed to him he had only dropped off to sleep when he was wakened by another nun. He caught a slight glimpse of her face – she was young – when she beckoned him to follow her, but he caught more than a whiff of suppuration. There was a jug of goat's milk, black bread and a hunk of cheese on the table in the outer chamber. "Is this for me?" he asked but when he turned, she had gone.

A few minutes later Blackbeard appeared. "It's time to leave. Put what you can't finish into your wallet." It was cold outside, not quite dawn, and a low cloud hugged the land. They returned by a different route and reached the bank further up the river. "How will I travel from here?" Christopher asked. His guide nodded towards a boat that floated in the water, then strode off and disappeared from sight.

Chapter eleven

The grey-clad boatman dipped the oars and the hull scraped the shingles. "Did I not promise to come for you?"
"Where will you take me now?"
"Up-river, beyond and to the other side."
"And will I find what I seek on the other side?"
"You will find what was and is no more on this side."
"I'll cross with you then."
"First you must pay me. You know the fee."
No more was said as the craft slid through the smoothly flowing water. The sky was a pale blue vault, each bank was smothered in green and here and there small white houses peeped shyly from behind clumps of osier willow. Larger houses with chequered facades and many windows stood back from the river edge, as if disdaining to dip their toes in the mud; and behind them, where the land rolled gently up and towards the horizon, spires and wisps of smoke signalled the presence of villages and hamlets. From far away came the living sounds of a dog barking, cattle lowing, a woman calling and a man shouting.

The boatman rowed like one taking a leisurely outing on a placid lake; feathering the oars on the ripples for the duration of two long breaths after each stroke. After travelling for a mile or more, the old man veered the boat to the right and began to chant in a language foreign to his passenger. When the boat skimmed over the shallows and slid towards a landing, he abruptly ended his song.

At first sight, the view from this point was so similar to the disembarkation place of yesterday, with granite steps leading up to a two-pillared arch at the top of a mound, that Christopher's mental compass became confused. Several men standing under the arch waves and shouted halloos. "Who are they?" Christopher asked.

"In one particular, you'll discover that soon enough but in

another particular, you'll never know." The boatman gave his passenger a cloth visor. "You must wear this before you land."

One of the men, also masked, came down the stairs. "Welcome, a thousand welcomes, my friend," he said and reached out to help Christopher from the boat. "You must be hungry after your long journey."

"I've had a meal earlier today. I brought along what I could not eat." Christopher opened his wallet, but the bread and cheese were greeted with a contemptuous cry. "This is fit only for scavengers. See, it's slimy with green mould." The masked man grabbed the food, threw it into the water and then, laughing, ran up the steps to his companions.

"Is this what you promised me?" Christopher asked the boatman.

"It was not I who promised. It was so designed." He dug his oars into the water and pulled out to mid-stream.

The high-spirited group above beckoned and called to Christopher. They were dressed in rich but not ornate clothes and though masked – as was everybody else he would meet that day – their movements betrayed their youth. They effusively welcomed him as if he were a boon companion and, linking arms, marched as one body towards the castellated and crenellated frontage of a large solid-stone house.

There was a vast throng of men eating and drinking at a long table in the capacious dining-hall and the hubbub was so loud that it was a wonder anyone could hear himself.

He who had first greeted Christopher seemed to have taken on the role of mentor and guide. "What shall we call you, my friend?" he asked.

"I am – "

"No, not that name inherited from those who had engendered you, cursed or blessed as they may be. To join our congregation, you must be baptised again." He stood at the end of the table and shouted, "In the name of Belzebub, I pray silence. Children of Lilith, we have an unbaptised one among us. How shall he be named?"

Tankards were banged on the table and several called out, "Summon Merlin, the name-giver." A small, crook-backed figure, dressed in gaudy patchwork clothes with a painted face-mask to match, appeared from behind a curtain, hop-skipped drunkenly across the floor and onto the table, picked up a full tankard and drank down its contents in one go.

"Did I not vouch you magic?" he squealed and then giggled. "Look, I've poured a quart into a pint pot. How can I serve you now, o masters?"

The guide laid his hand on the new arrival's shoulder. "Conjure from your black bag a name for this stranger so that he may be baptised according to our ritual and thus be fit to eat the forbidden fruit."

The little man jigged down the table, chanting, "Baliol, Belcher, Beelzebub and Banio, guide my guile." When he reached the end, the besotted hunchback crouched with his hands on his knees, burbled, "I, Merlin, in the spirit of Nephriti, pronounce him Icarus," and then slowly toppled over on top of Christopher.

Chanting "Icarus, Icarus", the boisterous crowd, with Christopher in the middle, shoved and scuffled their way through the curtains into a circular room. A marble font, ornamented with bas-reliefs or gargoyles, griffons, writhing dragons and rampant bulls, was set in the centre of the tiled floor. Instead of baptismal water, the basin was heaped with smouldering charcoal.

Christopher was left standing near the font while the jostling revellers formed a disorderly circle. His guide announced in grave tones, "As commanded by sozzled Merlin, our new entrant shall be dubbed Icarus. Who will be devil-father to the choice?"

A very tall man, covered from head to foot in a mauve cloak, pushed through the mob. Suddenly everybody fell silent. "I, whose name cannot be spoken, will be such a one," he declared. Christopher's heart beat faster and for a few seconds he feared that this was not just an outrageous masquerade. Would lightening flash? The heavens rend? The earth gape?

A third man, attired in mock-Papal raiments and carrying a large, wooden-covered book, stepped forward. In halting Latin he read out a lascivious passage from Ovid's Amores and then asked the tall man, "Do you, whose awful name shall not be spoken, swear to be the Satanic guardian to this child, now known as Icarus?"

"I do."

"Then so be it. In the name of Adonis, Bacchus and Zeus's golden shower, Icarus you are and Icarus you shall be till Helious' burning orb melts your wings and you fall, like proud Lucifer, to the depths beyond redemption. Bring forth the censers and the water of life."

Full tobacco pipes were produced and lit with lumps of charcoal held by silver tongs. Christopher sucked on the stem but as soon as the fumes touched his throat, his eyes smarted and the inside of his head seemed to spin like a child's whirling top. He was given a small goblet, told, "This is the water of life" and urged to drink it down without hesitation. The liquid was clear, had the sharp smell of fennel seeds and raisins and rasped his gullet as if he had swallowed a bundle of flaming thorns.

The rite now completed, the crowd surged back to the hall to enjoy the next diversion. The long table was converted to a stage and a troup of actors, dressed in what was imagined to be ancient Greek costumes, began to cavort in a Priapean comedy. The crudely-spoken play was a far cry from anything produced at the Theatre but the grossly exaggerated gestures were greatly appreciated by the spectators.

Christopher tried to suppress the nausea gurgling up from the pit of his stomach but the noise and heat threatened to overcome him. As the gathering roared at the ribaldry, he sidled round the wall and ran towards the entrance.

"Whither do you fly, O Icarus?" His guide and erstwhile greeter approached the portico with a company of riotous-looking men of substance.

Christopher replied that he had felt faint. His guide laughed. "It's your belly fainting for sustenance. Come with us to another room where there's food in plenty." They turned into a second, smaller dining-room where a table was laden with meat, pastries and flagons of wine. Snuffling and snarling like a pack of starving dogs, the new arrivals stuffed fistfuls into their maws.

Christopher stood back from the melee. "Are you not hungry, Icarus?" he was asked.

"I've no wish to compete with those snouts in the trough."

"Have you no sin? Neither lechery or gluttony tempts you?"

"You've tempted those men to become swine."

"They are swines by nature and temper."

A man who had torn at a chicken breast with his teeth began to choke on a bone. He reeled across the table, upsetting plates and goblets, fell on the floor and rolled and gasped in agony. His companions continued to ravage the food and did not give the writhing man a second glance.

"He'll surely die," Christopher said but the cold reply came: "Let him. He is, as we all are, the instrument of his own salvation and his own destruction. Come with me, Icarus, and leave them to gorge their fill."

"First tell me, friend, since I am dubbed Icarus for this occasion, what is your given name?"

The man hesitated. "Calcobrina, the grace-scorner. But come, Icarus, let's take that bald sexton Time by the forelock and feast our eyes on temporal richness."

They went down a long corridor and entered a windowless room at the end. Tapestries, carpets and pictures covered every inch of the walls, ivory, marble and onyx statues, gold and silver cups, vases and chalices filled every flat surface and, as if flung pell-mell by an angry sprite, coins, gems, pearls and jewels were strewn all over the floor.

"I've business elsewhere," said Calcobrina, "and will return presently. Meanwhile, take a measure of this wealth."

Christopher picked up a chalice and wiped off the patina of dust. It was heavy with its own gold, the embedded blood-red carbuncles and the pearls and coins inside the vessel.

"With one such pearl I'd be lord for a month, with two a king and with three an emperor. Those who now slight me for my poverty would drool and slobber with envy and beg me to throw them a pittance. They would say, 'There goes the great, the mighty, the munificent Christopher Marlowe.' All they say now is, 'Look at Kit Marlowe, the sometime poet, with his arse sticking out of his breeches, on the look-out for someone to buy him a drink.'"

He held up the chalice and stared at the inflamed shafts of splintered light through the gems. "But then, if I was burdened with such an outward show of splendour, they'd creep up at night to slit my throat."

"Truly, Icarus, but I could have sworn I saw a Papist priest performing his holy office." Calcobrina had silently returned. "But it was you, I think, worshipping at a different altar. Tell me, what does this boundless wealth mean to you?"

"It's all dross. Where are your tomes of learning?" He held up a pearl. "One printed page is more precious to me than this lump of a diseased oyster. Give me knowledge and you give me an omnipotence and a dominion that stretches beyond any empyry."

"Icarus does not seek a deity, he seeks to be a god. You have Lucifer's ambition and his untrammelled pride. And I feared you were without blemish. Wait. I hear voices. We'll hide behind this drape."

From their covert they saw two men enter the room. Their clothes of brocade, silk and lace, their bejewelled fingers and their well-filled bodies showed that fortune favoured them. "Didn't I tell you?" said one, "There's a king's ransom here." The second man uttered an oath. "No, no, ten kings' ransoms is nearer the mark."

With increasing excitement, they rooted through the piles. "But this is a Roman coin." "Here is a Spanish piece." "This comes from the Indias." They grew more intemperate and, with the playfulness of children running through autumn leaves, tossed coins and gems into the air. After several minutes of levity, they became quiet and thoughtful.

"Is there an account of all this written down in ledgers?"

"Judging by the way it's scattered, I'd say not."

"I desire that gold coin. It's from the days of Julius Caesar."

"It would be a sour return for our host's generosity to take it."

"Rather I would say it's a just reward for his poor stewardship."

"True, true. What is not marked down is not counted. I have a fancy for this ruby. It fits snugly in my purse with room to spare. I have a good mind to add this and this to keep it company."

Greed overcame any prudence and they stuffed gold coins and gems into their purses, tucked plates into their jerkins and wrapped goblets in their cloaks.

When the two men waddled out with their load, Christopher and Calcobrina came out from their hiding place.

"Will you not challenge them?" Christopher asked.

"But what have they stolen? In your words, dross. Would you have me spit them on the point of my blade? Is that the sum of our endeavours? To kill a man for this?" Calcobrina laid a pearl on the floor and smashed it to pieces with the base of a chalice. "What, Icarus, amazed at this vandal act?" He flung the chalice down and stamped it flat with demonic fury. "Now, my friend, I've shown you gluttony, lechery, greed, my wrath and your pride. What other sins shall I exhibit?"

"Sloth and envy are left in the tally."

"Sloth is plentiful enough in high places and when you return to your London companions you'll have your bellyful of envy. Let's leave this midden heap and join the revellers but before we go, taker this for remembrance." He pressed a gold coin into Christopher's hand. "Hold it tight in your fist and inspect it where there is more light."

They walked down a passage towards the noise of music, singing and drunken bellows. When they reached the door, Calcobrina said, "Now look at your remembrance." Christopher opened his fist and saw that the gold paint had melted from the lead disc and smeared his palm. "Nothing in that room, Icarus, is true to its pretended nature or vaunted value. As it is in this world and shall be forever, even to the power you seek with your waxen wings of knowledge." He flung open the door, marched into the hall and was lost to sight among the rowdy assembly.

The lord of misrule reigned supreme. Many men had donned women's clothes and were prancing obscenely around like spare whores from the Bankside stews. Others hopped and leaped in a grotesque imitation of courtly dances, some had exchanged their cloth visors for goat-head masks and not a few were dressed in the popular images of devils.

The Merlin figure sat enthroned on a high chair placed on the table. He had a sceptre in one hand, a globe in the other and a crown on his head. He shouted obscenities and demands for drink; and when he screamed he needed to piss, a devil-person undid his breeches while a man-woman minced forward and lifted out the hunchback's penis with a pair of silver tongs. The high trajectory of the ensuing gush of water was greeted with raucous applause.

The rhythmic notes of a large bell in the near distance eventually penetrated the uproar. The tall figure of he whose name should not be spoken appeared in the entrance and held up his arms. As the din decreased, he called out, "Foul and fair is the hour with wanton wiles upon midnight's fading breath. Bring forth our craven king of the day and pray our true lord and master accepts this misshapen lump as restitution for all our sins."

Staves were placed under the hunchback's chair, four men hoisted this ready-made palanquin on their shoulders and the load was carried out of the house at the head of a turbulent procession towards the arch and a prepared pyre. Merlin continued to bawl and sway and many hands reached out to prevent him toppling from his throne. At the arch the tall man raised his arms again and cried out, "It strikes. It strikes. The twelfth hour is with us. Elements dissolve. Soul fly. Let it be consummated."

A torch was set to the pyre and palanquin and passenger were placed on top of the blazing pile. For a few seconds the hunchback sat there in drunken stupor and then, when flames took hold of his clothes, screamed and seemed to fall into the burning sticks. A swirl of smoke blinded the cheering mob and Christopher was knocked off his feet by a small, smouldering figure hurtling towards the river.

He remembered little of what happened after that. He felt depleted, as if his blood had flowed out of an opened vein. Leaving the crowd, he lay on a slope facing the water. He dimly recollected that as the fire died down the inflammatory excitement was dampened. Later, as he dozed off, people passed by, talking in subdued tones. There was a splashing of oars and, occasionally, a shouted farewell.

Was it a dream? An hallucination?

No, there was the arch, the granite steps and the imposing house with its ostentatious battlements. And there had been a fire. The arch's pillars were soiled with soot, charred sticks were scattered on the ground and a thin wisp of smoke rose from the still-glowing embers.

"Westminster ho!" A brawny young man wearing the flat cap, badge and regulation costume of a ferryman called out from his boat. Christopher went down the steps, asked the fare and checked his money to make sure he had enough. The lead disc nestled among the coins.

"What's that?" the ferryman asked.

"Nothing of any value. A curiosity I found." He dropped it into the water as he boarded the boat. Two men, one very tall and dressed in a long mauve cloak and the other not unlike Calcobrina, stood under the arch, watched the boat for a few seconds and then turned and disappeared.

"Friends of yours? Come to see you off?"

"No, I've never seen them before."

"Just as well if they're from that house. Queer things go on there, I've heard, and if they're not careful, the same fate'll befall them as happened to that wizard's house in Mortlake. Flying in the face of God, that's what I say."

He was a garrulous fellow, with firm opinions on many matters, in particular foreigners. "Should never be allowed in the country. They creep into nooks and corners, like fleas in a strumpet's shift, sucking good trade from honest men with their shoddy wares and not giving a ha'penny worth of value to scratch your itch." The man's tireless chatter flowed over his passenger but he seemed not to care whether his stream of comments, fragments of news and forecasts of doom caused a single ripple.

Though a Westminster man – "Born and bred and proud of it" – he was as one with the citizens of the rival town of London in elevating the young Earl of Essex, the Queen's 'white boy', to the status of a national hero. He saw the youthful adventurer as the instrument of deliverance from the predicted doom. "If the Queen herself will let him have a free hand with the Lisbon expedition, he'll sweep all before him." The ferryman had not a good word for Ralegh – that know-all babblemouth – whom he blamed for fitting the Lisbon expedition out in Plymouth instead of Tilbury. "Making trade for his own friends, that's why."

Westminster hove into sight and the ferryman paused long enough for Christopher to ask, "Is the old boatman who took me up the river yesterday your father?" A look of fear flashed in the man's eyes and he pressed his passenger to describe the ancient. "Yesu help us if he's plying the river." He refused to add any more to that and gruffly said, "Take care, friend, and when you come this way again hire none but them who wear the badge."

Chapter twelve

London, flower of all cities in the words of the Scotsman Dunbar, was in a festive mood. Trade had been good, prices had remained steady and, a singular blessing, the warm summer had not provoked a major outbreak of any endemic sickness, in particular the dreaded pestilence. True, the news from abroad was not to everybody's taste. The Lisbon expedition, which had proudly set sail from Plymouth with the intention of putting paid to the arrogant ambitions of Philip of Spain once and for all, had ended in shambles and volleys of accusations and counter-accusations of treachery and incompetence. "A foolhardy, costly and ill-advised escapade," said some, many of whom had invested in the enterprise and called it 'God and England's glorious avengement'.

On the 24th of August, there was little thought given to the Lisbon debacle. St Bartholomew's Fair was in full swing and crowds streamed into the city from all directions to buy gee-gaws, sticky cakes and wooden dolls, to gape at the jugglers, laugh at the freaks and try their luck at the trick-of-the-loop and other games of chance.

The taverns were packed and none so much as The Mermaid in Cheapside where the so-called University Wits Christopher Marlowe, Tom Watson, Thomas Nashe and Robert Greene, plus fellow writers and actors such as the renamed Will Slaughter, were squeezed into a tight huddle by the press of bodies. They had agreed among themselves to leave and perhaps find more pleasant and less congested sport across the river on the green sward, vulgarly known as 'Whores-lie-down' by St Towley's church. But for the present they were well and truly trapped in the crush.

Suddenly, above the hubbub, came alarmed calls and wild words of, "Murdering rebellion" – "Hundreds of rogues" – "Thousands of armed men". The tavern crowd milled around and Nashe asked, "What new garboil is this?" Garboil or garbled, some sense was made of the incontinent shouts and the cause of the commotion was made clear. A large band of armed men were marching up Cheapside. Within seconds, the tavern had lost more than half of its customers.

"A blessing on this come-lately Jack Cade, whoever he is," said Thomas Nashe. He was a plump, jovial person and it would take an earthquake of disproportionate measure to disturb his equanimity. "He's put rout to these once-a-year revellers and has given Bacchus' most constant disciples room to breathe and replenish our tankards."

"Cade was a Puritan before his time, Tom," said Robert Greene and, glancing slyly at Christopher, added, "and worse, he was a Kentish man."

"I couldn't give a tinker's curse," retorted Christopher, "whether Cade was a come-early Puritan or the misbegotten son of a Kentish sheep-shearer. His error was to demand money from the London merchants instead of their wives and daughters and thus had the gates closed against him."

What remained of the tavern's customers were clustered by the lattice window. There was little they could see through the clumpy glass. When the trembling potboy refilled the tankards, Marlowe, Nashe and Greene strolled over to join their cowering companions at the entrance. The crunching of many feet on the cobbles, the disturbed bee-hive buzz of many voices and the explosive chanting of many futile demands now sounded very near the tavern. Not a few of the window watchers dashed out by the rear.

"See how the rabbit scuttle to save their mangy fur," sneered Greene. "Shall we, too, vanish down a hole or, with the true curiosity of enquiring minds, investigate this alarums-off in all its rabble rage?"

He pushed the door open and, in spite of cries for prudence from their more cautious friends, Christopher and Nashe followed him. In less time than it took to shout "Down with Drake," the three were swept into the ranks of this turbulent and ragged army on its march towards St Paul's.

The majority of the men wore the tattered remnants of soldiers' and sailors' uniforms. Devon and Cornish accents were dominant among the mariners and guttural Celtic words were bawled by many of the erstwhile warriors. The rest of the mob consisted of idle apprentices, roustabouts and street toughs: a typical London rabble who could always be relied upon to turn out for any riot. Order of a sort was maintained by club-wielding thugs who marched on each side of the procession and threatened any potential looter with a cracked skull if he stepped out of line.

By now Christopher had lost sight of Nashe and Greene. He had also lost his ale-pot: it had been snatched from his hands as soon as he was engulfed by the crowd. He was pushed from behind, hemmed in on both sides and nearly deafened by the loud chants of, "We want our pay!", "Essex for commander!", "Death to Norris!" and "Death to Drake!"

A burly seaman glowered at him. "Has the cat caught your tongue?" he asked, then grinned and said, "Why, it's Kit Marlowe. Remember me, Jack Marlin, and that bit of ruction we had on this very spot in Cheapside?" He lowered his voice, "This is a rough lot and you'd better yell with the rest of them or they'll think the worse of you."

From then on Christopher was as loud as the next person.

When the marchers pressed into the area round St Paul's Cross, he was separated from Marlin. To save himself from being smothered in the crush, he pushed through to the first rank facing the plinth. Nashe and Greene were a few feet away; both looking as if they had had an encounter with a thorny bush.

"Let's hurry from here," urged Nashe. "There's trouble on the boil and I've no wish to wait and be scalded."

Greene's high domed forehead glistened with sweat and his eyes glinted with excitement. "Rein yourself in," he said, "and let's listen to what this mouth-almighty has to say."

The 'mouth-almighty' on the plinth was Richard Chomley. "Fellow soldiers and sailors of the ill-fated and thrice-betrayed expedition," he began.

"I don't recall him," muttered a sailor.

"Chance he was on another ship," said a second sailor.

"Maybe he was and maybe he wasn't or maybe by chance he was warming his arse at another man's fire."

"Aye, and giving it a poke to make the sparks fly."

Chomley, in his best rhetorical style, dwelt on the courage, the suffering and the resolution of the warriors and the inglorious end to the Lisbon adventure.

"Devil take the glory," a soldier shouted. "We want our pay."

Chomley was well into his stride. "Where is the promised booty? Where is the Spanish gold? Where, I ask you, is your just reward? Fellow soldiers and sailors, while you hunger and want, while you march, footsore and weary, from Plymouth to London town, while your wives and children famish, there are connivers and intriguers in this kingdom, gracing high offices, who can open their coffers and count, from now to Saint Nicholas's Day, those very gold coins that should be jingling and jangling in your purses. Yes, I say to you, those greedy men of little faith (Cries of 'Who? Who?') are in the pay of the Spanish King and are hand-in-glove with the Papists and the Jesuits."

"This bellowing fool touches on treason," Nashe said.

"Is it any wonder they tried to stop the one man who, alone, if he had had full command, for he lacks nothing in wisdom and courage, would have brought you victory, glory and filled your bellies and your pokes. And who is this noble man, you ask?"

"What I ask," said the sailor to his companion, "is whose belly did he fill with his poke?"

Chomley's question was answered by a small group, Marlin among them, near the plinth. "Essex, Essex," they chorused.

"This is politics and has nothing to do with my money," a soldier grumbled and repeated the refrain, "Where's my pay?"

"Where's my pay, this good soldier asks. We know where your pay is, Essex knows where your pay is and when Essex returns, he will spoil the spoilers and give to each and everyone his just desserts; and I tell you, some will not escape a whipping." Though his cronies cheered the last remark, the rest of the crowd were becoming restless. "We can't eat words," one shouted. Chomley changed tack. "Fellow soldiers and sailors, today is St Bartholomew's Day, a day to be remembered and avenged and as the good citizens of London disport themselves at the Fair – "

"They disport and we go hungry," a sailor shouted. "There's plenty of food at the Fair." Others cried, "To the Fair." Chomley's speech was lost in the uproar as the roused mob heaved and shoved. Marlin and his companions tried to hold back the surging mass but the unfortunate dry-land sailor was smashed on the head with a cudgel and disappeared under the trampling feet.

Whatever rags of military discipline had clung to the discontented sailors and soldiers when they marched up Cheapside was now torn to shreds and flung to the four winds. Bellowing "To the Fair," they stampeded like a blind and furious dragon round the cathedral, overturning stalls and crushing everything that stood in their way.

The first strong opposition presented itself at the Newgate end of Cheapside. A hastily assembled squad of London's red-coated militia, strengthened by a line of blue-coated horsemen, stretched across the road. Martyrdom was not the option chosen by the rabble, least of all by the London apprentices and street-toughs. "Back, back," those in front yelled. "To the Fair," persisted those at the rear. For a minute or so the crowd milled in utter confusion before turning to swarm in the opposite direction; but again their way was barred by another militia squad.

The three friends were like twigs caught in the vortex of a whirlpool. Greene and Nashe, both deathly pale and staggering as if drunk, held onto each other, while Christopher, who had picked up a discarded sword, struck out left and right in an attempt to force a way out of the tumult.

Suddenly a volley of shots rang out from Cheapside, followed closely by another from Newgate. The crowd recoiled and ran towards St Paul's as if to seek sanctuary; but hardly had they gone five yards than a third and more deadly volley came from Paternoster Row. Men fell, screaming and cursing, and the horsemen rode in to slash and jab at every person in their way.

"Run, run," Christopher urged his companions, but Greene, weeping and gibbering with fear, collapsed in a faint and pulled Nashe down on top of him. A horseman made a cut at them and then turned to slice open the head of an apprentice. A small red fountain of blood spurted from the stricken youth's skull, he fell against Christopher and they both sprawled on the ground. The rider forced his horse to step on the bodies and then, losing interest in the sport, galloped off into the melee.

Both Greene and Nashe lay very still and a riverlet of gore coursed down the latter's face. "Are you dead, friends?" Christopher rose groggily to his feet. "Forgive me for leaving you without a prayer."

He sprinted this way and that way, but wherever he turned he was met by knots of fighting men, foam-mouthed horses, militia stolidly reloading their cumbersome guns or huddles of terrified women and children. "Here, here." A blowzy woman clutched his arm and pulled him through a narrow doorway. "God save us this day, but you're drenched with blood." She dragged him through the tenement and out to an open space. "Over the Wall with you and go to Bart's. They'll patch up your wounds there and never ask a question."

Two short ladders and a rickety scaffold-tower leaned against the crumbled brickwork of London Wall. Christopher climbed up the rigging and had almost reached the top when a tumbling yelling gang of rioters burst, like pus from a boil, into the space below. Those in front heaved themselves up on the bars, those behind grabbed at the feet above them and those at the back frantically punched and shoved to gain a foothold. As Christopher quickly clambered onto the Wall, the tower shuddered, began to sway and was only saved from toppling by a length of hemp wedged by two massive stones.

"The rope, mate, pull in the rope," a sailor on the upper section called out. Christopher turned away. "Why should I endanger myself for you rogues," he said to himself. From this point he could see the quiet countryside dotted with houses between Holborn and the Fleet and, in the near distance, a party of riders trotting towards the city from Clerkenwell.

There were several lean-to sheds on the other side of the Wall and as he half-jumped, half-slid on the roof of one, he could hear the crash of the collapsing tower and the screams of falling men.

Christopher hid in a ditch until the horsemen passed. They were a fox-hunting party returning with the pelts of the day's kill and their tired dogs showed little interest in the blood-smeared man lurking in the undergrowth. The hunters called to the hounds and one raised the rallying cry of "So ho." Their new quarry was not Christopher, as he had feared, but a scurrying rabbit; but they quickly abandoned their half-hearted chase and continued on their way.

Christopher emerged from his covert and, dodging between bushes and trees, ran towards a wall on his right. It was too high to climb over. He followed its course away from the city until he came to a turret and a small, heavy door set under an ornamental arch. Turning the ringed handle, he entered the building and decided to climb the stone spiral stairway to the top in the hope of finding temporary refuge until dusk.

He found himself stepping into a round, bare room where an old man knelt, praying loudly, his face towards a narrow, pointed window, his back to the intruder.

"How easy it would be to crack that eggshell, without anger, without fear, without reason, and walk from the brutal act with no more regret than a distaste for the brain-yoke staining the floor." Christopher shuddered and was appalled that the mayhem he had witnessed this day should have engendered such dreadful thoughts.

The ancient bowed three times, kissed a flat brown purse hanging from his neck by a leather thong, slowly rose and turned to face his visitor. He was very old and frail and his glazed skin appeared to be pasted to his bones.

"Aleicham." The alien greeting surprised Christopher. "I have made my peace with God and I am ready. God will the dead to life again restore. Praise be his glorious name for evermore." He spoke slowly and enunciated every syllable in a firm voice. "As with the bride awaiting the bridegroom, I knew you would come and had purified my soul. Yes, every man has his sword upon his thigh because of fear in the night. Are you alone or have you company, lusting to witness your sin?" He bowed his head and, with a touch of bitterness, said, "But then, is it not a principle of Christian faith that it's no sin to kill a heretic, an infidel or a Jew?"

"I cannot make sense of your blabbering, old man." Christopher leaned against the jamb and breathed in the cool, musty air. "Keen your contritions and prepare your quittance in your own manner, it's all one to me. I've no desire to kill and even less to be killed. I only ask to rest here till the hue and cry dies down."

"But you've slaughtered, bloodied youth. Your jerkin reeks with gore."

"An unfortunate wretch died in my arms; his head split with

the ease of a chopped turnip. I assure you, I've seen enough slaying today to last me a lifetime. Why should I wish to add your bones to the pile?"

"Because I am a Jew."

Christopher stared hard at the skeletal face. "You're mad," he said. "If you're a Jew, you're insane to be in London and if you're not, you've lost your reason to proclaim yourself so. Either way, you're a madman and we don't kill madmen in England. We make them kings, judges, commanders of our armies or if they're poor in substance and rank, we send them to Bedlam."

"True madness is a divine gift. All the saints, prophets and visionaries were divinely mad. I am deranged with sin and guilt but I am not mad. Look upon me. Here you see a born Jew who has denied his birthright, a false Christian denied his faith. To whom shall I bare my soul and confess my errors? To whom shall I bend my neck for the stroke of the avenging sword? I have waited and you have come to stand by my door, as bloody as the sons of Rimmon before David. Are you not God's dark angel of retribution?"

Christopher smiled wryly at the celestial appellation. "I'm not a wanderer from the heavenly host nor, if it goes to that, a lowly member of Satan's cohort, but a mere mortal whose divinity is circumscribed by fallible flesh. I am one whose limited learning had dubbed him a scholar and I earn my sparse pennies by scribbling passable dramas for the entertainment of this town's kings and commoners."

"And to whom are these passable dramas attributed?"

"Why, as I've just said, to me, Christopher Marlowe. And who are you?"

The old man's eyes widened and he trembled. "I know of you, Christopher Marlowe, and you will have heard word of me. I am Doctor Lopez, surgeon of this hospital."

"I've heard more than a word. I've heard a multitude of words praising your skills, your learning and your charity. You are not a Jew. You are a Christian Portingale who fled from the terrors of the Inquisition."

"Are you so blinkered, Christopher Marlowe, that you fail to recognise a Hebrew without the guise of long, red hair, hooked nose and talons clawing for gold and silver?"

"Red hair, hooked nose and talons were one-time stage devices to make it simple for the unlettered to mark out Judas when such dramas were performed during Holy Week."

"Judas, Jude, Jew. How simple are the ignorant in their unlettered hate. But you, Christopher Marlowe, are not kindred to simpletons. You've studied these matters and you know my profession is counterfeit. You have told the groundlings so. Do we not walk abroad at nights and kill sick people groaning under the walls? Do we not poison wells? Do we not enrich the priests with burials and keep the sexton's arm strong with digging graves and ringing dead men's knells?"

"Those were my words, I grant you, but – "

Lopez spoke with unhurried anger. "As put into the mouth of Barabas, the Malta-Jew. Yes, yes, a play is just a passing fancy and all is grist to the mill, a stage device to winnow the seeds for dark, forbidden bread. And now, tell me, scholar, how have you spent your time? Setting Christian villages alight, binding galley slaves, cutting pilgrims' throats? Oh no, leave that to the rough soldiers, the scum from the tenements, the tow-headed louts from the unploughed fields. Christopher Marlowe is a sweet poet steeped in learning."

"Old man, Doctor Lopez, it was not my intention to offend you or your people – "

"No, no, it is I who has caused offence." Lopez' soft words were like the whisper of a wind blowing through a broken window. "For my own benefice I have spurned the children of Abraham."

It seemed to Christopher there was nothing he could say that was neither trite nor banal to comfort this injured spirit. But then, was it important? The convulsions of the roaring mob still echoed in his skull and the cleaved head and gushing blood of that unfortunate youth by St Paul's rose before his eyes as if it were painted by an Italian master on the bare wall. Had he not seen the disfigured beggars, the rotted bodies of living lepers, the scab-encrusted children swarming in London's alleys and the bloated starvelings festering in the ditches? What was this ancient's anguish compared to their sufferings? And what was their offence? If he should have slighted a thousand old men or even a kingdom in his plays, his sin was venial when weighed against the mortal crimes committed against humanity.

The glazed face in front of him appeared void of life and the incantation which came from the lips was spoken as if by a ghost impatient to fly the aged shell.

"I have seen the ranks of men marching, O Jerusalem, terrible as an army with banners, trumpets were their mouths, burning coals their eyes, stones were their hearts and their feet trampled the lilies of the fields as they marched, marched against the wooden walls, to tear apart the vineyards, to sunder the temple and throw the ark among the swine. O children of Israel, mourn, rend your clothes, the Lord has raised a whirlwind and has scattered your seed abroad on the barren deserts and the fields of strangers. Did we not burn in York, in London, in Prague, in Venice, in Barcelona? Did we not rise from the embers, our hair soiled with ashes? Great is my sin among the multitude for I have turned my face away lest my tears betray me, denied my father, donned the cloak of the murderers so I could live out my span in shameful servitude. I am as a dead dog." Light and life returned to Lopez's eyes. "If scheming, Machiavellian Barabas was vile, as portrayed in Marlowe's mighty lines, then I am twice, thrice as vile, for even in the limits of his torture he did not renege his faith."

Christopher had nearly become entranced by the rhetorical flow. "Doctor Lopez, you make a great occasion of my poor play. It's nothing but a scheme of windy words roared by ranting actors from a wooden stage on a dry afternoon. Your people, if they are your people, may hold fast to their faith but if they don't have the strength of arms to hold fast the power of office, then they will perish. For my part, I would be a Jew, a Moor, a Musliman or any of the twenty contentious breeds of Christians if, by an outward show of reverence and ritual mumbling, I could live and have access to books, pen and paper. The tribes of Israel are not alone in their pains. The tribes of Africa are hauled from their homes, chained and sold as black gold to slave away what remains of their miserable lives. The Christian Spaniards blasted the American savages from their cannons. Old Essex slaughtered the Irish on the island of Rathlin because he lusted for their land. The heretics of Languedoc were burned to cinders. I could give you a list as long as my two arms and would not have told you the half of it. Think on them and then lament."

"They are not Jews?"

"No, they were not."

"In their suffering they were Jews."

Lopez turned to face the window, knelt down and placed the scapular round his neck. "Are you still there, Christopher Marlowe?"

"Yes, but I shall leave presently."

"And the sword is in your hand?" The congealed blood had glued the hilt to Christopher's palm. "God has sent you to test us both. I am well past my years of sin. Come, smite this wretch in his hour of contrition and purification."

Christopher brought the blade up and took a step forward. His eyes were transfixed by the thin, white hair and the blue veins pulsing on the skull beneath him.

"Strike, I pray you, strike. The hour is nearly past and my resolve weakens with every retreating minute."

A swallow crashed against the window in futile pursuit of an insect. Christopher slowly lowered his arms, tore the hilt from his sticky hands and let the sword drop to the floor.

"You hesitate. You do not strike. You have failed me. O God, for what divine purpose have you granted me this reprieve? Have I not been absolved? Have I not lived long enough? Must I on the morrow counterfeit my beliefs and walk among the Christians as one with Christ? Marlowe, you and I are damned."

Christopher backed through the doorway. The light was nearly gone from the turret room and the shape of the kneeling man merged with the shadows. The keening prayer drifted down the stairs.

"O Jesu, forgive us our sins for we know not what we do."

Chapter thirteen

Three weeks after the so-called Battle of St Paul's, Christopher and Tom Watson were spending an idle September morning in The Theatre, watching the rehearsal for the afternoon's production of The Malta-Jew.

It was rare for a play to be shown more than two times in the one year at the same venue but Burbage, usually so cautious, had gambled with this popular drama earlier in the spring by presenting it twice within the space of a month. Producing it again in less than twelve months was an even bigger gamble but he was confident that the Londoners' thirst for treachery, murder, devious scheming and ultimate terrible retribution (on stage) had not been slaked.

"And what of my fellow skirmishers?" Christopher asked. "I've not seen them since Bart's Day. Have they recovered from their ordeal?"

"From all reports they're alive and kicking. Nashe did suffer a crack on the head, as you know, but it would take more than a spent ball to damage his skull and it's not cured him of writing scurrilous tracts designed to scald the thick skins of the Puritans."

Christopher was of the opinion that Nashe was wasting his talents on cheap politics. "It seems to be the fashion among our scribbling brothers to fart loud and long with more stink than sense whenever their bellies swell with wind. And what about Greene?"

"I've heard he's deserted his lawful wife to bed and board a Bankside whore. Perhaps when he wetted his breeches on the day, the dampness soaked through his clothes and softened his brain."

While they gossiped, another heated exchange between Ned Alleyn and James Burbage was enacted on the stage. As this was a regular event, few took much interest in the argument. Even Burbage's son Richard – a lanky lad who showed great promise as an actor – ignored the squall and was at that moment deep in conversation with two other players.

"They're as thick as thieves now," said Christopher. "I thought Will Slaughter slaughtered Will."

"To name but one, namely the Stratford crow, thief is the right word," said Watson sourly. "Take care he doesn't purloin your baggage."

The acidic comment from the usually affable Watson surprised Christopher. Did he resent the bit-player's humble origins or lack of university learning? "Oh, to me he's a jovial enough fellow with his country saws and sayings and his speech as thick as his native loam. I grant you he's no great shakes as a spear-carrying player but he's harmless." He paused. "Though I must say, he does pester with his pretensions to be a writer."

"And it's these hot pretensions that have made Dick Burbage and fiery Redbeard warm to the turnip-trotter. There's talk of a drama he's writing with prime parts for those two pretenders. Actors are like cats: they'll curl up on any lap that promises cream and succulent scraps from the table."

The bitter row between Ned Alleyn and Burbage came to an end with the actor declaring he would not rest content till the matter was settled to his satisfaction. The manager stalked out of the building, muttering, 'So be it. So be it.' The unsettled matter was the actors' share of the takings.

On cue, the lolling players rose, stretched their limbs, yawned and prepared to take their places. Richard Burbage and the other two strolled over to Christopher and Watson.

"You're a sight for sore eyes, Kit," said Richard. "I've heard all about your adventures at St Paul's from Greene and Nashe. By their account, you were a veritable noble Roman three pitted against Tarquin's horde."

"It doesn't take into account our tails between our legs. I've had a bellyful of alarums and excursions to keep me well fed on that fare for a month of Sundays."

"Then make your experience of that day the meat and drink of a new drama," suggested Richard. "Wasn't it on St Bartholomew's Eve when the French Papists massacred the Huguenots in Paris?

Now there's a theme of treachery and murder suitable for your pen."

Before he could reply, Richard was called up to the stage. "It's the last act," he said, "and I've the part of Ferneze."

"And I, too, have a hand in this." Will Slaughter grinned. "I have the measure of many feet for I march on and off as a knight, reappear as a shuffling, cowled monk, trot around the back and return as a mincing courtier, then a quick scamper away and once more present myself as a scowling, stomping soldier." He sighed. "In all I'm dumb with not as much as a grunt or a passable greeting. I do wish Alleyn would use me better. Why, in my time I've made the rafters tremble with my orations." He slapped Shakespeare on the shoulder. "Will here has promised me a wordy role, a brave and noble knight, in his drama."

'Indeed I have," Shakespeare said with what appeared to be a smirk. "Sir John Fastolf is most apt to your bearings."

"And I'm marked down for Harry the Sixth," said Richard Burbage, preening himself with pride, as he and Slaughter went up to the stage.

"And you, Will?" Christopher asked Shakespeare, "What's your role in the present production?" The actor grimaced and pointed to a soot smear on his forehead. "Only the unspeakable part of a Turk." He did not seem to be too upset by his minor role. Neither did he appear to have noticed that Watson was shunning him. The silence made Christopher uneasy.

"I've a question of a philosophical nature to lay before you both." Trimming his story to the bones, leaving out names and pretending the event concerned a third party, he told them of his meeting with Doctor Lopez. "Then this ancient, having purged his soul with sincere contritions, begged my friend to be the instrument of his death. Of course, he spurned such a foul deed and fled from the chamber but wasn't this a grievous sin when, with sword in hand, he could have dispatched this purged soul to its heavenly reward?"

Watson snorted. "God's mass, Kit, in company with Nashe and Greene, your riotous knocking has addled your brains. Whether the cause is just or unjust, I would not stain myself with another man's blood."

"And you, Will? What do you say?"
"I would not be a party to that old man's death."
"You, took, shrink from taking life?"
"No, that is not how it stands. A shriven soul has paid its passage to the heavens, but aren't we enjoined to live all our days in grace? If this man had enjoyed many years of evil, I say let him live to sin once more and when he's drunk, or in a rage or in a whore's bed – if he's not too withered for that sport – then, if it's God's will, dispatch his unpurged soul so that it may plunge to hell without delay. That is the final and most just retribution."

Alleyn, in the role of Barabas the Malta-Jew, was dashing about the stage with a hammer and shouting instructions to the carpenters. It was close to Shakespeare's cue and as he rose to go, Christopher invited him to a drink that evening in the Mermaid. The bit-player declined the offer, pleading a severe headache.

"He has excuse after excuse to avoid our drinking company," Watson said. "Though he values our conversations, all is grist to his mill, he values his pennies more. But he's the least of my concerns. If you've no other business in this place, will you walk with me down Shoreditch? My wife worries if I'm away from home too long and she has fearful reasons. I'll tell you when we reach a quiet corner."

But Watson only spoke when they had gone through the Hole-in-the-Wall and stood in Hog Lane. "My wife's family the Swifts and Ned Alleyn's brother are in legal dispute with the Bradleys, the tenants of The Bishop's Tavern in Holborn. The Bradleys' partisans have enlarged the quarrel with brawling threats of violence. Anne keeps fearing I will be attacked in the street."

"Such threats are more bombast than muscle and are common in the course of litigation," Christopher said. "My own father has had promises of a drubbing and worse but nothing ever came of it."

"Tom! Tom Watson! A word with you." James Burbage's fat face appeared from behind the gatepost. "Yesu," muttered Watson. "What does the old windbag want with me? He'll keep me talking for hours to no avail."

"I'll walk on and when I'm out of sight, you pretend to remember a message you have to give me from, say, Thomas Walsingham. You know how he fawns on the nobility and that should be enough to escape from his blabbering."

Christopher strode off as if eager to be gone. When he reached the curve and the high bramble bushes, he slowed down to a saunter and inspected the hedgerows with the untutored eyes of a town-dweller. "So our Stratford churl is making a drama about Harry the Sixth," he mused, laughing a little at the impertinence. "Should I stir myself to raid the ancient chronicles of our kingdom for material? As for Dick Burbage's idea about the Paris massacre, perhaps a full-blooded drama of murder and mayhem could prove to be a better attraction than a bear-baiting."

He was unaware that he had spoken his thoughts aloud. A gang of youths stared at him and one shouted, "Listen to the loon from Bedlam, talking to himself."

Another said, "Let's take him back to his cell."

A third countered with, "Careful his nails don't infect you with a mad contagion. We'll pelt him home with stones."

When a pebble flicked his cheek, Christopher turned to face them. "Do you want to joust with me?" he asked truculently, determined not to show fear. He put his hand on the hilt of his sword. One spat on the ground and the rest looked sullen. "Then I'll bid you good day," he said curtly.

The spitting youth called out, "You're Marlowe?"

"I am. What of it?"

"Who's he?" another asked.

"Marlowe the scribbler, that's who. Where's your fancy man, Marlowe?"

"I don't care for your tone. Whom do you mean?"

The youth mimicked Christopher's speech. "And I don't care for your tone." His companions guffawed. "You know who I mean, mouldy Marlowe. Watson, he's your fancy man. Tell him when you find him that Will Bradley is waiting for him."

"I'll tell him that a stinkard risen from a rat hole squealed his name."

Christopher made a mock bow, turned and walked back the way he had come. As he quickened his pace, a bulky form emerged from the bushes and stood in the middle of the path.

"What's your hurry, Marlowe?"

"Baines!" Christopher felt the same anger a diligent gardener feels when he discovers a slug in his cabbage patch. "Are you spying on me?"

"I've better things to do than spy on you," Baines blustered. "I can't go behind a bush to piss without some streak of misery yelping, spy, spy."

"Piss in whatever sty suits you, Baines, but don't piss in my pocket." Christopher stepped sideways but the other stoutly barred the way.

"Not so easy, Marlowe. You won't slander a God-fearing and loyal Englishman without answering for your lies."

Christopher drew his sword and prodded the belly in front of him. "Out of my road, you putrid priest, or I'll stick you for sure this time and damn the consequences."

Baines sneered. "How brave you are when faced with a weaponless man." He looked past Christopher and shouted, "See how I'm accosted by this ruffian and he knows I'm a man of the cloth with nothing but my bare hands to defend myself."

"If it's a good fight you're after," said Bradley, running up to Christopher, "turn to me and I'll bandy with you."

"My quarrel is with this fat-gut, not you."

"But my quarrel with you, Marlowe, is this. You're Watson's friend and all Watson's friends are sewer-scum-suckers, shit-eating, whey-faced gallows' meat. Answer that with your sword."

Bradley lunged forward and his blade sliced the air an inch from Christopher's nose. Encouraged by Baines, who shouted, "Fight fair now. Man to man," the youths circled the combatants and loudly urged their champion to finish off the weasel. Bradley wildly swung his weapon this way and that. His supporters chanted, "Slash. Slash. Cut. Cut," while less bellicose spectators cried out for the fighters to desist and called for clubs to beat the weapons down.

Watson burst through the ring. "Bradley, what call have you to brawl with Marlowe?" he demanded. Bradley snarled. "He's your consort but now you've come, I'll make music with you." He yelled a mad halloo, cut his new opponent's left arm and followed through with a berserk windmill of slashes, jabs and sweeps; none of which found their mark. Watson was forced back to the verge and stumbled into a shallow ditch. As he struggled to his feet, an onlooker pulled him up by the right arm and another pushed him from behind. Bradley rushed forward, his sword raised above his head, and with the force of his charge impaled himself six inches above the right nipple on Watson's blade.

A total silence fell as the stricken youth slowly keeled over.

"I fear you've done for him, Tom," Christopher said.

"I fear more that he's done for us," Watson replied.

Chapter fourteen

The coroner's inquest was held the day after Bradley's death and Tom Watson and Christopher were committed to Newgate Prison to await their trial, fixed for December 3rd.

To one fresh from the outside, the concentrated gaol-stench of urine, defecation, fungoid walls, rotted straw and festering bodies was so suffocating that many thought their first day would be their last. From dawn to dark there was a continuous uproar and at night, when even the most vociferous sought ease from their distress in slumber, a chorus of growling snores and whimpers arose, chains clinked and an occasional scream tore through the opacity.

The brutal jailers could only be distinguished from the ugliest of prisoners by their comparative freedom of movement, their cudgels and bundles of keys. In the morning they woke the sleepers with kicks and yells, counted the living and removed the dead. Even this simple task taxed their intelligence: for two days they had missed the corpse of an old man half-buried beneath a pile of rags. When all the wretches were standing in line, a jailor read out the day's punishment list: so many whippings, so many brandings, so many hands to be lopped off, so many ears to be chopped. The condemned bawled their protests and tried to hide behind their fellows. After they had been hauled away, a second and usually shorter list was read. Unlike the violent reaction to the first, those named either put on a brave smile and swaggered out or slunk abjectly after their escorts.

"Are they freed?" Christopher asked a fellow prisoner.

"In a manner of speaking they'll soon be free." The man grinned a toothless smile. "For now, they'll rest a day or two in Limbo."

"Limbo? Isn't that the place for the unbaptised halfway between heaven and hell?"

"Could hell be worse than here, I ask you?" The prisoner contemplated the relative merits of this world compared to the nether world and brought up a ball of phlegm. "Our own Limbo is a pitch-dark room above the jail-gate where them laddoes are shackled till they're trundled off hell-bound for Holborn and the high gallows. Many a happy time I've spent gawping at the gibbet and giving friends and enemies alike a good send-off with a rousing cheer. Better than the playhouses any road, and what's more doesn't cost you a penny unless, of course, you've paid your coin to dance the hangman's jig."

The third and last list that morning was for those set at liberty. There were only two. One of them had died the day before and the second, a lumbering lout destined to return within a year, shook his fist under a jailer's nose and slouched off to freedom. Then crates of fish and bread, bought in part from money donated by charitable citizens and in part contributed by the Fishmongers' and Bakers' guilds, were dragged into the centre of the hall. Whatever shreds of civilisation still clung to these creatures were flung to one side in the few minutes of mayhem as they fell upon this stale manna with the snarling yowls of famished dogs.

Neither Christopher nor Watson moved but the toothless man, who seemed to have adopted them as his 'pals', disappeared into the scrummage and emerged within seconds clutching a lump of black bread and two shrivelled fishes. "When I've baked this pair," he said, "we'll eat royally, we will." On his return from the gridiron with the skin-crackling food, he offered to split it three ways. Christopher and Watson politely declined the kind offer, each pleading a loss of appetite. "I fear my stomach has become a clenched fist," Watson said.

Old Toothless conducted them over to his corner and made room on his ration of straw. He floated the black bread in a bowl of water – "It's as hard as Belzebub's horn, it is" – and, tearing the fishes to shreds, flung some into his gob and stowed the rest inside his jerkin. "Our humble fare's not to yer taste then, you being gentlemen," he remarked. "Mind you, hunger's a good sauce and tomorrow or the next I reckon you'll scrabble and scratch with the best of them to grab a morsel. Unless – " he shot them a sly glance, "unless you're well provided to buy in dainty dishes." They protested their poverty. "Never mind, me pals, seeing as how you're not the usual run of Newgate fodder, your friends outside will see to your belly furniture." He sighed gustily. "As for me, I've nothing to rattle in my poke now I haven't the means to make myself rich and easy as I was down by Moorgate. Then, I tell you, I had friends in plenty."

"It's a short walk from Moorgate to Newgate," Christopher said. "Were you taken on this journey after taking a few purses on another journey?"

"Who are you calling a cut-purse? Who are you calling a common thief?" The man was most indignant with this apparent slur on his character. "I'll have you know you're talking to a master craftsman, fully indentured, fully served and fully marked for his masterwork. John Poole is the name and coiner is my trade. Ah, how sad and unjust it is to be made a felon for such clever handiwork. Doesn't it stand to reason that if there's more money abroad, more goods will be bought and sold and everybody is much happier and wealthier?"

His listeners were not sufficiently versed in economics to dispute the man's logic, though Christopher did remark that if the Queen could have coins made, then every man had the right to do likewise.

They confided the cause of their incarceration. Poole waggled his head. "Your crime is of no account and I reckon you'll be home and dry before the year's out. Now, if you'd done as I did, forged a few coins, or as others have done, spoken out of turn, I wouldn't give a tinker's spit for your chances. But to kill a rogue in a fair fight, why, that's nothing."

As the forger had predicted, someone did come to their aid. That day and every day following, a parcel of food was brought to them by a jailer. "Give him a sweetener," Poole advised. With great reluctance, Christopher handed the surly brute a coin. "Better to do so than have half your meat down his gullet. He's the biggest robber born and he'd rip the hair off your head for the sake of a penny. See, he's up to his tricks now." He nodded to where the warder was chopping off a young whore's tresses. "I have a rare old laugh when I see them elegant ladies flaunting their perukes and them not knowing the lice-ridden scalps that grew their finery."

The two friends found it impossible to become reconciled to

their situation or the misery and squalor that surrounded them. Tom Watson felt a double anguish. He grew sick with worry about his wife and children who would have no funds to buy food and drink while he was in jail. Christopher tried to comfort him – friends would rally round, surely her relatives would keep the family – and cited their daily parcel as evidence that they had not been forgotten. The last did little to console Watson. He would rather sup on news about his family than chicken breast any day. He sat on his haunches, hands between his knees and head bent low. "Rats, lice, fleas, slimy worms, bloated slugs making spittle-paths across the sodden walls," he intoned. "I dare not breathe lest I suck in a belly full of this foul air."

"Your trouble is you're gentle-born and bred," Poole said sagely. "But, Lord bless us, it's second nature to many rotting here. Home from home, you'd say, and with just as much liberty to live, starve and die. You're tender to its taste now but you won't know its stink from new-mown hay before you're much older."

There was an element of truth in the old forger's philosophy, though their tolerance of the human abuses they witnessed was due more to resignation of will than any conscious acceptance of fate. They had even taken to listening patiently to Poole's rambling tales.

His stock theme was the wiles of a well-proportioned wife cheating on her fool of an old husband. Mostly her tricks consisted of either giving him an obnoxious brew to make him blind to her wanton ways – pissing in a pot of boiling cabbage came up more than once – or dressing her young lover in female attire and pretending to her befuddled spouse that the deep-voiced youth was her niece. At another time and in another place his interminable anecdotes would have seemed crude and tedious to their ears but here, in these circumscribed and savage surroundings, he had taken on the stature of a Homer or a Chaucer. They had also become quite fond of the old codger.

Christopher did try to divert their minds by provoking debates and contentiously questioning whether heaven and hell actually existed; but Watson was apathetic and Poole a poor, ill-learned foil.

In this human cesspit known as Newgate Prison where every hour was an eternity of despair, heaven was an extra crust of bread and hell a bleak prospect of present reality. Bodies and souls suffered and it needed a great faith, blind courage or beast-like indifference to keep even the smallest of sparks glowing.

Day by day, Tom Watson spiritually declined and physically wasted. He barely ate a scrap of food, spent sleepless nights with a rasping cough and enervated days sitting with his back to the wall. On the tenth day, Christopher and Poole had to hold the sick man upright during roll-call and later found it almost impossible to force water through Watson's clenched teeth.

"I tell you, poor old Tom's a goner with the Newgate fever," Poole said. "I've seen it take the strongest by the throat and wither them to a dry stick in the space of a week or so." Christopher dismissed the man's dire predictions but he spoke with more confidence than he felt and his heart sank at the sight of the black circles round his friend's eyes. "Send messages to your pals," suggested Poole. "Don't you number them with power among your cronies?"

"We've a power of cronies," Christopher replied with some bitterness, "but none appear to count us among their number." He put an arm round Watson's shoulder. "Come, Tom, this pugatorial detention will be brief and soon we'll be downing a bellyful of ale in The Mermaid."

Watson showed a flicker of his old self. "We'll be downing or upping, Kit, but not in Purgatory, not since Cranmer declared it void and without substance."

But towards the latter part of their second week in jail, he was overcome by a fit of shivering. Christopher hugged his friend in an attempt to impart some warmth into the feeble body. "Am I shaking or is the ground crumbling beneath our feet?" Watson asked.

"Perhaps Bradley's knocking from below and raring to continue our bout." Christopher said with forced jocularity. "The burning coals up his arse will make him leap and hop but there's little chance he'll freeze. I dread that the demons are labouring to tear me limb from limb before I cross the barren desert." Another fit of trembling surged through Watson's body. "If I should die – "

"Don't say that, Tom. You won't die."

"But I must as you must and all these fetid bodies who surround us must. Swear to me, Kit, if I fail to walk from this pit of despair, you'll bend every effort to care for Anne and my children. Swear to it, Kit."

"I'll take any oath to set your heart at ease but let's not talk of you departing from us."

The next morning when they rose from their rancid straw beds to stand in line with the other wretches, Poole nudged Christopher and said with a smirk, "I've had word I'm to be freed today. It's just an inkling, mind you, but a nod is as good as a wink. Old scraggy-top who brings your parcels said one of us is to be let out and seeing as how you're here till the trial it must be me."

The first list was quite short. Three sailors from the St Bartholomew's Day riot and a prostitute to be whipped out of town, two cut-purses to lose their left hands – "They've still got their right ones," said Poole – and a blaspheming drunkard to have his ear nailed to a post outside the jail from dawn to dusk.

The jailer then read out the second list of those destined for Limbo and the gallows. The fourth name he called out was John Poole, coiner.

The old forger managed a wry smile. "I said, didn't I, I'd be let out today. Ah well, to Holborn and hell is my lot. When I'm toasting my toes at the devil's griddle, Kit, I'll tell old Nick what you said about there being no everlasting punishment and he'll have a good laugh, he will." He looked very small and shrivelled when he followed the other condemned men to that final dark chamber.

The starvelings were impatient with the drawn-out ritual and were only prevented from pouncing on the mouldy bread and stinking fish by the warders' threatening cudgels. The head jailer read out the third and shortest list. It consisted of only one name, Christopher Marlowe.

"Come on, Marlowe, out of here. You've been bailed."

"And so should Tom Watson. We came together and we'll leave together."

"Yours is the name here, not his. Go or stay, it's all one to me. Two respectable citizens, Richard Kitchen, attorney of Clifford's

Inn, and Humphrey Rowlands, maker of lantern horns of St Botolph, Bishopsgate, are your sureties. The way you're carrying on, they needn't have bothered."

Christopher had never heard of these respectable citizens. "What do you say, Tom?" he asked.

"Do what best fits your conscience, Kit." The faltering reply was almost drowned in the rising howl of the prisoners swarming onto the food.

"I can't bear to leave you alone in this sewer, Tom. But outside – " Christopher waited till the uproar had subsided. "But outside – " But outside there were clean beds, dry rooms, food on tables, ale, beer, wine, conversations with friends. "I'll be free to carry news to your wife, see to your family's welfare, find sureties for your release. If that fails, I'll press for your transfer to a part of the prison that's more suitable to your rank and health. Have faith in me, Tom." He flung his arms round his friend and gave him a fierce hug. "You are my dear friend, Tom. You are my brother." He turned and walked quickly towards the exit, stopping for a second to look back and wave. Watson did not return the farewell salute but stood blankly gazing at his departing comrade.

Christopher's release was the excuse for a rather rowdy party held in the upstairs room of The Bull tavern. The celebration had reached the stage where even the most reticent competed to have his voice heard. The air was thick with fug, bellowing and witty aphorisms.

Will Warner had arrived late and was unaffected by the gusty merriment. "It'd be better if you lie low till the trial, Kit," he advised.

"Does that come from your heart, Will, or are you an errand boy from the gods?"

"The gods, if you so wish, suggest that a journey to a more pleasant clime would benefit your health."

Nashe overheard the last remark. "A journey to a pleasanter clime, did you say?" he roared. "I tell you, Kit, travelling is a curse and only Englishmen and the damned go traipsing off to unknown countries."

Thomas Deloney, a pedlar of gee-gaws and rustic tales, said,

"Robert Greene has traipsed to Poland, Germany, France and visited the dour Danes and is none the worse for it."

"Trust a Norwich man to speak for a Norwich man," replied Nashe. "The question is, are the tow-headed Polacks, the sour-cabbage Germans, the flibberty French and the dreary Danes any the better for his visit?"

Warner fluttered his hands in a vain attempt to regain Christopher's attention.

Greene banged his pot on the table. "I've had better profit trawling those shores than any Lowestoft layabout ever gained scratching the shingles for driftwood to shore up his leaking craft. If you haven't the virtues for such tours, stay at home and roast your cockles by your own fireside."

"Virtues?" Nashe snorted. "A traveller must have the back of an ass to bear all, a tongue like a dog's tail to flatter all and the mouth of a hog to eat all that's set before him."

"If you could fly like a sprite and vanquish distance, would you hazard a journey?" Christopher asked.

"How, in God's name, could that be accomplished?"

"Not in God's name but with Mephistophilis giving you Mercury's wings."

"The devil take that for a lark," said Deloney. "I'd rather fly to my own hearth, home and the hot haunches of my good wife than take wings with demons."

During a lull when the pots were being replenished, Warner, by dint of urgent whispering and plucking of sleeve, cajoled Christopher over to a quieter corner. "I won't take offence, Kit, if you think of me only as a mere messenger, but knowing, as I do, how matters stand, there's the weight of my own concern for you in what I say."

Christopher sighed with impatience. "And the weight of my concern is for poor Tom Watson rotting in that midden. Good advice butters no parsnips and doesn't make his caged days any sweeter."

"He killed a man. The slain has friends."

An outburst distracted them. Greene was glaring at Nashe. "You dare compare me to an ape, you baboon?" His vehemence merely provoked further hilarity.

"No, I protest, I did not liken you to that monkey." Nashe's wide grin simulated a simian grimace. "I had said, with respect, that you differed."

"In what respect?"

"Inasmuch as you are bald before and an ape is bald behind."

Greene subsided under a fresh downpour of laughter and Christopher longed to rejoin them. The insistent Warner sat too close to him. "What are your intentions?"

"Yesu, Warner, what is it with you? Why must you pry? Haven't I had enough of ferrets like that fat failed priest by the name of Baines, a scullion's whelp, a bane on all pleasantries and one-time whinger of spying tales, the same who sought to brawl in The Gilded Lily tavern as you should remember. It was he who caused the Hog Lane affray by provoking clod-headed Bradley to flourish his blade under my nose."

"I have heard of this Baines," Warner said. He appeared perturbed by this additional information. "I did not know he was present at the fight."

"It seems to me that there's little you do know," Christopher snapped. "Tomorrow I'll do as I've done today and yesterday, send messages to Walsingham, asking, no, pleading for Tom Watson's rescue from the Newgate cesspit. And I'll try again to find his family and see to their welfare. Those are my intentions."

Warner pursed his lips and spoke quickly. "Contrary to what you may think, Kit, we are also concerned with Watson's condition. There's little more Walsingham can do at present except send provisions to the jail –"

"So it was him. He could do more. He could muster up bondmen to have Tom bailed, as he did for me."

"Our sodality, not Walsingham, was the agent for that act. Tom Watson is not among our fraternity and he must depend upon the small mercies his friends can afford to dole out. There have been disturbances in the city. It would not do for Walsingham to favour one faction against the other by releasing a murderer."

"What justice is this to judge Tom Watson fit for the gallows before he has stood trial?"

"There are urgent matters of state needing attention. What is the life and death of one poet worth when hourly confusion threatens to grind the kingdom to dust? Should the miller's wheel be stopped to save a butterfly when the harvest is ready to be brought in?"

Chapter fifteen

Anne Watson had disappeared. It was not a simple matter of her falling down a hole in the ground or being taken up to the heavens in a fiery chariot; she was still in the land of the living, Christopher was sure of that. But on all sides his search was frustrated by denials and evasions. He paid three futile visits to the Watsons' lodgings in Bishopsgate and each time the old woman who owned the house glared at him and muttered, "They're not here. Come back tomorrow." Seething with exasperation, he tramped the streets from morn to dusk and, more by chance than design, came to the dull frontage of The Gilded Lily.

He sat at a table, ordered ale and asked the potboy if Kate Quick was about.

The pimply-faced lad pulled his earlobe, scratched his crotch and grudgingly admitted she was on the premises. When he returned with the ale, he was accompanied by a cross-eyed character who amiably asked his business. Christopher decided that perhaps an ounce of tact could be worth a ton of information. "I'm Kit Marlowe. I thought Kate could help me find Dick Chomley." "Can't say I've heard of him. Chomley, was it? And you're Kit Morley?"

"No, not Morley. Marlowe." Having shot off one name, it would not make much difference to fire off a few more. "How about Jack Marlin? And John Poole?" He waited for a second. "And Watson? What of him?"

The man beckoned to his companions. As one, they rose and Christopher was surrounded by a circle of grey faces and passionless eyes.

"What's them names again, Morley?" asked the wall-eyed one. "My mates didn't hear you the first time. Well, if it's all the same to you, I'll tell them. This gentleman, called, so he says, Kit Morley, is asking the whereabouts of Kate Quick, Dick Chomley,

Jack Marlin and – what was the last one? – oh yes, Watson. A very curious cove is our Kit Morley."

Christopher began to rise from his seat but two heavy hands on his shoulders forced him down again. "You're not thinking of leaving us, are you, Kit Morley? And we've so much to talk about. Old friends, you could say. It's not every day we've someone walking in here to ask about dead men. Least, some are and some will be. Chance is you'll be attending their funerals."

"In the name of St Judas, what's going on here?" Kate Quick barged through the encircling men, gave the potboy a clout and glared at Christopher. "What cat brought this in?" She gave the potboy another clout. "Move your scabby arse, fart-in-the-bag, and when I'm asked for, come to me first. Well then, you gawping loons, if it's me he wants, it's me he'll talk to. Be off with you."

"It's like this, Kate, he's asking questions. He says he's Kit Morley."

Christopher protested his true identity and Kate blasphemed with a particular bitterness. "No need to tell me you're not Morley. I know that gallow's-meat and God help me, if I ever lay hands on the streak of misery, I'll skewer his belly to the bench and stamp on his sniggering face so hard his own mother won't be able to tell him apart from a dog's dinner. It was him, blast his pox-riddled heart, who had my Jack killed, it was. With his dying breath he told me it was this Kit Morley and two of his kidney who led the roaring fools rampaging onto the Fair last August and left my poor Jack trampled and trashed at the height of the ructions."

"God's truth, woman, is Jack Marlin dead?"

"Where've you been hiding this past month not to hear how my Jack was crushed and beaten at St Paul's? In gaol? Ah yes, there's a touch of the Newgate yellow round your gills." She sat down on the seat so recently vacated by the squinter. "Ah, me lovely Jack. I fed him. I watered him. I clothed him. He was to be my fourth husband in troth and plight and now it's my plight to be alone." The shade of sadness passed. "And tell me now, Kit Marlowe – but wait, I recall a Kit Marlowe once in this very tavern – listen to me running ahead of the hare. What's your business with me?"

Christopher told her of his search.

"Anne Watson? With her airs and graces, you'd never think her family once sold fish from an open stall down by Cheapside. I remember you, too. You had a brawl with the fat pig in this tavern the day the sheriff's bully-boys came wrecking and raiding. And you were mixed up in the Hog Lane murder. There'll be a dagger stuck in your brown eyes before you're old enough to hobble home on two sticks."

She looked shrewdly at him and reached a decision. "Tomorrow at midday, pass by but don't come in. I'll have a lad ready to take you to where she waits for callers, God help her."

The next day Christopher followed the Gilded Lily potboy towards Cheapside. When, for the third time, they passed a dead brindle hound on a rubbish pile, he was sure he was the victim of an elaborate wild-goose chase devised by Kate Quick. He caught up with his guide and told the youth he did not care for this joke.

The potboy shrugged his shoulders and looked to the left and right. "We were followed but he's gone now."

"Followed? By whom?"

"Dunno. A lump of lard on legs, I reckon. We've lost him. See over there where the boy's cutting a stick by the door. That's where you're to go."

The stick-whittler moved to one side and Christopher entered an empty hall. A thickset man came down the stairs and jerked his head backwards. Upstairs on the first landing a plump, middle-aged woman with long straggling hair leaned against a door-jamb and nestled a cleaver in her folded arms. She looked him up and down and then nodded towards the room behind her.

Inside, Anne Watson was sitting on a chair, an opened prayer book on her lap. As if unaware of his entry, she continued to read for nearly a minute; her finger moving along the text as she droned the words. Then she closed the book and said, "You've come then. You've taken your time."

Christopher was stung by the injustice. "I'd have been here earlier but none would tell me where you were."

"They have their reasons. And what are yours? To find another to replace my poor Tom in your affections? What use is he to you now? You've taken what you could from him and now he lies wasting."

"He's worried sick about his family and he had asked – "

"Do you imagine I lack news? It would be unnatural of him not to worry. Judge not others by your own conscience." She went over to the only window in the room. "I also suffer imprisonment. Guarded day and night, every move watched and every caller checked before he or she enters this cage. But worse than bars, bricks and locked gates are the shackles of hate, greed and sin which chafe every soul on every side."

She turned from the window and her voice was charged with the ringing passion of a preacher. "And I pray my Tom will be with God's grace when he walks from that temporal prison and shuns the ways of men and sinners, the abominations of the flesh, and through his tribulation, find the true path to eternal joy. Yes, I tell you, it is straight and narrow, beset on all sides by evil spirits, false doctrines and vile temptations, but they who carry the cross and wear the crown of thorns and cast not their eyes to the left or right shall enter through the narrow gates to eternal salvation." She paused and stared hard at her visitor. "And this I say to you, Christopher Marlowe, hide where you will, your wickedness shall root you out and on that dreadful day, the earth will gape beneath your feet and the demons of hell shall tear you limb from limb."

"People such as she are the fools of martyrdom," Christopher thought. "Why do you condemn me? You know nothing of evil if you think me wicked," he said.

"With your presumptuous questioning of God's divine purpose, you, Christopher Marlowe, have damned yourself from your own mouth and you and your kind are lost to perdition. You've turned from truth and seek that which is forbidden."

He should have closed the debate there and then but the devil of contention spurred him to ask, "What is forbidden and by whom?"

As if he had ceased to exist, she reopened her book and began to intone passages like an ill-learned priest mumbling his hocus-pocus. Suddenly she clapped the book shut.

"Why don't you go?" She spoke like one dismissing a flunkey.

"You haven't answered my question."

"Questions, questions, always questions. Isn't the revealed truth enough?"

The harridan burst into the room and shouldered Christopher to one side. "Stand away from the window, Mistress Watson. There's a parcel of Bradley bullies loitering in the street and there's only myself, my husband and the lad to hold them off if they've a mind to make a raid."

"Why don't you number Marlowe here among the defenders," said Anne snidely. "He's famous for his brawls."

"This scrimp-shanks?" The woman looked at Christopher with disdain from beneath her black, slug-shaped eyebrows. "He couldn't wipe a one-legged fly's arse, never mind crack a hard-boiled head. It wasn't you who led them here, was it? With all our caution, they seemed to find their way with ease." She lifted the cleaver two inches from her bosom. "If it wasn't for Tom Watson rushing to save your skin, you'd have been pricked good and proper and he'd be with his good wife and lovely children instead of rotting in Newgate. You'd better get away from here. I'll give the word when they're gone."

When she left, Anne came quite close to Christopher and spoke in a sibilant whisper. "My guardian bitch wards away the Holborn curs but the slavering hounds of hell wait for you, Christopher Marlowe."

"Why should Satan honour me as his favourite guest rather than you or those alley whelps?"

She drew back from him, her eyes dilated, and once more spoke with the fervour of a demented preacher. "Should it be God's will for my Tom to suffer Newgate prison for the rest of his mortal life and be spared your demonic company to free his soul from eternal damnation, I'll fall on my bended knees for my remaining years to offer up prayers of thanksgiving. May the Lord be praised."

He was saved from further harangues by the reappearance of the plump woman. "They're still about, God's blast on their thick hides. Come with me and keep your gob shut." She clutched Christopher's sleeve, pulled him down the stairs, through a backyard and out to an empty alley. "You're safe for the present. As for your woman upstairs, she's distraught, poor soul, and there's no sense in her sermons. Be off with you, now. We've enough botheration with poverty and illness without a touch of your affliction, Kit Morley."

Chapter sixteen

On December 3rd, the morning of the trial, Christopher rose early but was too nervous to eat. The landlady called up from the well of the stairs, "There's three gentlemen waiting for you, Master Marlowe." To her, everybody who called for Christopher – he being a scholar – must be a gentleman.

Two heavies and Will Warner were Christopher's escort to the Assizes.

When they passed by the south side of St Paul's, a group of Bradley partisans were beadily watching their progress. Further on the cross-eyed man and his friends from The Gilded Lily lined the route, while Anne Watson's protectoresss took up space with her entourage near the court.

"The slum scourings have come out to greet us," said Christopher anxiously. "It's a wonder they haven't tried to stop us."

"Less than a wonder, Kit," replied Warner. "Those gutter-swaggerers haven't the heart to tangle with our Essex hirelings."

What political ebbing and flowing had brought about such a sea-change that the Earl of Essex would loan his bodyguards to protect a Walsingham man?

"Those roughnecks kept their distance," said Warner, "but I fear they'll be in a fury after the hearing."

"If it goes in our favour."

"Have no fear on your account, Kit. It will."

A thin man with a smooth cherubic face and the dull-brown clothes of a well-to-do clerk came over to them at the courthouse. "Christopher Marlowe? Am I correct? But of course you are. How could I mistake you for another."

"My apologies, sir, but I do not recollect – "

"Richard Kitchen, attorney of Clifford's Inn. I have often listened to your witty discourses at The Mermaid."

"Forgive me, Master Kitchen, for not remembering you. I owe

both you and Master Rowland an immeasurable debt of gratitude for my bail surety."

"It was our privilege to assist you from that odious place. But privilege has its price." The smooth face puckered as if Kitchen had tasted a sour gooseberry. "There's the small matter of our account to be settled before the hearing."

"Account? Surely I've discharged my bail debt?"

Kitchen simpered and patiently explained the custom and practice of charging interest on the sum put at risk. "Master Rowland and I are not demanding a jug of blood or a slice of your flesh, only a just recompense for our venture, and it would be most unpleasant for us to press legal action to recover our money."

"This is usurious," he said angrily. Warner stepped forward and counted the required coins into Kitchen's open palm.

The attorney inclined his head. "And if there's any other service – a witness, perhaps? There are professionals present – " he indicated with a flourish of his hand a group of men who each had a single straw sticking out of his boot "- who are prepared to take an oath, for a consideration, of course."

As if from nowhere, Will Slaughter, Dick Burbage, Nashe, Greene and others appeared in the foyer, surrounded Christopher and pushed his party into the packed courtroom. The stentorian usher, using his bellowing voice to its full, had to repeat his call of "Put up Christopher Marlowe and Thomas Watson" four times before it was heard above the hubbub.

Watson had wasted to a shadow. His shabby, smelly clothes hung lankly from his skeletal frame, his facial skin was white and shining like a winter's moon, and his once-thick hair was reduced to thin wisps. He did not turn his head when Christopher was hustled up to the dais to stand beside him but stared fixedly at the bench where the three presiding judges sat in whispering consultation.

The usher called for quiet and an official announced that Sir Roger Manwood was to speak. Christopher vaguely remembered he had been present at the sodality induction ceremony in Scadbury House the previous September.

"We'll deal with the case of one Christopher Marlowe first," Manwood pronounced. "From the evidence laid before us, we find that the said Christopher Marlowe suffered an unprovoked attack from William Bradley – " Some brave person in the thick of the crowd shouted, "He's not here to defend himself." There was chaos as court officials waded into the thickly packed crowd.

After three innocent fishmongers had been ejected, Manwood continued. "Yes, yes, Marlowe had suffered an unprovoked attack -ahem -ahem- instigated by a person unknown and the accused Marlowe had made every effort to avoid an affray. Furthermore, when the aforesaid William Bradley suffered the fatal blow, the accused Marlowe, having failed to prevent the second accused, Thomas Watson, from entering into an engagement with William Bradley, was standing some distance away. Therefore, we find the said Christopher Marlowe not guilty of causing an affray as charged nor of being party to the death of William Bradley, and he may now stand down."

Shouts, catcalls, hisses and cheers greeted the verdict. "You're pardoned, Kit." Hands grabbed Christopher and he was hauled outside. His friends urged a hasty departure from the building. Will Slaughter offered to return to the courtroom to find out Watson's fate and came back looking downcast. Tom had been sent back to Newgate to wait another hearing.

Christopher was stunned by the news. "It's all too true, old son," said Slaughter. "His wretched wife near-screamed the place down. I don't know what's to become of her."

"I must go in to speak for Tom." "Too late. Too late," cautioned his minders, bundling him across the square and thrusting him into a carriage. Flung unceremoniously on the floor, he became aware of the second passenger.

"Thomas Walsingham! You're a long way from Chislehurst."

"And you, Kit, are further still from either Cambridge or Canterbury." The young man emitted a whinnying laugh and dabbed his mouth with a scented silk handkerchief. The horses broke into a gallop and the carriage shook from side to side. "Stinking London is truly a cesspool of pestilence, vice and purulent humanity." He peered out of the window. "Where are we now? Fleet Street or is it the village of Charing? I know little of these parts and have no wish to know more. If it's not swamps, it's fetid mires or a thousand clogged rivers filled with dead dogs and still-born babies. Yesu, what madness induced them to build Westminster on Thorny Island's bog?"

Christopher was so shaken by the day's events and this rattling box that he had no feelings to spare for his fellow passenger's precious sensibility. "He'd change his tune after a day's sojourn in Newgate," he thought, "but then the likes of him are never guests in that sty."

Walsingham continued to talk and Christopher strained to hear his words above the clatter of the rocking vehicle. The only sentence he caught was "Consider your circumstances, Kit." He raised his voice to reply but Walsingham, pouting with displeasure, had put his head out of the window to tell the driver to slow down.

When the horses ambled at a more leisurely pace, he ordered the carriage to be driven around St Giles in the Field.

"My circumstances are, in the first place, that I've escaped imprisonment by a whim of fortune and – "

"No, Kit, not a whim," Walsingham interrupted. "Wanton fortune is too much of a harlot to allow for the chance beneficence of her grace."

"Then to whom do I owe a debt of gratitude and in what coinage do I pay? I have not much money to my credit."

"There's no need to worry on that score. I arranged with Will Warner to see to your bail-bond interest and on that account you owe nothing."

"So I'm in pawn to your grace's favours?"

"You may pledge yourself for my favours, if you desire. It is always redeemable."

"It's Tom Watson who needs your grace and favour. He'll scarcely survive Newgate."

Walsingham dabbed the corner of his eye with the silk cloth. A sharp speck of dust had brought a tear to his eye. "How sullen are the clouds over St Giles," he said and drew the curtain over the window. "As sullen and as dour as you, Kit. You should be celebrating your freedom."

He paused, sighed and then spoke in the serious tone of a man who had come of age and abandoned all frivolity. "Neither you nor I can afford to become embroiled in the feuds of tavern-keepers and stall-holders. Tom, by his ill-judged marriage, is involved with them and there we must leave him – by contrary chance in prison – until those turbulent bands are suppressed or dispersed. Idle young men are ever a danger to the peace and order of the kingdom but we'll fit their bodies in the red cassocks of London soldiers and send them abroad to clout foreign pates for a change.

"Until such time – we are never short of small wars for small men – you must retire to your parents' Canterbury home. We have arranged for you to be carried there without hindrance. When Tom is free, you and he will stay as our guests in Scadbury House."

The horses jog-trotted down Holborn towards Smithfield.

Walsingham chortled. "I do not visit common playhouses, but others have told me about the just punishment inflicted upon the scheming Barabas in the broiling cauldron. Why, even the Earl of Essex himself has commanded your Malta-Jew to our Queen."

"I was not aware you were privy to the likes and dislikes of the Earl of Essex. I remember a time – "

"Censor your remembrance, Kit, and select only that which is profitable to you. Your present standing among discerning men promises well and there are many who had a high regard for your genius. Ralegh, for one, so I have heard, has made mention of your provoking lines in favourable terms. There are a number of such men whom it would pay you to cultivate. Young Cecil, he is a coming man. Francis Bacon, there's one to suit your mettle. It would be a pleasure for me to hear the substance of their wit and who better to gather the grain without the chaff than you, Kit?"

"Who better, indeed. A parrot would promiscuously squawk in his cage, a jackdaw would fly away and a goose would eat the grains but Christopher Marlowe, preening his feathers and with a ready quill, could redeem his pawned honour to the Walsinghams by translating private conversations into written matter for the eyes of his masters. To use simple words, to pry, to spy."

"You have offended me, Marlowe, and I had mistakenly looked upon you as something of a kindred spirit."

Walsingham lapsed into a sulk and did not speak again until the carriage had turned towards Aldersgate.

"We'll rest a while in my uncle's Seething Lane house and then you will travel on to Canterbury. Let there be no bitter words between us. Our regard for each other must come from the heart. Today Essex is the Queen's golden boy. Yesterday it was Ralegh. Tomorrow? Young Cecil? But yesterday, today and tomorrow the Walsinghams were, are and shall be the nub, the fulcrum of the kingdom. Consider this, Kit, whether the tide is in or out, the Walsingham harbour will always shelter your bark. Where would you be otherwise?"

Chapter seventeen

Catherine Marlowe was like a clucking hen with only one chick to tuck under her wings. She gave Christopher the best cut of meat, heaped his plate with second and third helpings, plied him with questions and admonishments about his health and nagged him to keep warm, clean and dry.

"You stuff him as if he were a gander being fattened for the festivities," said Ann one day at dinner.

"Listen to our plump goose talking, will you, with enough fatty flesh on her to make festive meals from St Nicholas's Day till the Eve of the Holy Innocents." As if to spite her daughter, Catherine piled the last of the apple turnover on Christopher's plate. "Kit's had a lean time in London and there's no call for your to begrudge him a mouthful. You've a table and a man of your own and it's there you should be stuffing your husband's belly with a well-cooked meal."

"By the size of her, I'd say our goose has had her stuffing," said Dorothy with a tinge of acidic envy.

"If you'd opened your legs as wide as you open your mouth," Ann replied, "you'd have a fine cock of your own and less chance to brood on your empty nest."

Margaret turned her eyes up to the ceiling. "You wouldn't hear such vulgar talk up in London, would you, Kit?" A subtle change had come over her since her return from the city. She affected a superior air, pretended to refinements, presumed an affinity with Christopher and spoke at great length on the grand company she had met.

"Hark to Lady Muck," exclaimed Dorothy. "By the pout of her you'd think she had gooseberries for breakfast."

"And I don't need to traipse abroad to learn my manners," said Ann as she wiped her greasy lips with her sleeve. "There's them born in humble houses with gentler ways to their backbones than others living in castles. Our Lord God was born in a stable and who are we to ask for better."

"I've been thinking Kit himself should be settling down with a good wife to wed and bed," Catherine said. It was not the first time she had broached the subject but on each occasion he had made light of it.

"Who'd have him, I ask you, who'd have him?" Ann shrilled.

"I know of no frisky mare he could mount," Dorothy said. "He'd be thrown before he could use his riding crop."

"Unless he leaped on her from behind," Ann added. She and Dorothy collapsed into giggles.

"Shut your gobs, you brazen fools." Catherine slammed a knife down on the table. "I won't have lewd tavern talk in my house."

Margaret looked up from her interminable embroidery. "There's no need for Kit to take a wife to see to his linen and put meals on his table. I'm free to lodge with him in London to see to his needs."

"Free is the right word for you, young woman," said Catherine. "There's little enough in your dowry chest to hobble you from taking flight and that's only half the botheration."

A loud belch served to remind them that the titular head of the house, John Marlowe, was among them. He awoke from his post-dinner doze, belched again and glared at his family. "What's this blathering about London? Haven't we enough trouble on our plate as it is?"

"Now then," said his wife soothingly, "there's none of us wants to set foot inside that cursed city and I'm sure Kit's got better things on his mind."

With an air of triumph, she announced that she had in mind a highly respected and rich family of Canterbury whose only daughter – one who was the wonder of the world for her civility and chaste modesty – was of marriageable age.

"Why should you go traipsing here, there and God only knows where to seek your fame and fortune when the very same can be had here in Canterbury itself. With your learning, you'd be a great catch and if you were to marry into a rich family who lacks a clever man to manage their estate, why, you'd have your foot in the door, your arse warmed at the fire and yourself lolling in silk and satin. As for them little dramas and interludes you're fond of writing – I know you've your heart set on them – there'd be plenty of time to exercise your pen when you're wealthy with leisure."

She stared hard at her son to gauge the effect of her plan but he did not betray his feelings. His father's grandiose schemes were loaded with talk, empty of action and rarely lasted beyond the third pot of ale, but his mother was made of a different metal. A determined woman, she would work her devious ways like a ferret down a rabbit hole. Very rarely did she fail to clutch her prey by the scruff of the neck and drag it out of the burrow.

"It's a shame for Kit's costly education to be wasted in a London hovel and him starving and perished with the cold for the want of a stitch in his coat, while we're here scrimping and scraping and not knowing which way to turn for the next penny."

"It's all the fault of them foreigners with their cheap shoes," John Marlowe grumbled. "The sewing comes apart at the seams at the first sign of dampness but can you tell people they're buying rubbish? Oh no, anything for a bargain, so they think, and meanwhile English craftsmen are driven to desperate plights and have to go begging to the town's coffers for a crust to put in their children's mouths."

"And there you have it, the upper, the lower, the sole and heel of it." Catherine looked hard at Christopher. "You've heard from your father how his trade is going to rack and ruin and it's your bounden duty, as our only son, to save us from dreadful penury."

In his present mood of despondency, he felt like an exhausted sailor lying on the sea shore as the incoming tide lapped round his body.

On the contrary, Catherine was in full sail. "Please God it'll turn out for the best and wouldn't it do my heart good to see our Meg and Dorothy making ready their linen chests for their own weddings." Dorothy's face shone but Margaret kept her head down.

There was nothing he could say. He was surrounded by pink leeches, their eyes wide with avarice as the juice of his soul was sucked down their maws. And what was this Christopher Marlowe – so well fattened for the sacrifice – to be? Poet? Scholar? Or snivelling clerk perched on a stool scribbling numbers, stocklists and market prices? Nausea rose within him, a sudden sweat soaked his clothes and his limbs grew cold. He struggled to his feet.

"What's the matter, Kit?" Margaret asked anxiously.

"Dear heart, he's over-excited with his prospects." Catherine hurried to his side.

"It'll sour our chances if he turns weak on his feet and in his head," said Dorothy.

"Let him be," said Catherine. "Kit's our loving son and your faithful brother and he'll do his best for all of us. Off with you now, dear heart, and if you're not any better in the morning, I'll make you a purging concoction."

He heard Ann asking the name of the rich family. There was no mistaking Dorothy's exclamatory shriek, "Yesu, but their daughter's a crippled chit."

Chapter eighteen

On St Thomas's Day Catherine rose from her bed with the first church bell and woke the whole household with her noisy bustle. By midday her unwilling female recruits were worn and weary but Catherine's store of energy seemed undiminished. When Christopher entered the dining-room, she was busy festooning the walls with holly and ivy.

"Are we to have a pagan ritual?" he asked. "Where's the Yule log for the sacrificial virgin?"

"You'd be hard put to find a virgin in Canterbury." She caught sight of her husband quietly leaving the house. "John, where are you going?" He mumbled something about checking the shoe prices in the market but she curtly reminded him that there was little marketing today except for the wood-sellers and ordered him to buy a yule log. "An ash is best and make sure it's not green. And don't be late home and don't have no more than two pots of ale with your cronies."

When the door slammed behind John, she turned to Christopher and held him at arm's length. "Let me look at you. Though I say it myself, you're a credit to my cooking. You've filled out in every measure. Do me more credit and change into a fresh set of clothes and, for my sake, don't go traipsing out into the streets today. The rain's coming down in dribbles and drabbles but I fear it threatens worse."

He assured her he had no intentions of stirring from his room and pretended he had a complex document to translate for Sir Francis Walsingham.

"Sir Francis Walsingham, did you say?" She rolled the name thrice on her tongue. "Didn't I say you'd make a name in the world."

He lay on his pallet, stared at the ceiling and contemplated his immediate past, his pointless present, his unknown future. Of the last, a thick mist, like grey drapes, hung across every path he tried to map. Out of this fog lurched wraiths. Faraway voices called.

Tom Watson looked down on him, pale, wan, a rebuking spectre. Anne Watson's distraught scream echoed. Poole, toothless grin, rope round neck. A joke, my friend, this final jig. Lopez, old Jew, awaiting Maccabean fire, the Christian boiling cauldron. Naked children wallowing in shit, mire, urine. The mob surging. Kill, kill, slash, slash. Crushed bodies under trampling feet. Legless beggars. Blind man clutching. Festering sores. Mildewed bread. Screams of fear, hate, anger. Kiss of worms crawl through lips. Straw rots, men rot. Bellies bloat, explode, stench. The spirit of God moved over the sewers and the cockroach was made in his image.

"Kit, are you there?" Margaret called from the landing.

"Of course I am," he replied testily, "and I'm busy writing."

"Clever as you are, you've not learned to see in the dark." She placed a candle on the table, sat down on the foot of the pallet and bent over her embroidery.

"Why do you spend hour after hour with that frippery. It doesn't clothe men, feed beasts or make a rainbow bridge to eternal glory."

She pulled a red thread through the frame and knotted the loose end. "Each has been favoured by the Almighty with a special talent which he or she should practise for God's eternal Glory." He leaned on his elbow to stare at her. Was this platitude-spouter his sister Meg, famous within the city walls for her inventive language when roused to anger, or was this a devilish succubus sent to tempt him into profanity and blasphemy? "You with your writing," she continued, "father's shoemaking, the carpenter with his cabinet and coffin joinery, the weaver, the tanner – "

"And the butcher, the hangman, the cess-pool cleaner," he rudely cut across her list. "What's come over you, Meg?"

"Small chance, given our fortune, for anything other than the chaste blanket of my virginity to come over me. But then I care little for them hereabouts with their pretended gallantry. Do not forget – " she paused long enough to slip into her affected accent, "I have conversed with noble, virtuous and gentle persons in

London, miles above Canterbury's clodhoppers. Robert Greene, for one, is well spoken and sincere."

"And well-spoked his marriage by deserting his lawful wife to live with a strumpet from the stews. In all sincerity, I don't doubt."

"And there's the gentle Warwickshire lad, a noble soul."

"Him? Gentle and noble?"

"He's a gentleman, if not by rank at least by nature. He thinks highly of you and said he measures all he writes by the yardstick of your verse. He pressed me to hurry back to London."

"Yes, Will would have his will and, I wouldn't wonder, pressed you most quickly and willingly."

Margaret smiled. "According to gossip, he has a wife in Stratford. An old dame, by all accounts. It was a speedy bedding, a speedy wedding and then, with all speed, away with Will to foreign parts."

She held her frame up to the light. "I'm sure the mare had a good gallop for her money and wouldn't begrudge her rider keeping his hand in on the flanks of a younger filly. I'd have taken Anne Watson to heart as a sister but, Lord save us, she made every second word a sermon. Her husband Tom loves you like a brother and – " She could have bitten her tongue for mentioning this forbidden topic. She violently tugged and swore at an obdurate thread, then broke the knot and the awkward silence. "As for my embroidery, Kit Marlowe, it is said it's the accomplishment of a serene soul."

"One prick leads to another," he retorted petulantly. "God's brother, Meg, have you come to aggravate me?"

"Save your tantrums for others, not me. I came to warn you. They're here. Your bride-to-be giving a limp start to the evening and her parents heaving their barrel bellies into our best chairs. When you go downstairs, be your own man and only do and say what is in your heart. To act contrary to that would be the height of immoral philosophy."

"Philosophy? That's a rare and wonderful word for you to be trotting out, Meg. Have you been reading books?"

"No, but I met the scholars coming home from school."

"Then with your new-found land of learning, tell me what's immoral in marrying wealth? There's no sin in a full stomach, warm and clean clothes and a tiled roof over one's head. If it were so, every bishop in the kingdom would be bound for perdition."

"It's a sin to make a sacred vow before God to hold and cherish a girl whom you've not laid eyes on before today while in your heart of hearts, your only desire is her money. I was told to tell you to come down as soon as you had finished your document though I'm blessed if I can see laid-out papers and wetted quills. Take her, and the devil take you."

When Christopher came downstairs, he nearly collided with Mary May in the dining-room doorway. Before he could interpret her enigmatic signals, Catherine emerged and grabbed his arm.

"There you are at long last," she said. "Didn't Meg tell you we had guests?" She affected a bantering tone as she pulled him into the room. "But then, I wouldn't wonder. Time means nothing to you when you're deep in your reading and writing."

"So he reads and writes then. Very useful indeed, very useful." This came from an over-dressed man with a face like a sad horse. His swollen body was crammed into a carved oaken chair and when he leaned forward like a large bag of grain gently toppling over, the seat moved with him.

"Well may you say Kit reads and writes," Catherine chantered on. "He's been to Cambridge and earned both his BA and MA."

"There's such a thing as being over-educated." The man agitated his jaws as if masticating this profound truth. "Am I not correct, John Marlowe?"

"There's a deal in what you say," John replied. He appeared to have exceeded the alcohol level ordained by his wife.

"And Kit's very well versed in Latin and Greek," continued Catherine.

"Not much call for them dead languages in our line of business." Again he turned to John. "A string of Latin never sewed a leather shoe, Master Marlowe, or a Greek tag nail a loose heel, hey."

"And our Kit's travelled to foreign parts." There was an edge of desperation in Catherine's voice. "He's been to France, Germany, the Low Countries and has more than a smattering of all them tongues. Isn't that so, Kit?"

"Well then, there's sense in that and I could do with a bright spark to make useful contacts for the furtherance of my trade."

"And what is your trade, sir?" asked Christopher.

"I'm not called upon to answer your questions, young man. My dealings are with your parents."

"Deal with them, then, to your haggling soul's content. I'll not stay to trade words with you." Christopher strode out of the room but he had hardly gone five paces when Catherine caught up with him and pinned his arms to his side in a wrestler's grapple.

"Kit, Kit, dear Kit, why are you doing this to me? You'll spoil our chances."

With some difficulty, he managed to break her hold. "I won't stand being paraded like prime cattle in the market so that bullneck can prod my haunches."

She stroked and brushed his clothes. "If I'm parading you, as you say, I'm only doing what any proud mother would do who has such a clever son. Don't let's give them the chance to think the worse of us." She linked her arm in his and they slowly retraced their steps. "And you haven't greeted his wife and daughter, have you? What a sweet and gentle creature their Joan is."

Directed by his father's waving hand, Christopher became aware of the other two guests sitting on each side of the dole cupboard. Mistress Faulds was a gross bundle of taffeta and silk, with a round pudding face and two eyes like dried raisins. The second person was a small, pale, almost ethereal girl dressed completely in white. Was it possible these two balls of suet pudding had engendered this weed?

When he approached Faulds' wife, she raised a podgy hand for him to kiss and as he stooped over the extended paw and gazed down on the dirty fingernails, she giggled, squirmed and said, "How gallant he is."

The sniggers of his sisters were drowned by Catherine declaring: "With his training and learning he can turn out with the best in the land and there's many in high places who've made demands on his service. Why, this very day he has been preparing an important document for Sir – Sir – Francis Walsingham, himself."

"The Secretary of State," added John Marlowe helpfully.

"I know who Sir Francis is," Faulds grumpily retorted. "No need to tell me. I've had dealings with his estate." John Marlowe winced when his guest gulped down the rich Rhenish wine and held out his goblet for a refill.

Catherine wheeled him towards the girl. "And now, dear Kit, we've left the brightest flower in the garden for your undivided admiration. Isn't she the tenderest and sweetest rose ever to bloom within our city walls. Your lovely Joan brings to mind a poem our Kit wrote. Now, how does it run. He was likening a girl to a swan. Why, it could have been written with Joan in your thoughts."

He corrected her, quoting " 'And she to whom in shape of swan Jove came.' " It was Margaret, not Christopher, who supplied the next two lines.

" 'And she that on the feigned bull swam the land,
Gripping his false horns with her virgin hands.' "

The Marlowe girls shrieked with laughter while the Faulds gaped at them with great perplexity. Catherine's cheeks flamed scarlet. "Shut your gobs, you pair of harridans or I'll – " She suppressed the desire to box their ears, quickly regained her composure and lowered her voice an octave. "Shush, now, my linnets. Our guests are not here to listen to your chirping. Come, Kit, finish the poem for Joan's delicate ears."

His sisters could barely contain themselves while the elders turned their collective gaze on him as he completed his translation of Ovid's Eligia.

" 'So likewise we will through the world be rung,
And with my name shall thine be always rung.' "

Catherine clapped her hands, hugged Christopher and beamed at the assembly. "Praises be to God, he has spoke the words of betrothal and before witnesses. Am I not the happy mother on this blessed day and you, gracious lady – " she waltzed towards Mistress Faulds, "your heart must be leaping with joy. I give my son, my ship of Asia, willingly and gladly, to your daughter, your thrush and your precious treasure."

"Speaking of treasures – " Faulds began as he tried to rise and leave the chair behind.

"Be easy in yourself, Master Faulds. We'll not spoil the flavour of the occasion with the ins and outs of the marriage settlement. Rouse yourselves, Dorothy, Margaret, our guests' goblets are parched dry. And you, Kit, take your place by your betrothed's side and acquaint one another with your pleasures, your thoughts and your hopes."

Christopher was stunned by the speed with which his mother had trapped him into a false promise and the Faulds into a false hope. Standing beside this inert girl, he felt awkward, gawky and bereft of words. Joan, who was not much older than 14 years of age, could have been mistaken for a large waxen doll. A wisp of a smile appeared and she slowly lifted her hand. For a second or two she held it suspended and pronate, as if expecting him to repeat the act of mock gallantry he had perpetrated upon her mother. Then, with the hurt look of a child unjustly chastised, the smile vanished and the hand dropped back on her lap. She was staring passively at his sisters. They had been surreptitiously tasting the wine and were, to their mother's chagrin, "behaving beyond decency".

"Kit, Kit," Margaret shouted. "Tell this strumpet. Did you not write a drama about Canterbury?"

"Who are you calling a strumpet, you rancid dollop of half-baked dough." Dorothy thumped her sister's arm.

"Now, now, girls, don't put us to shame in front of our guests," said Catherine. "Why don't you go down and help Mary May to bring up the food. I'm sure we'd rather enjoy the roast fowl than watch you flapping your feathers."

Margaret would not be silenced. "It was about Canterbury, Kit, wasn't it? Tell her and shut her gob."

"No, Meg, the scene was Malta." Christopher was more than glad of this diversion. "It's called The Jew of Malta."

"Jews!" Faulds snorted. "Heaven forbid they ever return to Canterbury, with their big houses in George Street and their sneaking usurious ways. Bad enough with them Walloons swarming all over the place."

Margaret was on her feet. "You may say Malta, Kit Marlowe, but I know better. Barabas the Jew described the hollow rock and the running stream by Holy Cross Church, where the Stour comes into Canterbury and also the Dark Entry in the Priory leading into the Green Court. You know it, we all know it. It's where the ghost of poor Nell Cook walks every Friday."

"God's mercy be on us." Dorothy squealed in simulated girlish fright.

"And if you meet with the lost spirit of poor Nell Cook, who was so wronged by the monks and was slaughtered by them, you'll be dead within the year." Margaret grinned at the young girl. "In your delicate state, Joan, I'd take care not to be next, nigh or near that dreadful place."

It needed all Catherine's brute force and strategically placed pincer movements to hustle the slightly tipsy girls towards the kitchen to fetch the feast.

Christopher asked Joan to accompany him to the table but she shook her head and looked appealingly to her mother. "Is she a mute?" he wondered. "Likely she has little to say and that's a rare virtue in a woman."

Her mother bent over Joan to listen to the girl's rapidly whispered words. "Joan wishes you to pardon her but she's so overcome with excitement her appetite has completely deserted her."

"But of course," exclaimed Catherine. "Would we be so churlish, I ask you, to demand her presence at the table when her mind is on more pleasing prospects?"

"But her company is our pleasure. Is that not true, Dorothy?" There was a malicious glint in Margaret's eyes as she rose from her seat. "Come, sister Joan, let me help you over to your rightful place between your father and my brother."

Joan was revealed to be as tiny as she was thin. She summoned up her small ration of courage. Taking a deep breath and dragging her deformed left foot, she limped grotesquely across the floor.

Chapter nineteen

John Marlowe was a happy man and whenever he passed a reflecting surface he congratulated the false image on being so acute in business matters. "Say what they will about me but John Marlowe knows how to put a fine pair of heels on an upstanding contract." Faulds and he had come to a signed and sealed agreement in which the merchant would pay any of the shoemaker's debts whenever creditors pressed too strongly. The accumulated amount owed would be deducted from the dowry when Christopher and Joan married. Of course, Faulds would add interest, a puny amount said he, to the final total, but this was custom and practice in commerce and the expected price to pay for putting another man's money at risk. What risk? The wedding would take place. O joyous day to come.

Occasionally a nagging thought would intrude to spoil his new-found contentment. Were the debts greater than the stated dowry? John had carried out several hasty calculations but stopped when the figure came dangerously close to the limit. Perhaps he had made a mistake? Tomorrow or the next day, he promised, he would study the ledgers again.

The coming event had re-established Marlowe's standing with his many acquaintances and some who had lately shown a remarkable shyness in greeting him now pressed their old friend to join in various ventures; to be fully discussed, of course, in a nearby tavern. Even Capal the weaver had hinted that his second son was anxious to marry either Margaret or Dorothy Marlowe. Capal always asserted he was English but his parents were Flemish refugees and John was not sure he could allow his daughters to marry a foreigner.

One night during the Christmas festivities when he was returning home after several hours of deep and thoughtful discussions with his comrades, John met the three horsemen. He was humming a jolly tune to himself when a shout of "Ho, there, you drunken sot" startled him. He felt the flecks of foam from the snaffled horses on his cheeks.

"I beg your pardon, gentlemen," he said. "I had weighty matters on my mind." They could be thieving rogues or the Puritan sheriff's hirelings ready to arrest revellers for debauchery. Either ways, it did no harm to promote them beyond their rank at this hour.

"I reckon you've more weighty ale in your belly than matters on your mind." The speaker laughed. This was reassuring. Neither rogues nor Puritans, if you could tell the difference, were given to laughter.

"Indeed, I've been merry with my companions and I fear we've overspent our time and money."

"Even to the grave, these tradesmen think only of money." John did not care for the surly tone of the second rider. "What, in particular, have you to celebrate?"

"That which is foremost in all our thoughts during this festive season. The birth of our Lord and Saviour."

"Why then," replied surly voice, "it's a mean thought to honour the Son of God with the belches of piss-sodden windbags."

"Who are we to judge, Robin?" said the third horseman. "Each man is free to show joy for Christ's birth in his own manner."

"It seems the devil is your judge, Ingram," retorted Robin. "Or have you been taking counsel with Kit?"

At the mention of Kit, and in spite of the champing horses surrounding him, John felt impelled to share his good news with these strangers. "And secondly, sirs, my friends have taken the occasion of my son's betrothal to wish a proud father well in his fortune. My son is an esteemed scholar and is to wed into a respectable and prosperous Canterbury family. Have you, by chance, heard of the merchant adventurer by the name of Faulds?"

"No, nor have I any desire to mingle with grocers and fishmongers." Robin jerked his nag's head. "We're wasting time gabbling with this drunken tradesman. Look you, fellow, direct us to a decent hostel. Not one of your tossed-straw, bastard-ale and lice-ridden hovels but one where gentlemen may rest in comfort, eat without vomiting and have their horses fed and watered."

"There is the eminent inn," hiccuped John, "where our glorious

Queen, may God keep and preserve her, laid her royal head when she graciously honoured Canterbury with her noble presence in the year of our Lord, 1573."

"I wonder who paid her royal reckoning?" inquired the third horseman facetiously.

"Ssh, Nicholas. Lead on, fellow, lead on."

John went ahead, the horsemen followed and in less than a minute they reached the gate of the inn's yard. "I'll leave you here, gentlemen. I pray God will grant you a pleasant stay and a peaceful night."

"What's your name, fellow." Ingram asked. "I'd like to know to whom we're beholden."

"John Marlowe, master shoemaker and freeman of this parish."

"Marlowe? Is this town clogged with Marlowes?"

"There's been Marlowes in Canterbury long before St Augustine ever set foot on our holy soil but I fear we're few and far between these days."

"And you have a son?"

"Indeed, sir. Didn't I say he's to wed?"

"It's surely not him," one said and chortled. "Our Marlowe's more adept at handling himself than fingering a maiden." They said goodnight to John and rode into the yard.

The nocturnal encounter filled John Marlowe with foreboding. After the last occasion when two characters accosted him in the George Tavern and asked for Kit, nothing but bother followed. If this meeting should presage trouble, the marriage plan could crash to the ground and Faulds would foreclose on the debts.

Since the Faulds' visit, a rare quiet had fallen on the Marlowes' household. Christopher had sunk into an apparent apathy, either lying in bed for the best part of the day or sitting by the window staring at nothing in particular. Catherine trembled to think he was going into a decline and, like her husband, she went in dread of any unforeseen blow that might wreck her schemes.

The following day at dinner, John recounted his encounter of the night before. Christopher roused himself from his torpor and asked him to repeat the names of the riders. "Do you know these strangers?" Catherine asked anxiously. Christopher shrugged his shoulders. "They're commonplace names," he replied. He then appeared to lose interest in the incident. Later he asked his father for details of the Faulds' estate.

The elder Marlowe began by expounding on the Faulds' munificent generosity to church and town. He touched only lightly on the man's investment in the slave trade. Christopher listened to him with seemingly rapt attention but instead of discussing how he would fit into this life of commerce, he rose from the table. Without another word, he did what he had not done for three weeks and left the house.

A burly man with rolled-up sleeves and a leather apron strung round his large stomach stood in the doorway and demanded to know from Christopher where he thought he was going, adding for good measure that the rear of the inn was for scullions and road-sweepers. Christopher tried to push past but the man shoved him hard in the chest.

"Kit, Kit, come in." Nicholas Skeres appeared. "How dare you treat my friend like that," he said to the doorkeeper, grabbing Christopher's arm. "Tell me, Kit, was it by chance you came to this piss-hole or were you doing the rounds of the taverns? The devil take it, Kit, but is it any wonder foreigners think of us as beer-bloaters and ale-swallowers? What else is there, I ask you, to be done in this town? Whatever else Canterbury lacks, it is not short of toss-pots," he said when they reached a corridor of curtained alcoves. It was quieter here with only low murmuring, subdued laughter and an occasional female squeal to be heard behind the drapes. Skeres stopped at the third one on the left and pulled back the cloth.

Robin Poley was busily tearing the flesh of a chicken's leg with his teeth. On his right, two young women with bared breasts were engaging in a rowdy game of groping with Ingram Frizer. At the sight of Skeres and Christopher, one of them cried out, "Ooo look, our wandering boy went out with his widgeon in his hand and came back with a whelp at his heels."

"Throw these trollops out," Poley shouted and began to belabour the nearest with the carcass of a fowl. "They stink of stale fish."

"But of course they reek so," said Frizer. "They've been trawled from Dover."

"Hark to Tom Tit-dibbler," sneered one tart as they sidled out of their seat. "You'd have less cod and more mackerel if you'd a bigger worm for bait."

"Out! Out! Out with these whores." Poley seemed overcome with both rage and repulsion and while Skeres and Frizer laughed and pinched the female flanks, he showered the women with leftovers. During the commotion, the doorkeeper poked his head through the curtains. "Everything to your satisfaction, sirs?" he asked and looked with suspicion at Christopher.

"No, it's not," replied Poley. "Clear away this mess and those harlots and fetch us wine that's not as sour as your face."

Skeres and Frizzer were in an excitable mood but Poley was as dour as a dyspeptic clergyman conducting an early morning service. He did not speak to Christopher until the debris had been cleared from the table.

"And what chance brought you to this inn?" he asked.

"The fair chance of your meeting with my father last night."

"It was he then who guided us here. The best in Canterbury, says he, one graced by our glorious Queen."

"Heaven forbid we ever need to rest in the worst," belched Frizer helplessly.

"You're welcome to rest in the dungeon beneath the city walls."

Frizer suspected a hidden meaning in the remark but subtlety was not his strong point. "We'll rest content behind any wall, Kit, if you'll tell us the truth and shame the devil."

"The truth? I know of no devil who's ashamed of the truth."

"Your father said you're to wed commerce."

The servant returned with a beaker of wine and stood in the entrance while Skeres filled four goblets. "Well, fellow, why do you wait?" Poley asked.

"The reckoning, sir."

"God's blast, man, we'll reckon with you when we've reckoned this wine. Go and leave us in peace."

Christopher blandly extolled the virtues of a steady and settled life. It was not in Poley's nature to trust simple statements and he was suspicious of this encomium to stolid middle-class prudence.

"Is this not evidence that Kit Marlowe is wise beyond his years?" said Skeres. "With his last drama, whatever it was, he's blasted away all his powder and shot and now his ordnance is emptied, he retreats to this safe haven."

"Indeed," said Frizer. "Another man less clever than Kit would have stayed to pester the playhouses with an abundance of dull versification but our friend, in his wisdom, voids the field in the face of more talented writers."

Their darts pricked Christopher's vanity. He had not left the field to any upstart crow of a rival, he asserted, and neither was he void of talent. He was working on several new dramas. The last was a lie because he had not put pen to paper for many weeks now. Finally, he defended his new-found fervour for commerce as a means of putting money in his purse.

Frizer and Skeres continued to goad him with acerbic remarks about reversing the order of nature by turning a gaudy butterfly into a grubby caterpillar and selling his honour so he could stuff his gullet with prime beef until the day he would die of a surfeit. Christopher reminded Skeres that his father was a tradesman, a tailor, and Frizer earned his keep by counting bags and bales in his management of the Walsingham estates.

Tempers were becoming frayed and the exchanges grew louder with each word. The doorkeeper hurried down the corridor, poked his pugnacious face through the drapes and deferentially asked the gentlemen to lower their voices as the clamour was disturbing the other customers. Frizer turned his wrath on the man, said unkind things about the low-class patrons of the inn and demanded another beaker of wine.

Poley had taken no part in the increasingly vociferous arguments. He brooded over Christopher's motive for converting to trade and suddenly saw the answer.

What better disguise for a wily spy than the pack-bag of a merchant peddling his wares from city to city, country to country? Traders crossed borders from state to state even when governments were at each other's throats. Walsingham received valuable information on the gathering of ships for the Armada from Italian merchants trading in the Spanish ports. A devious one like Marlowe could insinuate himself into courts and chambers and while exchanging credit notes for the easy passage of cloth and grain could pass and receive secret documents. Poley sourly wondered for whom he was working.

When the servant returned with fresh wine, Skeres, looking directly at Christopher, remarked that it was typical of certain tradesmen and their base-born breed to gulp down their betters' wine and never part with a penny towards the reckoning.

Christopher flung a coin on the table and attempted to depart. Poley restrained him. "You're our guest, Kit, and it's not fitting you should pay. Come, take back your money. Have another drink."

"Let Marlowe go and wallow, like a pig in shit, in his earthy paradise," said Skeres. "We've more pressing business than his market-stall bawling. I want to press those Dover bawds between hands and thighs," replied Frizer. He pulled back the drapes and called out, "Hey, you fishmongers' spelt, let's see your tails wriggle." Poley slid along the seat. "I feel in need of fresh air, Kit. Walk with me till my spirit is revived."

It was dark and damp outside and neither spoke as they walked down St George's Street. Christopher asked himself why he had set out to meet these people. He did not love them nor they him. Poley had, in the past, endeavoured to harm him. Yet, tonight, the man had displayed rare affability. Why?

When they were in the Long Market, Poley laid his hand on Christopher's shoulder. "So, Marlowe, after your purgatorial year in London you've reached, as Skeres aptly said, your earthly paradise." The voice was rasping, like a bad file rubbing a rusty chain. "But will it end there? Doesn't the river continue to flow beneath the frost-rime layers?"

"And are you angling to break a hole in the ice in the hope of pulling out a fish or two? What do you expect to catch in Canterbury? Since the monks were driven from the town we cannot boast of many fat trouts in our streams. And even if they were plentiful this is not the right season."

"Tell me then, Kit, when is the correct season? I must prepare my bait."

"You're wonderfully ignorant if you imagine a charnel-house worm skewered on your hook is sufficient lure to capture a river-salmon. Try your skill in the season of swarming Spanish flies."

They walked another ten paces before Poley spoke again. "Are you not curious about why we are in Canterbury? You and I, Marlowe, are of the one kind. We keep our secrets to our breast, we trust nobody, we suspect everybody and as it has been proven time out of mind, with the most excellent of reasons. The loyalty of those drunken and lecherous sots is unreliable at the best of times. Their metal is soft and pliable. But we are forged differently, Marlowe. We keep our own counsel. Yet have we not a common mission? Do we not strive to take this benighted kingdom from the realm of darkness into the eternal light of the one true faith?"

"That's Papist preaching."

"The Church of Rome is riddled with heresy, greed, lust and its vaults echo with the ranting music of Satan. It will be put to the sword and flames, its marble walls smeared with the lascivious portrayal of naked flesh will crack and the ranks of graven idols will be cast down. Then, and only then, shall the one true Catholic Church rise from the ashes. I have spoken to you, Marlowe, as one apostle to another. Now tell me how you fit into the sacred scheme of divine retribution."

"Only if you're willing to be entertained by the ramblings of an idiot. Only a dumbstruck loon on free leave from Bedlam would listen to your blow-hard preaching of fire and destruction. And if I gave voice to any wayward thoughts on the matter, would it stay with you? Or would it be carried to those with ears for hints of sedition and heresy and tortuous devices for the blabber-mouthed fool who spoke out of turn?"

Suddenly Poley swung him around and held a dagger against his windpipe. "Then, Marlowe, mark yourself down for twice, thrice a fool in choosing to walk with me through these dark and deserted streets. What is a slit-throat corpse lying in the gutter but another body to be cleared away by the garbage collectors." The blade's point pricked Christopher's skin. "I give you grace to blabber-mouth a final prayer but do not ask for grace to live another day."

A trundling cart laden with night-soil loomed out of the shadows on its way to Newingate. The concentrated stench was too much for Poley. He staggered back, dropped the dagger and covered his face with both hands.

Christopher quickly hid in a wall recess and waited until the cart had passed. His antagonist, after shouting, "I'm not finished with you, Marlowe," disappeared down the murky street. Then when it was safe to move, Christopher went through an alley towards Burgate and, to avoid another unfortunate meeting, decided to go home in a roundabout way through the Cathedral grounds. But what if he should come upon the ghost of Nell Cook lurking by the Dark Entry? Would that restless spirit be also exorcised by a load of excrement?

Chapter twenty

January was a cold, damp month and as day followed dreary day, the nightly hours of darkness decreased by minutes and the morning chill increased by degrees. In the Marlowe household, there was an uneasy atmosphere of muted expectation and, with the girls, a sense of suffocating boredom.

"Make a shape to your day," Catherine urged her daughters as she set them to some domestic task. Five or ten minutes later she would whip the brush or cloth from their hands and rail against them for their slovenly method. "God alone knows, I'll be glad to see the back of the pair of you." Occasionally she mentioned the tanner Capal's interest in one of them marrying his son – a rather gormless character – but neither girl showed a spark of enthusiasm. "When you're wedded, if ever you are, and I'm thinking a nunnery is the only place for jilted jennets like you, you'll learn a thing or two, the same as your sister Ann." Ann was very much pregnant with her first child.

She was deeply concerned about her son's apparent lassitude. When she lay in bed at night she poured her worries into John's ears.

"I fear the Faulds'll think twice when it comes to taking him for their son-in-law if he proves weakly. Mind you, given a high wind and a sharp turn in the weather, their daughter will be swept into her grave before the winter's out. But what will that matter once Kit has his feet under their table and his arse warmed at their fire. Are you listening to me?"

John Marlowe would prefer to sleep. Even better, he would prefer to wake up in the morning and discover his fretting anxieties about the match were a troublesome dream. His credit had been good when word of the proposed wedding was first out but as days and weeks went by without any definite date being set, people began to doubt the veracity of the news.

"Have you been to see the Faulds of late, Kit? I'm no stranger to all this legal fiddle-faddle, as you well know, and I say, have the matter signed, sealed and settled with sturdy witnesses to your mark before the sea breeze makes them grow cold."

Christopher's reply to his father's urging was a lethargic, "There's time and plenty."

"Where'll you be if some fellow-me-lad jumps in there, with more life in his breeches than you, while you're studying your belly button? And suppose the worst comes to the worst, and God forgive me for ever giving the thought house room, and that frail chit was to fade into her grave before a single penny of her dowry is paid across the counter? Where would we be then?"

A harbinger of this disaster appeared one evening towards the end of the month when Catherine burst into the house in a distraught condition. "We're as good as ruined entirely and it's your shilly-shallying, Kit Marlowe, that's to blame. There I was in the Fish Market when this high-faluting voice rang out in my ears. And who was it but herself and her with a serving girl in tow to do her fetching and carrying. I asked with all due politeness, 'And how's your beautiful daughter, sweet Joan, keeping this fair day?' She sniffed, turned up her nose, God's truth, it's turned up enough as it is, and she squeezed a few tears from her blubbering eyes. 'Well you may ask, Mistress Marlowe,' says she. 'Well you may ask and she poorly and pining and not a visit from your son.' 'As for him not calling,' I said, 'he had many documents to prepare for them in high positions and important offices.'

" 'That's contrary to what I've heard,' says she. 'I've been told by them who know, he's out of favour and none, be they riding high or low, will suffer his service for the cost of a penny and him spoken of the length and breadth of London for a rowdy tavern-brawler with the taste of prison on his mouth.' Then she goes and says, 'My poor child, my darling baby, my treasure,' she cried. 'Every day her heart is hoping and waiting for him to call or, at least, send a letter or even a poem. But not a word, not a sign. And with this and that and the dark nights upon us, she's relapsed into a decline and her grieving father and myself fear and dread that the ever-merciful Lord will call her to her heavenly place before the first lambs scamper in the fields.' I didn't know where to look for the shame I bore my bone-idle son."

Catherine was ablaze with frustration and thwarted plans. She regretted the passing of the years that did not allow her to take her son by the ear as she did when he was reluctant to go to school and haul him off to the Faulds for immediate marriage.

"I've small humour to wed and less to couple with the lame daughter of a Canterbury bagman," was all he said.

January rode out on the hump of a frost-haggard cloud and February slid in, bright and garish in the attire of a false Spring.

Early one morning Jem the Carter called into the kitchen with a sealed letter for Christopher. Catherine tried to make out the emblem impressed on the wax by squeezing it on a ball of dough but only succeeded in smearing the missive with damp flour.

The letter was not from the Faulds.

'To Ch Marlowe, esteemed scholar.
My dear Kit,
We bring you glad news. Tho Watson is at liberty and to the design of his good health he is to reside among us at Scadbury House till he is fit and hearty. It is our pleasure to invite you here to greet your fond friend. Also, to this matter, we have diverse concerns affecting our kingdom's welfare to discuss. We will send another letter when the stars are in the ascendance for your proper attendance. Do not fail to come.'

The letter was marked 'As written by Culbert, Clerk to Walsingham' and signed in a sloping scrawl 'Tho Walsingham.'

Exactly seven days later another letter came from the same source. It stated that he must be ready to travel in two days' time. A horse would be sent for his journey.

His mother took the news with commendable good grace. "You do as you see best, Kit, for your sake and ours. You'll have no trouble finding the path to your own home when you've had a bellyful and there'll be that sweet girl waiting to welcome you when you come through the East Gate."

She failed to tell him that she had 'borrowed' the first letter to show the seal to the Faulds as confirmation of her story. They were impressed enough to give Catherine a gift of a bolt of cloth.

"Dear Joan is on the mend, thanks be to God," Catherine continued, "and we did all agree the marriage be delayed till she's hale and hearty and you've made a name for yourself. Of course, you're as good as married. You've pledged yourself before witnesses and there's no escaping that."

Chapter twenty-one

Christopher's companion on his second journey from Canterbury to Chislehurst was a Walsingham house servant, a rather talkative Londoner by the name of Archer. They arrived at Scadbury near midnight and after being ushered to his room by the yawning lackey, Christopher fell on his bed with exhaustion and slept till well past noon of the following day.

Thomas Walsingham came to see him later in the afternoon and they chatted for some while on trivial matters; each one, for his own reasons, unwilling to touch on any serious topic.

Thirty minutes later Ingram Frizer appeared and made a great show of welcoming the new guest. There was not the smallest mention of the unpleasantness in the Canterbury inn – perhaps he was too drunk to remember – but, to Christopher's surprise, he asked when the proposed marriage was to take place. Prompted by Walsingham, whose apparent ignorance of the matter seemed real or well simulated, Frizer was able to give detailed information on the Faulds' business, wealth and the delicate state of their daughter.

Frizer quipped that Christopher's writing career began with the drama of a shepherd's lame son and was now set to end with a comedy of a wool merchant's lame daughter. Walsingham, in his turn, commended the astuteness of his guest for marrying into money. "Fair words, even if they are Kit Marlowe's, butter no cabbage," he said, and then went on to tell, badly, a story of a miller's daughter betrothed to an old farmer. Frizer capped this with a bawdier tale of a carpenter's wife and a student of divinity. For half an hour the three indulged in ribald yarns.

"I've a fund of such anecdotes," said Walsingham, standing up and wiping a tear from his cheek, "and if I had the leisure I'd spend the day listening and telling. But Ingram and I must, as the devil drives, be about our affairs and leave you to your own pleasures." He stopped in the doorway. "Tom Watson will be with us within the week." He and Frizer rode off late in the evening and it was some days before either of them returned.

The pleasures of Scadbury House were limited to eating, drinking, listening to the musicians, conversing with the other guests and visiting the library. The Walsinghams were inordinately proud of their books.

The other house guests were not a prepossessing lot. Most seemed to be poor relations of the Walsinghams who flaunted the reliques of past grandeur and bickered endlessly about who should take precedence at the table. The rest seemed to be merely waiting for their host to set them to some task suitable to their low rank. They sat at the bottom table.

Christopher shunned the company of both groups and whiled away his time in the library. Most of the books were of the orthodox devotional kind, dull in the extreme and apparently written by men whose piety was greater than their prose, but he also discovered volumes dedicated to tales of epic voyages, adventures in strange lands and stories of wondrous beasts and man-like creatures.

The only other visitor to the library was an old clergyman. On the fourth day, Christopher was reading a hardly credible account of one-footed giants roaming the plains of India when he was distracted by a sniffling sound followed by a cough. Looking up, he saw a shabbily dressed young man enter. With just a glance in Christopher's direction, the intruder turned right to wander by the shelves and at every tenth volume stopped to override the clergyman's snores with harrumphing and throat-hawking.

"Sir, why must you exercise your phlegm in here?" asked the irritated Christopher.

"You're Marlowe, aren't you?" The man picked his nose and hawked again.

"I am. What of it?"

"People often mistake us for each other. Did you know that?" He spoke with a London slum-dweller's nasal twang. "It's on account of our names being so similar. Good Lord, how I've suffered on that score. Oh no. Mind you, not so much the same as similar. You understand my drift?"

"No, I neither understand your drift nor care if you should float, swim or sink."

"Our Marlowe's clever with words." The man had the sullen tone of a resentful underling. "It's alright for high and mighty Marlowe. He's well in with them who've power while the likes of me and your friend Tom Watson are stuck in gaol."

"Listen to me, spittle-face or whatever your name is, you annoy me and – "

"Don't you touch me." The man shouted and backed away towards the doorway. "If you want to know, I'm Christopher Morley."

He remembered Kate Quick mentioning a Christopher Morley.

"So, Morley or Marley or Marl-dung or whatever name your mother gave you when she whelped you in a ditch – "

"Are you any better, son of a Dover fishwife?"

Christopher grabbed the man's jerkin and shook him hard. "I've a mind to haul you before Walsingham and have you thrown in the cesspit."

Flecks of foam appeared on Morley's lips and his breath smelled of decay. "Let me go," he squealed. "I could tell Walsingham a thing or two about you, Marlowe, and then we'll see who has the best of it. He'd like to know it was you with sly Dick Chomley who led the rebellious riot down by St Paul's on Bart's Day, shouting your heads off for Essex. And they they said it was me because that drunken sot Marlin spluttered my name before he died and now the hunt is up for me in Cheapside and I was in the Clink on the day. You owe me for my ills, Marlowe."

"I could pay you ill for your insolence, Morley," Christopher replied, "if I told Walsingham a thing or two about you. When I was last in The Gilded Lily, I heard about one Kit Morley who ran with the hare and hunted with the hounds and peddled his favours to soldier and sailor alike in the manner of a rank Wapping whore."

Morley sneered. "You've been listening to Kate Quick's tittle-tattle, you have. If you hare after that whore-hound's bitch, you'll end up pox-ridden and raddled with her lies. I'm no Hoxton hot-boy for soldier or sailor."

"I'm talking about peddling favours of a different kind. I reckon she had in mind Ralegh the sailor and Essex the soldier. Walsingham isn't earning full credit from you for his money."

Morley shrugged his shoulders. "What if I earn a penny from Walsingham, another from Ralegh and a third from Essex? Are your hands clean? Poor people like us are glad of any crust thrown our way and it's little enough, God knows, after what they've robbed from us. Are they any better than us? Does their shit smell any the sweeter?" Morley moved towards the doorway. "Let's agree on this, Marlowe, you and I have more than names in common and if you don't blow the wind on me, I won't fart in your face."

When Morley left, Christopher fell to wondering why the man had troubled to seek him out. Was he seeking an ally? And for what? Or was he sent by someone else in an attempt to trap Christopher into an imprudence?

"The devil take it," Christopher shouted and banged the table with his fist. "But I'm seeking Machiavellis in every shadow."

The sudden noise stirred the snoring clergyman. He raised his hand in benediction, muttered, "Sanctus. Sanctus. Sanctus," allowed the weighty tome to slip from his grasp onto the floor and then returned to his wheezing.

Christopher picked up the fallen book – a dull and morbid work dedicated to the joys of death – and as he did so, a handful of loose sheets tumbled out. He glanced at the headings and then, excited by his discovery, sat by the table to read them.

They were translations of heretical tracts written by an uncle and nephew, Laelius and Faustus Socinus from Siena. The authors' argument was that any doctrine not based on human reason should be rejected. To that end they boldly denied the Holy Trinity, the personality of Satan and the existence of eternal punishment.

Christopher tucked them back into the book but it was three days before he had an opportunity to lay his hands on them again. On the first two days the somnolent clergyman had kept a firm hold on the book but on the night of the second day he succumbed to a seizure and was tasting the ineffable joys of death when Christopher entered the library on the third day. He had settled down to a deeper study of the papers when he heard a noise outside. Hiding the papers in his jerkin, he went to the doorway.

Morley stood in the entrance. "A word with you, Marlowe." He seemed worried. "There are rumours upon rumours and I'd value your counsel. We're to be dispersed to the four winds."

"We?"

"Yes, we who sit at the bottom table. Down-at-heel clerks, failed scholars, one-time clergymen, bankrupt nobles, runners and fetchers and all in debt to the Walsinghams." Morley sniffed in a vain attempt to dislodge the glistening drop on the tip of his nose. "I fear I'm destined to hang or to be hauled off to a rotting jail." He came closer to Christopher. His breath had not improved over the last few days. "It's said Sir Francis Walsingham is dying."

"The same was said last year and the year before but he still lives."

"It's certain now. And when he does, who'll be Secretary of State? Not young Walsingham. Essex? We all know he's set his heart on the post. Robert Cecil? That dwarf is small enough to wriggle through any mousehole to gain entry to the Queen's chamber and her favours. And that's another matter. No amount of primping and painting will disguise the old Queen's age, let the poets say what they will, and it's rumoured she's taken to her bed with a chill. What if she died? Who's to succeed her? The gangling, stuff-mouthed Scots barbarian with his clutter of fancy boys? Or Essex?"

"Prate sedition, Morley, if you must but my counsel is for you to keep your tongue to yourself or the hangman will tear it from its roots."

"That's the nub of it. I'm commissioned to go North with a sealed letter. If I'm caught I'll be hanged and I'll be hanged if I refuse. Let this be between you and – " Morley quickly glanced over his shoulder and disappeared down the hall.

"Rough company for a smooth scholar, Kit." Frizer stood a few feet away. "I cannot imagine you and he were discussing the finer points of Plato's Dialogues or Ovid's Amores. Be warned, the man is an infamous liar and his bad breath exhales stinking slander."

"I wonder, then, such a disreputable character should be given house-room in this place."

"We've had worse here." Frizer cracked a smile. "Forgive me, Kit, if I seem to pry but many a purse has been emptied at the behest of his ill-fortuned tales. He would wheedle pennies from crippled beggars." Frizer reached out and plucked the tracts from Christopher's jerkin. "What have you here? Ah, these again. Have you read them? But, of course, Marlowe would. You found them in the library?"

"Yes and I intend to return them."

"No, Kit, don't. Burn them when you're alone. We had hoped to net those who had the writings translated but it's of little consequences now. We've bigger fish to land than some miserable heretical penk." Frizer yawned. "I've ridden hard this day and I'm dog-tired. I'll find myself a soft bed for an hour or two's sleep." He stiffly walked a few paces away and then stopped and turned. "Even in your scholarly seclusion, Kit, you must know that matters of state are galloping to a close. Many men of rank and standing in our kingdom shall be gathered in this house. I trust, Kit, you'll be as one in our endeavours."

"And if I keep trust with myself and choose to stand to one side?"

"Choose what side you will, Kit, but when the harvest is called in the reaper leaves no blade standing."

Over the following two days, Frizer's predicted flood of guests was the merest dribble and he was a picture of fretful anger. When, late on the second day, Christopher asked him about Tom Watson, the reply was an irritated, "Watson? What of Watson? Yesu, there's room enough for twenty Watsons and as it is, we'll have to scour the highways and by-ways to make a round dozen for our debates."

Two stout, red-faced men approached. "May we have a private word with you, Master Frizer?" one asked. The three went into a huddle. Frizer, stepping out of the group, shouted angrily, "Go, if you wish, and wallow with your pigs. We'll suit ourselves to better company."

"There's the spring sowing and the lambing," protested one, "and if we're not on hand there'll be the devil to pay."

"And the devil never pays the rent," added the other.

Frizer turned on his heels and strode furiously down the corridor. Christopher trotted after him and they did not stop until they reached the library.

"By the blood of all the martyrs, at this time, Kit, when we need men of iron – " For a moment Frizer seemed lost for words. "What have we to call upon? A regime of petticoats, fat farmers, dry-land sailors, stay-at-home merchants, the rag-tail and bob-tail of London slums."

He began to strut up and down and orate like one possessed. "Where are the warriors who fought at Crecy, Poitiers, who stormed the infidel citadels, who waded knee-deep through blood, to snatch the Frankish banner? Give me the company of one hundred such Englishmen and we'd take Paris, burn Madrid, cage the Pope in Rome and plant our flag on Jerusalem's flat and burnished towers." He dismounted from his dreams of ancient chivalry. "There's not ten of equal merit in the whole of England. Is it any wonder we're harried by the tow-headed Irish savages, suffer the disdain of the prancing French and the sneers of foreigners from Calais to frozen Moscow? We've grown soft on sweetmeats and spices, Kit, fat on beef and stuffed geese, turned our sinews to silk and are like suckling babies, podgy on women's milk. I fear for our kingdom."

Sounds of shouts and hearty laughter echoed down the corridor and Frizer bestirred himself. "God be praised, they've arrived, fully armed in heart and mind to set the nation to right."

"And Tom Watson?" Christopher asked. "Is he among the company?"

"Tom Watson's been with us since early morning."

"I did not see him at the table."

"He's had his bellyful of noisy crowds and eats alone."

"Where is he now?"

"Why, in there." Frizer waved towards the library. "I wonder you didn't know about it. He has exchanged one prison for another and is, at present, jailed behind a wall of books."

Chapter twenty-two

Tom Watson sat on a high-backed chair at the far end of the long, narrow chamber with a large wood-backed volume propped up on the table in front of him. His clothes were sombre black and his hands and face were alabaster white. He did not look up when Christopher entered the library.

"Tom. Tom Watson! When were you released? If I had known the time of your arrival, I'd have gone a mile down the road to greet you."

A white hand turned a page. "You travelled many miles to distance yourself from me recently. Why did you betray me?"

Christopher gaped at him, shocked.

"You denied me. Isn't that a betrayal?"

"What's this incestuous coupling of denial and betrayal? Surely you don't damn me for seizing the chance to get out of prison?"

"That was the first denial."

"Even so, I kept my pledge to help your wife and family. I would have done so if she had not spurned my aid."

"That was the second denial."

"Do you insist that I cover my head with ashes and walk abroad in sackcloth? Why should I repent for taking whatever fortune offered me?"

"That is the third denial."

Christopher found this piling of sin upon sin quite vexing. Perhaps the man before him was a fabrication made in the shape of Tom Watson or an actor of similar appearance primed to speak certain lines? Or did the foul air of prison sicken the flesh and disease the spirit?

Possibly a Parthian shot might rouse him from his morbidity. "Tom, there are three kinds of men whose company none enjoys. Monks, madmen and lepers. The first has a mange on his soul, the second a mange on his mind and the third a mange on his body. Which are you? Even the dogs enjoy the company of their fleas. Cast off your prison skin, Tom, and you'll cease to itch with the Newgate distemper."

Watson turned another page of the book and continued to read as if deaf to the world.

Christopher was too disheartened by this encounter to join the assembly in the main hall. With bread, cheese and a jar of beer, he went up to his small room in the tower. When he came down the following morning, the house seemed remarkably empty. There was nobody in the library and the long hall and corridor echoed to his footsteps. Suddenly a big blustering man dressed in breastplate and helmet stomped towards him.

"Hey, you, boyo, fetch me wine,' the figure commanded. He had a rough, scarlet, pox-scarred face, fierce blue eyes and a mottled beard and exuded a smell of old leather, dried horse-sweat and unwashed clothes. "Do what I say, you gawping loon, or, by St Tavy, I'll roast your hide."

"I'm no servant," Christopher replied.

"What! What!" The large man shook as if a petard had exploded under his feet. "Hell's blast and blood, you gutless snipe, fetch me wine, I say."

"I have it here, Sir William." Archer hurried up with a flagon and a goblet. The soldier grabbed the flagon, stuck the spout in his mouth, threw back his head and marched down the corridor. After twenty paces he stopped, belched and dropped the emptied vessel on the floor.

"Who's that drunken lout?" Christopher asked.

Archer wrinkled his nose. "That stinkard is Sir William Rogers, a Welsh bully-boy. His leek-ridden brain can't tell the difference between friend and foe and thinks every house is a besieged city ripe for looting." The servant cautiously looked from left to right and lowered his voice. "He's a close friend of the Earl of Essex."

This was not the first sign of collaboration between the Walsingham and Essex factions. 'There's more than Rogers' ordure in the wind,' Christopher thought to himself as he followed Archer towards the main entrance.

"We've been up and about before cockcrow," said the servant, "running about like scalded cats to make them ready for the hunt and they're still prancing around outside."

The whole household seemed to have gathered on the sward. Horsemen cracked their whips, hounds bayed, nags neighed and bystanders shouted; but there was no real effort to set off on the chase until Sir William mounted, gave a wild hulloo and charged across the fields in the direction of Sidcup village.

When the hunt disappeared, the remaining crowd returned to the house. The last to come in was Thomas Watson. Less waxen-faced than yesterday, there was even a slight flush to his cheeks. He barely glanced at Christopher as he walked by.

"Tom, what is the matter with you?"

Watson stopped. "Rather, what is the matter with you, Kit Marlowe, that you should fritter away your talents and gifts in the mean politics of these intriguers? They're enmeshed in their own ambitions but why should you risk your genius on the throw of these rash gamblers? The fox they chase is less wily than the fox they wish to join the pack. I speak of Essex and I speak the truth. How can this assembly be innocent of guile when it has such arch-tricksters as Francis Bacon in its midst?" he said contemptuously. "He's fit to be on show at the Fleet Fair. He can stand on one foot on the sharp point of any dispute, toss a dozen beliefs and loyalties from hand to hand and sing anybody's song – if they pay him – with the skill of a trained juggler."

Nothing Watson could say could diminish Christopher's excitement at the prospect of meeting the infamous philosopher, scholar and statesman. "So Francis Bacon is among us. I'd go a long way to be acquainted with him."

"Then you go your way. I'll take a different path."

Christopher had no wish to follow Watson into the library. He wandered around the Walsingham estate and returned to the house when the dinner was already in progress. The servants buzzed up and down like demented flies.

"You can't sit in your usual place," Archer said, a smirk on his face. "You'll have to sit at the bottom."

"I'll sit where I will or I'll not sit at all."

"It's one less bother as far as I'm concerned."

Ignoring the insolent servant, Christopher strode towards the top table. He would, he resolved, thank Thomas Walsingham for his hospitality and then depart.

Lady Frances, who wore her widow's weeds lightly, sat in the host position with her cousin, Thomas Walsingham, on her right and Sir William on her left. Edmund Walsingham, Thomas's elder brother and the nominal host of the gathering, was too ill to attend. Frizer and Skeres sat next to the blustering soldier and were firing a volley of impertinent questions at a man with his back towards Christopher.

"Whatever your Italian Galileo proved," Skeres shouted, "by my sight a feather floats gently to the ground while a lead shot plummets in the space of – that." He snapped his fingers. "Now tell me, clever Master Bacon, were I to leap from the musician's gallery, which would hit the floor first, my body or my hat?"

"It would depend on whether you fell on your arse or your head," Bacon replied, "but, to my knowledge, you've always contrived to fall on your feet."

As the others applauded, Skeres scowled and selected Christopher as an easier target. "Why, here's our Canterbury scribe wearing out his father's shoes. Truth, I had mistaken him for a servant and was in mind to order fresh meat."

"Truth, Nicholas Skeres," said Walsingham, "you mistake the order of your place. Make place for Kit to sit with us. No, let it be between you and Ingram."

Skeres viciously poked the person on his left in the ribs and all those on that side suffered an immediate reduction in rank. Christopher took the grudgingly vacated place and sat opposite Francis Bacon.

Bacon had dark bushy hair, a high forehead and restless eyes; but the handsome symmetry of his upper face was contradicted by a large nose, scraggy beard and wide, sensual mouth. He smiled at Christopher and said something but his words were drowned by the tumult.

All Europe denigrated the English for their immoderate eating and appalling table manners and the present dinner lived up to that ill reputation. The odorous Welsh warrior was the worst offender with his belching, guzzling, ribald remarks and campfire expletives; but the others, including Lady Frances, competed hard for second place. It was obviously not the time for philosophical questions into the nature of falling bodies or dynasties.

The noise abated a little when, at the end of the meal, earthenware jars and pipes were brought in. "Ah, the devil's weed itself," roared Sir William. "Fire in the mouth, fire in the belly and we'll all shit cinders." He rallied those reluctant to try this new-fangled habit: "Whoresons and hell-shakers, stick it in your gob and to blazes with your beards."

Christopher had no liking for the smell of smouldering compost and less for the scorching sensation in his mouth after an inhalation but in this boisterous company one would have to be very churlish, very brave or very sick to spurn the tobacco pipe. He sucked in a puff of fumes and immediately his stomach seemed to revolve. The surrounding faces turned into floating pink blobs. He persevered and, in spite of the welling nausea, nodded and smiled to show he found the effect most enjoyable.

"Does it not cool the brain and refresh the vitals, Kit?" Walsingham asked.

"He's a boy or a fool who does not like tobacco," said Christopher. He quickly gulped down a full jug of ale in the vain hope it would soothe his mouth and settle his stomach, but when the company turned to another diversion, he crept out of the house and disgorged his meal behind a rain-barrel. Giving himself time for the retching to stop, he dowsed his face in the water and returned to the house; a bit shaken and weak in the legs.

Only Bacon and Thomas Walsingham remained seated. "Have I traipsed all the way from London to witness these rowdy schoolboys?" Bacon asked.

Most of the men, under the chaotic supervision of Sir William, had formed two opposing lines down the length of the hall. At a command from the sodden soldier, some clambered on the backs of others and, at a second command, the two rows charged across the floor. It was impossible to hear a civilised word when they clashed and bodies sprawled and tumbled into untidy heaps.

Walsingham bit his lower lip as he watched the lines reassembling. "Bear with us a while, Francis," he said anxiously. "They're as good as any gathering of men you'll find in the kingdom and when they've exhausted their exuberance they'll be ready and willing to join our debate."

"That, in itself, I would debate," Bacon replied. "Rather their exuberance was for learning, then the sinews of their minds would be whipcords and lashes, a scourge against ignorance and a strength for the true governance of the state. What can you shape from a rabble but a rabblement?"

Frizer had come over while Bacon was speaking. "Would you have us neglect the art of war then, Master Bacon?" he asked. "We'd have a short shrift of it indeed if we brandished quills instead of swords."

"And shorter shrift we'll have if we mimic the bull beast and in brute panic charge upon our adversaries with our heads to the ground and our eyes closed. Do you dispute Caesar was a learned man?"

"There's no disputing Caesar had not learned to tell friend from foe and died bloodily as a consequence," Frizer replied. "For my part, give me one hundred men who – " Walsingham stopped him with a gesture and asked that Sir William be restrained. "I'd have more chance of restraining a wasp-maddened horse than halting our knight's gallop." At that moment he was called over to rejoin the boisterous crowd.

"There's one person here who has held onto his wits if not his dinner," Bacon said. "A dozen lambent lines of Christopher Marlowe, in my book, are worth a thousand lion roars from your bellowing bullies."

"Have a care," said Walsingham, "lest you figure in a mad Marlowe drama."

"Let's all have care," replied Bacon, "lest we figure in a drama made from our own madness."

Sir William's lines of centaurian cavalry charged. "By your leave, Thomas," Bacon said, attempting to make himself heard above the noise, "Marlowe and I will take the air."

Christopher followed the philosopher-statesman out to the herb garden. "Tell me, Marlowe, have you studied the multitudinous benefits these humble plants offer to man's weal and health? Or, like so many Latin-laden scholars, do you spurn such learning as may lie beneath your feet?"

In truth, Christopher had never thought of roots, weeds and flowers as being within the province of his studies. To him they were only within the lore of crones living in damp hovels with cats and toads, preparing their potions and poultices for credulous peasants. Secret lore or not, unique, or so it was said, to alleged witches, Bacon appeared to be well versed in the hidden knowledge.

"Consider the comfrey," he said, pointing to a tall plant growing in a wet patch. "Pluck the root fresh from the soil, bruise and peel it into a concoction and it'll bring relief to wounds and raw sores." He continued to list the medicinal uses of various herbs. Coltsfoot for coughs, petty spurges for sore throats, wild mint for tiredness, foxgloves for weak hearts. "There are many others said to be favoured by sprites and gathered by the love-lorn and the lack-love to bring fortune where virtue fails," he concluded, "but those are simples for the simple." Then, quoting from Tamburlaine, he said, "As like the moon's reflected light." He turned to face Christopher. "Tell me, Marlowe, have you studied cosmogony?"

"I've read what I could in whatever books are available."

"Are such books available or have you been exploring beyond the permitted boundaries of knowledge?"

"Only the ignorant and the superstitious set boundaries to knowledge."

Bacon smiled. "And Marlowe counts superstition but a childish toy and holds there is no sin but ignorance."

"Machiavel said so; but he counted religion, not superstition, a childish toy."

"In his prologue to The Malta-Jew, Machiavel had only said what Marlowe wrote. I reckon Marlowe's written words are demon children of his thoughts sent out to prick us with their forked meanings." He looked towards the house and scowled at a fresh outbreak of noise. "Suffer little children. I misquote to suit my argument. Religion, superstition, are they not twins engendered by the same parents, ignorance and dread? But on a different matter, Christopher, would I figure in some fresh drama of yours?" There was a touch of vanity in the question. "Pray, do not make me bombastic or one given overmuch to rhetorics."

"I would liken you to Socrates."

Bacon's frown indicated he was not pleased with the comparison. "I'll drink my hemlock in my own time and not at the behest of the mob. Christopher Marlowe, it is said you are a rash and imprudent young man, given to barbed and provoking words, yet I take you to be an innocent and I fear for you. Be guided by me. Put the snakes and adders of your words into the mouths of your invented characters who will, at the close of the last act, be victims of divine retribution. In this manner, you'll explore your ideas, prod the fat belly of complacency, enrage the obtuse and lash the ignorant with your tongue and yet, in the end, when damnation looms, divert the arrows from your hide and give pleasure to the groundlings. But why should I presume to tutor you in your own well-crafted art?" A swelling roar came from the house. "Suffer little children to come unto me. Suffer? It is my despair that man will always suffer because man will always be a child."

Chapter twenty-three

Much to the chagrin of the Walsingham clique, the Scadbury House concourse of like minds had come to nothing. Bacon was the first to leave and the other guests, having heavily feasted on beef and beer and lightly supped on political intrigue, followed him in dribs and drabs over the next few days. When Christopher decided to depart and return to London, only the poor relations, their host, Skeres, Frizer and Tom Watson remained.

April in London that year was balmy and though some feared the dry and warm weather could signal the early arrival of the plague, most others were glad the cold damp was evaporating. They could lay aside their remedies for the rheumatics.

Christopher's life in the city was simple, frugal and almost monastic. As soon as it was light, he rose, ate a sparse meal – usually bread and cheese washed down with ale – and then continued writing until it was too dark to see pen and paper. After which he would leave his lodgings – a poky room in a Bishopsgate tenement – and go to The Bull tavern where he would have a more nourishing meal and meet his friends.

His present play, based on the infamous slaughter of the Huguenots in Paris, was not a patch on anything he had written before; but he hoped it would prove both profitable and popular. Given the existing political climate in England and France, the proposed drama was topical – but speed was essential to catch the fickle mood of the times.

It had taken him just seven days to finish the first copy and he was feeling quite pleased with himself that evening when he entered the tavern.

Kyd, as usual, was fulminating against foreigners. Today it was the Dutch, whom, he asserted, accosted decent women in the streets with lewd suggestions in their guttural tongue. His listeners asked for translations for future use but, being a remarkably humourless man, their jocular request threw him into a sulk.

Nashe nudged his neighbour to make room for Christopher. "How are you, Kit?" he asked as if he had not seen him for weeks. "So Tom Watson is still enjoying the fine air of Chislehurst, is he? I've heard there's nothing to fear now for the pair of you from the Bradley rogues. Some have been sent to France, and the French deserve no better, others are bond and bound for the Americays, two have danced a last jig outside Newgate and the biggest braggart of all has taken the Essex colours."

Though Christopher was mildly curious about his identity, he did not press Nashe to enlarge on the subject. It was sufficient for him to know he could walk abroad without the danger of being ambushed by an avenging gang.

He enjoyed the loquacious company of his friends and rivals. Recently Greene, who was feverish with moral rectitude when not called upon to practise it, had taken to greeting him with, "Hail, mighty dandiprat, how go our Hoxton friends?" It was an obvious reference to Christopher's apparent lack of interest in women; Hoxton was a notorious area for deviant behaviour. On the first occasion Christopher pretended not to have heard the jibe and the titters it attracted, but later he retorted: "And hail to you, Robert Leno (Leno being the cant name for a male brothel-keeper). And how goes it with your very own Winchester goose? I hope she hasn't strayed to pluck at another man's tufts." Winchester Geese was a common name for Bankside harlots and Greene was living with a prostitute. The dart had struck home and its victim secretly began to worry about its implication.

The broth of the day was a viscous pottage of haricot beans, cabbage leaves and chunks of meat. Impossible to tell if the stringy flesh was cow, sheep or goat – it could have been horse, and the rump end of an old nag at that – but it satisfied Christopher's hungry stomach and he sopped up every last drop of the liquid with thick lumps of rye bread.

Red-bearded Will Slaughter was now the centre of attraction. The bit-player had an unshakable belief in his histrionic abilities and was more than willing to declaim in sonorous tones, with much hand-chopping of the air, solemn passages from antique interludes. His offering for this night was Jupiter's opening passage to Heywood's The Play Of The Weather but when he spoke the first line, "Right far too long as now were to recite" mock-groans and cries of "True, true, far too long" rose from his listeners. Undeterred by further heckling, he continued to roll out the stanzas and only stopped to glug a pot of ale.

During this rare gap, Nashe asked Christopher, "And who's this clown newly come to entertain us?" He nodded towards where Nicholas Skeres stood at the edge of the crowd, nervously going through a pantomime of beckoning gestures.

"Clown is one of the names I'd give him," Christopher replied as he rose and, without much enthusiasm, ploughed through the press.

"I've searched for you high and low, Kit," said Skeres, "but I'd have saved myself a lot of bother if I had asked Robin Poley."

"Poley? I've not seen him for months. How should he know where I am?"

"How indeed? You may ask." He drew Christopher to the other side of the room and told him to peer round the corner. The unmistakable obese form of Richard Baines sat, half-hidden in the shadows of a nook, at a table by himself. "Could this be the answer?"

"If that rancid ball of lard is spying on me, I'll slit his gullet, I will," Christopher swore.

"It may not be as it appears," said Skeres. "Perhaps he's innocently chosen your tavern for a quiet and private hour of meditation. He still retains the habit of saying the office of his church. Pay your reckoning, Kit, and we'll leave. If he follows us, we'll know his purpose is otherwise."

"Let him and his purpose serve the devil, for all I care and may he rest and rot in his flea-ridden Papist surplice."

Skeres sighed. "It's no concern of mine whether he rots or rest. I've other matters to discuss with you and this is not the place I'd choose for our talk. I'll treat you to a glass of Dutch brandy-wine elsewhere."

Christopher's curiosity was roused, though he felt it would be an ill-favoured choice to share any drink, be it hemlock or brandy-wine, with Skeres. They had gone about ten yards when Skeres pulled him into a doorway. "See if he comes."

Baines emerged from the tavern, stood for a second under the sign and then strode in their direction. Skeres and Christopher stepped out of their hiding-place.

"Richard Baines, what fortune brings you here? Are you, by chance, taking the same road as us?"

Baines stepped back, startled, but he was not one to be discomfited by an ambush. "Can't a respectable citizen take an evening stroll without being accosted by the snivelling sons of bankrupt tradesmen?"

Skeres drew his dagger and pointed it at the fat man's bulbous nose. "Careful, Baines. Your tongue could help to cut your throat." Baines moved out of arm's reach. "Tell your master and hound-keeper, Robin Poley, that we've no patience with any cur he sends out to sniff our trail."

"Tell him yourself, Skeres. You've paid more than one visit to his kennel before now." Baines retreated a few more paces and his lips rolled back from his teeth. "As for you, Marlowe, you untried whelp among cunning dogs, the coursing whippet by your side is as likely to bite your arse as lick your paw."

"Have you no wells to poison? No suffocated corpse to bury?"

"You're poison enough, Marlowe, to sicken a thousand wells," Baines shouted as he quickly turned and trotted away.

"I wonder before God and man if any cause is justified that employs such toads," Christopher said. "His very skin reeks of venom."

Skeres grunted and replaced his dagger. "In the great divine scheme of things, even the gadfly has its reason. But now I'll be brief. I see you're anxious to return to your companions." They strolled on a bit further away from the tavern. "Kit, you are a novice in our sodality."

"Are you questioning it? You and Ingram were my sponsors to that antique ritual."

"Antique ritual or not, you did swear to serve your novitiate in accordance with our precepts. How many sodality meetings have you attended? Two? Three?"

It was four, but at the first three the subjects chosen for debate were fit only to delight charlatans and impress the gullible. He had been invited to give a lecture on religion at the fourth but when, in the course of his talk, he threw doubt on the Bible's chronology and the accepted belief of the earth's age – 4000 years – his audience became restless. When he said that Moses was a juggler and had tricked the Hebrews into wandering in the desert for forty years so that those who knew of his conjuring trick would perish and only a great superstition remained, his listeners murmured loudly and one shouted that Marlowe was a damned atheist.

Christopher had expected scholars and philosophers at this so-called School of Night, not dull men with suspect ambitions and limited intellect who stifled yawns when faced with complex ideas. They only woke to irritation when provoked by such as he and showed obsequious attention when one of greater rank than they joined the company.

Christopher knew that Skeres would neither understand nor sympathise with his reluctance to attend fraternity meetings, but he was somewhat annoyed that they should send a messenger to reprimand him. "Am I a serving man who must be chided for neglecting his duties?" he asked testily.

"No, I'm not here to admonish you," Skeres replied. "But if you'd been attentive to your duties, I would have no need to tell you of our present disarray."

"Disarray? Who's in disarray? The sodality or the Walsingham cohort?"

"Both. Remember that you are one with us and by sacred oath a member of the sodality, yet you play the stranger with each party. All is not going well in our endeavours and we cannot afford deserters or laggards."

"Am I being warned?"

"Listen, Kit, there are divisions and dissensions within the brotherhood and the factional quarrels of politics are threatening to tear us limb from limb. Sir Walter Ralegh, for one, with his crew of alchemists and wizard earls, is arrogantly attempting to suborn the very spirit of our sodality. As for us, whom you are pleased to call the Walsingham cohort, we are weak and dismayed by fortune's enmity. Are you sure you'll not share a bottle of brandy-wine with me, Kit? Another time then? Perhaps after the funeral."

"Funeral? Are you interring your great cause? Shall I prepare an epitaph?"

"Write whatever dirge you wish, Marlowe, but there's no paean sufficient to salve our wound. Sir Francis Walsingham is dead."

In a few succinct phrases, Skeres related the last few days of the Secretary of State. The great manipulator of men and plots, scourge of traitors and rebels and father of the secret service had suffered the scourge of a prolonged illness, was wracked by the insidious agents of death and had finally succumbed to a bladder disease.

"And on the stroke of midnight two days hence," Skeres concluded, "honourable men will assemble at St Paul's and you are to be one of the party. But, be warned, not a word to any Dick or Hob."

"For what reason should I be there?"

"For the reason of the funeral." With that curt reply, Skeres turned and disappeared down the street.

The remnants of the company were being firmly ejected from the tavern when Christopher returned to The Bull. "Hail, mad and scoffing poet," Greene drunkenly shouted. "Hail, Merlin's spit."

When, two days later as instructed, Christopher approached St Paul's Cross from the direction of Bread Street, Ingram Frizer emerged from the shadows to greet him. "Why should a man so esteemed as Sir Francis be interred with only the midnight owls' screeching to render his obsequies?" he asked.

"No ding-dong bell shall be the debtor's knell," Frizer replied, giving a grim twist to the children's rhyme. He reminded him of the custom of creditors, who would attempt to seize the body and prevent it being laid to rest until all monies owed were paid. The corpse of Sir Philip Sidney, Walsingham's son-in-law who had died a hero's death in battle, had been abducted and hidden for over three months until his debts were cleared.

"God above, but it makes my heart sick," said Frizer, "to think of Sir Francis, whose private purse was emptied to assure our realm freedom from tyranny, being hauled through the back alleys of Cheapside in a box of unvarnished wood as if he were a pauper.

Yesu wept, but it would serve us better if these stones cried out for shame."

Two more men known to Frizer appeared and he allotted the three of them various posts. "Stand and be on your guard against strangers. Ask one such, gently if it is your wont, what he is about at this hour and if his answer does not please you, don't hesitate to draw a second breath. Clout him hard on the pate."

"Perhaps he has a friend or two in tow?"

"Then call out sharply. We'll be close at hand to put intruders to rout."

Christopher's station was by the chapter-house entrance on the south side of the Cathedral and he soon became aware, from the sounds of whispering and snuffling coming from between the buttresses, that he was not alone. Cautiously he went over to investigate and saw, in the fleeting moonlight, what appeared to be untidy bundles huddled against the wall. He smelled a sour mixture of urine, sweat and mouldy clothes. He retreated back to his post, fast losing stomach for this nocturnal task and the ubiquitous company of the human detritus which crouched and lay in every hole and corner of this massive monument to Christianity. These were not the intruders of whom Frizer had spoken; they were the poor, the destitute, the dregs: none of whom came within the politics and reckoning of state affairs.

Suddenly and silently a group of hooded figures appeared and gathered in a semi-circle by one of the larger bundles. Christopher at first feared he had come upon the ghostly return of long-dead monks but the curses that came from the cowled figures, the blows and kicks landed on the bundles and the whimpering cries of the vagrants soon disabused him of that. Screwing up his courage, he shouted, "Ho there! To the watch," and marched towards the disturbance. He was immediately grabbed by the raiders. "Who's he?" one asked. "Tried to trick us, he did," said a second. "Let's scrag him," suggested a third. "And have his mates fall upon us?" objected another. "Listen, cully," said the first man. "We'll have no snappers spoiling our traffic, so look to your footwork." He gave Christopher a vicious prod in the chest with his stick.

A cry of "Kay-vee, kay-vee" came from a few yards away and the gang began to melt into the shadows. The first man smacked the stick across Christopher's fingers. "When I find the trugging house who's paying your loot, it'll be the worse for them and you." He shouted to one of his disappearing comrades, "Have you taken a drab?" The raider turned to show he had a girl vagrant by the hair. "Let's scarper or we'll be nabbed."

"What's this ruction?" Poley emerged from the dark recess of the cloister door. "Ah, Marlowe, it's you. Never happy unless you're tangled in a fray."

Christopher wondered whether he had been standing in the doorway from the very beginning, only making his presence known when the danger had vanished. Two other guards came hurrying round the corner and Christopher told them what had happened. "What have these unfortunate wretches left to steal?" he asked.

"Gold coins, for one," a guard said. "Some starvelings cling to the relics of past grandeur and sew coins in the hems of their cloaks to pay for their funeral rites."

"As for the chit of a beggar girl," continued his companion, "she's fresh flesh for the whorehouses where those alley-creepers will sell her."

Poley raised his voice. "Oh wrathful God, as you did to Sodom and Gomorrah, do so unto this vile city for it is not a little place and its sins are grievous."

Frizer appeared, followed closely by Skeres and several other men. "Hush, Robin," he said. "This is not the time for sermons. Our own ceremony is finished and the vigil is ended. God alone knows what tomorrow will bring but now we'll go back to Seething Lane to refresh ourselves. We'll disperse from here and go our way in twos and threes."

"Can you find the path in the dark, Marlowe?" Poley asked.

"With you as company, Robin Poley," Christopher replied, "all paths are darkly shaded."

"It's not as far as Babylon."

"Will I get there by candlelight?"

"If you're nimble and don't take fright. My man shall strike the spark and be our guarding light." Poley called out, "Baines, prepare your link-light and walk on. Kit Marlowe and I shall be close behind."

"Baines? I'd rather break wind with those beggars than follow the whiff of his breeze."

Poley chuckled a humourless dry laugh. "Keep to his footsteps, Marlowe, and you'll not drift into the shallows. Is he not akin to your guardian angel, forever hovering by your side?"

"Forever crawling after my arse, you mean. Have you no better employment for his talents?"

"What would you suggest?"

"A frizzled slice of bacon to catch Papist mice."

"God grant we catch Bacon to entertain the Protestant cats with sufficient frizzled meat to keep their claws in trim." A candle-lantern flickered and moved away. As they turned to go, a vagrant lurched out of the gloom and clutched Poley's sleeve. "Help me, sirs, help me," he pleaded. "Those rogues have stolen my daughter, my only help-meet."

"You old fool," Poley snarled. He hit the pathetic creature across the face. "What's your drab daughter to me?" His fingers dug into Christopher's arm. "We must hurry from here. I've vowed to pray for Sir Francis's soul before the light of day."

Chapter twenty-four

Following the deaths of his uncle and brother, Thomas Walsingham became titular head of the estate and inheritor of the Secretary of State's political empire – though without his power. The young man was strong in purpose but weak in abilities and sought to confirm loyalties through bribery instead of his late uncle's subtle mixture of intrigue, blackmail and threats.

In his uneasy roles as patron and leader, Thomas doled out benefits to his favourites, ostensibly for services to be rendered, and to this end gave Christopher a small amount of money with a promise of more generous allowance when the financial affairs of the estate were settled. The declared reason for this retainer was the future translations of scholarly documents at present held in the Scadbury House library. In the meantime Christopher was invited to call in to the Seething Lane house whenever he felt in need of a good meal. But at the end of April Walsingham suddenly departed for Chislehurst, left no message and – what was worse – no money.

The officious servant at the door informed Christopher that the house was the sole property of Sir Francis's widow and she was not in the habit of sharing her table with strolling players and out-of-work clerks. The man added, wrinkling his nose with disdain, that if the caller was in real need he could join the other beggars at the back door.

The month brought Christopher another disappointment. Alleyn and Henslowe had taken up his drama The Massacre At Paris but as yet had not produced it and therefore not paid him. The new censorship laws, the vociferous campaign by the city's moral guardians against plays and playhouses and the Government's entanglement in the turbulent French politics had made theatre managers fearful of presenting new dramas that could be regarded as controversial. Old and safe dramas were revived, comedies with gaudy clowns and buffoons falling all over the stage became the normal diet for the groundlings and insipid romances of lovers and mistaken identities set in mythical forests were now fashionable among the upper classes.

These were poor days for playwrights and Christopher's Bull Tavern comrades were prolix in their grumbles. They laid the blame for their short commons squarely on the shoulders of the miserly and spineless playhouse managers, but there was no comfort to be gained from their complaints and they could only bide their time until the audiences tired of the sweetmeats and floss they were offered.

One evening Thomas Kyd sidled over to where Christopher sat. "Listen, Marlowe," he half-whispered, "I've a matter of utmost secrecy which – " he furtively looked around "- if I tell you, will you swear on your mother's grave – "

"May God preserve the good woman in years of health to come," Christopher said loudly and heartily and again Kyd quickly looked round to see if anyone was paying heed to them.

"Then on your grandmother's grave."

"When I travel in that direction I'll willingly swear upon her mouldering mound, which, if she knew of it, would please her mightily. In her heyday she was champion swearer of all Dover."

"Swear upon what you will, Kit, but will you keep my secret?"

"In what proportion?"

"In the whole proportion. How could it be otherwise?"

"No, I differ. If I shared this pot of ale with you, as you've offered to share your secret with me, my portion would be that much the less. Therefore, does it not stand that the proportion – "

"The devil take you for a Gotham fool, Kit Marlowe," Kyd shouted with annoyance. "I had thought you'd welcome a chance to earn a penny or two." He was, as the saying went, a little pot and soon hot; and true to that, he folded his arms and lapsed into a sulk. For several minutes he retained his petulant pose then, seeing that nothing came of it, relented and asked, "Would you join with me in a venture, Kit?"

From time to time, Christopher had been pestered by Kyd and others to collaborate on writing plays, but he had no desire to be a buttress for their frail structures. "I've a drama of my own to complete," he replied evasively, "and I'm urged by Ned Alleyn to present him with a fair copy."

"I'm also working on a new play," Kyd said. "It's the tale of a Danish prince whose kingly father had died at the hands of his brother, the self-same brother who, by insidious argument, enticed the queen and now widow to – " he stopped, fearful that he had said too much. The pilfering of plots among writers was as common as purse-cutting at a country fair. He leaned forward and spoke quickly. "But that's not the venture. It is this. There is a certain noble lord who, though he does not lack a name, lacks talent and has pretensions in surfeit. Namely, this noble lord has pretended to a surfeit of literary pretensions and when not too pressed by other duties would, if pressed, make it his duty to exercise his pretentious talents." Kyd, when roused, tended to speak like a character from his plays.

"Let's not dwell on this unmentionable noble's pretended talents," Christopher said. "I do not lack a name but I am sore pressed by my own lack of talents and nobles."

"Indeed, Kit, you speak for many of us. I also suffer from the want of an angel to bless me. But before we speak further on the coins of the realm in our fists, let me press on with the matter in hand. When pressed to pen a sonnet, our noble lord failed to press a talent's worth of juicy verse from his dutiful head. So he called upon me."

Christopher laughed. "Why? To change a goose into a swan with your quill?"

"Rather, Kit, to goose a swan. He's asked me to write sonnets for him but, at present, I've my own play to write – '

"And I've mine to complete." Christopher drained his pot and rose.

"Wait, Kit, wait. Allow me to replenish your ale." Kyd's rare offer to buy a drink was too tempting to refuse.

His scheme was simple. He would write out several lines of a particular theme and then Christopher – "With your esteemed eye for a smooth form," he said – would shape the work into a sonnet. When the completed poems were sold to the unnamed lord, Kyd and Christopher would have equal shares of the profit. "Of course, Kit, if you should spurn this chance to earn some extra money, thinking perhaps that the task is beneath your talent, I'll look elsewhere. I've heard that Will Shakespeare has a fancy to make a name for himself as a poet, he not being too fancied as an actor, and I'm sure he won't need a second asking."

At first Christopher made a show of reluctance but eventually agreed to visit Kyd's lodgings near Cripplegate in the afternoon of the next day.

The room was a mess of scattered clothes and papers and it took Kyd several minutes of frantic search to find what he had written. The half-dozen lines on each sheet were impeccably laid out – Kyd had been apprenticed to the scrivener's trade – but none were of any merit and Christopher was appalled at the crudity of the verses. It gave him malicious pleasure to openly criticise Kyd's work but even so, within an hour he had shaped and polished three sonnets based on the man's puerile efforts.

"And when shall I see my profits?" he asked.

"Soon. Very soon," Kyd promised. Two days later in The Bull he gave Christopher a handful of coins and said his noble lord was so pleased he had urgently requested at least another six sonnets. On this occasion Christopher composed the poems without any assistance or hindrance from Kyd. The only part the other man played in this enterprise was to transcribe Christopher's scrawled copy into immaculate exemplars of the calligraphical art. More requests and more money came and the pair were kept very busy. One day Christopher brought the heretical tracts he had found in the Scadbury House library with the intention of showing them to Nashe that evening, but when he reached The Bull tavern he realised he had left them in Kyd's chaotic lodgings; now, in all probability, lost in that midden-heap of clothes and papers.

After three weeks, the demands for literary compositions ceased. More than likely, the noble lord had sufficient for a small book, which, in his conceit, he would publish under his own name. None of this worried Christopher. The work, while it lasted, was profitable. Not quite as profitable as he had been led to expect – did Kyd cheat? – but it had put money in his purse.

It was about this time that Jem the Carter called in to The Bull with a letter for Christopher. It was from Catherine but as she had little learning in the ABC and less patience to sit moidering with pen and paper, it had undoubtedly been written by either Dorothy or Margaret.

"She said as how you'd pay the cartage fee." Jem held onto the missive until his favourite brew, Lambeth Bastard Ale, was ordered and drawn. The letter read as follows:–

'My dear and one true son,
God in his mercy look over you as He does us. Yr sister Ann had brought forth a man-child and it being alive to this day as I write they be in good health thank the Lord Almighty. Yr father is in good health. Yr sisters Dorothy & Margaret are in good health as I am truely yet I suffer small times with arm aches and Mary May complains of sore legs but I do not raise my voice against the Lord it being damp with much rain in Canterbury. Yr betrothed Joan Faulds is taken abed with shivering sickness. Her father, quoth he, if there be no wedding he'll call in yr father for monies owed.
Yr loving mother
Catherine Marlowe
Hr mark.'

Jem plonked his now-empty pot on the table. "A man'll gather a mighty thirst while waiting to start or finish a long journey. I'll hang on if you'd like to scribble a reply."

"Tell my beloved mother – ' Christopher began.

"Hold your horses there, young Marlowe, and tell her yourself," insisted Jem. "Put your hand to paper and pen for I'll as likely as not forget every word you say. I'm as dry and as footsore as a weary cow in the market-place after having a taste of the salt lick." Christopher called for more ale to help the carter put his memory into good trim. Eventually they agreed that Jem should convey an unwritten message to Catherine; in brief, her loving, attentive and dutiful son was chasing bright prospects in London Town and dare not return to Canterbury any earlier than Christmas.

"And what wonders have you brought from Kent this day, Jem?" Christopher asked. "I trust you didn't lose any passengers on the way this time."

A sly grin cracked Jem's corrugated features. "Ah, I see your drift, young Marlowe. You're talking of the time I left you with your gentlemen friends on the London Road, eh? Well, no matter. I knew they weren't Chatham roughs straight away, I did. You can't fool me. If they weren't gentlemen, I'd have shown them a thing or two, mark my word. Jem the Carter is a holy terror when roused." He scowled a fearsome grimace. "As for my passengers this day, a pair of strapping Broughton wenches, they were, with haunches that would do a heifer proud. Not like that poor snipe your good mother passed on to me, God help the unfortunate weed. Yes, them two sturdy strumpets are finely settled in The Barge Bell and Cock, much to the pleasure of Ned Alleyn. You know the man?"

"The Barge Bell and Cock is a brothel hard by The Rose playhouse. Surely you're not acting the bully-boy to force innocent country girls to be wanton whores? And what is this to Ned Alleyn?"

"I'm off to finish my deliveries." Jem heaved his bulk from the seat. "Force them, did you say? I reckon you're the innocent, young Marlowe. Them frolicsome Broughton fillies were rearing to gallop into the stew with all haste and hope and without a backward glance. As for Ned Alleyn, he's part-owner of The Barge Bell, not to mention other tenements butting on to Bankside, and his good wife takes care of the rent. He's an upright man who always pays straight on the nail with never a quibble or grumble. There you are then, young Marlowe. I'll offer a prayer to St Marlin to keep your shoes well shod and preserve you from all evil."

With that pious farewell, the carter trundled out of the tavern, leaving Christopher to contemplate the venality of friends and relatives. Ned Alleyn, for example, an incomparable actor, numbered among his many roles offstage that of moneylender, landlord, playhouse manager and, as now revealed, a whore-house procurer. With all those profitable professions under his belt, he could not fail to become Lord Mayor of London.

Christopher re-read his mother's letter and discovered a postscript from Margaret hidden in the folds.

'My loving brother Kit,
Do not venture home to wed Joan Faulds. She is bereft of health

and wealth, her father's richness, it is said, having sunk with
the slaver ships of the ocean and she's fast sinking to her grave.
yr sister
with all her heart
Meg.'

Chapter twenty-five

"Tamburlaine, Tamburlaine, Tamburlaine," chanted the line of children as they weaved behind a shambling boy-simpleton through the crowded streets. At Bandyleg Walk he turned, his flat features distorted into a beastly grimace, growled and lumbered towards his tormentors. They screamed and yelled in pretended terror, scattered and then rallied back to poke the unfortunate with sticks. Some bystanders were amused by the hectic game but the bawdy-baskets, pedlars and cheap-jacks were annoyed with this disturbance to their trades and shouted abuse at the children.

"I've a mind to visit Paris Gardens this coming Sunday evening," Christopher had said to his friends. "I've heard there's a monstrous bear fresh from Asia, a massive, savage and cunning beast they've called Tamburlaine. If it truly lives up to its infamous name it'll make short work of the baiting-dogs. Who'll come with me to witness this scourge of God in its wrath?" But each one found a different excuse for being elsewhere.

"I've no stomach for the gory mangling," Nashe had said, "and I do wonder, Kit, how you, with your gentle spirit, could find relish in that brutish sport."

"It's a tonic for my jaded soul."

The pit's equivalent to a play's prologue came to an exciting finish just as Christopher took his place on the scaffolding. An old blind bear had been tied to the stake and, instead of being baited by dogs, was beaten by three men with canes and whips. The shabby animal suffered the blows with miserable groans and whimpers for several minutes and then, with a sudden show of ferocity, lashed out and tore a gobbet of flesh from its nearest assailant's arm.

"He'll surely die," some said. It was not clear whether this referred to the bear, now being dragged out, or the injured man who was also being hauled away as he bawled and clutched at his torn flesh in a vain effort to stop the gushing blood.

The arena quickly filled up with latecomers and there was much shouting and shoving. The vendors were busy selling pies, fruit and hazelnuts and gamblers laid bets on the outcome of the next and most important event. Nobody was taking money on whether Tamburlaine won or lost; they all agreed he would certainly be the victor. What was worth a wager was the number of dogs the famous beast would kill or maim.

"Have you seen Tamburlaine?" Christopher's neighbour, a chatty tailor, asked.

"O mighty and godless Tamburlaine," Christopher intoned in a mock-histrionic style. "He who rose from fierce Scythian plains to march against the Turks and smote the caliph and kings of Asia. Tamburlaine is king of kings and shall not die."

"What are you yawling?" The tailor gawped at him. "Here we bait bears, not kings." He turned to his cronies. "We've a right loon here who thinks he's at the playhouse to see Ned Alleyn rant and rave."

"He must have been pricked out at The Rose," said one.

"More than likely, he's been pricked outside The Rose and has a rash of red flowers on his crotch for keepsake."

While two boys sprinkled fresh sand on the pools of blood, the crowd raised a steady chant of "We want Tamburlaine." As was the custom, the bearward entered the ring to advertise the coming bout but jeers and yells drowned his voice and a pie crust struck his neck. He was a thick-set man with a brutal face so akin to his charges that many swore his father had lain with a she-bear to save the cost of a wife and he was the resulting whelp. Though he shouted with all his might, it was hard to compete with the hubbub of impatient spectators, the vendors' calls and the shrill whistling of small boys, but this did not deter him from finishing his announcement. In conclusion, he cracked his whip, made a grotesque bow towards the better-off section and marched out; his departure accompanied by cat-calls and a few more pie crusts.

The so-called better-off section was usually occupied by the sons of rich merchants. They affected the airs and graces of the upper classes and hoped, by doing so, to be mistaken for nobility; but today there was one among them with whom their pretensions could not compare. In the very first row a young man, frilled and flounced in fashion's highest degree, leaned languidly on the barrier and spoke to none but his companion. The companion, dully attired by contrast, was Tom Watson.

At the rolling of the drums, the clamour subsided. Presuming Christopher to be innocent of the baiting rites, the chatty tailor elected himself expert informant. "They'll parade the champions first so we'll have a measure of them. Ah, here they are." A burly man, a near-twin to the bearward, marched in with three snarling hounds held on long leashes. "The brown mongrel is called Belzebub, the scrawny brindle is named Mephistophilis and the jet-black hell-hound was christened Lucifer. They keep them on short rations to make them that much more evil." Another man brought out three more dogs, younger and smaller than the leading trio. "Them's the taunters, learning their trade, you might say, and they'll work the bear up to a terrible rage."

Now everybody went deadly quiet, every eye was fixed on the entrance and every breath was held in excited anticipation. They had not long to wait for Tamburlaine's fearsome appearance.

None was disappointed at the sight of this monstrous auburn beast, this ursine king. Four strong men, each tugging on the end of a tarred rope wound round the animal's chest, pulled the creature into the middle of the arena. The chain dangling from the brute's neck was made fast to the thick wooden post, the ropes were slipped and the men hurried to the barriers.

Tamburlaine was alone, the locus point of a thousand stares. He sniffed the sweaty smells of agitated bodies, looked with short-sighted gaze at the watchers, uttered a grumbling growl, scratched his back against the post and rubbed his nose with his paws.

His respite was brief. A whip was cracked and the taunters sprang forward. One snapped and snarled at his feet, the second circled to bite his rump and the third leaped for his face. The bear struck the jumping dog a glancing blow and crushed the second against the post. The last hound turned tail and scampered back to the barrier.

With canine cunning, the dogs yelped beyond the chains' length and pretended to make forays over the boundary. "At him. At him," the crowd shouted. At the signal for the second assault – two cracks of the bearward's whip – the curs repeated their manoeuvres, but Tamburlaine was ready for them. He ignored the one at his feet and the second tearing at his rump and waited for the third. When the dog sprang for his snout, he crouched as if to allow the attacker to fly over his shoulder and then, in a movement so quick nobody saw the beginning or end of it, he ripped open the animal's stomach. Even before the torn corpse had hit the ground, Tamburlaine turned and dug his claws into the second dog's spine. The handlers struck out with their whips but it was too late to save the dog and it, too, ended its career in a gory mess. The third dog, less brave but more sensible, retreated out of reach to bark defiance from a safe distance.

The crowd went wild. "Send in Lucifer. Send in Belzebub. Send in Mephistophilis," they chanted. Tamburlaine returned the roar with a roar and showed the assembly his naked yellow teeth and claws. The bearward signalled to the handlers and the champions were released.

They did not waste time snapping, snarling or circling but, as one, jumped straight for the bear's face and chest. He opened his arms as if to welcome them to his bosom and then, when the three bodies crashed against him, he embraced them with a crushing hug. Belzebub screamed as his ribs cracked, Mephistophilis slid from under the grip to dig his teeth into his antagonist's belly and Lucifer locked his jaws on the brute's nose. Tamburlaine fell to the ground and rolled over, smothering the hounds under his hairy weight, but the attackers held fast. He rolled over again and again, only restrained by the taut chain, and then struggled upright to a standing position. Lucifer was still clamped to his snout, Mephistophilis clung on to his belly like a leech, its hindlegs tearing at the lower flesh, but Belzebub lay on the ground, hardly twitching in its final agony. Now Tamburlaine raised his arms, dug his claws into Lucifer's eyes and flung the stricken animal ten feet across the arena.

Two valuable hounds were lost and the third was in danger. The bearward distracted the enraged beast with his lashing whip while the handlers tore Mephistophilis away; flesh, skin and fur clamped between its teeth.

"Wasn't that a famous victory for Tamburlaine?" The tailor was hopping with joy. He had laid a side bet with a cooper on four dogs being killed.

"If he's true to his mighty name," Christopher said, "our Tamburlaine will not rest content with the slaughter of a few mangy curs."

Tamburlaine was, once again, alone in the centre, the blood of his slain enemies spattered on the ground around him. His nostrils were torn, his matted fur damp with gore and ribbons of skin and flesh hung from his belly but, as if unsated with his easy triumph, he roared like one thirsting for further combat.

The bearward and handlers, with ropes and tackle, cautiously closed in on him from all sides. He turned this way and that way, tried to sniff the scent of his new foes through his lacerated nose and then, when the first neared the radius of restraint, bellowed, lurched forward and the chain snapped. Tamburlaine was free.

Sticks, staves, ropes, whips were dropped as the handlers scrambled over the barrier and only the bearward and the bear were left to face each other. "Whoa there, boy. Whoa!!" the man shouted and to help the beast recall the retribution for ursine sins, slashed his whip across the animal's face. Apparently subdued, the bear went down on all fours, his shaggy, bleeding head lolling from side to side and it seemed to the spectators that even the mighty Tamburlaine could be vanquished.

But his full fury was not yet spent. From within the cavern of his chest came a deep growl that grew louder and louder till it climaxed in an almost human shriek. Then, with the speed of a leopard, belied by his ungainly bulk, this behometh of the Siberian wastes charged and crashed his massive skull against his master's stomach. The cursing bearward fell flat on the ground, but the beast's rush was unstoppable and suddenly those in the front row were staring at gaping jaws. Afterwards, many swore they could even smell the bear's fetid breath.

Panic reigned as those nearest scrambled up to the second row and those on the second leaped up to the third, while those on the fourth pushed the others back and those on the fifth stood up because they could not get a better view. The wooden scaffolding trembled with the turbulence, then cracked and the collapsing structure carried seats, spectators and furious monster down into the arena.

The fit and able, Christopher among them, trampled over the unconscious and the injured and fled, helter-skelter, out of the bear-pit. Attracted by the cries of "The bear's escaped. The bear's escaped", people came from all directions; and soon the streets and alleys were blocked by the curious who listened, open-mouthed, to the extraordinary tale of the event. At the junction to Green Lane Christopher stopped to catch his breath and saw Watson and his companion approaching. The young man appeared to be highly excited.

Christopher called out to Watson who returned the greeting with a wave of his hand and then spoke to his companion. The youth nodded, shrugged his shoulders and then stood in the middle of the crossroads, his hand on his sword hilt and his eyes fixed in the direction of the bear-pit. At that moment shouts of, "The bear's coming," went up and people scattered in the manner of terror-stricken fowls. It was a false alarm and as they re-grouped in small huddles each told each that their hasty flight was merely to make sure aged parents were safe and small children were out of the savage beast's reach.

"You're a sight for sore eyes, Tom," Christopher said. "When did you return from Chislehurst?"

"Recently," was Watson's short reply. He stood half-turned away, his gaze on his companion.

"And who's your young friend?" Christopher was determined to provoke a conversation.

"Him? He's the Earl of Southampton, of lately come into his estate but still in wardship." Watson sighed. "He has the body of a seventeen-year old, for that's his age, the impetuosity of a ten-year old and the sense of a toddling five-year old. For my sins and for my keep, I've been charged to be his wet-nurse."

Once more, the alarm went up but this time Tamburlaine did appear, trotting from the Paris Garden on all fours, the broken chain dangling from his neck. The bearward ran along by the animal's side, red-faced, panting and blaring, and hitting out with a stave in an attempt to turn the beast back.

"Yesu, he's set to challenge the bear," Watson yelped. Southampton stood in Tamburlaine's path, his unsheathed sword in is right hand, his silken cloak wrapped round his left arm. The crowd cheered and egged on the youth, though one irreverent person said it would only be a fair combat if the bear also had a sword.

"Kit, help me to pull the fool away."

Christopher thought otherwise. "I'll not risk life or limb for any noble idiot."

Tamburlaine sat back on his haunches, myopically seeing only the irritant of bright, flapping clothes, and raised his naked claws. The bearward grabbed the chain and tugged hard but, in spite of the choking effect of the iron collar, the bear pulled in the opposite direction. His keeper held on while men with staves, pikes and a net hurried up to surround the beast.

Southampton was angry that his attempt to have a killing to his name was frustrated and when Watson dashed over to drag him from the battlefield, he turned on his tutor-cum-guardian.

"How dare you lay hands on me, Watson."

Watson was not cowed by the youth's arrogance. "Better I lay hands on you now, Henry, than you be bereft of hands, legs and arms. Come away. They have it cornered and it's finished."

But it was not finished. The net was flung over Tamburlaine, men struggled to hold the ends down, but within seconds he had torn the mesh to shreds. Now twice as furious, he had to use all his ursine cunning to break through this trap. He charged one way, the crowd in front scattering and tumbling over each other, the street dogs harassing him from behind, then he wheeled, slashed at the curs and charged in another direction.

"They'll tire him first and then make him captive," Watson said.

"I'd have vanquished the brute with one sure thrust but for you, Watson." Southampton pouted in a sulk.

"It'd take more than one callow youth," Christopher muttered, "to vanquish mighty Tamburlaine." The baying and taunting of the rabble and the stupid pride of this young man doubled his championing of the beleaguered beast. "Go to it, Tamburlaine," he shouted (and he was not alone in doing so). "Tear them limb from limb."

There was a lull in the skirmishing. Tamburlaine stood like an exhausted bull, his shaggy head lowered, his nose near the ground, blood and saliva dripping from his jowls. Emboldened by this apparent mixture of fatigue and defeat, the encircling men closed in, staves, pikes and ropes at the ready. Another net was fetched and a string of baiting hounds was brought down from the kennels. The onlookers murmured, some with fear, some with expectations of finality and a few with sympathy for the subdued animal. The bearward cracked his whip, the hounds were unleashed, the net was thrown and in an instant there was a whirling confusion of broken staves, torn net, tossed dogs and a cacophony of screams, yells and growls. When the maelstrom died down, Tamburlaine the undefeated stood alone.

He roared, sniffed the breeze and then, again on all fours, charged, without opposition, down the lane leading to the Paris Garden Stairs. "He's for the river. He'll swim across," the cry went up and the crowd surged towards the Thames. Southampton waved his sword in the air. "I'll put an end to this troublesome Tamburlaine," he boasted. "Make way. Make way." He ran down the lane.

"Yesu, this troublesome youth will put an end to me," Watson said desperately as he and Christopher followed Southampton. By dint of much shoving and pushing, they managed to reach the front rank of the multitude standing by the ferry steps. The bear was at the extreme end of the jetty – the boatmen having quickly rowed out when they saw him approaching – and was sitting back on his rump, his front paws dangling between his rear legs and his snout pointing to the sky. He softly howled a long single note of despair.

The bearward was arguing with an official-looking person. "Send those people away, I pray you. I tell you he'll be tamed in a thrice."

"He's a danger and a threat and there's none to control him."

"I tell you, I'll master him. Give me leave – '

"It's too late. I have my duty to do."

The official signalled to three bowmen. The first flight of arrows sailed over the bear's head and plopped into the water. Of the next three, only one found its target – it immediately fell out – and another grazed a boatman's cheek.

The onlookers jeered, made insulting remarks about the bowmen's abilities and, fickle as ever, encouraged Tamburlaine to take to the water. As if he understood their advice, he waddled towards the edge but before he could leap off, the bowmen found their range and three arrows pierced his back. He yelled a cry that had the quality of human anguish as he turned to face his attackers. The next three shot into his chest and as he lurched towards the source of pain, the following three struck his throat, jaw and right shoulder. But still he came on.

"Shoot. Shoot again," barked the official.

"Our quivers are empty," said one bowman. "We weren't prepared for this."

"We'd only enough for practising at the butts," explained the second.

"And who'll pay for our lost arrows, I'd like to know?" asked the third.

Staves and pikes were brought to the fore. The bear took two more staggering steps, roared, clawed at the protruding shafts and then, with a pitiful moan, toppled over.

"So Tamburlaine, the scourge of God, must die," Christopher said.

The bearward was the first to reach the fallen beast. He crouched down, stroked its head and began to weep. "Oh, my beautiful boy, my hero, my Tamburlaine. Fit to kill a thousand hounds from hell and now, flesh only fit to feed those scraggy curs."

Chapter twenty-six

The midsummer heat seemed to have sucked the breath from the city's maze and turned the shadeless areas beyond the walls into dry-dust patches. The ululation of distressed hounds, sweltering in their kennel-jails, wafted across the tenters' fields and was counter-pointed from the ditch side of Moorgate by the rasping screech of a fiddle and the whining dirge of the fiddler's woman.

"Thus is the strophe and antistrophe of our epitaphs," said Watson wryly.

After their chance meeting at the Paris Garden bear-pit, Christopher – reluctant to encounter Anne Watson's tartaric tongue – had sent messages to Tom's lodging, asking his one-time friend to come out for a drink, see a rehearsal or go to a lecture. Until last week he had not received a single reply. He was surprised and somewhat puzzled at a written invitation from Tom to meet him at Moorgate the following Friday at noon. 'We'll walk to Finsbury Court to view the archers at their practice,' the note read, 'and if the weather is temperate and our conversation agreeable, we'll stroll past Mallow Fields to the windmills.'

Since Tom Watson's return from Scadbury House, sightings of him were rare; never in a tavern and only occasionally at a playhouse. Whenever he visited the latter, he was in the exclusive and excluding company of the foppish Earl of Southampton. According to reports, he was hired to be the youth's tutor; a rather comelately task, some said, for the young man had more airs than a Morley composition and less grace than a market stall-holder. It was also said that the Earl was a jealous person prone to fits of excessive tantrums if his mentor spoke more than a half-dozen words with any of the writing and acting tribe.

Renewing their once-close friendship was near to Christopher's heart, but Tom's lukewarm greeting and morose face were not good omens. It was as if he had screwed up his courage to perform an unpleasant task and was determined to carry it through to the end.

Moor Lane's ruts were baked dry, cracked and dusty, and Moor Field, which was normally covered with stretched sheets and shirts, lay yellow, barren and empty under the glare of the scorching sun. Christopher would have preferred Bankside where there were enough taverns for an army of over-warm sufferers, but the only shelter he could see here was a large tent which an enterprising ale-seller – undoubtedly without permission – had erected opposite the moated farmhouse.

He looked longingly at the drinkers by the entrance, wiped his damp brow and said, "On such a thirsty day, I envy the savages of Americay who run naked through their endless forests."

"In their pagan ignorance, they have no true knowledge of sin," Tom replied, "and will live and die in dreadful darkness unless they accept the light of God as contained in the words of our preachers."

Surely this pious statement was said in irony, Christopher thought, but Watson's face was as stiff as his remark. Was this the comrade with whom he had shared the questioning of accepted beliefs? Old men on their death-beds were wont to repent their wild days with solemn declarations; they were petitioning for a licence to travel to the next world by the straightest route; but it boded ill when one so young as Thomas genuflected his intelligence to the extremities of piety. They walked on in silence as if they were strangers who had by accident taken the same path as the same time.

Like the opening salvoes of a dozen cannons, a rumbling noise resounded from the heights of Hampstead Mills and they turned to watch an enormous anvil-cloud, suffused with blinding flashes, spreading rapidly over the city. The aerial artillery approached the walls, a dark-mauve curtain swished across the roofs and demonic sparks spat and crackled round the snub steeple of St Paul's.

"I must return, Kit," Watson said and began to stride towards Moorgate. "I dare not leave Anne and our children alone to face the danger."

"Hold your horses, Tom," Christopher cried as he quickly trotted after him. "You're walking into the storm. And what danger is there if they're safe and sound under their roof?"

"You don't understand, Kit. She firmly believes that thunder and lightening are God's voice and fury made manifest and she lives in mortal dread of the Almighty's wrath."

The vanguard of the storm, a spattering of rain, fell upon them as Christopher grabbed Watson's arm. "It's a wonder to me that one so manifest in her Christian faith is so manifestly pagan in her fears," he said. To save them from a total drenching, Christopher dragged the reluctant Watson under the ale-tent's portico. "It'll soon pass," he repeated in reply to Tom's plaintive "I must go to her." Eventually tiring of the refrain, he declared, "Then, Tom, if you're set on a good soaking, I'll go with you. I won't have it said against me again that I deserted you in time of trouble."

Watson appeared embarrassed with this offer of damp martyrdom. "As matters stand, Kit, I'd rather my good wife did not know we've met. She has certain – I'll explain fully at a later date."

Christopher was not to be put off. "Come on, we've time and plenty to discuss any matter. The head of the tempest should now be giving Greenwich Reaches a mouthful while still emptying its piss-pots over us."

"I'll go when it eases but I fear it'll return."

"And so will the Spanish Armada."

"Will the Spaniards return then?" A plump woman asked. "With King Phillip on board?" Her husband, a thin man half her bulk, laughed. "Pay no heed to my wife, gentlemen. She has delusions affecting Spain. Don't you see, Martha, it's only said in a manner of speaking. And speaking of manners, the manner of my thirst is without words." She simpered girlishly. "You're a dry one, Jack-a-Dandy." He grinned and smacked her rump. "Why did you strike me?" she asked. "It was not you I struck, my sparrow," he replied, "but the bold flea that dared mount the mound I've claimed with my unfurled banner." Encouraged by the chortles of those nearest, he raised his voice. "Contrary to what you've said, my minnikin, I'm dry inside and wet outside but in a thrice I'll be double dry inside and outside and wet again inside." She frowned at the riddle. "How can that be, Jack, unless you've wetted your breeches?" He nodded towards the interior.

"Why, in there the warmth will dry my clothes. I'll be both dry on my outside and dry inside the tent and when I've had my ale I'll be wet inside." He looked around to see if his wit was appreciated. "And then you'll slash it against the wall," his wife retorted, "and contrary to what you've said, you'll be neither wet nor dry and still be an old soak."

When they disappeared behind the drape, Christopher said, "I've a mind to figure those clowns in a drama. Perhaps as a king and queen. Crowned heads are akin to clowning heads and both are apt to tumble. Or a king and his lover? Or, more apposite, a queen and her lover. Is that too near the bone for the sensibilities of our present politics?"

The drumming of the rain on the tent-roof was almost deafening at first but Tom appeared to relax a little.

"Now, Tom, to the point. You've shunned our company – '

Watson began by evading the point. "As it is with all women, so it is with my Anne. They have their seasons and their fancies and the passage of their moods is peculiar to the passing of the moon." He took a long swig of his drink. "As matters stand." And the matter was that Anne had laid the blame squarely for their misfortunes on the God-mockers with whom he had kept company. To her, Christopher was prime among their number. With outraged rhetorics and dire threats of departure, she had forbidden Tom to consort with the "riff-raff of the scribbling rascality".

"It's a great sorrow to me, Tom, to see a man cut off from his friends at the behest of a woman. The Pope's singing eunuchs have more freedom than you. Are you sure you've not been gelded?"

It was a jocular remark but Watson did not take it as such. "Your insolence is offensive to my wife and myself," he retorted and stomped towards the exit. Within seconds he returned, his face glistening with the spattering of the persistent torrent. He resumed his seat and called for more ale. "I'll treat you as you've treated me, Kit, and suffer no obligation. Another potful is not a carouse." He sat sideways, his lips clamped tight and his eyes fixed on the doorway drape.

Now exiled from his companion's confidence by a palisade of

silence, Christopher fell to wondering how a man who managed to be a scholar, a poet and a roustabout with the best of them could be so circumscribed by a woman ensnared in religious delusions. As he recalled, his initial meeting with Anne had not augured well.

It was the winter of Christopher's first year in London and he was lodging in a ramshackle tenement owned by the widow of a once-prosperous cloth merchant. She eked out a meagre living by letting off rooms to tradesmen and poor scholars, but it was not sufficient. She therefore schemed to decant her current tenants and replace them with refugees, three or four to a room, charging the unfortunates an exorbitant rent. And she took advantage of Christopher's enforced stay in Chomley's Thames Street hovel. The door was bolted and barred against him and his few belongings were left outside on the step.

Tom offered to put Christopher up for a few days until a more suitable place was found. The Watsons' rooms were cramped and overcrowded – they had two children – and they could ill-afford the space given to their temporary lodger or the cost of an extra mouth; but Tom never gave so much as a hint that their guest was a burden. Anne, for her part, left Christopher in no doubt about her views on playhouses, players and those who "earned their meat by scribbling lewd and impious prating for the clod ears of penny-stinkards, for they are an abomination to the Lord. They who hunger for forbidden fruit shall, on the last day, sup with Satan."

Just before dawn on his third day in the Watsons' home, Christopher woke in a sweat from a recurring nightmare in which he was thrown from a precipice by a cowled figure with the voice and appearance of Baines. The dream-cries he had heard from the abyss changed to the raised voices of Tom and Anne coming through the thin partition.

"Oh, faddle-me-rue, what do I care for him?" she said. "I only care for my own, Tom Watson, and so should you." There came the clump-clump of someone crossing the floor. "Now what are you doing?" she asked. "You'll waken the children if you're not careful and I've had enough trouble as it is with them vext beyond sleep with their coughing and retching. Not that that should worry you. They're only your own flesh and blood and not some pretty boy you've picked up from the gutter, reeking of sour ale. And you never give a thought to any pestilences he'd bring into our home."

"It's you who's in danger of waking the whole house with your slander." The sound of tinkling water accompanied Tom's reply.

"Mind you don't splash it over the floor. It's me who has to mop it up. I wish your aim was as straight as your charity."

"Mary Magdalene was a whore but Christ didn't turn his face against her. It was she to whom he appeared again on the third day."

"That's right, talk of the great whore of God and your own wife lying beside you. You're not turning peculiar, are you, in your distraction. Mind your elbow digging my arm. You're all skin and bones with little flesh and less brains. I can't say I wasn't warned by my cousins but now I'm suffering for my sins. Yesu keep us, I can't go back to sleep and do you know the price of flour is twice what it was last week and the carriers are asking eight pence for a barrel of water. Bad enough to have to put up with every stray from the streets you care to bring in to lap at our plates."

After one or two heavy sighs, they became quiet and Christopher, now very cold with the morning chill, decided to gather up his belongings and leave the house. He tore up some work that did not satisfy him, threw it in the fireplace and began to rip up a second when Anne's cry of "What's that scrabbling?" stopped him.

"Scrabbling? I can't hear any scrabbling," said Tom drowsily.

"You're deaf as well as daft. I tell you it's a rat of monstrous proportions ripping the plaster."

"It's the proportion of your monstrous dreams," Tom muttered.

"How can that be so when I've not slept a wink since you and I had harsh words," she answered peevishly. "If you love me, as once you said you did, you'd take the glimmer and rout that devil's beast from his lair."

Tom grumbled, padded round the room and, afflicted with early-morning flatulence, fired off a cannonade sufficient to frighten an army of rodents. "There's nothing here but bloodsuckers crawling up the walls. I'll deflagrate them. See how they run with the fire on their tails. You fat bugs, would you bloat on my flesh? This is good sport."

"If you want good sport, there's nothing wrong with my flesh. A kindling stick would put it ablaze and set fire to my tail." Tom began to sing in a low voice a ballad about a lady called Suzannah who had married a man from Babylon. "Hold your whist, Tom. Do you want the neighbours to join in the chorus?"

"I could sing a better tune with a fiddle."

"My fiddle is well-tuned and is waiting for your bow to play a jig," said his wife coyly.

"I'll snuff the candle. One hot wick is plenty."

Christopher quickly tied up his books and clothes, his ears burning and his limbs trembling as the sounds beyond the partition became more hectic. But to leave the house, he had to pass through their room. The tumbling stopped.

"What's put a stop to your gallop?"

"I fear we'll waken Kit."

"What of it? He'll think we're fighting like Noah's cats on the Ark."

Christopher tip-toed by the wall, crept down the stairs, quietly drew back the bolt, lifted the latch and went out to the grey streets.

"Kit, Kit, have you fallen into a trance?" Having apparently thrown off his carapace of sulkiness, Tom Watson now seemed eager to converse. "I've asked you for gossip but you seemed lost in meditation."

Christopher called for more ale. "The affairs of our friends change like the weather from drought to deluge. For a time, in fear of censors and their own profits, Henslowe and company dare not buy a new drama. But when the distracted multitude tire of faded, jaded, bombastic plays, the managers cry out loud for new entertainments to earn them pennies."

To meet this sudden demand, the playwrights had combined to churn out dramas, comedies, interludes, prologues and so on by the score. Their method was simple though chaotic. A plot was stolen from the ancient Latins and Greeks and each writer would, in turn, contribute several pages to the script. Then the resulting hodge-podge of blood, murder, revenge, lust, terror, carried forward on waves of ranting and raving, was presented as a brand-new play by one or the other of the 'scribbling tribe'.

Watson listened attentively and then looked up to the canvas roof and said, "Rain, rain, go to Spain."

"I beg your pardon, young gentlemen, for this rude intrusion on your conference." The plump woman called Martha stood by their table and spoke with the strained vowels of one who does not wish to be thought vulgar. "I couldn't help but overhear you mention Spain and as you're learned – ' she looked directly at Tom ''- for I know you live in Holywell Street where all the educated people reside, I said to myself, I said, I'll ask this scholar to settle an argument of royal weight and, once and for all, shut the gobs of the mockers and scoffers." She turned to glare at her grinning husband, sat among a party of his cronies.

"Shut your bleating, you laced-up mutton, you," he shouted.

"Will you listen to his mouthing, I ask you, and him a shiftless horse-currier daring to slander a woman of royal blood. But wait till I tell how I know you're from Holywell Street. I'm the very woman who takes care of your shirts and sheets for sun-drying and bleaching. A humble trade, but being a laundress is far beneath my rightful and proper station in life. I am – " she paused for dramatic effect ''- I am the bastard daughter of King Phillip of Spain and I was begat when last he visited these shores."

"Take a care, you fat drudge," her husband called out, "or you'll be whipped to the arse of a shit-cart for your presumptions."

"Presumptions, he says. He must have been listening to the playhouse ranters to learn to spout such big words. Why should I presume when I've proof positive right here for all who care to see." She opened her blouse and bared her right shoulder. "You're scholars and you'll know what these marks signify. And what's more, when I was pulled mewling from my mother's womb the very first word I spoke was in the Spanish tongue. Would you credit that?" She leaned over, one stout arm supported by one red hand on the table, and showed them her massive naked shoulder.

Christopher had the best view. "Ah, now I see it in the proper light. Your ladyship, do forgive me for my blindness in not recognising the haughty Castilian manner in your composure and my deafness in not hearing the proud regality of your voice."

She smirked and waved a podgy hand. "There's no need, young gentleman, to crave my forgiveness. I grant it from the goodness of my heart. But as for them sniggering sneerers, they'll wait a long time before I favour them with a pardon."

He placed his hand on the nape of Martha's neck and pushed her head down so that her nose nearly touched the table. "See there, Tom, the red marking of the letter M and below it a star cluster of three moles."

The woman gently removed Christopher's hand, righted herself and buttoned up her blouse. "Isn't that proof positive? What do you make of that?"

Her husband shouted that she was branded like the buttocks of the Queen's horses and that that was the extent of her royal pretensions.

Christopher pretended not to have heard the man. "Your ladyship, with your leave, I'll put certain questions to my colleague. Tell me, Tom, whence sprang Phillip of Spain?"

"From his mother's womb pricked on by his father Phillip of Spain."

"And whence sprang the father of Phillip?"

"Likewise from his own mother's womb."

"She being Mary and her sire being Maximilian."

Watson gasped as if suddenly struck by enlightenment. "Hence the mark of M upon our ladyship's delicate shoulder. And it surely follows, without a doubt, the three moles are the three stars enshrined in the escutcheon of noble Phillip, son of Phillip, son of Maximilian and Mary, denoting the three kingdoms of Spain. Your ladyship, we are overwhelmed by your august presence and humbly crave leave to depart in order to recover our disturbed spirits."

"God grant me such subjects as you two to serve me well when I come into my proper estate." She dismissed the pair with a queenly wave.

"God's truth, Kit, there's a power of idiocy in that deranged woman." But when the merriment of the moment drained from him, Tom returned to his sombre state.

The storm was spent and the only reminders of its torrential fury were the placid pools and the thin haze rising from the walls and fields. Watson stepped from the ale-tent and splashed into a puddle. "But is there not a power of idiocy in all our pomp and ceremonies? Do we not, each one of us, suffer our own delusions of grandeur? Were we wrong to encourage the absurdity of that poor woman?"

"Nothing will shake her certainty. Tomorrow, when her brawny arms are steeped in boiling water, she'll conjure regiments forming in the steam and think of her doltish husband as a gallant come to pay court. I'd rather have the harmless delusions of a poor washerwoman from the parish of St Helen's than the illusory rights of kings, popes and princes that lead to the clamour of war and the slaughter of kin by kin."

"The rain has eased. I'll be away home." Watson staggered and clasped his forehead.

"What is it? Are you ill?"

"It's nothing but a slight headache. We must part here, Kit, and, if you please, don't insist on accompanying me."

"Che sera, sera, Tom, if you needs must exile me beyond your borders. You do know, Tom, that if you starve, I feel the pangs of hunger and if you sicken, my bones ache."

Watson walked on a few paces, stopped and looked back. "And if I die, Kit?"

Chapter twenty-seven

When Christopher told Tom Watson about his collaboration with Greene, Kyd, Nashe and others in jointly writing plays, he had not mentioned the bad news. Pulling the plough as a team was quite foreign to writers and soon there were squabbles, acrimony, accusations and counter-accusations of plagiarism – a nice paradox from those who happily looted plots and storylines from the Italians, Germans, Greeks and Romans – and eventually to splits and partings. Former boon companions now refused to say a good word about each other. It was not uncommon to see two people sitting one day with heads together over their script, like a pair of children looking at a butterfly, and the next day at opposite ends of a tavern as if a chasm separated them.

Irascible Robert Greene was the worst of the bunch and though he reserved the main spite of his venom for actors who presumed to write plays – and one in particular whom he called an upstart crow – he managed to insult everybody. In the end he was left strictly on his own. Part of the fault lay with the playhouse managers who welcomed dramas which did not offend the authorities but insisted that only one author's name appeared in the advertisements.

Greene had been given the credit for one play that proved remarkably unpopular. The groundlings revolted against the tedious speeches and pelted the players with orange peel and hazelnuts.

In truth he was responsible for the over-long and pompous passages but refused to recognise his effort and laid the blame for the disaster on his collaborators.

Christopher had enjoyed the teamwork at first but eventually became tired of the carping. Greene was the most wearisome of them all. To do the man justice, he never stinted his praise for Christopher's talent – "Famous gracer of tragedians. Excellent wit" – but his snide personal comments became increasingly irksome.

One day when they were discussing a scene in which two ill-fated lovers met in a forest, Christopher suggested a more sensuous turn to the dialogue. Greene snorted. "Tell me, Marlowe, what do you know of the sweaty passions of limbs tangled with limbs?" he asked and added, with a leer, "I speak only of what is natural between man and woman. Of the others I leave them to wrap their sweet infections between unsavoury sheets."

Christopher put a rein on his rising irritation. "I know as much as any who goes around with raggle-taggle alley girls. Aren't you acquainted with my translations of Ovid's Amores?"

"I don't number them among my acquaintances. Do they live in Shoreditch?"

"I will quote – "

"Oh, says he, I will quote, as if to acquit himself like a capon among cocks with a greater clucking to their crowing."

There was no profit in this for Christopher. Like everybody who had a taste of Greene's acidity, he left the bad-tempered writer to his own devices. Greene took himself off to live a secluded life in a hovel with a prostitute and it was rumoured that he was suffering from dire penury and a raging fever. Some likened him to the fabled scorpion that poisoned itself with the sting of its own tail. Nashe also retired from the enterprise to fritter away his talents writing polemical pamphlets against the Puritans. With dissensions and desertions, the great play-writing scheme diminished and barely survived through to the autumn. There were exceptions. Kyd had recruited the Oxford-educated poet Peele to help him with a drama about murder, mayhem and incest in a Danish castle; but most of the writers returned to what was best suited to their nature, the sole begetters of their own creations.

Christopher had abandoned his fellow-writers to their faltering scheme. Then, to his dismay, he faltered and writing abandoned him. Nothing he saw, heard or read served to inspire or stimulate him and it seemed to him that his much-vaunted genius had, like the dried ink in the well, crumbled to black powder. Was he spent? Was the summation of his talent a handful of plays and a parcel of student poems?

For several weeks he shunned all company. Every day, for hours on end, he paced the floor of his poky room; turning over a dozen ideas, a dozen themes. The nights only brought darkness, doubts and fitful sleep.

At times he thought of the riches that could be his if he exploited his Cambridge education. The Church, for example, had rare openings for learned men, burdened as it was with semi-literate clergymen. For those blessed with a nimble brain and a silver tongue – and not too encumbered with a rigid faith – the benefits were beyond sanctity. Who would say no to salmon and trout every Friday, haunches of venison for the Sabbath, brocade and silk for bed and body and foreign wine for the belly? 'Christopher Marlowe. Archbishop of Canterbury.' That would stun those beer-swilling roustabouts of Shoreditch and Bankside. He laughed at the preposterous image – yet was it so outlandish?

"Let's put a brave face on it. I'm depleted, I've nothing more to say or write. Why not?"

There was no sense in brooding. He decided to seek out his one-time companions for a valedictory celebration.

His first stop, The Bull, was depressingly empty. Next he called into the Crosskeys. Once it was a lively place, noted for the comic turns put on by Tarleton, the famous clown, and later for the jigging capers of Will Kempe. The city fathers had suppressed these jollifications and the tavern was now filled with dour drovers, colliers and fish merchants. He visited Saba, The Boar's Head, the Bell and three other taverns in Gracechurch Street, drank a pint of ale in each and never caught sight of any friend or acquaintance. When he reached Bishopsgate, he was quite merry and full of good will towards humanity.

A hurrying group of women, heads bent and covered with black shawls, approached him. "Where do you wander, shrouded ladies of dark and dreary demeanour?" he asked them whimsically as he lurched across their path. They huddled together, whispering to each other, and the foremost said, "Sir, you have a kind and gentle face. Let us pass. We have a solemn duty to perform." Her voice was soft and soothing."

"I'm not of Agamemnon's cruel tribe, sweet sorrowing women of Troy." He staggered and threw out his arms. "If you seek to bury your dead, I'll be silent."

"He's drunk," said one. "We'll go another way," counselled a second but the first woman demurred. "This is our ordained road." To Christopher she said, "Our dead are buried, sir. It's their souls we seek to release."

Even in his befuddled state, he knew that they were Papists, going from foreign embassy to foreign embassy to participate in the forbidden rite of All Soul's Day.

"Hallowed be they names, daughters of Oedipus, sisters of Polynices. I won't betray you to tyrannical Creon or the mighty Argive army." He bowed to the confused women and stepped to one side; a gallant gesture spoiled by one foot tripping the other.

As they went by, shawl-fringes clutched to their breasts, eyes glancing warily in his direction, their apparent leader murmured, "God preserve you from all harm, sir. We'll remember you in our prayers."

"I'm not yet dead," he shouted after them, "but walk among the lost and the damned. For what is that portal – " he pointed towards Bishopsgate, "but hell's own vestibule, for is it not incised on the lintel, all hope abandon, you who enter here."

A group of ragged-arsed children howled with derision at this oration, basketwomen screeched with laughter and the local constable barged through the crowd. "What's this ruction? You're the cause, are you, cully? Drunk and disorderly, are you, cully? Asking to cool your heels in the keep, are you, cully?" Another drunk, a young man of about eighteen with brown wiry hair and straggly beard, wrapped his arm round the constable's shoulder and slurred in bad Italian, "Maestro, il senso lor m'e duro." The lawman glowered at the youth. "Assault an officer of the law, would you?" The drunk grinned inanely. "Maestro, e quel ch'i odo?" The constable rewarded these friendly overtures by giving the fool a hearty push in the chest. "I'm attacked by foreigners in an English street," he shouted. "Who'll help me to take them to the magistrate? Right then, I'll be back with more men." He began to push through the crowd then stopped, turned and gripped Christopher's jerkin. "You! I know you. You're a trouble-maker and a Newgate rat."

"There you have the advantage, sir," said Christopher insolently. "Are you Jem Scabarse or Bill Blowhard?" The crowd hooted with laughter but the beak did not appreciate the witticism. He shook Christopher and bawled, "I know you and – "

The young drunk, who seemed to be discarding his inebriation as rapidly as a Bankside whore pulls off her shift, laid his arm across the lawman's chest and said, "Sir, your speech is tedious and offensive to the ear. I beg you, change your song to a more pleasing tune." His companion, a slightly older man, shouted, "Go to it, Ben, my trusty Flanders swasher, while I entertain these people with a madrigal." He began to boom out, to the air of Haul In The Bowlines, 'I know you and you know me/ O, what a rollicking compan-ee/ Come, my roistering roaring boy/ We'll tumble maiden proud and coy.' He was greeted by raspberries from a tone-deaf audience.

Distracted by the cacophony and Ben's intervention, the constable released Christopher and stepped back, his face puce with rage. "You're part of this tow-rags' band, you are," he said to Ben, "and you shut your gob. Street singing is not allowed." He turned to Christopher. "As for you, Marlowe, you won't escape proper justice this time."

"Marlowe?" asked Ben. "Is this Kit Marlowe?"

"Watch your lip," advised the constable. "You'll fester in Newgate with him and God help you if you do. He's brave enough to kill a young lad in Hogg Lane but he doesn't frighten me. And this time his high and mighty friends won't help."

"Kit Marlowe," said Ben decisively, "will go with us this day to Shoreditch." He pulled back his jacket to reveal the hilt of a sword. "Have you a writ equal to mine?"

The constable was not over-burdened with courage. "I've my duty to perform," he said with sulky pugnacity, "and I'll have you know it's against the law to carry swords within the city walls."

"Then I'll take my sword, myself and Kit Marlowe without the city walls, by your leave." The crowd pressed in closer, not daring to miss a moment of this drama. Suddenly a stentorian voice shouted, "Make way. Make way for the watch." The watch always arrived mob-handed. They had a well-deserved reputation for brutality when they came upon what they regarded as a riotous assembly; and the gathering needed no urging to scatter in all directions. In the confusion Ben and his companion grabbed Christopher by the arms, ran through Bishopsgate and did not slow down till they were in sight of St Botolph.

"By the blood of Christ," said the second man, "that was a fine caper to give a man a roaring thirst." The other two followed him into a nearby tavern. The sad-faced landlord looked at them warily as if they had just been allowed out of Bedlam for a carouse.

"I am Gabriel Spencer," said Ben's companion, "actor, orator, some-time songster and owner of a thundering voice." He grinned and bawled, "Make way. Make way for the watch." The landlord was now sure that at least one of his customers was a licensed loon.

"He's a gabbling dispenser of bad verse," said Ben, "and his thundering voice farts more wind than an ordurous swine."

"Will you listen to that cup-shotten leather-sweating lump, Kit. He talks like a tubster, yet our Ben Jonson has little talent beyond the bloody strokes of a sharp blade and the blunt crush of club on skull."

Christopher was by now sober enough to take stock of his newfound comrades. The actor was easy to assess. He was one whose roles were less than his ambitions and greater than his abilities; a third duke, a second murderer, perhaps a vanquished king executed five minutes after the prologue and, when times were hard and parts scarce, a voice in the chorus, a brandisher of spears.

Ben Jonson, the hireling soldier, was a raw youth with the hard swagger of one who had seen battle, untimely death and had walked knee-deep in gore. Coldness, cruelty and arrogance were stamped on his features. Though he joked, he never laughed and his rare smile was a predatory grimace.

"Which Kit Marlowe are you?" he asked.

"If you've heard of another bearing my name, I'll bear him no grudge if he does not begrudge my honour. Which Marlowe suits your honour?"

"I've heard of two in one person and perhaps an honourable ghost would make a perfect trinity. One is a spy and the other a poet and playwright." He then spoke as if quoting, "Spies, you are the lights of state, but of base stuff, who, when you have burned yourself down to the snuff, stink, and are thrown away. End fair enough."

"I am Marlowe, the poet and playwright. Is that fair enough for your end?"

Spencer sensed a quarrel brewing and hastened to keep the peace. "Our fearsome fighter cares little for scribblers who've never savoured a skirmish and yet stuff their bombastic verse with cannonade and alarums." He lowered his voice to a stage-whisper, glanced slyly at his companion and said, "Our Ben reckons to turn his lance into a quill and do battle with the writing craft but, alas, in spite of his book-learning, he has little art beyond the butchering or bricklaying trade."

Jonson scowled. "I'll skewer you, Gabriel Spencer, one bright day if you fail to check your waggling tongue." With that, he turned his back on them.

Spencer shrugged his shoulders and leaned towards Christopher. "Ben is in a sulk now but when the tantrum's passed, he'll be his own merry swasher again. It's a sore point with him, which I fancy to scratch now and then, but his stepfather is a rude mason and would rather Ben laid brick on brick for his mother's sake than pile body on body in a muddy Flanders fields."

Jonson abruptly stood up and swallowed his drink. "Hey, you ha'penny actor," he shouted, "stir your rump and close your prattling hole. Better for your purse, if not your craft, to go prancing on Burbage's stage as you promised." He marched out of the tavern as if to lead an assault on the bastions of Shoreditch.

Spencer swallowed his drink in one gulp but Christopher left most of his in the pot. Jonson was far ahead, bawling out a marching song as he stolidly tramped down Bishopsgate Street.

"I was in your Tamburlaine drama, Kit," said Spencer as they hurried after the trooper. "I played Zenocrate but, alas, I'm too old now for women's parts and the tenor of my voice has taken a harder note." They were now in sight of The Theatre's roof. "Thanks be to Yesu, the flag's not up. I'll be in time to take the stage, that is, if the drama is performed. Skinflint Burbage cheats the players of their fair share and he has scarce few to fill the day. He sent me out to search high and low for recruits to man his stage army but only Ben was willing."

"What drama is this?"

"Oh, a roustabout brew concocted by that sometime bit player, Will Shakeshank, called Harry The Sixth. It's a veritable stew of alarums off and has more parts in it than there were soldiers before the walls of Orleans."

Jonson was waiting for them at The Hole-in-the-wall. "Come on, you laggards. Gallant Talbot is eager to hunt the French witch-bitch and tear her strumpet shift to shreds."

"How about you, Kit?" Spencer asked. "There's the price of two pints of ale for each who carry a wooden sword. Just copy the swashing gait of our friend Jonson and you'll be a fine braggart soldier."

At first Christopher protested he had a play of his own to write. "And a grand piece of work you were making of it, Marlowe," said Jonson,"when we met you sot-sodden at Bishopsgate. But leave the stage to Stratford Will if that's your will. He's certainly willing to take your part. For my part, where there's parts for bloody warriors, I'll blood my will to the part." He waved his sword in the air. "To your metal, you slogging infantry. For Harry, for St George and for England. Charge." With that, he ran down the path towards the playhouse, followed by Christopher and Spencer.

Chapter twenty-eight

Jonson had said, "Even if Marlowe were soused in a barrel of malmsey, he couldn't have written a worse rigmarole than this Stratford scribbler's hotch-potch."

The Harry the Sixth play did not deserve the full brunt of Jonson's acerbity – and he also had a lot to say about the sloppy bearing of the stage soldiers – but its style and structure did little to win applause. Fortunately for the players' lives and limbs, The Theatre was less than half-full and a sudden downpour dampened the groundlings' discontent. By the end there were more actors than audience.

When Burbage grudgingly doled out their pay, he announced that he was withdrawing the drama until such time as the writer saw fit to excise or amend the many flat verses and dull passages. The author himself sat apart from the others, a thoughtful expression on his placid face. He looked more like a man contemplating some minor domestic problem than one suffering the inner anguish of failure.

Jonson's mordant remarks goaded Christopher into extracting from England's bloody and turbulent history some dramas worthy of his pen.

But what king of this land could equal Tamburlaine? Few were possessed by the all-consuming lust for power and the rage to be the scourge of God. They were either weaklings and simpletons bullied by their wives, minions, bishops and courtiers, or they were petty tyrants, squabbling and intriguing over trifles. For all the glory of their regality, they might as well have worn paper crowns on their empty skulls.

But if, among this parcel of religious clowns and mendacious princes, the chronicles lacked a Tamburlaine, was there, then, a disciple of Machiavelli? One who smiled and murdered while he smiled? One who shamed the chameleon into envy with his profusion of colours?

Two seemed fit for the role. The first was Mortimer, who had shared his schemes and bed with Queen Isabella and had plotted to overthrow and kill her effete husband, Edward the Second. The other candidate was Richard the Third, dubbed Richard Crookback, born, some said misbegotten, to the house of York and, according to Thomas More's biased history and the Croyland Chronicler, a man as deviously twisted in body and spirit as an eel on a string.

As he had done in that October month of vacuity and futility, Christopher shunned all society, ignored the Christmas festivities, sent a message to his mother by Jem the Carter that he was detained in London on important business of state and told his acquaintances he was returning to Canterbury for the holy season.

By the second week of January, he had two dramas ready for the eyes of Henslowe and Alleyn, or, if he drew the short straw, Burbage.

Richard Crookback, the title he gave to the first, was eminently suitable as a treatise on the strength and ultimate failure of Machiavellian teaching. Cunning and conniving, Richard planned his predetermined moves like a chess player; but when the game went awry, he thought nothing of overturning the board. Without mercy or pity to friend or foe, he allowed no impediment to his path to the throne; but when the crown was on his head, he fell at Bosworth, pierced by lances and betrayal.

Christopher did not quite believe all that was said about Richard the Third. Where were the bodies of the murdered princes in the Tower? But to exclude this alleged incident would diminish the garnish. Even the best-cooked goose needed a fair sprinkling of herbs and spices.

In the second play, Mortimer the regicide (which was the title Christopher had thought to give the drama) had entered fully armed, a rough uncouth soldier, void of subtle thought or clever plots. It was Queen Isabella, the woman he possessed who in turn possessed his soul, that was the Machiavellian schemer.

It was a muggy day, surprisingly warm for the month, when Christopher tucked the two scripts inside his jerkin and set out with the intention of crossing to Bankside. The streets were crammed with traffic and it seemed to him that there were more carts, wagons, carriages and people abroad than ever before.

He was struggling through the crowds in Fish Hill Street when he heard his name called out. Turning, he saw what he thought was a familiar fat face and purple nose. A rowdy bunch of apprentices swept him back several paces. Whooping and jeering, they continued on, leaving him at the entrance of a narrow alley. 'Perhaps the gods are telling me to abandon my journey for the day.' He had gone about six steps when something soft struck his head and a hand was placed in his.

"It is I, Kit Marlowe." He looked down at the over-large face and grinning thick lips of a dwarf. "I've been told you were abroad or was it with your parents in Canterbury, but when I called at your lodgings, the woman there said you had just stepped out. My, but your shanks eat up the road. I was hard put to keep you in sight. And where's your companion?"

"Companion?"

"Indeed. A stout man with a sour face who kept a careful ten paces behind you. Is Marlowe so rich he can afford a servant, I ask?"

Another missile, a carrot, landed at their feet. "Hey, cully, are you taking the monkey for a stroll?" The rowdies were grouped at the alley entrance.

"I'll teach those scum-scourings to mind their mouths," Christopher said but the dwarf pulled him away.

"Don't bother with them. Their words only fly over my head." He chortled at his self-mocking joke and stuck his tongue out at the youths. "Let me treat you to a drink."

The passageway opened into the rear of a tavern and the dwarf was already sitting by a table and calling for service when Christopher joined him. A buxom woman came out of the door, her sour expression changing to a glad smile at the sight of the little man. "There y'are, me darling dandiprat, and what's your pleasure today?"

"It'd be my pleasure to pleasure you," he replied.

"Away with you, you pint pot. You'd never reach higher than my belly button."

"I'd go higher than that if you lay on your back with your legs to the north and south."

She cackled. "I'm more inclined to face east and west, the same as the church. My husband says it's my religious bearings when he comes under me portals and sprinkles me with holy water."

She took the order for ale and went back into the tavern. "She's used to my ways," said the dwarf, "and as long as I've coins to rattle in my poke, I'm welcome to poke my rattle on the quiet. She says big men and small men are all the same size and many a night she's sat here with me under her skirt and none were any the wiser. I've heard some say, and me wrapped in darkness, 'Why are you squatting on your haunches and rocking yourself like a ship at the tide's turn?' and she saying, 'It's me shift's at half-tide and I've a flea biting me belly.' And when she sighed with relief at the end, she'd say, 'There now, didn't the wind blow hard?'"

Christopher could hardly credit the preposterous story but when the woman returned with their ale, she did not object to the dwarf fondling her rump.

"So Kit Marlowe is saying to himself, 'Who's this lecherous midget who dares to presume familiarity' – yet, recall, Kit, are we not both members of -?" He showed the faint scar on his thumb. "But I'm not here to bother with that. I've sought you out at the behest of one who's expressed a great desire to meet Kit Marlowe, famed creator of Tamburlaine and the sly Malta-Jew. Go to it, Merlin, said Walt, and bid the estimable poet to my table."

"Merlin?"

"Ah yes, those that are entranced by my magical mathematics dub me Merlin, whereas others, dull sticks and clod-heads, jeer and snipe at me. They've even compared me to that Satan's spit, Richard Crookback." Christopher's hand shot up to his jerkin. "What have you there?"

"The rough copies of two dramas I've finished and taking to show Henslowe and Alleyn – "

"Stay your journey for another day, Kit. Walt has an eye for such things and it would double his pleasure in meeting you to see your new-made lines fresh on the page."

"Walt? Who's this Walt?"

"Surely you know Walt?" He thumped his empty pot on the table and called for a replenishment. "You don't do honour to your reputation by being tardy with your drink." He was still shouting when the woman bustled out with his order. "Hold your horses, me sprightly mouse," she chided. "You're forever in a hurry, jumping the ditch before you come to it and losing your whip in the water."

Again they exchanged ribald remarks. Christopher now remembered seeing Merlin at a sodality meeting, trying to explain the intricacies of a mathematical theorem to a group of glazed-eyed listeners. There was also the recollection of another so-called Merlin, drunk and gaudy, leaping from a pyre.

"She mocks me gently," Merlin said when the woman had returned to the tavern. "Did you hear her threatening to smother me in her bosom? What a joyful pressing that'd be if it were not for the fleas. Those blood-suckers, how I envy their sucking, have a greater fondness for womanly flesh than the hard hide of man." He scrambled up on the table and raised the pot to his lips. "I drink to mortal flesh and all Eve's daughters. May they flourish to tempt us forever more to the succulent fruit of forbidden knowledge." Without pause, he drank down most of his beer and poured the remaining dribbles on the ground. "A libation, Kit, to the gods of chaos."

The little man's caper now convinced Christopher that he was indeed the drunk-sodden hunchback from the debauched revelry up-river.

"Hee, hee, Kit," giggled the dwarf and flapped his arms. "If I had your wings, Icarus, I'd challenge the sun with my daring."

Three men entered the yard and sat at a nearby table. "What's the manikin doing?" one asked. They did not appear to be enthralled with Merlin's antics, but he seemed pleased by an extra audience. He produced from his satchel a strip of paper formed into a closed circle. "What do you see in my hand? Why, one ring. Yet, with careful cutting I can make it into two. Watch closely." He next took out small scissors and slowly snipped along the edge, till, with a cry of triumph, he held up a pair in intertwining rings.

"That's Belzebub's black magic," a man shouted.

The woman came out to take the men's order. "Hold your whist," she said to them. "There's no harm in the dandiprat."

"What do you know of these matters? He's a changeling and we know where they come from."

"And I'll know where you'll go if you can't keep your tongue to yourself. Give me your order or give me the sight of your backside as you leave."

The men eyed her muscular arms. One muttered, "The misshapen lump is a devil's whelp."

Christopher sensed danger in the men and said, "Let's be away. Didn't you say Walt expects me?"

Merlin did a little jigging step. "Walt awaits and Walt will wait till I've finished my lecture. It's my bounden duty, as a learned man, to bring edification to the untutored." The untutored trio scowled when he turned to them. "My friends, there's no magic, black, blue or pink." He produced a second ring of paper. "It's a cunning trick of eye and hand which even you, if you had the art and mind, could do at your leisure. Bear with me and as I transform one ring into two, you'll see how those who pretend to miracles fool the innocent and the ignorant."

The men growled and rose from their seats. "Who's he calling ignorant? Are we going to sit listening to this whelp of hell?"

Christopher managed to grab Merlin's legs but the little man refused to budge. "Whelp of hell, did you say?" he squealed and produced a bell-muzzle pistol from his pouch. "Then I'll show you devil's play." He poured white powder into the pan, flicked the flintlock several times until the granules began to sputter into a thick yellow smoke and then, as the men lurched forward, threw the fuming powder towards the bravadoes.

The woman came out of the tavern and screamed as the rowdies backed away, choked and nearly blinded. Christopher grabbed Merlin round the waist, tucked the shrieking dwarf under his arm and ran down a passageway. He did not drop his burden till they had passed through another backyard where the washerwomen gazed at the fugitives with some astonishment.

Christopher was breathless and sweating from his exertions when they re-emerged into the crowded streets. His companion, on the contrary, was not in the least perturbed and his excitable chatter continued as if there had been no interruption. 'God's truth, does he never stop talking?' Christopher wondered.

To avoid the worst traffic, they threaded their way through the back streets. Only in the environs of St Paul's were they free to walk without being bumped and shoved. Some women turned away at the sight of Merlin and surreptitiously made the sign of the cross and a pregnant girl fell into a faint.

Near Ludgate a party of drover lads, sticks under their arms and cow-dung up to their knees, jeered Merlin; but when he darted towards them, they scattered with yells of fear.

"I'd have sworn we were trailed by your fat follower," he said as he returned, "and I thought to invite him with us on the last leg of our journey but he scampered off when I approached." He grabbed Christopher's hand like a child. "Come, Kit, we've a short step to go."

By now they were strolling along Fleet Street, a comparatively open highway only restricted by the market place. Further on the road widened and followed the curve of the river. Though there were houses on each side, the area was not so cramped as the City and a traveller could walk abroad without suffering the crush of the crowds or the noisome fumes from the multitude of sea coal fires.

The hunchback did most of the talking. "I reckon I put the fear of God, or rather the terror of the devil, into those tavern louts with my Satanic fumes. And yet it was only a subtle fusion of differing powders common to any apothecary. I've a mind to sell the device to playhouses for the dreadful exits and entrances of their stage fiends. Write such a drama, Kit, with proud Lucifer and swaggering Mephistophilis appearing and disappearing in hearty gusts of coloured smoke, and I'll warrant every groundling will go home with wet breeches." He then went on to explain his great scheme to fight superstition and ignorance where it was most rife. He had devised a mountebank's 'magic' tricks to catch the mob's attention. When he had a gathering, he would launch into his 'lecture'. Alas, it was at this point that a riot would break out.

For the first time that day, Merlin appeared downcast as he considered the obdurate love of ignorance by the ignorant. "Why can't they see that there are no miracles and no magic. What Moses and Aaron did were tricks of the trade. They were jugglers and conjurors and Hariot – you know Thomas Hariot, Sir Walter Ralegh's man? – can do better."

"I've heard there are certain formulae, which if repeated, can conjure up Mephistophilis."

"Repeat what you wish but devil a dark spirit will appear." He stopped by a side gate leading to a large house. "And so we have arrived, in part by chance, in part by design. The chance being my short legs keeping pace with your long shanks and your willingness to abandon your journey to Bankside. The design being my mission to invite you to this eminent dwelling and the welcome of Walt."

"What is this place? And who is Walt?"

"Are you a dung-spattered, straw-chewing rustic up for the day from some manure-reeking hovel?" inquired the dwarf archly. "This is Durham House, the London home of Sir Walter Ralegh."

Chapter twenty-nine

So by pre-designed fate, by capricious fortune or the conjunction of certain stars, Christopher had travelled the unsure and sometimes hazardous path from the cloisters of Cambridge to the vestibule of the most famous and infamous house in all England.

The long, empty gallery in which he now stood, gaping at the faded escutcheons on the varnished oak panelling and the overblown nymphs painted between the arch-ribs of the barrel ceiling, had given passage to many who entered by one door with power and authority in their fists and left by another door to meet shame, disgrace, defeat or an untimely death.

Simon de Montfort, of whom Henry III had said, "By God's head, I fear thee more than thundering and lightning", had chanced his arm against his king and lost his head at Evesham. Katharine of Aragon, who was, according to the old rhyme, divorced by Henry VIII for using too much tarragon, lodged here. Butcher's son, prince of the Church and eminent statesman Cardinal Wolsey – who had the sense to die on the stroke of eight o'clock before suffering the stroke of the axe – had resided here for two years. The adventuress Anne Boleyn had been allocated the house by her doting paramour, later to be her royal husband and later still to be her accuser. Cranmer had concocted reasons for his king's divorce as he paced along this gallery and then, for another royal ruler's reason, had been burned at the stake as a heretic. The marriage of Lady Jane Grey to the oafish Guildford was executed in the house chapel, but hardly had the nuptial bells ceased echoing than the bridal pair heard the executioner's knell.

Merlin had gone on ahead, chattering like a child going towards an expected treat, and was now standing at the foot of a spiral iron stairway. "Watch me, Kit." He jumped up, grasped the balustrade, hoisted his legs above his head, stuck his feet between the rails and hung upside down. With his cloak flapping around his ears, he reminded his lone spectator of a belfry bat. After a few seconds, he reversed the order of his acrobatics and landed nimbly on his feet. "It does wonders for straightening the spine," he said by way of an explanation. "Now we must go aloft to meet our captain."

The dwarf's limbs were too short to do much more than take one step at a time and their progress up the winding stairs was slow and clattering. At the halfway mark, he stopped to inform his companion that Walt had the steps specially built to keep his sea legs in trim. The stairway ended at what appeared to be a stage trap-door. When Merlin clambered through the opening, he was greeted with, "Ho there, what have we here? A hobgoblin?" When Christopher's head and shoulders followed, the same person said, "And what's this driftwood you have in tow?"

"Not driftwood, captain," Merlin replied, "but one Kit Marlowe, famed poet and scholar and begetter of mighty Tamburlaine. Did you not say, 'I fancy this man for my crew?' "

"I dare say I did. Let's see the rest of you, Marlowe. Have you legs long enough for our deck or are you foreshortened like our swab of a numerating runt?"

Christopher heaved himself up through the hatch and took in the speaker. The man had obviously seen service in foreign lands: the face was rough and brown from exposure and there were wind-creases round the eyes: but the domed forehead, the steady gaze and the neat beard denoted more the thinker. Naval artifacts such as a telescope, an astrolabe, compasses and rolled charts were scattered on the rough wood table behind which he sat. A freestanding globe was on his left and behind him a copy of Ortelius's world map, Theatrum Orbis Terrasus, hung on the wall. The sitter was splendidly accoutred in a mariner's sturdy clothes: knee-high boots, leather over-jacket and a shining bandoleer. As clean and bright as the day they were bought, none had ever been wetted by a single drop of salt water.

"Well, lad, I think you've made sufficient study of the longitude and latitude of my phiz. Go and rest your pegs till I've settled a navigational problem with Francis Bacon."

Bacon said he would rather rely on authorised charts than the imagined course set out by half-baked sailors and scribblers seeking gainful employment.

Christopher wondered if the last dart was intended for him. He went over to join Merlin, perched on a wall-seat, and asked in a low tone, "Who's this dry-land mariner spitting brine with every word?"

Merlin climbed onto the seat and gazed out of the slit window. "On a day when there's neither mist nor fog, it's possible to see as far as Greenwich from here. Are you a dunderhead, Marlowe? He's Sir Walter Ralegh and it would hurt his pride, and God knows there's plenty of that, if he thought there was one person in the whole kingdom who did not recognise him. In his conceit he's made this turret chamber into a captain's cabin. While you're here, humour his vanity. He'll call you lad till he sees fit to take you for a fellow sailor and then you'll be on first-name terms. But a word of caution, it's only the fashion within this room."

Looking at the sluggish Thames, the lead-grey sky and the brown-green fields of Lambeth Marshes, Christopher doubted the claim that Greenwich could be seen on a bright day. One would be fortunate to glimpse London Bridge and even then be deprived of the sight of the heads and limbs spiked on the battlement.

"And I tell you, Sir Walter, – " There had been a rumbling behind the window-watchers. With the sound of Bacon's raised and angry voice, they turned to see and hear the cockfight. The circular room, with its bare, rough-stone walls, strangely resembled those pits where spurred fowls tore each other into ribbons.

"Francis, dear Francis." Ralegh stressed every syllable. "In this sanctum sanctorum – " Some of the men smiled to hear the turret so described" -we're all equal before God, man and the uncharted oceans."

"If you insist on this play-acting, Walter, give me leave, then, to write my part of the script in words you'll understand. The wind has veered against your face and the admiral of the fleet, namely our sovereign Queen, has a mind to put a more dashing captain at the wheel."

"You're very apt with your metaphors but very inept with their use." Ralegh spoke in the hearty manner of an old sea-dog. "If that's the limit of your marine lore, I wouldn't hazard to sail with you; not as much as a wherry from here to Paris Garden. And talking of sailing close to the wind, word has been blown down to me by the very same north-easter that you've shown immoderate haste to climb aboard this dashing captain's leaky brig even though you've little stomach for his crew. Tell me, Francis Bacon, are you proposing to become first mate or a paying passenger?"

Christopher could only guess that the 'dashing captain' they referred to was the young Earl of Essex.

"As for your crew, Captain Ralegh." Bacon looked at each man in turn and when his eyes fell on Christopher, he pursed his lips. "As for your crew, from what skulking harbour and disarrayed pirate ship did you recruit them?"

"That's unjust, Bacon." Percy Northumberland, known as the Wizard Earl, spoke up. "You should not need to be told we're all honourable members of our sodality, a fraternity which – "

"Your sodality!" Bacon made no effort to hide his disdain. "Your supposed fraternity. Your School of Night."

"We may not enjoy your wit and learning at our meetings, Francis Bacon, something we can only deplore," Northumberland retorted, "but we do enjoy each other's trust and confidence. Can you say the same with your clique?"

"Don't denigrate our sodality, Francis," said Ralegh smoothly. "You'd be welcome within its ranks."

"And a right rank welcome that would be, Walter." Bacon's brusqueness was proving an irritant to the others. He walked over to the hatch as if expecting evil spirits to rise through the hole. "I care not for the savour of your present henchmen, Walter, and I hope for your sake they're equipped to man your ship and that you prove a better captain on this voyage than your first on the Falcon." This was an unpleasant and deliberate reminder of Ralegh's disastrous expedition to the West Indies. Bacon carefully lowered himself down the first rung of the stairs and then stopped. "I never allow questions in the province of learning and knowledge to vex me overlong and, as far as I'm concerned, the tittle-tattle of gossip is best left to those with more dust to their heels than grit in their bones." Once more his eyes sought out Christopher. "But this I've heard, blown on whichever wind you fancy, that you, in your imprudence, have sent emissaries to the Scottish Court."

There was a collective intake of breath at this suggestion of treason. Ralegh slapped the table with the flat of his hand. "God blind me, Francis, if I don't repeat what I've said time out of mind, you'll never make a true mariner. You mistake a squall for a storm, a cove for a harbour and the piping cry of a curlew for the mewing of a thousand albatrosses. True, we've sent emissaries to Edinburgh. But it was in the office of our excellent sodality that our delegates journeyed North. They, on our commission, brought fraternal greetings to men of like mind who are endeavouring to form a body of our society within those four walls."

"I've heard different," Bacon replied.

"You've heard idle rumour, Francis Bacon. The world would be upside down if credence was given to every lie and half-truth sent scurrying from the back alleys of London. We have for our part dismissed with contempt the half-penny tale that your friends have sent craven letters of submission to tongue-tied James as he anxiously waits to place the crown on England on his lolling pate."

Bacon flushed. "I know nothing of that," he snapped. "I'll abandon this fanciful forecastle talk and be direct in speech. Leave this trumpery drama to scribblers like Marlowe. He could do no worse and I reckon he'd manage it in better style. As for you, Sir Walter Ralegh, it's my belief the only benefit these turret sessions will bring you is a sturdy rehearsal for a longer stay in the Tower." The Parthian shot came as his head disappeared from view down the steps.

None spoke as they listened to the diminishing sound of Bacon's footsteps on the iron stairway. When they were sure he was gone, only Northumberland made any comment. "Heavens preserve you, Walt, if you navigated by his faulty lodestone."

Two men joined Ralegh by Ortelius's map, Merlin produced a dice and short polished stick to explain an abstruse numbers game to another pair and Northumberland unrolled a bundle of anatomical drawings to show to a fifth.

Christopher felt ignored; worse, deliberately excluded. "Am I invisible?" he wondered. "They'd take more notice of a servant." He wandered over to the table and pretended a studied interest in the equipment. "Tell me, lad," said Ralegh, staring fixedly at him, "did you use this map in one of your plays?"

"Indeed, he did," Merlin called out. " 'Give me a map', said mighty Tamburlaine and into the warrior's bloody fist our Kit thrust Ortelius."

Christopher suddenly found himself popular. So that was the trick of it. In the enclosed world of this small room, Ralegh was captain and king. In spite of their pretentious display of free comradeship, his word was law, his rule supreme. Whomsoever was favoured by his grace was graced by the favour of all.

"And what else have you prepared for the stage?" one asked. "Lately there's been a glut of drolleries, not comic enough for laughter, not tragic enough for tears, and I swear I've spent more pleasant hours watching terriers tearing a tribe of rats to shreds."

Christopher produced the two plays from his jerkin.

"You'll allow, Marlowe," said Ralegh, "that I'm well versed in literary matters and, when affairs of state grant me a modicum of leisure, I've penned a few stanzas of modest merit." He preened his moustache. "I'd be happy to cast a weather-eye on your dramas, lad, and give you the benefit of my opinion."

"It was my intention to take them to Henslowe and Alleyn today."

Ralegh placed a hand on each script. "Delay hoisting your anchor till tomorrow's high tide, lad, and, in the meantime, I'll measure the worth of your writing with the compass of my judgement." Some of those present remarked that the writer was deeply honoured. Christopher thought otherwise. He did not care to have his work subjected to the scrutiny of any self-nominated critic and an unstaged play was not worth a plate of meat to a hungry dramatist. Ralegh, with an imperious wave of his hand, said, "Temper your sail to the breeze. I'll read them this evening and if the land stands fair, you'll stow them in your hold for the outward journey. Of course, you'll dine with us later in the day."

Was this an invitation or a command?

With the prattling hunchback by his side, Christopher spent an hour or so exploring Durham House. Whereas Scadbury House was a crude mixture of fortress and farmhouse, the London mansion had been built for grandeur. It was, in truth, a storehouse of loot, differing from the stalling kens of the common thief only in the moral and legal justification that the original owners were heretics, pagans, enemies of Christianity or the state and, worse crime of all, had chosen the losing side.

When they reached the library door, Merlin laid a loosely tied bundle of papers on the nearest table. "Isn't this the wonder of the world, Kit? Greek, Latin, Hebrew, Arabic, all gathered under one roof. We should be forever thankful to Sir Walter for so enriching the commonweal of our wisdom."

His hobgoblin presence engendered an uneasy feeling. Had not centuries of sculptors, wood-carvers and painters represented evil in this grotesque shape?

Merlin had untied the bundle and was laying out the sheets of paper on the table. "Cast your weather eye, as Sir Walter is wont to say, upon these. These are Sir Walter's poems and, though he'd be the first to disclaim their perfection, I've no hesitation in saying his poetry alone would place him among the laureate heads of our realm."

To Christopher's ears, the fulsome encomium had the false note of a cracked bell. The first three he read were well constructed with a clever use of words and rhymes, but they were trifles; more the work of a student. The fourth was different. Its manner, its strength, its rhetorics, struck a chord: a chord of remembrance. He, Christopher Marlowe, had written it. Not as it presently stood; there had been minor alterations in the copying from the original. Yet, in all other respects, it was one he had composed among the many he had given to Kyd for sale to that unknown lord. He read the rest with increased interest. In some he detected the hand of Kyd but of the remainder he, in his poky room, was the prime maker.

"What do you think, then, Kit?" Merlin asked, a wide grin on his face. "Has not Sir Walter an incomparable talent?"

Christopher shuffled the papers together and retied the bundle. "I am lost for words," he replied.

"And I, too, Kit, when first I laid eyes on the power and passion detailed in every line." He clutched the bundle to his chest with his stubby hands. "But don't mention to Sir Walter you've seen them today. He did not give me permission to show them to you. Wait till he should ask if you're familiar with his poetry and you'll reply you've by chance seen a copy of one or two and esteem them marvellously."

At dinner Ralegh was talking about his Irish estates and, in passing, spoke of Edmund Spenser, the poet and a near-neighbour in Ireland. "Take Spenser as your exemplar, Marlowe lad," he said, looking down the board, "and you'll be fit to take second in his rank." The gathering then returned to their debate on the ungovernable nature of the Irish. Each vied with each to give examples of that obdurate race's barbarism, promiscuity, animal cunning, neglect of pasture and husbandry, uncleanliness and stubborn fidelity to the old religion. Apart from Christopher, who concentrated on the food, all were loudly in accord with the solution to the Irish problem. Suppress by sword, rope and fire the unruly clans, clear the slovenly churls from the best agricultural land and settle the country with good, solid, hard-working Englishmen. Ralegh favoured men from Devon and Cornwall.

At the end of the meal, Ralegh called in the musicians and ordered them to play some of the more outlandish Celtic jigs; which they did with bad grace and much fiddle-scrapping and tabor-thumping. Merlin was over-excited by the heady wine and leaped onto the table to hop, kick and grimace in an ugly simulation of the dances.

Christopher was once more reminded of the revelry at the house on the Thames.

"Merlin is a clown, Ralegh's licensed jester, permitted to prance and jiggle his offence against nature. And is he alone in swelling the belly of his conceit with the flatulence of office? The honest actors in the playhouses earn their meagre crust by pretending to be kings and villains, but Ralegh and his kind have surpassed our creations. By lies, fraud and brute force, they have possessed the governance of the Theatrum Orbis, annexed the centre of the stage and orate their fraudulent speeches of honour, integrity and loyalty without a single blush of shame. How well Ralegh plays the mariner and yet he can't stand upon a swaying deck without heaving up his meals. How well he acts the warrior when faced with tow-headed kerns or naked savages in the Americays, armed only with sticks and stones. How well he plays the poet dressed in Marlowe's finery."

Chapter thirty

Two weeks to the day after his visit to Durham House, Christopher placed one of the plays with Henslowe. On his return from Bankside, he unexpectedly met Skeres and Frizer outside his lodgings. They greeted him with glad cries, said they were just passing by and insisted on liquid refreshment to celebrate this apparently chance encounter.

Still in an affable mood, they expressed concern over the rumours that he had given up writing and seemed genuinely pleased that he had completed two new dramas; one of which, Edward II, was to be presented at the Rose in ten days' time.

"And what about the other drama?" Frizer asked. "A tale of bloody schemes in a far-off land, I warrant. And will Henslowe the pawnbroker remit that for the stage in the near future?"

"It's the tragical history of Richard Crookback," said Christopher casually. "I need to change it before presenting it again. I've been advised that certain things may not get past the censor."

"Who presumes to be judge of that?"

"Sir Walter Ralegh."

His companions exchanged significant glances but Frizer, affecting an air of indifference, said, "Ha, Sir Walter's judgement is a worthy censure."

Christopher was disappointed by their calmness at his sly mention of Ralegh. The latter had returned the scripts that evening, obviously unread, muttered a few platitudes about "strong lines" and wished the author success in his venture. It was Christopher himself who had decided to hold back the play, mainly because some scenes cluttered the stage with widowed queens moaning and groaning about their unfortunate lot.

After an hour or so of ribald jokes, Christopher began to feel that in spite of past events, these cankerous schemers were really very jovial people beneath their acquired carapace. Skeres rambled through a story about a woman who had disguised her lover as her niece up from the country and had served her foolish husband with cabbage stew garnished with dog-piss.

Frizer neither laughed or smiled. He stared at Christopher and said,"Talking of stews other than the Bankside variety, Kit, I've a bone to pick with you."

"I've none to spare from my body for the picking, though I've little enough flesh on those I have to make a decent dog's dinner, never mind a cabbage stew."

"You've been so warmly dining with Ralegh's wizards, mathematicians and alchemists that you've coldly neglected your friends from the past. For instance, Thomas Walsingham has not seen or heard from you either in the flesh or the spirit for many months now. He's presently resident in Seething Lane."

"And he sent us to fetch you," Skeres blurted.

St Denys' church bell chimed. "We've overspent our time here. Come on, Kit, let's put our best foot forward."

When he walked between the now-silent pair, he felt more like a committed prisoner than an honoured guest.

Some of the loungers in the Walsingham house stood against the walls with contrived expressions of indifference like surplus players waiting to be offered a role; while others, having being thrown a few lines, gathered in excluding groups of threes and fours.

"Sir Thomas has many visitors today," Frizer said. "Wait here till you're called." He opened a double door and disappeared into the adjoining room.

"Tell me, Nicholas, have you ever reckoned the proportion of man's earthly life wasted in waiting?" Skeres gave him a wary glance and grunted. Undeterred by this grudging response Christopher continued. "Man waits nine months to be born, two years to be weaned and freed of his swaddles, twelve more to come into his manhood and then, until he reaches his dotage and waits to die, hangs back while his betters pass, lingers by lovers' windows, yawns between battle bouts, holds his patience for expected preferments and in between spends an age kicking his heels outside unopened doors. And if we were to believe the tenets of the old religion, he waits a hundred thousand years in purgatory before being called up to the celestial vestibule where, undoubtedly, he has to wait next to eternity while the angelic officials inspects his records."

Poley, followed by a second man, strode through the main entrance, beckoned to Skeres, gestured to his companion to stay put, flung open the double doors and entered the inner sanctum with Skeres by his side.

"Remember me, Marlowe?" Poley's companion had sidled up to Christopher. "We met at Scadbury House."

"Marley? Or is it Morley?"

"Morley, Christopher Morley. Famed by name, ill-famed by fortune. Do they still ask for me in the Cornhill tavern?" He came closer, coughed and sent out a gust of bad breath and spittle. "You and me, you know, Marlowe, almost the same name and by the same token, near enough the same nature. Grab what you can when the fruit's ripe and let the devil have the windfall. And talking of the devil's spelt, that was an artful trick of the loop you did to let it be known you were seen in Ralegh's coven. Soon as word of it was out, there was a deal of fluttering, as if a fox was found among the geese and your high-and-mighty Sir Thomas cried, 'Fetch me Marlowe this instant.' Dear o dear, weren't they in a sweat and there I was thinking you're as innocent as a new-born lamb. Take the advice of an old hand in the trade, Marlowe, whatever they offer you, hold out for more."

Christopher moved away from Morley's reeking breath but the man kept step with his step and it was necessary to turn aside to avoid the full flavour. If what his informant had said was true, he was being hauled back into the school of spies.

For a one-time alley urchin, Morley seemed well versed in the politics of the day and, in particular, the antics of the Walsingham clique. They were running here and there like rats harassed by a terrier, not knowing which banner to follow or which court favourite to adopt as an ally. "And we know, Marlowe, don't we," Morley whispered hoarsely, "about certain letters sent to a certain person to the North." They had wooed the young Earl of Essex, once their bitter rival, but he was in danger of falling out of grace again. Then they had tried to induce Francis Bacon into their ranks but that wily politican moved smoothly out of their orbit.

Morley's political tutorial had expanded to take in that supreme schemer and slippery statesman, Lord Cecil ('Another dwarf,' thought Christopher) when he was interrupted by a sudden commotion.

Poley was shouting indignantly at Frizer and Skeres. "Then I, for one, should have been informed. It's flagrant mistrust." Frizer and Skeres tried to pacify him but he strode over to Christopher and almost spat at him. "So you've wheedled and crawled, have you? You'll regret your return." He then marched out of the house.

"Robin Poley has had so few successes lately that even the smallest triumph in another offends him," said Frizer languidly. "I see you know our friend from the Cheapside sewers."

Morley had quietly and quickly slipped away.

"You forget he and I were guests together at Scadbury House."

"Yes, yes, that's true. Didn't I warn you against him? He's a liar of the first order but he has his uses. Like the cur he is, he can follow a scent from here to Durham House with only the whiff of an intrigue to guide him. Sir Thomas is free to see you now."

A high-pitched and querulous voice rang out. "Has he gone, I ask you? Has he gone?" Thomas Walsingham sat on a tall-backed chair at the far end of the long room, a silver wine goblet in his right hand. "I swear by the blood of all the martyrs, he's the most irksome fellow I've ever had the misfortune to encounter."

"He's stormed out of the house in a fine tantrum," Skeres said.

"What right has he to fly into a fine tantrum? Did you hear the insolent churl harangue me, and he my hireling, with, 'You must do this' and, 'You must do that'. Must I? And who is to say I must? Ingram, protect me from such immoderate and intemperate people from now on. I cannot and I will not deal with the Robin Poleys of this world."

Christopher was astonished and not a little perturbed by the changes wrought in Walsingham since their last meeting the previous April. The self-assured manner was replaced by a whining petulance and his features were ravaged by premature ageing.

"We have Kit Marlowe with us," Frizer said.

"Yes, yes, I know. I'm not blind. People act as if I were and not a few think I'm deaf as well. Bawling in my ears with their 'You must – '. So Marlowe, maker of mighty lines, has honoured us with a visit, has he?" Walsingham sipped his wine and wrinkled his nose as if he had tasted vinegar. "Cavorting with Ralegh and his covey is one thing, but call upon us, why, we'd have better grace asking Lucifer to join us in prayers. We're nothing to Marlowe, nothing, and after all that has passed between us." He placed the fingers of his left hand on his forehead and emitted a fretful sigh. "This is so wearying, this squabbling and arguing. My skull cracks with pain and I'm sure I won't sleep a wink tonight."

Frizer drew Christopher to one side. "Sir Thomas is unwell. Perhaps you should leave now."

"No, no, Frizer," Walsingham shouted. "By whore's spit and virgin piss, let it be you that leaves and not Kit."

"I, Sir Thomas? I? Withdraw?"

"Yes, yes, withdraw, go, leave, depart. Do it in whatever phrase you wish but go. And take your hangdog henchman with you."

"But – " For a second Frizer seemed lost for words. "There are men of substance and high rank waiting in the foyer, many since early morning. Be advised by me, Sir Thomas, grant them a hearing and send Marlowe away for this day. There's time and plenty to listen to his idle chatter."

Walsingham drummed the armrest with his fingers and raised his eyes to stare at the ornate ceiling.

"What a topsy-turvy fellow you are, Ingram Frizer," Christopher said. "Only an hour ago you were most forceful in your invitation but now nothing else will do for you except that I show a clean pair of heels. Aren't you interested in any tittle-tattle I have to relay?"

Frizer gripped Christopher's arm. "You're a fool, Marlowe," he hissed. "He's ill and is wont to fall – "

"Those hangers-on who plague me with their requests and their pleas fail to interest me. Go, go, the pair of you and leave me in peace. Don't I hire you to manage my estate? Then, steward, go and earn your keep."

Frizer hesitated, his cheeks red with anger, then, without another word, stalked out of the room, closely followed by Skeres.

"I'm not deluded by the rag-bag of fawners, place-seekers, fortune-hunters, adventurers and petitioners outside." Walsingham appeared to address a shadow by his chair. "Without honour, without grace, without pride. They think me pliant, supple to their venal causes, an open hand, an open heart, in short, an open head from which all sense has escaped."

"How could it be otherwise, Thomas?" said Christopher. Walsingham continued his intense study of the ceiling. "Are you not the sole inheritor of the Walsingham dominion? Where else would the flies cluster but around the exposed honey-pot?"

"And sole inheritor of the Walsingham debts. Why, the very pigs in their pens fatten to fill the Lombardy purses. As for the so-called Walsingham dominion of power, influence and office, it weighs on my shoulders like a cloak filled with lead pellets. The sword may rust in its scabbard for all I care."

Christopher now stood in front of the chair but nothing seemed to induce the sitter to look anywhere but the ceiling.

"You sang a different song, Thomas, when first I had the pleasure of being your guest at Scadbury House. If you recall, you sent bully-boys to waylay me on the London Road, as you did today in another place."

"Why bring up the past? As for today, it was not entirely my wish. Ask Marlowe, I said, to visit me at his leisure."

"Are you their master? It's a poor excuse to say the hounds dragged you unwillingly by the leash when you have the whip hand."

"Believe me, I want none of this." The voice had dropped to a near-whisper. "You neither will or wish to understand."

"What is there for me to understand? A year ago, no, less, political intrigue was your meat and drink. Has that changed? Hardly had I stepped inside the house when I was nearly trampled by that arch carrion crow, Poley, undoubtedly hurrying in with tit-bits snatched from the Westminster midden heap, and then I was accosted by another, a snivelling wretch from the sewers, who by a wink and a nod implied I had been recruited to join your clique. It's not you but I who want none of this. I've no desire to flap my wings by the gallows."

The wine goblet clattered on the floor. Walsingham began to gasp and clutch frantically at the cloth round his neck. "What's the matter?" said Christopher reluctantly. "Shall I fetch Frizer?"

Walsingham gritted his teeth, took a deep breath through his nose and seemed to have recovered his composure. "No, no, Kit, don't. It's nothing. A slight seizure, nothing more. A surfeit of wine, perhaps, or a surfeit of people. I think it's the stink of London." He stood up and slowly walked round the chair. "There was a time, Kit, when holy men with bell, book and candle would have gathered to exorcise the demon from me." He did another turn around the chair and sat down. "Have you been offered wine, Kit? I'm a poor host. Don't leave me, Kit. I need you by my side, to advise me, to make me privy to your thoughts. I'm weary of these scheming times and the clutches of ambitious and greedy men. I must have poets, scholars, musicians, men skilled in the arts. Leave London, Kit. It is a sty, a pit, a mesh. Think of those learned documents in our library that I have paid you a fee to translate. In Chislehurst, I promise you, you'll want for nothing. Soft clothes and feathered pillows for your bed, wild swan and trout for your dishes and warmth in every room. Compare that, Kit, with the hovel of your present lodgings and the hard crust of your daily bread. Come live with me, Kit."

"You are most gracious, Thomas," Christopher began. "But I must consider – "

"But, but, must, must. Those words are most hateful to my ears. Do I demand for you to throw away your pen or tell me lies for my diversion? Do I?" His eyes searched the face opposite. "Well, Kit, are you willing?"

"I am not willing to displease you."

"My pleasure is your willingness." Walsingham's voice grew higher and sharper as he read rejection in the other man's features. "Let's not be afraid to shame the truth. Do you despise my offer? Have you contempt for me?"

"I'd rather despise your offer than have contempt for myself."

"Contempt! Despise! What right have you to fling those words in my teeth, Marlowe?" Walsingham's tone was now quite shrill. "Why should I suffer the contempt of your despicable ingratitude. Me, of noble rank and you, Marlowe, the lowly son of a bankrupt cobbler." Walsingham stood up and began to gasp again. Every phrase he uttered was punctuated by peculiar clicking noises from his jaws."Spurn me – in your Lucifer pride – you've found favour elsewhere – Ralegh – false friends – false talk." He tore at his neck cloth. "Everybody despises me – weak – not like Edmund – " He stretched out his hands. "Help me – " His eyes rolled so that the pupils disappeared. "Help me – " He shivered violently, fell forward on the floor and his legs and arms twitched madly.

Christopher flung open the door and shouted for Frizer. As people rushed into the room, he left the house and quickly walked home to his lodgings.

Chapter thirty-one

"Did I do wrong?" Christopher asked himself over and over again. "Was my rejection brutal and offensive?" Come live with me and be – ? As Gaveston was to Edward II? He quoted from his own play, "Come, Gaveston, and share the kingdom with thy dearest friend."

"Am I brain-sick?" The shadows thrown by the candle were unable to resolve unanswered questions. "I am not so mean in spirit to play the pampered pet ornamented with silver chains." But this alone was not the reason for refusing Walsingham. He was repulsed by what he had feared to question, feared to answer, but which had been flung in his face by jibes, hints and caustic comments.

His sisters had said, "And talking of fowls of contrary nature, what of our own prize capon?" This had been echoed by the acidic Robert Greene: "What do you know, Marlowe, of the sweaty passion of limbs tangled with limbs?", adding, "I speak only of what is natural between man and woman."

It was a dull part of the week for the Bankside brothels when he stood inside the entrance to The Sugar Loaf. The whores in the house were specially selected for one quality only: fatness. Some were as white and as plump as geese gorged for the Christmas table and they waddled just like that bloated bird. These were the youngest, freshly plucked from the outlying villages of Surrey and Kent; their pink, smooth cheeks not yet raddled with the pox nor their thick and curly hair rotted with the yellow dye. Others, older, lolled on pallets; their fleshy mounds inviting cushions for bony customers. The elderly snuffled in dark recesses, their porcine skins and balding heads ready for less sensitive clients.

Business was slow and their only other patron was a toothless old fool. Podgy faces turned towards Christopher, contrived smiles crinkled painted lips and the house musician struck up a jig on his fiddle. The whore-ward, a coarse lump of a woman, told him to take his ease, inspect the assembled beauties and she would see to his need when she had helped the other gentleman to choose his blossom.

Tucking her hand under the old chap's arm, she helped him to hobble over to the pallets. "All our girls are flowers of the field," she said rather loudly. He was, it seemed, deaf in one ear and judging by the way he squinted, half-blind as well. "This is Asphodel, our golden lily. And here is Peony, never fear the wounds of the gods with her. For scholars, and you have the bearings of a learned man, sir, we have Pansie and for those who need to forget, there's Rosemary. Ah, I couldn't have made a better selection myself for this is sweet Briar Rose. Prick yourself on that elegant bloom." She hoisted the dodderer over his chosen flower and let him collapse upon the quivering mound.

Christopher did not wait to see or hear any more. He stopped at the top of the alley by Cardinal's Cap and wiped his brow. "Yesu, that old codger has a thin dibble stick. It'll do less to plant his seed and more to dig his grave."

"Were they not to your liking, sir?" A woman with a fruit basket slung under her large breasts emerged from the shadows. "And why should they be to the taste of a refined gentleman like yourself," she continued. "They're nothing but country heifers with the dung still caked to their teats. You wouldn't want to spend your night dangling on top of them smelly udders, would you? I've always said, a cow's rump is meat enough for rough merchants but mint-flavoured mutton is a delicate dish for a gentleman to savour."

With a continuous motion made perfect by practice, she unhooked her basket, laid it on the ground, grasped Christopher by his two forearms and pulled him against her bosom.

"Now, me young buck, if you want a lively jig for a penny, I'm your woman. I'll give you a good rub and if your spine holds out we'll finish with a gallop." Christopher was almost suffocated by the aroma of rancid lard and masticated onions. "You may squeeze my juicy apples and I'll fondle your bunch of grapes." Her right arm encircled his shoulders in a tight grip and her left hand fumbled at his crotch. "O dearie me," she said disapprovingly, "it's a bit of a periwinkle, son, isn't it? We'll have work on our hands to make that into a wriggling eel."

Her victim sent an anguished prayer to the gods to rescue him from this Amazon. Whatever divinity was his particular saviour heard his plea. Two whooping drunks rolled down the alley and grappled with the woman. "Yoo hoo," cried one, "we've caught a mare mounting a foal."

With an outraged bawl, she released her hold and turned to clout the nearest head. Hardly had Christopher gone ten paces than the trio fell to bargaining and by the time he reached Bank End Steps the woman and the drunks had disappeared. Feeling faint and weak, he leaned over the wall but though he retched hard and his stomach heaved, nothing came up.

"Why am I doing this?" Envy sharpened barbs; but one armour-clad with pride and confidence could deflect the worst if – if, unlike the Trojan hero, he was complete and wholly invulnerable. It was the fear that he was incomplete, lacking in nature as the jeers and jibes had implied, that had driven him to the Bankside stews. Recently he had received another nagging message from his mother about marriage. What if he should arouse their expectations but be incapable of rousing anything else?

Yet when he contemplated naked intimacy, abhorrence of the most violent kind churned within him. Equally odious was the florid language, the litany of false promises concocted to attain that brief moment of carnal ecstasy.

"I must be resolved. Screw up my courage. If only those lumpy trollops were in the image of Ovid's fair Corinna."

His mind went back to his student days when he had translated the Roman's erotic poems and his chambermates and he had boasted of bedding those beauties so skilfully portrayed. To an uninterested audience of perching seabirds he quoted a remembered stanza.

"Stark naked as she stood before mine eyes,
Not one wen on her body could I spy.
What arms and shoulders did I touch and see
How apt her breasts were to be pressed by me!

How smooth a belly under her waist saw I!
How large a leg, and what a lusty thigh!"

Somebody touched his shoulder and he turned to face a sparsely dressed girl who was as slender as a boy.

"Are you waiting for anybody?" she asked.

"I'm waiting for fair Corinna."

"And if she doesn't come? You can't stay here forever in the perishing cold. Wouldn't you rather have another?"

"Then let the gods bring me Cleopatra and her swarthy hordes or Salome to dance before me, each veil masking an enemy head on a platter, or even the wraith of Helen, faithless vision hurrying from the burning palace of Ilium."

The first two names meant nothing to the girl but she perked up at the last one. "How did you know I was Helen? Come on, let's go over there – " she nodded towards the last stew in the row.

"Is that the bastion of Troy, O Helen, daughter of Leda?"

"You say strange things. My mother's name is Helen, the same as me. Are you coming?"

"Jove send me more afternoons as this," said Christopher fatuously.

She told him to wait while she fetched their meal, disappeared behind a drape and within seconds returned with a laden tray. It was not a regal meal; the wine flagon was small and grubby and the scraps of near-raw meat were laid on a bread trencher.

A dour woman with a moustache limped over and held out her paw. "You'll pay now," she said. When Christopher exclaimed at the price, she replied, "Take it or leave it, me bucko, it's all one to me. The cost covers your bed for the night and if you want to cover her, that's your fancy."

With Helen leading the way and carrying the tray, they climbed a rickety stairway to a narrow room with a low ceiling.

"God's blood," grumbled Christopher as he crouched to avoid bumping his head, "it's as gloomy in here as the arse end of hell."

"If it's light you want, you'll have to buy a candle. Give me a penny and I'll find a glimmer."

Apart from making the squeaking rats scuttle back into their holes, the tallow candle did little to enhance the surroundings and only served to remind Christopher of the dire Thames Street hovel where he had taken refuge so long ago.

"We won't be interrupted," Helen said. "Let's eat first."

"I've no appetite for this."

She crouched down on her haunches and began to cram the food into her mouth, stopping only once to say, "You'll hunger for this before the night's out. There, I've eaten it all and there's nothing for you. But I won't touch the wine. That's fair shares, isn't it?" She rummaged at the foot of the straw mattress and produced a hairy blanket. "We'll wrap ourselves in this. My mother always says, 'There's no better way to catch a chill than to let yourself shiver and shake after a good sweating.' Are you ready then? What would you like to do?"

What should he do? It would be so easy just to walk out. Who would know? Only this scrawny prostitute. Sitting there in her grubby shift, her belly gurgling, her nails scratching her thigh, she would not care. But he would forever remember his failure to prove to himself he was a complete man. If only it had not been here in this squalid den with this starveling ditch-leavings but in some sylvan grove where myrtles and roses grow. Those sylvan groves of mud and mire, where brambles tore your hands and cheeks and midges swarmed to suck your blood.

"Come live with me," he quoted.

"Live with you? You're as mad as a cuckoo. What are you on about?"

"It's a line from a poem I've written."

"It's mostly draymen, colliers and bargemen here," she said indifferently. "They're a rough crowd and dirty into the bargain. You won't be rough with me, will you, master poet? I'll be making the bed straight while you take off your clothes."

He quoted another stanza.

"And I will make thee a bed of roses,
And a thousand fragrant posies;
A cap of flowers, and a kirtle
Embroidered all with leaves of myrtle."

"Will you listen to him." She giggled. "Me, on a bed of roses and with them thorns sticking in my arse, I'd be prodded from behind and before." She sat on the bed and held up the flagon. "Go on, have a drink before we start. I'll have a drop to keep you company and I promise not to take it all." She swallowed a mouthful and handed him the vessel. "It'll settle you. Do you really want to stay the night? If you don't, it won't worry me as long as the beak-bullies don't catch you leaving. You look gawky standing there. Come down here with me." But the cramped space on the mattress offered no comfort. She nudged him with her elbow. "You're a slow one. But my father used to say a slow trotter is a better ride than a bucking galloper."

If she were Helen, hair as red as the flames bursting from the burning topless towers of Ilium. If she were Corinna, ripe mistress of the poet's fervid imagination.

"And eagerly she kissed me with her tongue."

"So that's how you'd like to begin." She flung her spindly arms round his neck and pressed her lips against his. When she drew back, the breath hissing from between her teeth, he exclaimed with sudden awareness, "But you're only a child."

"No, I'm not. I'm a woman," she declared vehemently. "That's what you paid for and that's what I am." She sat up and slumped back against the wall. "Nobody's ever said I'm a child before. They're happy to lie with me and I've never had a word of complaint. I give them value for their money. Besides, there's them who like it young and tender. You've been diddering and doddering, spouting your poetry with not a single manly stir. Cocksure you may be but cock-proud you're not. I'll show you I'm a woman and I dare you to show me you're a man." She tore off her shift to reveal an emaciated body and then looked at him with plaintive, pleading eyes.

He stared at the shrivelled figure with a mixture of pity for her and disgust with himself and softly quoted, "Stark naked as she stood before my eyes, Not one wen on her body could I espy."

The girl's small oval face was blemished by an angry red sore on her upper lip.

"You've looked me over long enough. I've still got all my teeth and I'm sound in wind and limb."

He tentatively reached out, gently placed his fingers on her shoulder-blades and ran his hand down her arm. She shrank back, then went quite still and tried to smile. "You like what you see and feel, don't you?" she asked anxiously.

"What arms and shoulders did I touch and see.
How apt her breasts were to be pressed by me!"

They were small and surprisingly flaccid for one so young, with inverted teats. Her skin quivered under his touch.

"How smooth a belly under her waist saw I!"

"You don't think I'm like a stick, do you? The nearer the bone, the sweeter the flesh."

When his hand reached her navel, she pressed her legs together. The kneecaps protruded as if trying to burst through the mottled skin.

"How large a leg, and what a lusty thigh!"

"I'm nearly perished with the cold sitting here starkers while you have your fondle." She ducked down under the blanket and pulled it up to her chin. "Hurry up then while the humour is on us." Suddenly she raised herself on her elbows and asked with some alarm, "You've nothing to hide, have you? You're not mange-ridden with the French marbles, are you? The French marbles, the Spanish strawberries, the Dutch dimples, the pox, the pox! I won't risk the balls of fire to traffick with you."

"I've nothing to hide."

"By the way you're hovering there, you've nothing to show either. Is this – is this your first time? Yesu Christus and the bloody tears of Mary Magdalene, I should have known."

At that moment, the girl whore seemed to be much older than he. She took the loose folds of his shirt and pulled him to her.

"Isn't it better to stretch your limbs in comfort than to squat there like a grouchy toad? You haven't told me your name, have you? But then if you don't care to, you needn't. It's just nice and friendly, I've always said. Here, I'll loosen your belt." She undid the buckle. "You're shy, aren't you? That's the way with them who've been tenderly reared by a loving mother in a gentle home. It's a pleasure to have such soft sweetness in my arms, not rough and ready like them filthy draymen. I'd rather have a poet share my bed than the greatest in the land. I've had a few of them. Some have asked me to live with them, the same as you. Remember, you said come live with me and then there's the fancy talk about rose beds. Relax, there's no hurry. As my mother says – she's a widow woman with six hungry mouths to feed on the little I manage to send her – the more hurry the less speed. And my father always said, a rushed job is a botched job. We'll make ourselves comfortable then."

The hairy blanket irritated his skin, needle-points of straw stuck through the mattress and her cold body sucked the heat from his. He dared not think of the armies of fleas, lice and bugs that hopped, leaped and swarmed from every crack and crevice and he turned a deaf ear to the chorus of rodents behind the wall.

"If you'd rather, I'll snuff the glimmer. No need to waste the candle, is there?"

Outside, over the river, a storm rose and the wind buffetted the house.

"You didn't tell me your name, did you?"

"Robert." He told the lie without thinking.

"Robert? There was a Sir Robert here once – no, it was Sir Robin. A young man like yourself, except he had red hair. Like a fox. Not that he gave his name for all to know. Doll was the one that had him." A rumbling crash of thunder shivered the lathes. She clutched his arm. "God save us, I'm scared. I've seen a whole oak split in two in a flash of lightening. It's a warning, they say, of worse to come and a week to the day afterwards my father was killed when the cow shed fell on him. What's the rest of your name, poet?"

"My name is Robert Greene."

Chapter thirty-two

Three times Christopher went to St Bartholomew's Hospital to see Doctor Lopez. On the first occasion he called at the vestry gate of St Bartholomew's-the-less and was directed to a large hall crammed with poor people.

The porter looked him up and down. "The doctor refuses nobody on his day," he said. "If you've a mind to wait three or four hours, then do so and may God keep you from worse. Are you ill? You will be before the day's out."

Christopher gave the menial a coin and demanded that his name be given to Lopez.

A rag-picker made room for him on a bench but he declined the offer and for the next hour stood and watched with morbid curiosity as the old man and his neighbours compared ulcerous sores, deformed joints and diseased skins.

The porter reappeared. "Well, did you give Doctor Lopez my name?" Christopher asked.

The man shrugged his shoulders. "Yes, I did and he says, 'Marlowe? Poor Marlowe!' and I thought to myself, seeing as how you're poor you'll not mind waiting the same as everybody else."

Early the following morning Christopher banged on the closed hospital gate. The spy hatch opened and the porter's weasel face pressed against the grid. "I wish to speak with Doctor Lopez. Remember, I asked you to give him my name yesterday. Tell him I'm here. He knows me."

"And who doesn't he know? Come back next week." The hatch was slammed shut.

For the next few days Christopher stayed in his lodgings, bone-weary, distracted and restless. "Yesu, why should I be so punished?" His despair was the companion of rage. "That filthy slut, that reeking harlot! That mangy whore! May she be riddled with a thousand burning pox spikes and be basted on hell's griddle for ever more."

He had bought a jar of stinking unguent – reputed, according to the advertisements, to assuage all visible afflictions – in Apothecary Street and each night smoothed thick layers on the rash-ridden areas. Though the potion gave little ease and smelled strongly of sweating pigs, it raised hope that the contagion was being controlled. Every morning after closely inspecting the red clusters, he was convinced that here and there the lesions had diminished. Occasionally he turned from what he feared was the cause of his affliction to the possibility that he was the victim of some unknown bug brought into the country in the rags and tatters of foreign refugees. His only comfort was that, so far, the eruptions had not reached his face or hands.

On the morning of Doctor Lopez's 'day', he set off for the hospital well before dawn to be among the first few at the gate but more than a hundred people had already gathered at the closed entrance. A large woman with bared arms folded over her chest stood in his path and stared hard at him. Because she was apparently hale and hearty, he presumed she was a hospital worker and politely asked, "When does the medication begin?", adding rather lamely, "I am a friend of Doctor Lopez."

She scratched her left forearm, grimaced and signalled to those nearby with a jerk of her head. A section of the lame and halting came over to form a tight ring around them. "Says he's a friend of the doctor," the woman said. There were snorts and sceptical laughs. Some prodded him curiously with their knuckles as if they were at a cattle fair. "I'm ill, a slight distemper," he shouted. "I need a remedy from Doctor Lopez." The hostile circle was not prepared to accept that.

A noseless harridan screeched scathing remarks about cocks-of-the-walk who barged in as if they were persons of consequence. Decrepit fossils with running sores cackled that they'd let no rogue lay a hand on their doctor.

"What's going on here?" The porter pushed through the crowd. "Back to your places or you'll miss your turn," he shouted as he shoved the more obdurate out of the way. He gripped Christopher's arm and steered him several paces away from the grumbling mob.

"I don't know what you're after, a cure or a caution but whatever, you've picked a bad time. If there's as much as a nod or a wink that you mean harm to Doctor Lopez, those crotch-rotten cripples will rise against you and tear you limb from limb. To them he's a saint, a holy fool if you ask me, to be bothering with their scourings. As for yourself, going by the cut of your cloth, you're not short of a penny or two. For the sake of your future health, take my warning and seek a different leech for a remedy."

Christopher had no wish to return to the misery of his barren room and the tortured contemplation of his affliction but where else could he go? The morning mist obscured the bleak landscape and made hag-ridden wraiths rise from roofs and walls. Aimlessly, without sense of purpose or direction, he trudged though mulching heaps of decaying leaves and let his feet fall into every shallow pool. The worn route ran a wavering path round the hospital's sturdy wall and led Christopher to a familar door set under an ornamental arch.

Turning the iron handle, he quietly entered and climbed the stone stairway to the second door. The low chant of a man at his prayers came from the other side and Christopher hesitated, not willing to intrude upon this person's private word with God. The orisons stopped and the voice called out, "Enter, you who stand without."

The frail man who had risen from the kneeler stared at his visitor with the unblinking gaze of a blind person. "Aleicham. Peace be with you," Doctor Lopez said. "You have returned. Will there be a third coming, O dark, avenging angel of the Lord?"

"Don't you know me?" Christopher asked.

"That which haunts and harries the wicked, the unjust, the proud and the recalcitrant, has many guises."

"I am Christopher Marlowe."

"So you say and who am I to doubt it? Yet I could give you many names – no – not you whose shell of a born body is called Christopher Marlowe but the malignant spirit that the Lord has ordained to exact retribution for my sins against my people."

"Your people?"

"You know I am a Jew."

Was this to be the same prologue as before? Had he sought out the most skilful healer in the kingdom only to discover a meandering dodderer mouthing senile incantations and holy platitudes?

"Whether you're Hebrew or Musselman is irrelevant to my condition," he said sharply. "I've come here for a cure. I am sore afflicted with a – " A new-found shame made him stumble. "That which pleases you to call a shell – my body – has suffered – I have suffered the sting of a gall wasp. Of course, I speak indirectly – metaphorically." He drew in his breath and ended weakly, "I have a slight distemper."

Lopez held Christopher's hands, looked closely at the soft part of the wrists, then inspected the young man's neck and the skin behind the ears.

"Ah, imperfect man, forever stained with the sinful urging of our primal parents. And did they not also lust for the forbidden fruit? Can our flesh be other than corrupt, plagued with diseases, a prey to decay, rank in life, putrid in death? There's no cure for your illness."

"Am I damned then?"

"Damned! We are all damned. Cursed children of disobedient parents, cursed parents who engendered us. Beneath what fallen mountain can we hide from the heavy wrath of God?"

Christopher despaired of a doctor so possessed by his rhetorics. But having delivered himself of the final ponderous question, Lopez calmly removed and laid to one side the dark shawl he had worn round his shoulders.

"Perhaps, Christopher Marlowe, in the scourging of your flesh you'll find salvation. Come with me, this is the time when I walk among the afflicted. Be patient with my slowness. In babyhood we crawl, in youth we run, in manhood we march, in old age we hobble, in all we travel the same path towards the locked gate."

Putting his hand against the wall to steady himself, Lopez lowered his right foot onto the first step. When he was sure it was well placed, he followed carefully with his left. Once out of his cell, he was transformed from the God-fearing zealot into an garrulous old gaffer grumbling about the topsy-turvy times, the young failing to respect their elders and the new-fangled ideas flooding the country.

At the last step he paused for breath and, with a speed that belied his age, turned sharply left down a narrow passage, out to a herbal garden and through a door on the opposite side.

They entered a long room cluttered with a confusion of benches, shelves, coffers and numerous sacks opened at the neck to display crystals and powders of various colours. Scattered on every available flat surface were retorts, stills, stone jars, flasks, bottles of glass and leather, mortars, basins, scales and large books with wooden covers. At the far end, a boy clad in a leather apron vigorously worked a foot bellows and stirred the contents of a cauldron.

A medley of pungent smells smote Christopher's nose when he stepped over the threshold and his eyes watered with the whiff of acetic acid rising from an uncovered alembic. "A veritable alchemist's sanctum," he said, but Lopez would not have the place so named. "No, no, this is my kitchen. Here I brew, boil and bake a feast of potions, unctions and salves." He trotted between the benches, muttering and mumbling to himself, tapping a retort here, running powder between his fingers there, sniffing the contents of a flask and stopping now and then to turn the pages of a book. When he was near the furnace, he shouted, "Too much heat. Too much heat" and launched into a pantomimic dumb show to restrain the boy's energetic pedalling. "The lad's deaf and dumb," he explained to Christopher, "and eminently suited to my purposes. If he's questioned he cannot hear and if he understands the asking he cannot speak the answer."

"Who'd put him through such an inquisition?"

"Who else, Marlowe, but those charlatans and fumblers who pretend to inner knowledge with their gabbling Latin and stunted Greek and who drain the poor of both blood and money. They'd like nothing better than to steal my secrets and destroy my kitchen."

"Surely you're safe in your own domain? You've many friends among the rich and powerful and the poor who gather at the hospital gate would rise to protect you."

Lopez poured a scoopful of blue crystals into a mortar and began to pound with a pestle. "And who among the many your Christ had healed came forward to speak for him when he was condemned to die? Was he not denied by his own followers? But it's not the ignorant and desperate I fear." He shot a glance towards the entrance as if expecting marauders to burst in. "There was one like you, though beyond you in rank and wealth, who also suffered the folly of the flesh – "

"I had not told you the cause of my rash."

"Not in the particulars, rash man, but enough was seen and said to tell me the nature of your affliction. And you came creeping, as he did, through the back door. I tell you, Marlowe, fine lace, scented clothes and arrogant gestures will not suffice to smother the reeking stink of shame." Lopez poured a brown liquid from a flask into the mortar. The mixture bubbled and gave off a tartaric smell. "We'll let it settle," Lopez said. Leaving his sizzling concoction, he went from bench to bench, from retort to still, to flask and scales, weighing, measuring, pouring, all with the same fussiness of Christopher's mother in her kitchen.

The mixture had now solidified. He emptied the mortar onto a board, kneaded the paste with his knuckles and pressed it flat with a cylinder. "Hidden shame breeds hatred against he who is privy to the secret." He started to cut the dough-like substance into small squares. "And from that hatred rises madness to poison all rational thought with its venomous breath." He took one of the squares and rolled it into a ball between his hands. "And yet he had come to me, naked in his humility, his red hair blazing like the nimbus of a sun god, and with tears and pleading, begged me for a potion to ease his pain."

"And this you could give him?" Christopher's question was prompted more by hope than curiosity. He could only guess the identity of this unnamed nobleman. "Then grant me the same benefaction and, in your charity, ease my pain." In his eagerness, he reached out and touched Lopez' shoulder but, to his astonishment, the doctor struck the hand away, dropped the pellet he was forming and shrank back; a look of abject fear in his eyes.

"Surely I hold no terror for you?"

Lopez's trembling was replaced by an equally tremulous rage. "You – you, Christopher Marlowe, God's scourge, have you not unleashed your own terror? Does not your Malta-Jew rant, rave and connive in every playhouse in the land and re-light the fires of Christian hatred for the children of Israel? Go, suffer as my people have suffered and rot in the disease of your detestation. Go! Go and leave me to care for the innocent."

There was no hope for him here. The dejected Christopher slowly went out to the herb garden, but had hardly taken ten paces when Lopez called him back.

"No, no, by my oath, I was wrong to reject you. I have sworn that whomsoever seeks my health, I shall tend him as if he were my own flesh and blood, even if he be my vilest enemy." He scurried from pot to jar, shouted and made signs to the boy to prepare a steaming poultice and ordered his caller to bare the affected parts.

"Now, Christopher Marlowe, let this be a grim harbinger of the horrors to come when you've passed through the smoky mouth of hell. There is no lasting cure for you and no multitude of repentance will suffice. There is no end to the torment for damned souls and you, Christopher Marlowe, you are damned."

Chapter thirty-three

In the weeks following his visit to St Bartholomew's, Christopher never ventured far from his lodgings. Once a day he went to a common eating-house and on the way back bought bread and cheese in the market. The rye-and-bean bread was cheap and the eating-house catered for those with little cash and less taste. Nevertheless he was becoming dangerously short of money. Fortunately for him, his landlady was fairly tolerant about the rent. Procuring for her six daughters was more profitable than the meagre income from her tenants and besides, a lodging house with men coming in and going out day and night was an excellent cover for the tenement's real trade.

The memory of his return from Lopez's 'kitchen' was dominated by excruciating pain but the suffering, which lasted nearly twenty-four hours, was a small price for the results. When he removed the poultice, his skin was raw and tender but the rash had disappeared. The doctor had given him a jar of what he called Lombardy Balls with the strict instruction to swallow one a day after smearing lotion on the affected parts. The first was as hard as a marble knob, difficult to gulp down and vile-tasting, and the second gave off a stench of rotten eggs. The only effects Christopher now felt from his illness were a persistent ache in his jawbones and a looseness in his teeth.

Three weeks of seclusion passed and then one evening he had an unexpected caller in Thomas Nashe, who had brought a bottle of wine. Nashe was unusually morose. "The saints preserve us, Kit, must I number you among my stricken friends? You're as pale as painted lead and – " he sniffed, "I think you're decaying?"

Christopher laughed, invented a plausible story about being bitten by a dog and blamed the smell on the ointment he used. He said that the wound was merely a scratch and he had not yet taken to howling at the moon.

"You're fortunate it was no worse." Nashe opened the wine

and then related a yarn that Thomas Deloney, the one-time Norwich silk weaver and now itinerant pedlar and ballad-maker, had told him about an East Anglian village. It would appear that a vixen, in protecting her cubs, had chawed a lump out of a dog, the dog had snapped at a child, the unweaned child had chewed its mother's breast, she had nipped her lover's neck when her husband was in Flanders, and within the space of a month every person in the hamlet was yowling, keening and on their hands and knees like so many Nebuchadnezzars. "For my part," concluded Nashe, "there's little credit to be given to Deloney's tales from his ragman's roll."

"Yes, I've heard Robert Greene say of our Norwich poet that he is the seller of trivial trinkets and threadbare trash."

Nashe sighed. "As for Greene himself, I wish I knew what black dog had bitten him."

"You spoke of our stricken friends. Is it the plague?"

Nashe shook his head. "There are rumours of an outbreak in Cripplegate but since none can understand those foreigners' gabble there's no sense in running mad with panic. No, our friend Greene is fair eaten up with melancholic worms and has become insane with repentant ravings. He has abjured all he had written, swearing it reeks with sin, denounced the playhouses as being instruments of Satan's will, consigned his books to the fire and in these extremities of passion has abandoned his wife."

"Surely he did that some time ago?"

"He had deserted his legal wife to live with a known whore and it is she, whom we in our regard for him termed his wife, he has now rejected. He starves, has no money and yet will take sustenance from no one."

Christopher said that if he was in such a poor condition he would not be too proud to take a small donation and added, as an afterthought, that his purse at present was light enough not to be a weight on his conscience. Nashe pressed him to accept a loan. After a token display of reluctance, he accepted the gift.

When they both had a swig of wine, Nashe continued his litany of woes. The red-bearded actor Will Shakeshaft, or to give him his new name, Will Slaughter, had become so bloated from an excess of beer that he had almost lost the use of his legs and had to be rolled like a barrel from place to place. His near-name from Stratford had said, with rare wry humour, that the obese actor had taken his role as an infamous drunkard and lecher in the failed drama Henry IV more to his belly than his heart. Meanwhile two players had dragged their private quarrel onto the stage and in the midst of a touching love scene, when one was dressed as a maiden and the other her desperate paramour, they spat, snarled and cuffed each other round the head. "You know Ben Jonson, the bricklayer's son and recent soldier, and Gabriel Spencer? It was their fight and I fear worse is to come." Several of their acquaintances had taken to their beds with the sweats and the wife of a playhouse manager – Nashe hinted it was Henslowe – had been whipped behind the cart for keeping a bawdy-house.

"As for poor Tom Watson," Nashe slid a sideways glance at Christopher, "from what I've heard, he's sore afflicted with the shivers and the shakes. I don't know the whole truth of it for his wife has barred all callers. Her religious fervour is only equalled by his fever, I've been told, and she has put it abroad that his new illness arose when he went, contrary to her wishes, with a fellow scribbler – she names no names but – beyond Moorgate and was caught in a sudden downpour."

Christopher was distressed that Tom should be ill again but he was also annoyed that Anne Watson should once again blame him for their misfortunes. He diverted the conversation away from this unhappy topic by asking news of Thomas Kyd.

"I've often wondered if a mad dog had bitten his mother when she was belly-full with him."

"Kyd!" Nashe snorted. "That burnt-out quill of a scrivener's spit. Come, Kit, drink your wine. It's good tonic for a jaded spirit and it'll wet the head of our gossip. Kyd has converted his talent, such as it is, as one turns from light to darkness, to the writing of scurrilous pamphlets against aliens. Without a doubt, he'll contrive to blame the Flemings for the bad response to his latest play."

Nashe settled down on the pallet and his gloom began to disappear. "This drama, or if you like, this pottage, this par-boiled stew was halted in the very first rehearsal by Henslowe when Alleyn walked off the stage, declaring it was neither fresh fish nor blooded flesh and was more foul than fowl. Only one among those present thought it had merit, our friend Shakeshaft, and he was not in the least discomfited when Kyd flung the copy at his head and stormed out of the playhouse."

"I would not have reckoned Shakeshaft a fair judge of a foul copy."

"Curse this confusion of names. No, not our fatted Will but he who speaks as if he held a hot carrot in his gob and had a middling drama of Harry The Sixth put on stage by old Burbage."

"Shakespeare, you mean. A solemn person, not a drinker nor too great at shaking spears but a man of gentle nature – though not by nature a gentleman," Christopher could not resist saying. "But tell me the gist of this abused drama."

"Kyd's blinded eye had turned upon a dour Danish tale in which a prince, long in the tooth, for he must be near thirty years of age, would set out to avenge his father's supposed murder at the urging of a midnight wraith that spoke in the doleful voice of his dead and rotting dad. This gull of a regal clown did not question whether the roaring apparition was an evil spirit sent from hell or – "

"Or whether he himself was roaring wall-eyed from a bout of bastard ale."

Nashe laughed. "If you had tasted, as I have, what passes as Danish ale and I think what they sup is what passes from their incontinent horses – but I digress. Upon whom should this gawky – and, I should add, virginal – prince exact revenge, you may ask? Why, none other than the king's brother, his uncle, who had hardly waited for the grave to cool before he had hotly bedded the queen. Now, for two or three scenes, our hero swears dire retribution upon his uncle's wicked head in rhyming couplets. Does he cease his prating to skewer the offender on his sword? No, he pretends to madness and in his feigned demented state, spurns his beloved, invades his mother's bedchamber, slaughters his beloved's doddering father, schemes to have two university friends beheaded and in between these frantic activities, stops to tell the audience – if there had been an audience – how wearisome, how tedious life is."

"And in the end? Did he kill his uncle or did he discover that the ghost was nothing more than a fart rising from the Danish bogs?"

"Alas, there's more to come. The voice of his decayed father continues to haunt him, there are more comings and goings, plots, plans and questions. Is the uncle a murderer? Does the queen know? Is the prince mad? Are we mad? His beloved, having failed to lose her maidenhead and having lost her father, now loses her mind, wanders here and there in the bleak castle in her shift, handing out wild flowers to all and sundry, and then goes for a final swim in the local brook. Her brother suddenly returns from foreign parts, clutches his decomposing sister to his bosom – how grave are these incestuous Danes – and vows to kill somebody or another. At the behest of the scheming uncle, the returned brother challenges the clod of a prince to a play-acting duel. But treachery is afoot." Nashe's voice rose as he hurries towards the conclusion. "A foil is encrusted with venom. In the promiscuous sword fight the lout of a brother is smitten, the queen drinks poison intended for her son, he stabs the uncle, someone else dies, alas not the author, then our hero, spouting blood, sweat and bad verse, keels over and dies."

They both laughed at the preposterous tale.

"I doubt whether our Stratford lad could turn Kyd's stodgy broth into a comical pie," Christopher said. "Whereas Tom Watson, in his day – "

They lapsed into a brooding silence for a few seconds.

Nashe heaved a bronchial sigh. "I fear to tell you, Kit," he began, "that the signs do not favour us. Our friends moulder in illness and distress, the playhouses are berated on all sides by those who pretend to sanctity and now, there are moves to suppress the printing of books. Yesu help us, if the truth be known, they who bellow loudest against the stage and say it is an offence in the sight of the Almighty harbour silently within themselves all manner of lust and abominations." He rose as if to go and flung a cloth-wrapped parcel on the pallet. "Make what you will of this, Kit. It's a recent translation of a German tale but I, for one, found the words plodding and turgid. I left it unread midstream."

"And do you think I've a stronger stomach? Remember, I've been ill. Like a child-bearing woman, I'd prefer scarce Indian grapes, in or out of season, to dull Gothic dumplings." He removed the wrapping and read the book's title. "The Lamentable And Dreadful History of Doctor John Faust. A familar name but – let it stand for the moment. Could it be a misprint for Gutenberg's assistant, Fust? Or perhaps those guttural square-heads jest in Latin? Do you recall, Thomas, in your school days stumbling over the cobbles of the Roman tongue? Faust-ee, to mean luckily. Faustitas, faustatis, to be of good fortune of both the male and female variety."

Christopher continued reading out aloud, "History of Doctor Faust, the notorious sorcerer and black-artist: How he bound himself to the Devil for a certain time: what singular adventures befell him therein, what he did and carried on until he received his well-deserved pay." He laid the book aside. "I think this German story is more worthy of the comic touch than that obtuse Danish tale. Why, we could frighten every maiden-heart and make the groundlings wet their breeches by bringing on stage ugly hob-goblins, screaming imps and prancing devils. And for a further prank we'd dress Satan in Popish garb and make the foolish doctor a Puritan."

"Careful, Kit. I've heard it said that ill-fortune strikes any who tamper with this demonic tale."

"I'll turn the superstition to bite its own tail in this tale and name the learned doctor 'Lucky'. To confound the ignorant, I'll act the scholarly nomenclator with dog-Latin and title him Doctor Faustus." He flicked over a few pages and quickly read a couple of stanzas. "It is as you said, dull and plodding, not unlike those sour-cabbage eaters King Henry employed for their blundering guns. Thomas, I've suddenly remembered. Faust, that familar name, belonged to Socinus. They were uncle and nephew, heretical writers from Siena, and many of their tracts were smuggled into England. I discovered some when I was staying at – but no, for your sake I won't mention the place – suffice it to say I mislaid them some time ago."

Nashe lowered his voice. "Did you by chance lose them when you and Kyd were collaborating on – I know not what – in his lodgings?"

"It's possible. His room is a clutter of papers. As I recall, I had intended to show them to you."

"Thank God you didn't. It's likely they are the tracts discovered in his lodgings and which he has denied were his. Have I told you he has been questioned?" Nashe sucked in his breath. "Be warned, Kit, men like him wear their failures on the skin like envenomed toads and are poisonous to the touch. And touching on his imagined wrongs in spite, he'll spit your name."

"Who would believe him?" Who indeed? Those who wanted to believe. What chance had an impoverished poet if he were denounced?

Chapter thirty-four

What chance, indeed, had an impoverished poet if Kyd, to save himself from the extremities of the inquisition, bleated, "Marlowe owns the heretical tracts"? But these 'ifs' were suppositions, startled hares set coursing by the sound of a distant barking. Where was his covert? Who would hide him if the hounds came sniffing out his lair? When the political wind was in the wrong direction, even those in the highest places were dragged from their perches and hauled to the scaffold.

He believed enough time had passed for the grass to have grown over untended paths and resolved to make overtures of amity to one whose generous offer he had spurned with prodigal haste. Surely Thomas Walsingham would not continue to bear him a grudge? His clan was now close to the Earl of Essex. And was not that impetuous young man close to the Queen? One could be scorched by standing too near a fire but one's arse was not warmed by standing naked at the crossroads.

And that raised a more practical reason for renewing certain friendships. In short, he was short of money and his rent was long overdue.

Six days after he sent a note to the Walsingham house, he received a reply. The message was brief. 'Come to Seething Lane tomorrow at noon. signed Frizer.'

The last stroke of twelve was ringing over Tower Hill when he banged on the door. A manservant with blue lips and watery eyes mumblingly asked, "Who do you wish to see?", adding helpfully, "There's nobody here."

"Is that Kit Marlowe?" Frizer shouted from inside. "Come in, come in and leave the bad weather on the threshold."

A pettish voice asserted itself. "Yes, Ingram, I've every reason to be disconcerted by such discourtesy." Frizer pulled a face and turned to reply. "If you'll bear with me, Sir Henry, we have a caller."

"See to your caller, whoever he may be. It's no concern of mine. But first fetch me more wine."

Frizer shrugged his shoulders. "Is it really you, Kit Marlowe, or your ghost? You look ravaged and racked."

"Ingram Frizer, you are provoking. Where is my wine?"

"God preserve us from peevish, half-grown brats," Frizer muttered. "I'll be with you presently, Kit."

A tall youth with a preternaturally pale face and long golden tresses arranged himself delicately in the doorway. He was dressed in the effete and ostentatious manner of rich and idle young dogs. For a minute or so he maintained his elegant pose in silence then he sighed, straightened up and fluttered his rather long eyelashes. "Have you a tongue, fellow? Amuse me with rude, rustic adages and ancient saws. What do you say about the crimson sun at the fall of evening?"

"And what do you say about the moon reflected in your mirror?"

The youth stiffened. "You're uncommonly insolent. Who are you? Are you in the service of Sir Thomas? A stable lad, perhaps?" He pulled an ornate handkerchief from his sleeve and held it to his nose. "No, do not approach. I cannot bear the rank smell of ostlers."

He flounced back into the long room as Frizer returned. "So, Kit, you've become acquainted with the Earl of Southampton. Charming, isn't he?"

The name recalled the Paris Garden incident when this rash bravado tried to kill the bear Tamburlaine. "I've seen this gaudy parrot perform a pretty dance down in Bankside."

"Ever the irreverent and reckless Marlowe. It would pay you to be polite, even deferential, to him. He has come into his inheritance and has a mind to garnish his meat with the spices of poets and scholars. Tomorrow his fickle appetite may be jaded with that dish."

"I'm not a beggar."

"I'm not blind to your circumstances, Kit. I think we should go in before his lordship throws another tantrum."

Southampton was refilling his goblet. "See what it has come to,

Frizer. I'm forced to be my own servant. Your snipper-snapper – " he nodded towards the lackey, "is either daft or deaf."

"He's bothered in both senses, Sir Henry, but I fear he's all we have in the house."

"Why is the place deserted, Ingram Frizer?"

"Sir Thomas, in his wisdom and for his health's sake, decided to take the country air as a precaution. Have you not heard the rumours?"

"God's truth, the city is plagued with rumours."

"As you say, Sir Henry, the city is plagued with rumours. Rumours of the plague."

"Hell's scourge!" Southampton decanted a mouthful of wine. "My life is on a hazard and none warned me. Frizer, if you are at fault and I should suffer – "

"Be easy in your mind, Sir Henry. It's a mild outbreak of fever peculiar to those foreign wretches who swarm round Cripplegate.

"Those aliens are the cause of many ills." He turned to Christopher. "And you, what have you to say to this?"

"Christopher Marlowe is innocent of the facts, Sir Henry," Frizer said quickly.

"Marlowe? I've heard the name – now, let me think – in what respect?"

Frizer gave Christopher a conspiratorial smile. "Marlowe is our laureate poet as witness the Tamburlaine drama and the Malta-Jew play."

"Ah, yes, the Jew play. Robin Devereux told me it had given him great pleasure and plans to present a performance before the Queen. He contends that there is one such vile Hebrew, disguised as a Christian, who has found favour at the court and whom Robin swears is in the pay of our enemies. But this is politics and these matters weary me. Frizer, I won't stay another day in this festering midden. Get my carriage ready."

Southampton strolled round the room, hummed a tune and affected a studied interest in the Arras tapestry. His height was enhanced by thick-soled, high-heeled shoes giving him a stiff-kneed gait and he tapped his cheeks with his finger-tips as if to make sure the white paint had not flaked off.

"So you're Marlowe the poet?" He spoke over his shoulder. "I have one of your kind in my employ. He has an adept hand, as good as any trained scrivener, and when he's not writing his interminable sonnets, fills the post of my secretary. Now, what's the fellow's name?"

"Thomas Watson?"

"No, no, I no longer have to countenance Watson." The youth turned from his studies. "Marlowe, I need more wine."

Christopher knew he was expected to play the lackey but it was not in him to act the nursemaid for anyone. "There's two ways to fatten a goose," he mused to himself. "Cram its gullet with butter while it lives or stuff pottage up its arse when it's dead." Aloud he said with ironic courtesy, "Indeed, let us be pleasure-steeped in Walsingham's sweet offerings." He picked up a goblet from the table and filled their cups to the brim. "To whom or to what shall we drink? To the gods? Our glorious Queen? Your golden future? Or the death and disarray of our kingdom's enemies?"

"You assume the privileges of a court jester without any of his clownage wit." A faint smile threatened to crack the pargeting. "We'll drink to what remains of your short life, Marlowe, for it's my belief no one can be so filled with stubborn pride and hope to see the sun setting on his old age." He swallowed his drink in one draught but Christopher merely sipped his. "Set your mind to a brave and splendid epic, written with all the fine turns and leaps of your genius and designed, not for vulgar applause, but to delight the heart and intellect of one such as I. Dedicate in spirit and signature to me and it will prove most rewarding to you. Where is that Frizer? I swear, this reeking, fever-filled city stifles me."

When the young man had minced away, Christopher and Frizer sat opposite each other in the long room. "I'm famished, Kit, and I imagine, so are you. I've heard your belly rattle like a demented kettle-drum. And now to business. You wish to be retained in our service."

"I did not say that."

"Nor write it large in red lettering but it's marked in your face and clothes. And also in your note to us. The courtesy of the seasons, indeed. Rather the discourtesy of poverty."

Christopher mustered a show of indignation. "My greetings to Thomas Walsingham were sincerely meant. As for my service, it's not a geegaw hawked at the Fleet Market and I've no need to traipse high and low for a bidder."

"Do you think we'd haggle for your service? Have you had bidders? Perhaps our prancing earl? Help yourself to more of this. You'll wear out the bottom of the dish with your scraping. Did our noble lord here offer to smother you with gold, I wonder? He's rich in promises, they're cheaply minted, and generous with vows but you'll wait an age for a paltry gift from his purse. Young Essex, for political reasons of his own, is pleased with your Jew play but he has, I've been told, taken offence with your Edward II drama and says you mock him and his pretensions in the person of one Gaveston, the king's minion. Do not ask me to explain the ins and outs of it. I'm no judge of these subtle matters and I've not seen the play." He went over to the dole cupboard and returned with a ledger, quill and an inkpot. "Without any more shilly-shally, we'll arrange our affairs in the proper manner." He placed a gold coin by Christopher's dish. "In the final reckoning, it is I who must give a favourable account. Take the money and be witness I've marked both you and it down on the page."

"I'm not a hireling." Christopher's protest lacked conviction. The coin was more than he had received for his last two plays. "And in what way am I expected to repay this bounty? Smother babies in their cots? Poison wells? Slit a throat or two?"

"That's the stuff and clamour of your dramas, Kit. Let's put an end to this acting and put the money in your purse." He recorded the transaction and blew on the page. "I've neglected to buy drying powder. Now, Kit, as we've heard, you've been a guest from time to time of Sir Walter Ralegh."

"Your hearing is at fault or your informer is a liar. I've only been once at Durham House. Is there some law which forbids me being acquainted with Ralegh?"

"Heaven forbid there should be such a rule. Surely Ralegh is a man after your own heart. He's learned, a wit, a poet and he does keep scholarly company."

"And there's enmity between your faction and his."

"This unreasonable division, this childish animosity, is a cause of deep sadness and dire weakness when men of proven loyalty are called to be as one. We would be pleased, Kit, if you were to be a binding thread, a link. We urge you to cultivate your friendship with Sir Walter and his company and serve to allay our fears of anything being said or done that may endanger that noble gentleman or our kingdom."

The coin in Christopher's fist felt hot enough to burn and he wondered if, as had happened before, the gold would melt and leave him with a token of dross.

Chapter thirty-five

What can a gold coin buy? Dross? It bought Christopher the goodwill of his landlady, more palatable food than rye-and-bean bread, the service of a laundress to wash his clothes for the first time in six months and ease of mind to settle down to write Doctor Faustus. His ration of medication from Lopez was nearly exhausted but as both pain and rash had disappeared and he had become used to the jaw-ache and loose teeth, he was not too concerned on that score. To speed up whatever remedy was contained in the so-called Lombardy Balls, he swallowed two instead of the recommended one and after struggling with the welling nausea for several minutes, pressed out the paper and dipped the quill into the inkpot.

Though a creature of his own devising, Doctor John Faustus was proving intractable and would not wear the motley clothes of a capering clown. Surely his desire to suborn fate into granting him the giddy tenure of youth, his lust for the apparel of wealth and his half-baked quest for knowledge were subjects for derision not pity? Yet, for all that, Faustus's venal ambitions were in sympathy with the commonality of man. Who among the thousands swarming London's streets would hesitate to chance their immortality for a pot of ale, a platter of meat and a warm coat? Or a gold coin?

And what of Mephistophilis, this Secretary of State for the Satanic Kingdom, his ledger ever ready to mark down the demonic transaction? Rather than the dreaded, glowering figure wreathed in sulphuric smoke with pointed tail lashing in hellish rage, he came on stage garbed in saturnine gloom, a sad sombre angel who saw humanity as God's ultimate folly.

It was near evening and soon Christopher must choose whether to light a precious candle and take Faustus several pages towards his doom or, in the darkness, contemplate the life of Marlowe, the flight of Icarus.

He began to write, "Now that the gloomy shadow of earth,/ Longing to view Orion's drizzling look – " and his quill scratched across the paper till – "Then fear not, Faustus, but be resolute, and try the uttermost magic can perform."

Then what shall he say? "Come forth from your infernal – " Infernal? No, that is the baggage of ill-lettered scribblers. Would hell's emissary desert the pleasant company of poets and philosophers at the behest of an obscure German doctor who couldn't string a decent Latin sentence together?

"No, I'll give Faustus the learned speech of a Cambridge scholar. Without a doubt, Lucifer has attended those famed halls, either as a student or a divine, and will say to Mephistophilis, 'I am familar with that rhetoric'."

Christopher closed his eyes and began to compose the incantation according to Livy's strict rules of Latin Grammar.

"Sint mihi dei Acherontis propitii! Valeat numen triplex Jehovae! Ignei, aerii, aquatani spiritus, salvete!"

"What are you muttering, Christopher Marlowe?" a voice asked from across the room.

He knew he should have been angry with this uninvited intruder but instead he calmly replied, "Composing the words that will raise Mephistophilis. Are you he? No, he wouldn't manifest himself until the correct command has been completed."

"What arrogance to imagine divinity could be commanded. You're glutted with over-weening pride."

Christopher turned to face the vague shape in the shadows. "I didn't hear you enter. How long have you been there?"

"While you are, I am. Consider what you are about, Marlowe. It is a dangerous presumption for mortal man to conjure those ineffable powers from the depths."

"Why this solemn conference over a trifle? It's only a play, a long-winded drama with enough bombastical speeches to gain Alleyn the groundlings' applause, Henslowe a half-share of the takings and sufficient money to give me a week's provisions."

"For your sake and mine, for we are one, Christopher Marlowe, I would that it were so simple. But you've hazarded your life on lesser trifles and now you gamble your soul on the blind throw of a dice. Study what you have written and think about what you have yet to write. Surely Doctor Faustus, unhappily dubbed by you 'lucky', is the reflected image of unfortunate Marlowe?"

"I've no wish to debate with a shade. Present yourself. Who are you?"

The figure came forward till they were face to face, nose to nose. It was as if he held a mirror to his features.

"I charge you, whatever evil spirit you may be, whatever brain-fevered illusion you may be, to leave. Don't haunt my nights. Go, I refuse to gaze upon you." He closed his eyes and slowly spoke the names of the seven holy angels before opening them again. The morning sunlight struggled to shine through the grimy window.

In the following days and weeks Christopher only stopped writing to go to the eating-house where he listened with some disdain to rumours of fresh outbreaks of the plague. Themes of ultimate disaster were as endemic as the pestilence itself and were the stock-in-trade of every ranting preacher who saw the four horsemen of the apocalypse galloping around the corner. The world outside was dull, shabby, passionless and circumscribed, bringing the taste of ashes to the lips, while within his hermetical seclusion his universe expanded. There were no limits to space, no restrictions to time and he peopled his chamber with antique poets, philosophers and sages. In the evenings, when he tired of writing and the light had faded, he would converse with these shades and in their imagined shapes and forms they became more real than the owners of the disembodied voices that seeped through the tenement walls.

Prime among his nightly visitors was his own spectre. Rather, that which had been his obverse self in the beginning had become, by subtle transformation, Doctor John Faustus.

One evening, late in the second month of his anchorite life, his cell seemed crowded with an inordinate number of shades conversing among themselves. It was some time before he could gain their attention. Only the Faustus figure, now older and haggard like one who had overstayed his welcome on earth, came forward. "Is Mephistophilis among your company?" Christopher asked testily. "I'm not satisfied with what he says are the true movements of the celestial bodies. Do they move on one axle tree?

I've read that this is not so. For my money, Mephistophilis is both a liar and a braggart."

"Pray that he is, Christopher Marlowe, pray for my sake and yours. But am I not still damned? Will my audacious conjuring, my Satanic pact, my abjuration of Christ, be rewarded with the fires of hell? How will it end, Christopher Marlowe? No, no, there's no finality. All eternity gapes before me."

Christopher did not reply. Three times he had begun the final scene, three times he had written, "Ah, Faustus. Now hast thou but one bare hour to live," and each time he had crumpled the piece of paper in his fist.

"You do not speak, Christopher Marlowe. What terror possesses me?" A church bell rang in the distance and from below came a sudden outburst of wailing. "It strikes. It strikes. Oh, merciful God save me. They come! My God, my God, let me breathe a while!"

The flimsy door to Christopher's room was nearly torn from its hinges and his landlady stood swaying in the entrance, a horn lantern held above her head and her mouth working like a drowning fish.

"We're ruined. We're destroyed. Utterly," she gasped as she found her voice. "Sweet Yesu, what harm have we done, I ask you? By the blood of Christ, I swear on my bended knees and on the head of my unfortunate daughter that I'll lead a clean and holy life. This I'll swear if only she hasn't died from what we dread! I know you're learned. Look at her and tell us the truth, for God's sake. Haven't I heard you, night after night, talking to yourself in many voices? It's said when the Almighty's finger touches you with madness, you're granted other gifts to make a balance. Them whose minds wander wander free of the plague."

He was ushered into a room where her five daughters stood in a frightened huddle. The landlady pointed to a greasy curtain. "She's been in there for seven days now, and God help us, we couldn't afford callers with her moaning and groaning and she barely touching a scrap of food or a drop of water. Now she's quiet, dead quiet." She gave him the lantern. The sixth and youngest daughter was stretched out on the bare floor of the cubby-hole. There was a suffocating stench as if her entrails were exposed. Her parted lips exposed the gaps in her teeth, her nostrils appeared to be gnawed, raw sores clustered round her mouth and cheeks and a rash of red pimples covered her neck and breasts. He staggered, almost blindly, back to the adjoining room.

There were sufficient signs on their worried faces to show that more than one sister would depart from this den with similar scars of lascivious profit on her body. "She's died of the pox," he muttered.

The sisters embraced each other and their mother fell down on her knees with a thump that shook the floorboards, raising her voice in a loud paean of praise to the Lord God Almighty on High for sparing their humble dwelling from the scourge of the plague.

Christopher declined the offer of the surviving daughters as a reward for his expertise and returned to his room. He was stunned at the sight that met his bleary eyes. His books, papers and clothes were scattered as if a turbulent and silent wind had swept through the place. "Did my companions of the night greet the morning with a berserk revel of their own?" he asked himself. Searching among the debris, he found clean paper, the quill and inkpot and, crouching by the window, began to write, "Ah, Faustus, now hast thou but one bare hour to live, and then thou must be damned perpetually."

Chapter thirty-six

Christopher's wraiths were exorcised when he penned the final scene of Doctor Faustus's damnation and his room reverted to its true role of shabby, squalid lodging-place. He let a week or so elapse, amended a passage here and there – he preferred his draft to be more fair than foul – and then, with the manuscript in a satchel, set off to see either Alleyn or Henslowe at the Rose playhouse.

On the way down he passed the second youngest daughter busy scrubbing the stairs. She looked up at him with a crescent grin. "God keep you, sir. The sun's shining mightily today for sure." Her front teeth were missing. Downstairs her mother stood four-square in the street doorway.

"May I be stricken down on this very threshold by the hand of God if I tell a word of a lie," she was saying to a dour-faced man. "I keep a clean, neat, tidy and respectable house, I do, and though I say it myself, poor as we are, it's fit for the Queen herself to pay us a call."

"We've been told it's a brothel," the man said.

"Oh, the filth, the poison that comes from some vipers' mouths. God help me and isn't it all because I keep myself to myself and let off my rooms to respectable gentlemen to provide for my fatherless children."

"And what about your dead daughter? I was told she was riddled with the pox."

"And a right pox-ridden riddling, I say, to them slanderous scabfaces who told you that. Didn't I say to her, I said time out of mind, wrap yourself warm when you traipse out in the street, she being on the weakly side but would she, oh no she wouldn't, Yesu have mercy on the giddy girl, and to make matters worse, she picks up a terrible itch from the chicken feathers." The woman lifted her apron to her face and wailed, "Oh, my poor delicate flower. Yesu, Yesu, can't they let my lamb rest in peace?"

The man shuffled his feet, embarrassed by this public show of grief. "I'm only doing my job. You can't be too careful nowadays. And who's he?"

The landlady lowered her apron, stepped to one side and smiled benignly at her lodger. As Christopher walked away, he could hear her explaining that he was one of the fine scholars who rented a room in her respectable house and, though a little mad, was quite harmless. Indeed, as the girl said, the sun was shining mightily. London Bridge was crowded and the vendors did a roaring trade.

On the other side of the river, behind St Saviour's church and the approaches to Bankside, the picture drastically changed to dismal and deserted streets, locked-up houses and shuttered taverns. Christopher was so preoccupied with his own thoughts that he had reached Maiden Lane before fully realising how lifeless and empty the area was. Puzzled and not a little perturbed, he continued on to The Rose only to find it boarded up.

"You'll see nothing there today, Kit Marlowe." There was no mistaking the broad Warwickshire brogue. "I reckon it'll be a month of Sundays before there'll be any revels or antic hay this side of the water."

"So The Rose is not in bloom," Christopher said. "Will we have better picking in the Paris Garden, Will?"

Shakespeare's rustic expression of bucolic gloom and doom hardly altered. "It's more of a season for bittercress, goutweed and ragwort, I'd say. This touch of warmth will raise the wet to the top soil, there'll be hasty sprouting and then, I fear, the sudden frost will nip the buds." He sniffed the air. "There's a rottenness abroad, Kit. Can you smell it?"

"Bankside has a rare ordure of its own beyond compare, Will, even to the mulch of your Stratford compost heaps."

"Ay, for sure, there's nothing like mare's piss to make sour silage take a turn for the sweet and it's said a rampant stallion's shit – "

Christopher thumped the playhouse's bolted door. "Piss and shit, Will, why is it barred against us?" A spiral of wind-whipped dust danced down the empty lane. "And why are the taverns shut tight?"

"They're closing the whorehouses as well."

"It must be the end of the world."

Shakespeare seemed to ponder this possibility for a moment and then, with a muttered, "They're mucking out the stables right now. Come and see," he strode down Horseshoe Alley with the loping gait of one born to step over wide puddles. Christopher trotted after him.

A crowd had gathered by the river wall and were deriving free entertainment from the sight of officials decanting the stews. The Sugar Loaf had already been emptied and the last of its waddling beauties could be seen passing Deadman's Place on their way to the Clink. The Elephant and The Vine were being cleared without too much bother, apart from a few screams and ripe imprecations, but there were difficulties at The Beerpot. The entrance was barricaded and from the upstairs windows, the besieged bombarded their attackers with pots, pans, scraps of furniture and the contents of urinal buckets. The onlookers delighted in the discomfiture of the law officers and were vociferous partisans of the prostitutes.

Christopher and Shakespeare, the latter a little reluctant to leave the battle-scene, continued on towards the Bankside Steps. The raiders had not yet reached this stretch and the desperate tarts fled with their cloth bundles towards the Mint sanctuary, but some locals had taken it upon themselves to be law-enforcers.

A wisp of a girl tore herself from the grasp of a grinning lout and a stout shopkeeper and, running across the road, grabbed Christopher's sleeve. "Good sir, save me. Tell them I'm no harlot," she pleaded.

"Be merciful, Kit," Shakespeare said as he watched the vigilant citizens saunter over to them. "Pretend she's a country cousin, ignorant of the city, who's wandered from ditch to drift like a grazed turnip." Aloud he said, "Why, isn't this your brother's child, expected up from Canterbury yesterday?"

The girl and Christopher suddenly recognised each other. She turned to her erstwhile captors. "There, didn't I say I'm no strumpet and if you don't believe me ask my uncle Robert Greene. He'll confirm the truth of the matter."

Shakespeare smirked at the name of Greene and said, "Go to it, Uncle Robert, and confirm the truth."

Christopher looked with distaste at the upturned face of the young whore and the colony of red sores on her lips. "My friend is jesting," he said. "My name is Marlowe, not Greene. Do you think my family would own to a burning faggot? I don't know this baggage."

It was as if he had slapped her cheeks. "But you did say – come live with me – "

The shopkeeper grabbed Helen by the scruff of the neck and shook her so hard that her pathetic belongings fell to the ground. "It's your sort and them playhouses that's brought the pestilence on us," he growled. "Come on. You belong in the Clink." But the lout had deserted him to chase the whore-ward who had just then limped out of her brothel with a large bundle slung over her shoulder. The youth grabbed the woman, flung her to the ground and disappeared down an alley with the bundle.

"And when Peter was asked a second time, he said, 'I do not know this man'. Shall there be a third asking, Kit? For whomsoever denies one of these denies me."

"You prattle platitudes like an old woman, Will. Why didn't you prove your Christian charity and rescue the lamb? Could it be that the Arden poachers are not so ardent when the sheep are rotten with worms?"

"It was the deer that cost me dear, but I'll bend your analogy to ask why I should risk wool grease when our stout merchant is touched by holy grace? He's like the good shepherd who gathers in the lost lamb."

The shopkeeper was talking to her like a village elder chiding a wayward child while she stood with her head bowed and her hands behind her back. They then appeared to have come to an agreement and, instead of going towards the Clink prison, turned right down Deadman's Place.

"For his love, his reward will be laid up in heaven," Shakespeare said wryly.

"For his lechery, his reward will lay him down in the ground," Christopher retorted. "I'm tired of this futility. Let's find a tavern open to honest men and poets."

"Where better than where the whores lie down."

"Are you stricken with perversity, Will? Haven't you had your fill of strumpets for the day?

"Strumpets and trumpets shriek the same any day but today my belly shrieks for a fill of Lambeth Ale. I'm thinking of a place beyond St Olave's and near the ruins of Bermondsey Abbey. It's a green sward which the commonality – "

"Let's hope the taverns are not touched by the ordinance." He strode off in the direction of Winchester Steps and within ten minutes they were seated in The Crowing Hen.

They drank their ale in sips, spoke of banal subjects and fragmented their conversation with long pauses as if neither knew the other sufficiently to risk familiarities.

Yet in some respects they were similar, even in the year and season of their births. They were provincial boys seeking to root their talents in the uncertain soil of London's literary world. In other respects, they were dissimilar. Marlowe was the university wit, the creator of mighty lines, blazing star in his apogee, profligate of words and ideas, rash and impetuous. Shakespeare was the grammar-school boy, usually taciturn in company. a listener, a gatherer, a shrewd peasant. The first lit rockets. The second sowed seeds.

When they called for more drink, Christopher insisted, without too much objection from his companion, on playing the host. He had learned to be parsimonious with the little he earned from his writing but the remains of the golden crown, that Judas money, burned the seams of his purse.

They passed from polite trivialities to a tentative exchange of confidences. Christopher was not too surprised to discover the other was the secretary mentioned by Southampton – he had guessed as much – and there was a momentary look of displeasure on Shakespeare's face when Christopher revealed his hopes of benefiting from that erratic youth's estate.

With the tasting of the third round of ale, they fell to praising each other's work.It was true Shakespeare had not made a great mark with his first-produced drama whereas Christopher had the advantage of several fruitful years, but the latter felt it would be indelicate, not to say destructive to their amity, to appear to be condescending.

No such qualms bothered Shakespeare. Though a self-proclaimed admirer and avid student of Marlowe's plays, he stated firmly that the dramas lacked stagecraft; but, he added quickly, the magnificence of the rhetorics more than made up for that. He dwelled long and lovingly on certain passages which he repeated with relish as if to savour their full beauty. The line from Edward II, "And as a traveller goes to discover countries yet unknown," seemed to particularly intrigue him, so much that Christopher said jokingly, "As you love it so well, I'll grant it to you as a gift."

Having elected themselves the most praiseworthy poets in London, if not the whole kingdom, it was a short step to railing against those grasping people like printers and playhouse managers who cared more for money than merit. The writer, they both agreed, was not cherished. There was nothing for it but to replenish their self-esteem with more ale.

"And such are our circumstances, Kit, that – if I may quote once more from your drama – he must needs go that the Devil drives." It was, in fact, a mangled quote from Kyd's Spanish Tragedy which in turn was a clumsy translation from the Italian. Christopher allowed the error to pass without comment. "And we have to face the slings and arrows of intemperate fortune," continued Shakespeare, "when we ruffle a sea of trouble with the slights and scorn of chance offence."

"You have a talent for the apt metaphor, Will," Christopher said. To himself he thought, "And an exceeding talent for the mixed metaphor." He also wondered from whom his companion had borrowed it.

"And isn't your Edward II an exemplar?" Shakespeare slurred the last word. "For that red fox whelp, the young Earl of Essex flew into a tantrum and swore you mocked him in the person of Gaveston, the royal lover and minion. You've made an enemy there, Kit, and no mistake."

It was near to closing time when men who had drunk deeply ponderously turn to the serious problems that afflict the world.

Christopher deplored the bovine stupidity of the rabble, ever prepared to rise in riots of ignorance and bigotry, the merchants' obtuse philosophy of greed, the insolence of office-holders and the factional and divisive politics of the age. As a prime example of the folly of all these, he cited the blundering attempt to contain the plague by closing the Bankside brothels, taverns and playhouses.

"Would you cut off the little finger of your left hand if you had a headache?" he asked.

"Would you kill the geese if your wheat had rust?" was Shakespeare's rural question. For his part, he favoured the rule of an enlightened, benevolent and necessarily despotic monarch. Kingship was in the gift of God and, therefore, only the Divinity had the prerogative to exact retribution on those who abused their elevated position. To rebel or intrigue against the kingship, no matter how just the cause, was the same as raising your fist against the Almighty. As for the plague – if there was one – at times there was a need for a scouring, a need for a winnowing, a need for a culling. When, either through war or pestilence, the herd was diminished and the chaff burned, then those who remained had room to breathe, room to grow and all was for the best.

They staggered from the tavern towards the ferry steps, haggled with the boatman who only took drunks at twice the normal price, settled in their seats and spent the crossing in a pleasant blur of scurrilous songs and pot-valiant boasts. They disembarked near Billingsgate as a two-horse wagon surrounded by a small party of men approached.

"Whoa, you jades of Asia," Shakespeare impulsively shouted and stepped into their path.

One of the men shoved the exuberant poet to one side and snarled, "Whoa yourself, you cup-sodden cully, or you'll be taking a ride with them up there."

The pair could see the legs and arms of the ill-concealed bodies. With a chill that cooled his roistering fervour, Christopher recognised the scavengers of the dead and dying as those whom he had met in the outcasts' colony up the river. Was their day coming, as their leader had predicted in the ruined chapel?

The macabre encounter sobered the two men and they were silent until the sounds of the nags' clip-clop and the rumbling of the cart-wheels faded beyond the Postern Gate.

"They that are after the flesh," said Shakespeare in a low tone, "do mind the things of the flesh."

Christopher half-remembered the quote but could not place it in its context. He turned to ask its origin and was somewhat surprised to see his companion surreptitiously making the sign of the cross. 'Is our Will a recusant, a secret Papist?' he wondered.

"But they who are after the spirit are of the spirit." Shakespeare continued. "For to be carnally minded is death." He laughed. "We're like street ranters with our snatches of Bible fragments and if we stay here any longer we'll be tossing country sayings and old saws back and forth like a pair of midnight tennis-players. I'm off to my lodgings now, Kit, and I pray my landlord does not smell the beer on my breath. They are stern and forbidding Huguenots, strict in their strictures. When shall we meet again, Kit?" He grasped Christopher's two hands in his.

"When fair is foul and foul is fair."

"Then don't let our farewell be foul."

"Farewell, Will Shakespeare."

"Farewell, Kit Marlowe."

Chapter thirty-seven

With Bankside's pleasure-domes closed, Christopher had no choice but to offer his Doctor Faustus drama to James Burbage for production in the greedy manager's Shoreditch playhouse, The Theatre. But all had not gone well during the first performance. One devil too many had appeared on the stage.

"Swear by the blood of Christ it was not so." James Burbage's jowls quivered. Though he feared demonic visitations as much as anyone, his anxiety had a more rational basis. If the official busybodies, spurred on by the religious trouble-makers, were to hear of this, they would close his playhouses and lose him a lot of money.

"I did count them. There was Giles as Gluttony and Perse as Pride and – " The youth who had played Helen of Troy and had stammered Lechery's three lines began to enumerate the actors.

"To hell with you," James's son Richard Burbage shouted. "O, this feeds my soul. Yes, yes, the more devils the merrier. It'll bring the rabble down in droves to witness real fire-and-brimstone fiends and they'll delight in the dreaded rank smells of sulphuric damnation. Hurry back to your lodgings, Kit, and fetch for us one of those magical books and we shall conjure up a parcel of demons. Those leaping lumps of charcoal neither eat nor drink so they won't cost a penny. Then we'll be rid of these line-mumblers and stutterers."

"I've no need to fetch a tome for I've an incantation firmly fixed in my mind." He raised his arms and intoned a jumble of Latin and Greek words plus a few he had just invented. A few of the less credulous smiled at the joke but others stared at him with horror. One cried, "Stop, stop this blasphemy, Marlowe."

"You've cut short my diabolic invocation," said Christopher, pretending to be vext. "And I doubt if I've uttered enough to bring one of his Satanic Majesty's entourage into our presence."

Suddenly an actor pointed towards the entrance and yelled,

"Lucifer!" Even the cynics cursed at the sight of the dark shape in the doorway.

"Not Lucifer but a near-relative," replied the apparition. "I've travelled far and wide to meet him, or Satan, or Mephistophilis or Kit Marlowe. They're all one to me." Ben Jonson, dressed in the leather jerkin, broad hat and high boots of a Flanders soldier, swaggered in. "Will I not do as well as any warlock? Look," he brandished a long sword. "I can thrust, parry, chop, slice off a man's head, spill his guts and spike him like a stuck pig. Is there none who'll make use of my butcher's trade? How about you, sir?" He marched up to old Burbage. "I would stand guard over your coffers and smite down the widows and orphans who dare lay hands on your hoard."

"I'd rather lay in my coffin than – than -" Burbage blustered.

"By heavens, sir, you've lied for your coffers and you'll lay in your coffin before the week is out, judging by that raw sore on your nose."

As the manager's hand shot up to his face, the one-time soldier strode over to Christopher.

"What d'you say, Canterbury's Chaucer, Dover's Dante? Commend me to your friends. Tell them that there's a worthy fellow home from the wars, well versed in the art of slaughter and yet, unlike the commonality of brutal and ignorant warriors, he's a learned Cambridge man who can swear in Latin, curse in Greek and be damned in English."

"Bravo, Ben Jonson, bravo," Richard Burbage said, "but for today, warriors are the least of our needs."

Jonson assumed a doleful expression. "What then is to be my fate? Rejected, unloved, there is nothing for me but to wander abroad and beg for my bread. A soldier unarmed, a butcher cleaved from the meat counter, a scholar unread, a fiddle without a bow. Where will such a wretch find refuge and employment?" He grinned broadly as if struck with a brilliant idea. "Where else but here in The Theatre. I've so little to offer that there is nothing for me but to become an actor and a playwright." His dejected expression returned. "Alas,no. The stage will not bear Ben Jonson's light footfalls for many an age and the Theatre is closed to me. And I gravely fear it is closed to everyone else into the bargain."

"What are you blabbering?" Burbage asked. "Unless you're blind as well as bothered, you can see the playhouse is open and we're busy preparing for today's performance."

"Then prepare to perform a different rite. Trotting hard on my heels comes the magistrate and his bully-boys who, with joint and corporative voice, shall pronounce the temporal death of both The Theatre and Curtain playhouses." Some were prepared to take Jonson's words according to Jonson's merit, but others stoically accepted the expected blow. James Burbage flopped down on a seat, his face ashen, a shaking ball of dismay. Ben Jonson waved his sword above his head. "Gentlemen players, this sword is at your service and together we'll put these pinch-arsed officials to rout and drive them into Bedlam's cloisters where they so rightly belong."

None was eager to do battle and when the magistrate, an old dodderer wrapped in three fur coats, came with two burly constables to nail the suppression order on the door, the disconsolate actors were only interested in besieging old Burbage for their pay. As Christopher rose to leave, Richard Burbage asked him where he was bound.

"There's no profit in haggling with your father in his present state. I'm off to St Paul's. There's a bookseller there who owes me money from the printing of Tamburlaine."

"I'll walk the stretch of the road with you. I've business of my own beyond Ludgate."

"And Gabriel and I will take up the rear guard," Jonson said. The four set off down Bishopsgate Street towards the city. He was still in a high mood, laughing loudly, bragging, joking, calling out to every young woman he saw and challenging by word or look every brute who crossed their path. It would be some time before he became used to the fact that he was no longer a soldier in a foreign country.

"When I asked you to conjure a parcel of devils, Kit, it was only in jest," said Richard Burbage, "and little did I imagine they'd appear in the shape of the magistrate and his hirelings." He laughed. "Take care that your next invocation brings us a company of angels."

"And what about your company of players, Richard? Will they be dispersed?"

"It's only a squall, Kit, but, even so, we've made provisions against this misfortune and our wagons wait at Newington Butts to take us on a tour of the country towns. In a few days' time we shall be in Canterbury and you're very welcome to come with us."

Christopher was tempted by the pleasure of a journey on the London Road, that straight and runnel-scarred highway which once boasted the steady march of Roman cohorts, with the ebullient troupe of players. It would also be safer.

It was now more than two years since he had seen his parents; and there still lurked their cherished hope that he would marry some rich merchant's surplus child. Could it be any better or worse than living on the abyss of utter poverty, at the beck and call of such creatures as Frizer?

When Christopher and Richard entered the city through Bishopsgate, they deliberately put a fair distance between themselves and the rumbustious pair behind them. The outrageous Ben Jonson's prank was to accost any well-clad man who had an air of self-importance with a cry of, "Sir, I pray you. Stand awhile." Then, pointing his sword at the victim's face, he would loudly declare, "Sir, you are a danger to your fellow citizens and should go at once to the pesthouse. You have a large red spot on your nose."

Though some denied an outbreak of plague and others said that it was confined to foreigners, the rumours had brought out the doom-and-damnation mongers and they buzzed around the open space of St Paul's Churchyard like flies on a midden heap. When they crossed in front of a plinth, Christopher recognised a ranter's voice.

"See, see, there in our midst, crawls the damned Faustus' own creator, Lucifer's familar himself." Baines, in the fury of his diatribe, pointed out Christopher to the assembled gawpers. "It's this cursed whelp of hell with his blasphemous and atheistic conjuration who's summoned Satan's hordes to dance upon the scourged bodies of our beloved wives and children."

"Away from here, Kit," Richard Burbage urged, "or he'll have them tear you to bits."

At that moment Jonson and Spencer appeared. The one-time soldier strode forward and prodded the fat man's stomach with his sword point. "You, sir, are an epidemical abomination and a rancid suet pudding." He brought his blade up to the preacher's face. "Your nose, sir, is a purple festering wen and it's my duty, for the sake of all clean-living people, to take you henceforth to the pesthouse."

"And you're Asmodeus's misbegotten cur," the infuriated Baines screamed, "freshly torn from the rank belly of your whoring mother."

Jonson turned to the enraptured listeners. "Don't listen – to the black bilge spewed by this dog's vomit. To the pesthouse with him, I say, but be warned by me, let no man lay a hand on him lest he be defiled. Stone him, I say, stone him on his way. Who will be the first?"

"I'll cast the first stone," Spencer shouted and flung a pebble at Baines. A group of bored apprentices joined in the fun and within seconds the air was filled with missiles. Christopher left the turmoil and hurried around the cathedral to the bookstall area. To his chagrin, the place was empty.

Skirting the Cathedral's precinct, he returned to his lodgings. The gully of a street was unnaturally quiet and, except for two shawled women with the look of his landlady's daughters who quickly passed by, it was quite empty. When he began to climb the stairs, the landlady appeared and asked, "Where are you going?" Her face was deadly pale. "Gather your belongings or you'll be carted away with the rest of us."

She beckoned him into her rooms and pointed to where three of her plague-stricken daughters lay on the floor. Two were dead and the third, moaning and groaning, had not long to live.

"Hurry, hurry now," his landlady whispered and pushed him hard in the back. "Yesu, Yesu, why am I so cursed. Go, go and never set foot in this place again."

Chapter thirty-eight

If a fatted calf had been available at a reasonable price, Catherine Marlowe would have sacrificed it to celebrate her son's return to Canterbury. Instead, a few plump chickens went to the chopping block and, as a special treat, she bought in an extra supply of marchpane.

For the first week at home, Christopher spent the best part of each day with Richard and Cuthbert Burbage, business manager for their theatrical company The Lord Strange's Men. Their productions of The Malta-Jew and Doctor Faustus went well. Fortunately there was no more of the extra-devil-on-the-stage nonsense.

Late one dank and drizzly night before the company left for Ramsgate, he took a short cut home through the cloth market. It was the end of the trading day and the dealers were busy counting their takings and stowing bolts on the handcarts. The position of a stall was a measure of a trader's standing and success: the nearer the middle, the nearer the heart and the richer the pickings. The nearer the edge, the nearer the precipice and the poorer the crumbs. It was here that the Faulds stood behind their bench and displayed their marked-down bargains of off-cuts and shoddy cloth.

Christopher failed to recognise the once-affluent and now pathetic couple and would have passed them if the woman had not called out, "It's young Marlowe, wonder of wonders."

"Well, well, by my life, young Marlowe." The man spoke in the vague way of one who could not quite connect the face with the name. "So you're with us again, well, well." He lurched towards an old crone who was bent over a pile of remnants. "Excellent material, madam, excellent material and at our price, we're giving it away.

"Seize every opportunity is my motto," he said when he returned. "Only way to advance. Make every minute work, every hour profitable and at the end of the week you're nobody's man but your own. My guiding principle, aye, through thick and thin." He puffed up his cheeks and gustily expelled his breath. "Never mind what them moaning Jeremiahs prattle, trade is on the mend, I say, and with caution and careful counting – I speak the truth, don't I? I've always said you're a clever lad, young Marlowe, I have. You've brains to spare and when you're fit in yourself to come into the trade – " he slapped the bench " – I've a place ready and waiting right here for you."

His wife sidled up to Christopher. "And we know, don't we, who'll be overjoyed to see you again." She simpered. "And we'll fix the wedding day when you've joined the business. There's a contract, you know."

Catherine Marlowe thought otherwise. "Them and their contract. They haven't a leg to stand on." There was, of course, the vext question of the dowry which had been swallowed up by John Marlowe's debts. "As for that," she said dismissively, "they'll have to wait the same as everybody else. And fancy them thinking Kit'll be party to their business. What business, I ask you? A tu'penny shoddy-stall on the edge of the market. It'll go to rack and ruin the same as their other ventures. Didn't the old fool hazard their wealth in buying and selling them heathen blackamoors from Africa? Then the Almighty took a hand in their bargaining and scuttled the lot in the middle of the ocean without a trace. Do you think I'd have a son of mine wedded into a family of common stallholders? Kit's a better catch now than he was two years ago and with his dramas being performed right here in Canterbury."

Catherine had never abandoned her hope of a union with wealth and respectability; something she had not pressed too strongly with her daughters. Her youngest Ann, a tavern-keeper's wife, had given birth to three children and was now carrying a fourth, while the middle girl Dorothy had recently been married to a tanner's son.

Catherine put a brave face on it. "He's a fine, upstanding Christian and has great prospects in the leather trade."

John Marlowe cackled. "Tanners smell of dogshit," he said on one of the rare occasions that he spoke. He appeared to have shrunk with age and alcohol and his hands continually shook. Occasionally he would emit a peculiar snigger as if he found life a sad joke.

"Margaret's a grand comfort to me," said Catherine, looking benignly at her eldest and unmarried daughter who was scowling at her sewing. "What would I do if my lambkin was snapped up by a bold braggart? She's a precious pearl."

The precious pearl muttered a curse when the thread broke, gathered up her sewing and stomped out of the room. "She's vext entirely with her single state, God help her, and she growing older by the day. You're not a chicken yourself, Kit, but it matters less for a man if he weds at nineteen or ninety. When I've fixed you good and proper with a wealthy bride, see your way to putting a few gold coins in Meg's dowry chest."

Christopher had thought of his homecoming as an interval between acts, a time when the clowns gambolled and the audience made assignations and emptied their bladders. The presence of the theatrical company in the town had been a pleasant interlude; but now they were gone and with his mother rewriting her old script, his stay in Canterbury threatened to turn into a prologue to a stultifying play.

To add to his anxiety, the rash, not as virulent as before, had reappeared on his legs and arms and a nasty sore broke out on the corner of his mouth.

She was all for making a poultice composed of fermenting dough soaked overnight in the juice of young stinging nettles and foxglove leaves to draw the evil out of the sore but he said he would rather buy a soothing salve from the local apothecary. Nothing could be as effective as Doctor Lopez's Lombardy physics but he lacked an excuse to leave Canterbury and the means to make the journey to London. A week later Ann, seven months into her term, sidled in and gasped, "Have you heard? The devil take them and them conniving to force our Kit to marry the crippled chit and no mistake."

Faulds had been taken ill one evening at his stall and the next morning he was dead. His grave was still warm when his desolate widow took to her bed with grief. Within the week, she, too, had expired.

"God have mercy on their souls," said Catherine piously. "I'll always remember them in my prayers. They were kindness itself to the poor of the town when they had a penny to spare. All in all I'd say it was a blessed release for them and looking at the other side of the coin, it's also a blessed release for Kit."

"You'll sing a different tune when I tell you," said Ann. "With due power of notary, the Faulds' relatives – and that's half of Canterbury – have searched every screed and scrap of a paper to see who owed them money."

Even in his confused state, this was something John Marlowe could understand. "Debts die with the death of either the debtor or the creditor," he quavered.

"And well you know to the contrary, to our costs," Ann retorted. "There, on top of the pile for all to see, was a document signed and pledged by you, John Marlowe, and countersigned by Faulds himself whereby it says, as written and witnessed, that the dowry of their daughter was remitted to one John Marlowe on the promise of Kit marrying the gammy- legged girl."

Catherine was not lost for a reply. "As the old codger in Kit's play said, an oath sworn under duress is neither here or there and in the words of the law it is null and void."

"Has your memory gone as astray as your senses?" exclaimed Ann in exasperation. "Where was the duress when the pair of them were betrothed in this very room? That's as good as any wedding ceremony with book and candle."

"You've a lot of lip on you since you became a married woman, girl, but were you witness to the betrothal?"

"I wasn't asked to the feast," Ann replied with a touch of the sulks.

"And the Faulds themselves are dead," Catherine continued, "and there's no law living that'll take the word of a dead person."

"There's a lot living who'll give the word of your bragging about the grand match your only son had made.But – " Ann paused and looked hard at her parents with an almost triumphant smile on her lips " – but at the heel of the hunt comes the catch and that miserable, hopping wretch of a girl is now lodging in our tavern, my clod-headed husband being a third cousin of the Faulds on his mother's side. With the connivance of him and others, she's passing herself off as Joan Marlowe. There's some who swear they'll see her coupled with Kit rather than being thrown to the charitable mercy of the parish and I reckon you'll have an army of Faulds banging on your door before the week is out."

Once again Catherine's schemes lay in ruins and she reluctantly concluded that the best thing for all was for Christopher to leave Canterbury as soon as possible till this matter blew over. In the afternoon of the next day, Mary May came in to say that a man on horseback by the front door was asking for Christopher. Catherine immediately presumed that this was a skirmisher from the Faulds army and declared she would see the lout off the premises.

Nicholas Skeres was looking up and down the street with a fastidious expression on his face.

"What brings you here, Nicholas?" Christopher asked.

"By the blood of Christ, Marlowe, you'd tear a saint's patience to tatters and if my mission was otherwise – "

"Your mission, Skeres? You glorify your role somewhat. You're a messenger boy. Couldn't they spare a kitchen scullion or a stable lad?"

Skeres' face flushed. "Listen to what I've to say, Marlowe. Sir Walter Ralegh has arranged a meeting of his cohort in Durham House and you are to be there."

"I'd be happy to go if I had the money for the journey, if London was not cursed by the plague and if Sir Walter himself had invited me."

"As for the first, I'm permitted to give you what is necessary." Skeres fumbled in his pouch and pressed a coin into Christopher's hand. Either he was too agitated to know what he was doing or the paymaster was uncommonly generous, for it was another gold crown. "As for the plague, there's more rumour than pestilence and that should be the least of your worry. An invitation shall be delivered to you in due course. The gathering is to be a lodge meeting of the sodality and, as you should know, the London conclave hold Ralegh in great favour. You, alone among us, are acceptable to that faction, so you should be there. I've written the time and day for their assembly on this paper."

"And as you should know, Nicholas Skeres, a fraternity session is secret and is of no concern to those who are excluded."

Skeres handed Christopher the paper and mounted his horse.
"This concerns us all."
"Why should I go at your behest?"
"It's not mine alone. Walsingham desires it."
"Even so, why should I go at his behest?"
"You'll go because you're hired to go. You're paid to be a spy and as such you'll earn your keep."

Chapter thirty-nine

When Skeres had disappeared down the street, Christopher discovered his mother standing by his elbow in the doorway. She made no mention of what had passed between them but praised the rider's rich apparel and the splendid caparison of his mount for the benefit of those neighbours who suddenly found it necessary to sweep the dirt from their doorsteps.

The message provoked a stubborn defiance in Christopher. He threw the unread note on the fire and told his mother that he was in no hurry to leave Canterbury. With the extra money, he could afford to buy a large quantity of ointment for his hidden rash. The salve seemed to lessen the virulence of the affliction and the urgency to call on Doctor Lopez.

Ignoring his mother's pleas to stay safe and hidden at home, he went out to call on an organist called William Corkin who had expressed a wish to set some of Christopher's poems to music. As the evening wore on, they became more cup-sodden. When Corkin revealed that he was a relative of the Faulds, the conversation grew fractious. Insults were exchanged, swords were drawn and they were hauled before the magistrate, who bound them over to keep the peace.

Christopher feared this brawl was a precursor. He would have to leave Canterbury as soon as possible. The opportunity to do so arose two days later. A uniformed lackey brought a written message. 'Sir Roger Manwood requests the company of one Christopher Marlowe of this parish, to journey with the said Sir Roger Manwood in his carriage to London two days hence after matins, whereupon, on the conclusion of their travel the said Sir Roger Manwood and the said Christopher Marlowe will repair to Durham House in the tenancy of Sir Walter Ralegh, to assemble with such others who may gather in the said Durham House.'

The proud Catherine told the whole town in her inimitable way, never able to resist a nudge and a wink. "As for them others – "

By not naming 'them others', she hoped to exorcise the worry that haunted her. "Surely the Almighty, in his infinite mercy and wisdom, will take the poor, crippled wretch to join her unfortunate parents and then you'll be free of any distress in that direction."

For reasons of his own, Manwood had the carriage curtains drawn.

"Marlowe, are you awake?" he asked, breathing stertorously. "I'll not tolerate closed eyes when I speak. Closed eyes and closed ears are one and the same in my book." He lapsed into silence for another five minutes. "Marlowe, it's a cruel, harsh and ungrateful world we live in and no mistake. I've served God and our glorious Queen unremittingly these many years without one thought of self and the just rewards I've gained for my loyal service were not sought by me. As God shall be my ultimate auditor when I stand before the bench at that final and terrible tribunal, I do swear by the sacred blood, my own advancement was far from my mind when I sent proven traitors, heretics and criminals to the rack, gallows and the pyre. Fiat Justitia was forever my guide, my law and my conscience. Soon, as it will come to all of us, I'll cower before the throne of infinite justice and be called upon to give an account of my stewardship."

Another five minutes passed before Manwood spoke again.

"Did I speak of law and conscience?" He snorted. "We talk of them as if they were cousins of the first order rather than bastard children of disparate parents. The first was born in the powder wagon of a conquering army and the second was found under a bush in a monk's cloister. I tell you this, Marlowe, a man is a rogue who marries the first and a fool if he lingers in dalliance with the second. For my part, in all my dealings I've hearkened to the divine teachings and followed the precept: give and it shall be given unto you. Did I not build almshouses in the parish of St Stephen? Buy a peal of bells so the pious could be called to prayers and the impious reminded of God's omnipotence? Have I not built the transept chapel to hold my alabaster tomb? Were they the actions of a greedy man?"

Christopher did not deem it his place to comment. This cruel, avaricious man, in this joggling confessional box, was amending his plea and preparing his defence for what, with the onset of old age and crumbling decay of flesh, he most feared: the judgement beyond the realm of temporal legislators.

"You, Christopher Marlowe, will write my epitaph," Manwood commanded.

"What shall I write for your obsequies? That you were a good, noble, charitable man, that your untimely departure engulfed all those who loved you in a veritable flood of tears, left the widows and orphans distraught and your gracious memory will be forever enshrined in the grieving hearts of all who knew you?"

"Don't mock my funereal rites with obsequious lies, Marlowe. You know I'm hated and cursed by those very widows and orphans who mourn for those I've condemned and I'm reviled and scorned by the regiment of envious sycophants who crawl from beneath every stone. I'm a draper's son, as you are a shoemaker's son, Marlowe, and for that alone we've both had our share of odium. Write the truth, I tell you."

"Then I must fail you. If I write as I see fit, I'll offend you. If I do otherwise, it'll be a lie and if I write to accord with they who knew you best, friends a few, enemies a multitude, we'll need more than one slab of marble. Let what you have been be your epitaph."

"You provoke argument, Marlowe. What have I been? The terror of criminals. Write that."

They made two stops on the journey. The first was just past Boughton Street to extract gravel from the hoof of a horse and the second stop was on the far side of the River Medway where Pilgrim Way joined the London Road. While the horses were being fed and watered, the travellers entered an inn. After they had dined, Manwood demanded ink and paper and urged Christopher to compose the monumental tribute by which the judge hoped his ashes would be aggrandized as long as his marble sepulchre stood. He seemed pleased with what was written though his long neglect of the Latin tongue had made his use of it unsure and he asked Christopher to translate word by word. "Sad scourge of the profligate. An apt phrase, Marlowe, an apt phrase, but I would consider the epitaph complete if God himself received a mention. And have you written your own epitaph, Marlowe?"

Talk of any kind ceased entirely when they crossed London

Bridge and only when the carriage trundled into Durham House courtyard did Manwood seem to wake with a startled grumble. He reached across and clutched Christopher's arm.

"Sharpen your wits, Marlowe, summon your defence, prepare your attack, enter your plea. There's more at stake here than you've ever hazarded on the throw of a die." He grunted. "On the throw of a die. How apt, Marlowe."

"What's at stake?"

"Your life, Marlowe, your life."

Chapter forty

Northumberland greeted Manwood effusively but ignored Christopher. Sir Roger short-sightedly peered round the otherwise empty vestibule, mistakenly doffed his hat to a statue of Mars and asked, "Where are the others, Percy? I was led to believe – "

"They're assembled in the turret room."

"Better than a room in the Tower, any road."

"And we've waited your arrival to begin."

"What? Now? Have mercy on famished travellers, Percy. I've no stomach for any fiddle-faddle talk till I'm fed and watered. Don't you agree, Marlowe? Do justice to your belly, I say, and you'll do justice to man."

"My apologies, Sir Roger." Northumberland made a slightly mocking bow. "I'm a felon for forgetting the trials of hunger." He ordered a servant to lay out a meal for Manwood and his companion in a nearby room

Christopher pecked at the food but Manwood guzzled and became quite jovial in between belches. "I warn you, Marlowe, contrive never to stand in dock till well past midday. A short breakfast means a short temper leading to short shrift for the miscreant. In short, Marlowe, the belly speaks, the judge pronounces and the accused hangs." He had a fund of anecdotes on the theme and only paused when a touch of wind made him gasp and clutch his left breast. When he had clean-picked the bones and scoured the platters of every morsel, he gulped down a goblet of wine, cocked his head sideways as if listening and said, "I hear nothing and I see nobody. There's a void here, Marlowe, and I don't like it. And where's Walt, our honoured host?"

When Northumberland reappeared, Manwood asked him about the missing Ralegh.

"Sir Walter sends you his deepest regret for not greeting you on your arrival." There was a certain stiltedness in the reply which alarmed the perceptive Manwood.

"Is there trouble? I've heard rumours. I fear I'm in error in allowing myself to be entertained in his house."

"Entertain neither rumours nor fears, Sir Roger. A bothersome matter relating to his Devon estate had detained Sir Walter and he has urged us to continue our deliberations without him."

At the foot of the spiral stairway, Manwood drew back, aghast. "By Jezebel's sweat and Magdalene's bloody tears, am I expected to climb that? Is there no other way up or down? Why, we'd be trapped if – "

"If what, Sir Roger?"

"If there was a fire."

"We've taken due precautions. We have, as you see, a man posted here, a second further on and a third by the main door. Should there be a fire, we'll be warned in good time."

The turret room was now void of adornments and resembled a prison or a monastic cell, albeit an overcrowded one. Manwood was ushered to the table and Christopher was directed by Northumberland to the window seat. There were thirteen other men in the gathering. Apart from the hunchback Merlin who gave him a wisp of a smile, none showed any sign of recognition.

"Let me catch my breath before we begin," said Manwood. The climb had brought on an attack of wheezing. "Percy, is there a preamble or, should I say, a prologue?"

"This is not a playhouse, Sir Roger." Northumberland picked up a sheet of paper from the table and, after a preliminary cough, began to read. "Christopher Marlowe, certain charges have been laid against you, each by its implication and consequence heinous to a high degree – "

Christopher was astonished and angry. "Charges? Heinous to a high degree? What's the meaning of this foolery?"

"Sit down, Marlowe, sit down and hear us out," Manwood ordered.

"By your leave, Sir Roger, this is no court of law."

"No, no, it's not, not of the Queen's law. Percy, we'll have question and answer now."

"I've not finished the indictment."

"Finished? Great whore of Babylon, you've not begun at the beginning."

"But Sir Roger, I do protest – "

"And I protest you've ridden into the fray with your face towards the mare's arse. A ripe fart, I say, to your rambling indictment. I'll put the question direct. Christopher Marlowe, are you a sworn member of our sodality?"

"Is that my offence? Then I'll plead guilty and ask for benefit of clergy."

Manwood did not like pert answers. "Curb your tongue, Marlowe. The question was in the nature of a confirmation and only required a simple yea or nay. This assembly is a tribunal of our fraternity called to consider certain accusations laid against you in which – " he picked another sheet of paper from the table and peered closely at it " – in which you've brought ill-fame and disrepute to our sodality. I'll read them to you and we'll determine your guilt. In the first part. The said Christopher Marlowe preached atheism. Preached atheism, Percy? Is this within our province?"

"Yes. It was reported – "

"By whom?" Manwood asked sharply.

"That Christopher Marlowe did read a lecture to a gathering – "

"When? Where?"

"In which he likened Moses to a juggler and – "

"And so he was, by God, Percy, so he was." Manwood showed every sign of exasperation. "No, this will not do. You must produce time, day, place, witnesses, or this meandering evidence is inadmissable."

"You forget, Sir Roger, this is not the Queen's Bench. The same rules do not apply here."

"More's the pity. But since you've invited me as a learned justice to preside over this tribunal, I'll rule, by the articles of our sodality, that every charge against a member must bear substantial evidence in the shape of documents or the voice of a witness."

"The voice of our witness is mute to this tribunal. He is not a member of our sodality."

"Who's this straw man?"

Merlin piped up. "One Richard Baines, a defrocked priest, sidekick of the infamous liar and spy, Robin Poley, both being rancorous Papists and creatures of the Walsinghams."

The revelation enraged Manwood. "God's blood, Percy, are you in league with that boneless upstart, Thomas Walsingham? I tell you, he's not a patch on his uncle, Sir Francis, and it's come to a fine pass when one of his whelps is given first bite at our heels."

"You should know us better, Sir Roger, to imagine we'd employ such creatures as Baines," Northumberland replied, a little shaken by Manwood's outburst. "He had sent detailed reports to the Privy Council and through the good office of one whose duty it is to inspect such matters we obtained a fair copy of the documents and hoped to delay its exposure till we fully discussed the contents."

"Fully discussed, you should say, the consequences of its contents to you," Christopher said.

"Explain yourself, Marlowe."

"I shall be content to explain myself to myself and you to yourself."

"Content yourself with sticking to the point, Marlowe," Manwood growled.

"The contents of this secret document, which none but the Privy Council and half of London should be privy to, are presumably speculative ideas I advanced to a sodality meeting some time back." Christopher pointed to one of the men, "You attended the gathering, sir." While the man flushed and violently shook his head, Christopher pointed to another and another and another, "And you and you and you, you too were present." Finally he indicated Northumberland. "And you, sir, were not only present but joined in the debate most willingly."

"I deny ever being there."

"See, Sir Roger, you asked for a witness and here is one unwilling and disabled of memory."

"Yesu, Marlowe, are you inferring I'm a liar?"

"You are like one who lies on his right side."

"What riddle is this?"

"Riddle-me-ree, nothing less than when you lie, you contrive to be on the right side."

Manwood banged the table with his fists. "Enough! Enough! We're not here to watch two clowns bat tennis balls back and forth. My fiat is that this nonsense about a so-called speculative lecture is not relevant – "

"But, Sir Roger, surely in the matter of disrepute – "

"It is not relevant to the commission of this tribunal and not in accordance with the articles of our sodality. And furthermore, the attendance of each and everyone to a sodality meeting is marked down. If we need must discover who lies, we can inspect the ledger. I hope, Percy and you others, you rest easy when you lie on the right side. But we're wasting time. What's next?" Northumberland gave the judge another paper. "Hmm, yes, item two, no, three. The said Christopher Marlowe had agreed, on hire from one other, to carry from Sodality meetings all that which had passed therein." Manwood threw down the sheet of paper. "Are you saying Marlowe promised to spy on us? For whom, I ask you?"

"Ingram Frizer."

"Frizer is a sodality member," Christopher said. "There is no betrayal in telling him."

"There is for money. In an attested ledger it is written the said Christopher Marlowe was paid one gold coin by Ingram Frizer, steward and agent for the Walsingham estate, in a certain house in Seething Lane. Furthermore, in a street in Canterbury, the said Christopher Marlowe was paid a further gold crown by Nicholas Skeres who – "

"Who is also a member of the sodality." Christopher was amazed that such a transaction should be known and wondered who was the blabbermouth.

"Marlowe, do you deny receiving money from known Walsingham agents?" Manwood asked sternly.

"No, no, I do not deny – that is – yes, I did receive money from Walsingham and both Frizer and Skeres, in their various offices, gave me the amount due. But I'm no hireling spy." One man snickered and remarked to his neighbour that it was not every day you'd meet one willing to spy without the cost of hire.

"I'm a poet and playwright. Do you think I live on air and walk with the gods? For the purpose of translating learned documents, Thomas Walsingham has, from time to time, advanced me enough money to buy linings for my stomach and cloth for my back.

With those who cloak their intentions these days with fraternal greetings, I'd need to clothe my back with armour."

Judging by the stiff visages and glazed expressions, his listeners did not appear to be giving his defence their full attention.

Manwood grunted. "We'll note what you've said, Marlowe, namely you've admitted receiving money from known Walsingham agents. Is there more, Percy, or is this the sum total – ?"

"The sum of all the other offences would not rank so offensive in the total of this final abomination – "

"Yes, yes, Percy, but what is it?"

"Nothing less than that through the agency of Marlowe, in the flagrant abjuration of his avouched trust, the ancient and sacred rituals of our fraternity have been depraved, ridiculed and, by insinuation, our noble and honoured ceremonies have been likened to a Satanic pact."

"How was this done?" Manwood shouted across the hubbub.

"Forgive me, Sir Roger. In your Canterbury cloister there is nothing to disturb your contemplations other than an intrusive thrush."

"And I wish to God I hadn't been tempted to journey up to London. My health is not of the best these recent years and – "

"And you would not have heard the cackles, whoops and hulloes of our numerous enemies. What gave them such joy, you may ask? Why, a middling drama bellowed, as usual, by bombastic players at The Theatre in Shoreditch."

"I like a good drama myself," Manwood said to nobody in particular. "There was a company down in Canterbury recently. Now, what did they perform?"

"May I continue, Sir Roger?" Northumberland asked politely. He puffed out his chest, preparing to orate a denunciation of all those who earn their crust by oration. "Of what import, the question rises, is a middling drama bawled out to the four winds by bellowing actors? Are not such empty drums pounded out every day of the week for the delight of the flea-ridden groundlings? It amused the rabble, you may say, and while they're gawping at pretended kings and queens they are not rioting in the streets. But lately there appeared at the Shoreditch playhouse of one bankrupt carpenter and runagate, namely James Burbage, a drama – " He paused to favour his friends with a supercilious smile " – if one is so pleased to title such gallimaufry of alarums off, bleating verses and noisome quarrels, a drama – " He leaned over to pick up another sheet of paper.

"Yes, yes, I remember now," said Manwood brightly. "I recall one about a conniving Jew, a right rascal, but the writer did not know the ins and outs of the law. As for the second one, well, the devil take it – "

Northumberland read from the paper. "The drama is titled, 'The Tragical Life And Death Of Doctor John Faustus.' It is written by one Christopher Marlowe. Do you deny this, Marlowe?"

"What parent would be so cursed as to deny his child? Why should I deny that which I've engendered?"

"Why should you indeed? And do you deny that for the purpose of your scribbling play-acting you concocted rituals not unlike those by which we receive novitiates into our fraternity? And was it not made manifest to even the most ignorant of the gawpers that the ceremonies so portrayed, as similar to ours as brothers sprung from the one womb, were designed by Mephistophilis himself to entrap unwary souls into the mesh of Hell?"

There were cries of outrage from his listeners. Manwood thumped the table for silence. "What have you to say on this count, Marlowe?" he asked.

Christopher patiently explained that Faustus' Satanic compact, with all its rigmarole of Latin tags, was contained in the original German story. The similarities with the sodality's ritual were mere coincidence. Halfway through his argument, muffled sounds of voices came from below.

With all the pomposity of his office as presiding judge, Manwood announced, "We have paid attention to Marlowe's argument with due patience and forbearance and now, as is our bounden duty, we shall consider the nature of the retribution such crimes deserve." Being partially deaf, he had neither heard the rumpus below nor Christopher's speech. It was sufficient for him that the proper procedure had been followed.

There was much muttering among those present. "Marlowe, admits, no, he insolently proclaims," declared one heatedly, "his perversion and betrayal of our rituals. We'd be less than true to ourselves if we refrained from visiting upon this Judas the full weight of our righteous anger and contempt."

The hunchback, who had until then been staring with childlike curiosity at the sore on Christopher's lip, now scrambled to the middle of the floor where he could be both seen and heard. "And I say we'd be less true to ourselves if our judgement was spurred by wrath. We are men of reason, not a bigoted rabble. Marlowe has advanced a rebuttal to the charge by stating a priori cause to the ultimate effect. I say we should now let him enter a plea of mitigation."

Some agreed, some dissented and others said they should allow the dog a last bark before they hung him.

Christopher could barely suppress the surge of rage within him. Plea of mitigation, indeed!

"What do you expect from me? Humility? Remorse? That I should pray for your generous mercy and seek time to amend my grievous sins? This I proclaim. Those ancient and empty rituals which you grant so much grace and those hollow ceremonies and fatuous pageantries are fit only for the superstitious, the ignorant and the grovelling wretches who need must find salvation from their miserable state in the mumbling of bad Latin and the stink of incense, as it is with the Roman church. Are we not clever men gathered in a fraternity of learning? An honourable society which exalts natural philosophy and refuses to countenance any boundaries to knowledge? Yet, we indulge, no, we gallivant in primal rites as if we were naked savages and mutter hocus-pocus like credulous crones." Cries of "Enough" tried to silence him. "This, I state, is contrary to reason and, by every monstrous oath we take, is a perversion and a corruption – "

The last few words were drowned by an uproar and it was a good three minutes before Manwood, by dint of thumping the table and shouting, could suppress the tumult. "You've prated sufficient to hang, draw and quarter you, Marlowe, and if this tribunal had the power – "

"Let us put an end to this," some cried. Two wide-necked vases, one white and one black, were placed on the table and every man received a pair of small, wooden discs, again one white and one black. Christopher was solemnly black-balled.

"This then is your verdict?" Manwood said.

"There is only one who thinks differently." Northumberland held up a lone white disc.

"Christopher Marlowe, pay heed." Manwood produced a fearful scowl, one that had terrified thousands of unfortunates over the years. "This specially convened tribunal of our august fraternity has, after due deliberation and consideration, found you guilty of heinous betrayal and obdurate enmity, compounded by your intemperate words today, towards the body and spirit of our sodality and it is my awful duty to pronounce – "

The head of a lackey appeared through the hatch. "If it pleases your honours – " he began in a stammering voice.

"How dare you – " Northumberland strode over to the opening. The lackey ducked and shouted from a safe distance. "If it pleases – that is – it's Sir Walter and Lady Ralegh, they've been taken to the Tower."

There was immediate consternation and confusion and Manwood, for one, had all the appearance of imminent apoplexy.

"I mustn't be found here. I shouldn't be here. Why wasn't I warned? I knew there was something wrong. Didn't I say so to you, Marlowe?" His attempt to descend the stairs was foiled by Northumberland. "Let me go, I say. I'll be accused of being a conspirator and clapt in the Tower. My life's destroyed. They'll seize my property. A curse on this sodality and its arrant rites. It's brought me nothing but trouble. Marlowe was right, yes he was. Trust a Kentish man."

His colleagues were equally frantic and churned about like cattle hemmed in the hold of a storm-struck ship. Only three remained calm: Northumberland, who was quietly questioning the lackey, Merlin, who sat in a corner and giggled and Christopher, who was as indifferent to the fate of the others as they were to his reasoning.

"Gentlemen, gentlemen, there is no danger to our well-being," Northumberland announced. "The arresting officers have taken the Raleghs away, we believe to the Tower. Let us pray to God that whatever offence Sir Walter has caused is slight and redeemable."

"What about Marlowe?" Merlin asked.

"As you seem to have particular regard for the renegade, you take care of him. Marlowe, don't imagine this is the end of the matter."

Christopher and Merlin were the last to descend the spiral stairway. The long hall was as silent as a deserted mausoleum. Merlin led the way down a narrow, dark passage to a small doorway which opened into an alley.

"We'll part here, Kit, each to his own way. Have you lodgings for the night?"

"I'll beg a bed from Tom Nashe. Tell me, what'll that cabal do now? Not that I give a rotten fig for their mockery of a trial."

"They'll do you to death. You were too forward with the truth and none of us care to have it forced down our gullet without honey to sweeten the tartaric taste."

"May the truth choke them. And which of those brave warriors will forward my death?"

"None of them. Hired assassins are cheap and plentiful and in a month or more, when matters have returned to their proper order, the wish shall be executed."

"Their threat has more bombast than a shoddy jacket. I won't walk in dread of them."

"And I say to you, Kit, sit with your back to the wall and avoid dark passages."

"Thanks for the advice. And, before I go to try my luck with Tom Nashe, thanks to you for your token dissent."

"In what way did I show dissent, Kit?"

"Why, with that single white token in the black vase."

"That was not mine. At first I thought you were only a venial sinner, guilty at the most of being a fool. Then, when provoked to your final speech, you displayed an arrogant pride worthy of Lucifer, and that was not forgivable. It was not I but Northumberland who cast the white counter."

Chapter forty-one

"What haunts your dreams, Kit?" Thomas Nashe asked. "I heard you cry out last night."

"Was I so loud?" Christopher readjusted the cloth with which he masked the lower half of his face. "I slept badly and turned on my wrist."

"And the night before? And the night before that?"

"Maybe the midnight carts rumbling beneath the window disturbed me. Where do they go?"

"Through Moorgate to beyond Finsbury to lay their loads with the old bones of St Paul's Charnel House."

The overnight visit stretched to several weeks. Nashe, ever generous in word and deed, never once hinted that his guest had overstayed his welcome.

Thomas Deloney was less reticent."Twiddle-twaddle, Tom,- twiddle-twaddle. You're as soft as an unlaid pullet's egg. If I were you, I'd say to whoreson Marlowe, I'd say, 'Here's your bags and baggage, Kit, where's your hurry?' and I'd show him the door."

Nashe looked embarrassed. "Not many people understand the bond between Kit and I. We're both Cambridge men and – "

"Cambridge!!" Deloney almost shouted. "Good Lord and Maiden chaste, what contagion was there in those musty chambers that afflicted you striplings with this – this pious glow of brotherly love? Why, it makes common vulgarians of those of us who've never set foot within those mouldy walls." It was a sore point with him, as it was with Kyd, that the so-called University Wits, when it suited them, excluded him from their inner circle and mocked his limited education. "What prevents him from returning home? There's nothing for him in London other than the plague and closed playhouses."

"I've heard from a few people that there's a virgin waiting to wed him in Canterbury."

Deloney roared. "What? Kit Marlowe? Well, well, I'd hardly

credit that yarn." He prodded Nashe in the chest. "I thought his fancy turned to other antics, so rumours have it." He chortled."- Dear o dear, imagine Kit Marlowe fumbling his key in a stiff lock. If that's his trouble, I'd sell him a jar of unction squeezed from the belly of a virgin sturgeon. Why does he cover his face?"

"You saw him then?"

"There was one I took for him when I turned the corner but when I called out, all I saw was his startled eyes. What's the purpose of the mask?"

"All I could gather from his meandering tale was that he had offended a parcel of men who had sworn to kill him."

"He's mad."

"No, I swear, he's of good mind but sick in his body."

"Mad or sick, Tom, it's all one if, like a mad-sick dog, he bites your hand and you, too, suffer his distemper."

"Kit is not a diseased cur to be hung from the nearest hawthorn. He's a Christian – "

"There's many would dispute that."

"A learned scholar and an esteemed poet. Would you have me abandon him to the elements? Is that how they order these things in Norwich?"

"Ay, and in Norfolk, Stratford, Hertford – I could make a rosary for the damned and every bead would be an English town – but who weeps for them? The herdsmen, the cottagers, the farm labourers, each and every one cleared from home and hearth by a pestilence worse than any scourge rising from the London sewers. As Thomas More said, in this land the sheep eat men. Isn't the soul of one Norwich labourer equal, in the sight of God, to one crazed Canterbury scribbler?"

"I'm not competent to judge one soul against another. The mortal Marlowe is my concern. Of all those begotten either between sack cloth or silken sheets, he's unique in the opulence of his verse. His thoughts are exalted above the world of ignorance and all earthly conceit."

"That sounds like an epitaph. Is he dead then? Has he written his last word? It's surely the fortune of destiny."

"Destiny never defames herself more than when she lets an excellent poet die." Nashe rummaged among a pile of paper and handed a sheet to Deloney. "This proves he still retains that pure elemental wit."

Deloney grunted, read and then grudgingly said,"It's pretty, I give you that. I suppose it has merit for those who'd enjoy such elegant lines but it's not for my ears or Will the Dyer in the Bull Tavern."

"Nor is it intended to be recited to your ale-swigging tradesmen. This fragment is part of an epic poem called Hero and Leander that he's composing for the Earl of Southampton for a fee."

"Each is welcome to what he deserves, but I'd rather have a penny for a rude ballad in my fist than a golden promise stowed in an empty purse."

"Marlowe, in his stark moments of lucidity – "

"Didn't I say he's mad?"

"He has a fine madness which rightly possesses a poet's brain. When he's free from the rack of his illness or his fears, he is Marlowe, the laureate poet."

Deloney laid the sheet back on the pile and helped himself to more wine. "And talking as we were of demented poets, what's the news of my fellow Norwich man, Robert Greene? He's so taken with bile that he's like as not drowned in bilge."

"The branch is rotted. The fruit falls to the ground. Greene is dead," said Nashe soberly. "Between plague, the pestilence of poverty and the breaking of fine spirits, death has ridden a wide swathe through our ranks." He listed the number who had fallen before the three horsemen. "Remember Will Slaughter, the red-bearded blustering bit-player? And do you recall Brown, the actor? While he was away with his company, he was bereft of wife, children, even down to the meanest servant of his household. And most sorrowful of all, Tom Watson."

Deloney made the sign of the cross and thumped his breast. "What a massacre of the innocent. Tell me how Robert Greene died. I'll be a cursed man if I ever speak a bad word against him again."

The story of Greene's final days was pathetic, sordid and bitter. Alone and destitute, deserted by the whore for whom he had left his legal wife, he was reduced to pawning his sword and there were tales of him begging for ale and being refused in taverns where he once held court with his cronies. He had snarled at the world and it had turned to savage him. Sick, starving and penniless, he had collapsed in the street and was taken in by humble cordwainers in whose house he died.

"God has a way of twisting the tail of our fortunes," Deloney said. "In his days, Robert despised those base mechanicals and yet, at the heel of the hunt, it was their rough hands that wiped his brow and dampened his parched lips."

But there was one more twist to Greene's sad tale. In the hopes of earning enough to afford a Christian burial, he had written a pamphlet titled, 'A Groatsworth of Wit or the Repentance of Robert Greene.'

"A groatsworth of wit," Deloney repeated. "Even at his sourest, Robert could muster sufficient wry humour to make a donkey laugh, as long as you weren't the donkey favoured with the pricks of his pen."

"Whatever hilarity there is in this work it's well and truly buried with the author. No, it's an unhappy, angry mixture of contrition and barbed attacks upon his sometime friends and those he blamed for his misery. He had taken it upon himself to advise us in turn, though he mentioned no names, to mend our ways lest worse befall us."

"What does he say to me?"

"Nothing. I doubt if you were in his troubled mind."

"Even at the gates of hell he scorns me. What did he write about you?"

"Merely to enjoin me, in the gentlest of terms, to moderate my satirical pen. But before all he writes to Marlowe, he being foremost in fame."

"Marlowe again."

Nashe read out the particular passage and his voice rose as he neared the end.

"I know the least of my demerits merit this miserable death, but wilfull striving against known truths exceedeth all the terrors of my soul. Defer not, with me, till this last point of extremity; for little knowest thou how in the end thou shall be visited."

A groan came from the next room.

"Is that Marlowe?" Deloney asked in a half-whisper. "I would not have spoke so freely if I had known."

"It doesn't matter. His nights are full of torment, his days are exhausted and he sleeps like one whose soul has departed. So it is with lizards that lack water."

"Does he know about Watson? They were so close."

"It came as a hard blow. As a final act for his one-time friend, he wrote a dedication for Watson's book of poems. I have a copy here. A coldness had grown between them and Kit blames Watson's wife."

"God save me from priests, Puritans and holy women."

Another groan came from the adjoining room, followed by what sounded like somebody talking to a second and silent person.

Deloney lowered his voice. "Don't carry that load on your back. Better you carry a sack of stones than a bag of thorns."

"Hush, he's moving." Nashe cautioned. "Are you awake, Kit? Come and join us. Our Norwich weaver of silken ballads has honoured us with a visit. We're glutting ourselves on dry wine and spiced tales."

The muffled voice muttered that he would rest some more. Nashe shrugged his shoulders and encouraged Deloney to enlarge the story of Jack of Newbury which the weaver was writing.

Two hours later Deloney left to lodge near Spittle Fields with a first cousin and Nashe, now filled with better cheer and good wine, lay down to snore the night away. At midnight the laden carts trundled by the window.

Christopher gathered his sparse belongings into a cloth bundle, crept by the sleeping body of his host and tiptoed down the stairs. He had no plan but, not being deaf as the others thought, he was determined to be neither a sack of stones or a bag of thorns. He had hoped to sneak through the alleys unnoticed but when he turned a corner a wagon came to a halt in front of him and body-gatherers hemmed him against a wall. They, like him, had the lower half of their faces covered with rags.

"Why are you walking around at this hour?" one asked.

"To rob our corpses, why else," said another and plucked at Christopher's bundle. "What have you there?"

The biggest of the scavengers pushed through the crowd and

pulled down Christopher's mask. "Yesu wept," he exclaimed. "Could this be Kit Marlowe?" There was something familar in the man's voice and manner.

"And could this be Dick Chomley?" Christopher asked. "I only seek a place to rest, Dick."

"Tell your friend to join the other sleepers on the cart, Dick," suggested one, "and he'll have rest in plenty in Finsbury." Some of the men laughed.

"Don't mock, brothers," said Chomley. "We must complete our sacred task before morning. You won't lack a place to lay your head in this scourged city, Marlowe, but I reckon rest is beyond you in this life."

A woman's bare, thin arm swung down from the side of the wagon and a scavenger exclaimed, "There's a gold ring here for sure but it's welded to the flesh."

Chomley took out a knife, cut off the finger and put it into his pouch. "It'll be easier when it shrinks," he said and then ordered the horses to be whipped up and make all speed. Within minutes, the rattle of the wheels faded.

Chapter forty-two

"Where is this place men call hell?"

"Under the heavens."

"But whereabouts?"

He staggered to his feet, gazed bemusedly at the char-stained walls of the bare room and hugged the shoddy blanket tightly around his shoulders. Snowflakes drifted down from the broken ceiling and a sharp wind cut through the gaping window.

"Where we are is hell and where hell is, there must we ever be. Then hell is London for I am damned, and am now in hell." He shivered and flexed his hands. A little life returned and the tips of his toes and fingers began to tingle. "But is hell frozen? My blood congeals and I can write no more."

"I'll fetch thee fire."

There was a faint whiff of smoke and burnt wood in the air; a smell redolent of violence, panic and fear.

It was last night – no, no, it was the night before – or, perhaps, it was a week ago, he had been in another house, one crowded with outcasts, refugees and destitutes like himself, when suddenly there came an outburst of screaming and shouts of, "Burn, burn, burn." When he ran from the blazing building, men with raised clubs demanded to know his name and when he, scarcely remembering who he was, cried out that he meant no harm to anybody, they pushed him to the edge of the mob.

"Let him be," said a bully. "Can't you see he's English."

A woman shouted, "It's a shame, it is. Our own kind has nowhere to sleep while them godless foreigners poison the wells with plague and take over the best houses."

It was a particularly bright morning and the thin covering of snow's startling whiteness stung his eyes. He trudged through the narrow streets, with no thought of his final destination. Most people, like him, were muffled and cloaked.

"Yes, yes, I am in Nether Hell or London; or London is Nether Hell."

The thoroughfare broadened, the numbers of passers-by increased and the snow had turned slushy brown with the traffic. He recognised Cornhill. From all directions came the clamour of bells. Was today Sunday? But what was the week? The month? The year? The wind brought to him the enticing smells of baked bread, meat pies and stewed onions. "Is this the torture designed to tantalise the gluttonous?" Like a hound sniffing a trail, he followed the aroma till he came to the familar facade of The Gilded Lily. The sight of the tavern's dowdy exterior aroused a lurking sense of dread within him.

A haggard-looking woman with prematurely grey hair and pitted features stood before him and for the first few seconds he failed to recognise in her the once-stout, sturdy, smooth-skinned Kate Quick.

"What do you want?" she asked in a sour, irritable manner.

"Ale," he replied with the same lack of courtesy as he pushed by her and took a seat near the entrance.

"This isn't a tavern. Be off with you."

"It was a tavern when last I was here."

"By the shape of you, I'd say you've visited every tavern between here and Ludgate and been thrown out of them all. I don't want scratch-skins like you warming your arse for the cost of passing the day."

"I want food."

"I'm sure you do. Just like all them mangy beggars without a penny to bless themselves. You hoist your rags and tatters – "

"I'll pay." He knew by the weight in his purse that he had some money, but when he emptied the coins on the table, he was as surprised as Kate to see the gold piece nestling among the base metal discs. It seemed to him another world and another age when Skeres gave this to him in Canterbury.

"By the hanging Christ but you had me fooled and no mistake." Kate's truculence vanished and she spoke with the easy familiarity of the thieving fraternity. "And can you blame me with you wrapped in that filthy blanket? I've seen you here before, haven't I? With Sly Dick, wasn't it?" She nodded towards a group at a far table. "You'd better stow that away before they have wind of it. They're a lazy, scrounging lot, not a hard man like yourself, and they'd slit their grandma's gullet for the sake of a brass farthing."

He dozed off in the stuffy warmth and it seemed no time before Kate returned with a steaming bowl of thick broth and a chunk of bread. She placed these on the table, sat down opposite him and peered closely at his face when he lowered the cloth.

"Ah yes, you've been here before, a long time ago. And you've been away, have you? The Clink? Newgate? Or further? No, don't answer. I'm not asking. We've all got our own troubles. First it was them straight-backs having my place raided. You'd have to be up before the cock crows, and we're not talking about the risen cocks either, to catch Kate Quick with her shift above her haunches.

"I said to myself, I'll send my girls over the river to a place of mine by St Olave's, your man Henslowe and his trugging wife having the run of the Bankside houses. Mind you, I had the laugh on them when they were suppressed because of the plague. Ah, the plague, now that was a curse, taking away half of my best clients and didn't I have a touch of it myself, but thanks be to the ever-merciful Yesu I still have my health if not my beauty. And then them long noses closed all the taverns as well as the playhouses, they're worse than the pestilence. When they let the taverns open again, they wouldn't give me my licence back and I had to make the Gilded Lily into an ordinary and that's why you're eating your fill and not drinking your need. Remind me now, what's your name?"

"Kit."

"Kit, is it? Well, that's good enough for me." She glanced towards where two men stood in the doorway. "Kit, I don't suppose – " she drew her forefinger across her windpipe " – that's in your line of business?" He shook his head. "A pity then. They're on the look-out for a silent blade and the devil take it if I cannot find one suited to their satisfaction. You don't mind if these gentlemen sit with you for a while as they'd rather stay near the door."

The men were too well dressed to be The Gilded Lily's usual customers and they looked far from comfortable in these frowsy surroundings. "Kit?" said the first. "There's a likeness, I'll admit, but wasn't he carted off to the pesthouse?"

"It's possible we've seen this rogue some place else. Tell me, fellow, have you ever been before Manwood?"

Twice, Christopher could have replied, and the last time was in the turret room of Durham House where this pair were part of the tribunal.

"Is this Kit a dearly missed friend of yours?" The warm broth in his belly gave Christopher the strength to be provocative. "One whom you hold in as high regard as I do the blessed Sir Roger Manwood?" "He mocks us," the first man growled and made to rise from his seat but his companion stopped him and said, "We can't afford a brawl in this place." He looked hard at Christopher. "You've the cut of a man handy with a sharp blade. How do you fancy a gold coin clutched in your claw?"

"Not if it means evil for Manwood."

"Why does the memory of Manwood bother you?" "Memory?" Christopher swallowed the bread and wished he had ale to help it on its way. He quoted from the epitaph the judge had asked him to write, "Is he not the terror of vagabonds, the harsh scourge of profligates, a vulture to hardened criminals?"

"We've a dribbling idiot here. Don't you know Manwood's dead?"

"And when did the esteemed justice pass on to his final judgement?"

"The second week of December."

"December? What month is this?"

"You loon, don't you know it's January? Yesu, but we are the fools to have fallen in with a Bedlam runaway."

At that moment Kate Quick bustled back to the table to tell the pair she had found one who was willing to do their service. Christopher rose to pay and make a quick exit but as he handed Kate the coins, the first man also stood up.

"This is no babbler from Bedlam," he said loud enough for all to hear." I know him now. He's Kit Marlowe."

Christopher's flight was hampered by a multitude of people. They moved as one towards the cathedral and when they came to a frozen corpse – Christopher counted four between Bow Lane and Friday Street – there was no help for it but to step over the body. The dominant sound was the insistent clanging of bells.

His passage was barred by a trio of crouching beggars. The sight of the crone with outstretched claw, the one-legged ancient in the torn, red coat of a soldier and the sturdy lout with no arms reminded him of the unfortunate fracas into which he and Tom Watson had been hurled by a drunken mariner. The three miserable mendicants were very still and did not cry out their litany of woes.

"So, my three beauties, we've met again," he said. "I wish Tom and even that rough-neck Jack Marlin were with me. More's the pity, they're no longer sensible to wind or weather." But there was no response and he bent down to inspect their immobile faces. Their lives were finally vanquished by the frost and their blood was now ice.

His hope of escaping the throng by turning down Friday Street was frustrated by the appearance of an equally large number moving up from Watling Street. Fatalistically he allowed himself to be carried towards St Paul's.

'This is beyond human reason,' Christopher thought as another surge pressed him promiscuously against the bodies of strangers. Here and there arose a moan of distress or a shriek of despair as a man, or woman or child lost his or her footing and slipped beneath the trampling herd. He grew angry with this entrapment and his violent emotion gave him a ruthless energy, sufficient for him to push towards the churchyard.

Ranting preachers stood on various makeshift plinths. One cried out that the day of judgement was near, a second bawled for all to abase themselves in thanksgiving to the Almighty for the passing of the plague and a third declared that the pestilence was God's retribution for the evil brothels, playhouses and taverns which had turned London into a Sodom and Gomorrah, one city cursed with the sins of two.

"Surely that blabbermouth, that spoiled priest, is Richard Baines." Urged on by rage, he tore through those surrounding the orator and called out, "And I, Christopher Marlowe, I refute your lies, Richard Baines, and I defy your God."

The crowd raised their voices and intoned, "God have mercy

on us poor sinners. God forgive us our trespasses as we forgive them who trespass against us. God give us strength to fight Satan and all his works." Christopher's heart pounded, a dull drumming filled his skull and he staggered backwards to slump down on the ground in a faint.

Chapter forty-three

In the last week of April, the promised spring finally struggled through the clouds to warm the streets. To Christopher, now lodging in a hovel off Gracechurch Street, the past was a mutilated book in which the coherence of the story was disrupted by torn and missing pages and many words and passages blotched by blood and water.

When he woke from his faint in St Paul's churchyard, a swarm of urchins were attempting to liberate his clothes and bundle but they scattered when he shouted and struck out at them. With the beggars, vagrants, cripples and thieves, they searched through the detritus left by the dispersed congregation and pillaged the belongings of those unfortunates crushed to death in the press.

His blanket had disappeared. He staggered to his feet, shivered, brushed the snow from his clothing and walked a little unsteadily through the vast cavern of the cathedral to stand beneath the western portico. There, with the eyes of one who never expected to see this sight again, he gazed upon the neat houses on Ludgate Hill, the pleasant meadows of Holborn, now covered with a white patina, and the slow blue wind of the Thames.

In this plague-ravaged city, which had lost at least a thousand inhabitants each week, there were no difficulties in finding lodgings. At least no one in these squalid rookeries had any curiosity about him.

He threw the bundle in a corner and bought a candle to incinerate every flea, bug and louse he found. The rats were no problem: they had also died in their hundreds of thousands. It was now time to bend his mind to the practicalities of living. The gold coin would keep him for a while if he were frugal. But he had no way of knowing which of his friends had survived the pestilence. And would they welcome the risen Christopher Marlowe walking from the tomb to embrace them again?

As for his other sources of income, the book-sellers and printers had been swept from St Paul's concourse and the playhouses had all been suppressed.

What about his condemnation by the sodality's tribunal? Were they scouring every rogues' den for assassins to execute their judgement? He had had his bellyful of skulking in dark corners and scorned the fear they engendered.

"Didn't that effete fool Southampton promise to reward me for an epic?" The notes and draft of Hero And Leander that he had written so many months ago were still in his bundle and he spread the soiled and crumpled sheets out on the floor. "I'll make him think he's gazing on his own gloried reflection when he reads it. As I do now," he added bitterly, "upon this distorted image."

The face that looked out from the fragmented Venice mirror – a remnant from the spoils of a looting expedition by the previous tenant – was aged by rough and lined skin and the pits of dried-out sores.

But it was a week before he put pen to paper. "How shall I praise that prancing youth's hidden graces? Write,'Some swore he was a maid in man's attire.' No, that's too near the edge. 'His body was as straight as Circe's wand.' Not difficult with his spine held taut by stays. 'Jove might have sipped nectar from his hand.' If it's heavy with coins, I'd willingly sip ass's piss from that paw."

Once he had started, he wrote and revised with an intensity born of creativity. The picture of the gaudy, posturing Southampton faded and was replaced by the image of Apollo, sculpted in divine proportions by the ancient Greeks, painted in subtle colours by the Florentine masters, pure in form and measurement, undefiled by sensual lust, unblemished by age and sickness, a thing of the mind. When he turned to the portrayal of the female, he had exhausted the womanly description in the male and could only reflect her beauty in what she wore.

Within the month the first part was completed and ready to be presented to Southampton. Christopher dared not be the one to do so. He dreaded the disdainful grimaces when they looked upon his repulsive features. And as he read to the assembly, blinded by tears of humiliation, choked with chagrin, the languid spectators, deaf to his words, would mutter restlessly, raise delicate hands to yawning mouths and call for more amusing diversions;

a tumbling clown, say, with jangling bells or a dancing bear. He would rather burn than be rejected.

Perhaps he could find a messenger? He went down Cheapside to call into some of his old haunts but he only saw strangers. Disconsolate, he trudged back to his lodgings. When he reached Gracechurch Street, he sensed he was being followed.

"Kit Marlowe, wait," a voice called out. "I saw you leave the Mermaid and – "

A young man by the name of Simon Aldrich stood there. A Cambridge man, he had been on the fringe of the so-called University Wits' circle and lapped up every golden word like a greedy kitten.

"My sincere apologies, sir. I had mistaken you for someone else. I thought you were Christopher Marlowe. You resemble him to an extraordinary degree."

"I resemble him in every degree, even to the ultimate. I am Christopher Marlowe."

Simon flushed. "It's been a while since we met, more than a year, and I swear my memory is at fault. If you are he – "

"Do you need proof?"

"No, no, by God's truth. I should have said you have changed somewhat."

They went into the grounds of St Peter's where Christopher shamelessly blamed his altered looks on a plate of rank Colchester oysters. Aldrich, who was not blessed with a mercurial mind, appeared to believe him.

"May the Almighty be praised for sparing you, Kit Marlowe," he said in some awe, and told him the gossip about his whereabouts. According to one, he had crossed the waters to live in Flushing. Another said that from there he had gone on to Douai to enter the seminary. A third denied all this and stated that Marlowe had renounced all his writing, turned Puritan and had taken to commerce to earn his living. A fourth said he had been told by someone who knew somebody else in the service of the Cecils – or was it Essex – that the poet had been denounced by a fellow writer as a heretic and an atheist and was secretly taken into custody.

Not that Aldrich was agog for information. Being a collector of names rather than ideas, it was sufficient for him that at a later date he could casually mention that on so- and-so day he had met Marlowe the poet and one-time University Wit. He smugly listed all his highly connected acquaintances that had returned to the city now that the plague had apparently abated.

"And is the young Earl of Southampton in residence?" Christopher asked.

"I'm dining with him and his friends this very evening." He needed little persuasion to present the first half of Christopher's epic poem to the nobleman.

He did not reappear till the last week of April and Christopher was unable to hide his disappointment at the sight of the returned manuscript.

"It was not to his liking then?"

If nothing else, Aldrich had learned to speak in the euphemistic manner of courtly speech. "On the contrary, Henry was loud in his praises. Tell Christopher Marlowe, he said to me, I press him most urgently to complete the glorious task and he'll be handsomely rewarded for his efforts."

Christopher's unspoken thoughts were too acidic for any tongue to taste.

"As for the part he so graciously received, he feared you might not remember upon which point you should continue and yet he could not tolerate being divorced from those mellifluous words. To that end, he enjoined his sometime clerk by the name of Will – Will – "

"Shakespeare?"

"Indeed, the very man. So Henry enjoined his clerk to make a fair copy."

In the following days Christopher alternated between abject despair at his bleak prospects and a determined resolve to struggle out of this morass. In his despondent phases, he felt a strong affinity with Greene's sentiments though not with the man's deathbed repentance: he vowed never to abase himself before God or man. In his angry phases, he cursed idle aristocrats who thought – if they had any thoughts at all in their limited brains – of poets as less value to their households than their dancing master or hairdresser.

Then when his will to survive had cast out the demons of despair, his brave resolutions were shattered by the recurrence of several sores round his lips. This time he would not waste money buying lotions from an apothecary but go to St Bartholomew's Hospital and Doctor Lopez.

He muffled his face with a cloth and left the house but at the corner of the street a woman who lived below him barred his way.

"Yesu, sweet Yesu, be merciful to us," she moaned. "Why must we be so scourged? You do well to cover your mouth with a scented rag but we need more than rue to protect and save us from the pestilence." The woman began to weep."And after all our prayers and penitence, God has turned his back on us."

Chapter forty-four

Lopez's sanctum was as desolate as an ancient tomb and the herbal garden was smothered with torn pallets, soggy piles of rags and broken furniture piled as if for a bonfire. On the top of the last was the Doctor's kneeler.

Christopher strode towards Lopez's kitchen. The scene was one of appalling chaos and clamour. Sacks had been split open, others upended, stills and retorts had been swept off the benches and granules, crystals and broken glass were scattered all over the floor. Everywhere men and women were busy pounding pestles into mortars, scooping up spillage onto the flat surfaces, rolling pasty mixtures between grubby hands or filling small linen bags with powder. Shouting the loudest, as he threw another book into the furnace, was the porter from the main gate.

Much against his inclination to flee from this turmoil, Christopher threaded his way through the turbulence towards the porter and asked for Doctor Lopez.

"You wish to speak with that treacherous, scheming Jew, do you? You're not one of his poisoning spies, are you? If you are, we'll send you flying with a red-hot poker up your arse back to your master in his Holborn palace."

"I seek medication. I have an illness."

"We all have an illness, only ours is called poverty." There was a cackle of agreement from his comrades. "Not like them foreigners, buying up the grand houses and no wonder they can, the way they milk us dry. So you've an illness, have you? Let's see the face of it." He jerked at Christopher's muffler. "God's wounds, you have, a right pockful.I tell you, cully, there's no remedy here for your whorehouse fever." He poked Christopher in the chest with the pestle. "So begone and take your trollop's raspberries with you." At that moment Lopez's deaf and dumb assistant appeared with the Lombardy Balls in his cupped hands.

"You can have them, for all the good they'll do you," the porter said, "but you'll pay me first."

"Why should I pay you? I'll settle with Doctor Lopez."

"Has the rotting pox gone to your ears as well? Didn't you hear me say he's gone?"

"Then call down another doctor. Surely there's more than one in this hospital."

"If you must know, pit-face, them doctors couldn't wait to shake the dust from their heels when the plague broke out again. So much for your great Christian oath to heal and help the sick through thick and thin. And who's left behind? Just us, the dogs-bodies, the runners and fetchers, the cleaners, the cesspit men and the jake-men. Have we fled? By St Anthony's scabby arse, we haven't. Like the good Christians we are, we're sticking by to help the afflicted. Enough of this gab, give me money for them."

As Christopher retraced his steps, the porter followed close behind, clutching the pestle like a small cudgel.

Christopher stopped to have a last look at Lopez's kneeler."I'll let it be known then that when the rich doctors fled in fear of their lives, the humble labourers in the vineyard, true to Christ's teaching, stayed to bring comfort to their suffering fellow creatures."

They now stood by the stairway leading to Lopez's turret room. "With the plague running riot in the streets, there'll be thousands banging at the gate for a cure or a preventative. Thanks be to the all-merciful God, we're able to let them have concoctions to see them through the worse of the pestilence and all we ask in return is a few coins for our troubles."

"What if your concoction kills them?"

"And what if it cures them? Kill or cure, they'll pay for the hope and that's just as much as the doctors do." The porter's shifty eyes glanced up the stairway. "Did you say you're a friend of Lopez?"

"I knew him slightly but yet I thought of him as a perfect Christian gentleman. I recall you once saying he was a living saint."

"Maybe I did and maybe I didn't but I'll tell you this, beneath his Christian sanctus sanctus he's still a Jew and I've had my eyes opened to the conniving tricks of them Hebrews."

"And what opened your eyes?"

"Some drama I saw called The Malta-Jew."

Day after day the spring-time sun shone down on the plague-ravaged city with unaccustomed brilliance. Mangy dogs dragged dead rats through the gutters, the laden carts trundled on their midnight journey beyond Finsbury and the foul air in the rookeries was rent with cries of lamentation and despair. It was all one to Christopher. His own affliction, barely kept in check by the vile Lombardy Balls, was worse than ten pestilences and the miserable state of his purse led him to fear starvation.

A week later he was returning from an early morning foray down Cheapside to buy bread when he was accosted at the street corner by an affluent-looking man whose mouth and nose were swathed with a silken scarf.

"Kit? Kit Marlowe? By God, I nearly failed to – " It was Ingram Frizer. "I was told I'd find you hereabouts but my informant didn't say you'd taken to living in a pig-sty."

"Thank you, Ingram, for your generous praise from one so intimate with swine."

"Marlowe, it's not my wish to come here. I've been commissioned to warn you of grave dangers to your person."

"Surely we're all in danger of the grave."

"Are you aware that the Earl of Essex is now a Privy Councillor?"

"What of it? Why should I deny the golden youth his apotheosis?"

"Among the multitude of enemies you've gathered, Essex is foremost. Remember, also, that you are under sentence of death from Ralegh's friends. The bone and marrow of the matter is this, Marlowe. For your present well-being, Sir Thomas Walsingham has sent you this warning by me and offers you the sanctuary of Scadbury House. I have a carriage waiting beyond Southwark. If we delay, you'll be another nameless corpse thrown into the pits."

"I've learned to live with nameless men."

"And have you learned to live with the rack?"

"I've been racked by hunger and sickness. Name a worse torture."

"Shall I list those in the service of the Privy Council? Your sometime fellow scribbler and oft-time false friend Thomas Kyd has been persuaded by the Privy Council to name names. He has named you as a man of suspect loyalty and the owner of certain heretical tracts."

Chapter forty-five

Francis Bacon was angry. "This is madness. Would you harbour a rabid dog? Yet you shelter a man who can bring shame, disgrace and worse upon all our heads."

"You're somewhat overwrought, Francis," said Walsingham. "There's nothing Marlowe could say or do to implicate you in anything that would impede your ambitions. A dancing master could take lessons from you."

"That is uncalled for, Thomas, and does no credit to your discretion. Marlowe is unstable and it's sufficient for him to blab names. Each one so mentioned will be called upon to give an account of himself. Supposed guilt does not diminish when the questions are painfully pressed. Only yesterday I had occasion to speak with my lord Essex on the judicial paradox arising from such an inquisition."

"Here indeed is a paradox, Francis Bacon," said Frizer mockingly. "Only the day before yesterday you said that the very same Earl was unstable, erratic in his affections, possessed by a quick temper – " Bacon vigorously shook his head. "And furthermore, his rash impulses would one day guide him to the gallows."

"You've deliberately misconstrued a few harmless remarks I made at your table. Perhaps if you'd been more discriminating with those who share your wine-- Why do you impugn my loyalty to a man to whom I owe so much?"

Skeres sniggered and Walsingham turned away as Frizer replied, "Indeed, Francis, we all know how much your family owes." He paused and then added, "With respect to the Earl of Essex."

Bacon glowered."Where is Marlowe now?"

Marlowe had been summoned to appear before the Privy Council at morning sessions in Greenwich to assist them with certain enquiries. "And when he's not about the Council's business," continued Frizer, "he's held under lock and key. For his own safety, I should add. He is, at times, afflicted with convulsive rages arising from his illness."

Bacon looked startled. "Is it the plague?"

"It's a pestilence of a different order," said Skeres, "and as near contagious as the disease of heresy."

"Is he now accused of heresy?"

"A trifling matter blown beyond sensible proportions." Frizer contrived to be casual in reply. "When pressed by the Council, a fellow-scribbler swore that heretical tracts discovered in his chambers rightly belonged to Marlowe.

"Heretical tracts are commonplace among fools," said Bacon. "Why should this concern you?"

"Because, Francis Bacon, because – " Skeres refused to be subdued by Frizer's scowls " – those very heretical tracts were discovered by Marlowe in the Scadbury House library – " Two goblets of wine were overturned as Bacon leaped up from his seat " – with the idiotic compliance of one who should know better." He glared at Frizer. "Marlowe was allowed to take them away for further study."

If the house had been ablaze from wing to wing, Bacon could not have left any faster. Frizer stared morosely at the red pool on the table. "Master Bacon has a mind to change horses," he said, "and it's not yet mid-stream."

"He's too clever by half to do that," Walsingham replied. "For the present, he's content to ride in our ranks while the pace is a steady trot. He's one for the palfrey, not the high horse, and if Essex should call for a precipitous charge, Bacon will plead a lame mount and retire from the skirmish. When the dust has settled, he'll be on the side of the victor."

"And where shall we be on that day?" Skeres asked.

"With your mouth blaring like a badly primed cannon," Frizer snapped, "we'll be fortunate to retire with our skins intact." He poured a dribble of wine into the goblet from the near-depleted flagon. "But, God willing, we'll be here with our pens sharpened to write out our declarations of undying love and fidelity."

"To Essex?"

"To whoever wears the crown of laurels."

"Then let's keep the paper clean till the moment," said Walsingham. "We've been over-hasty with our letters in the past and the pigeon we sent North now threatens to be a carrion crow – " He stopped and frowned at the servant who appeared in the doorway. "What is it, Archer?"

"I beg your pardon, Sir Thomas. I came to clear away – "

"Clear away nothing till you're called. Fetch another flagon of wine." When the servant left, Walsingham said, "I don't trust him. He walks softly and is too willing with his service."

"Say the word, Sir Thomas," said Frizer, "and I'll dismiss him from our hire."

"No, let him be. If we dismiss all those who do not measure up to our trust, we would only be left with the three of us."

"Less than that, I reckon," said Skeres in the tone of a child who suspected he had not had his fair share of sweets. "How often have you excluded me from your confidence? Those imprudent letters sent to the North – "

"It was not our intention, Nicholas, to make you a stranger to our schemes but our concern for your welfare if – "

"If? If the badly primed cannon of my blaring mouth should blow – "

"If, by chance, the nature of our letters to Scotland – "

"Which, in their treasonable folly, vowed our support for one we expect to be our next royal master – "

"Be patient and listen to me, Nicholas," Frizer said. "Whether you knew little then or all now, you are party to our intents and, pray God, such knowledge does not go beyond these walls."

"As far as I'm concerned you can save your prayers for a better cause unless you have cause to fear someone else's primed cannon. Is that it? You spoke of a pigeon becoming a carrion crow."

"Yes, one who threatens to pluck out our eyes. We had thrust those damning letters under the wing of Christopher M--- "

"Christ save us," Skeres cried out. "How long must we suffer the insufferable Christopher Marlowe? It's not enough that Satan protects his own against plague and assassins' daggers but – "

Frizer reminded him of one Christopher Morley, a venal character who would fetch and carry for pennies. This London guttersnipe, whom they had entrusted with those letters, was now demanding a higher price for his silence.

"I know the man," Skeres said, "and I would neither trust nor pay him to exercise my dogs. Why employ him on such a mission?"

"In our cleverness we held his life cheaply," Frizer replied, "and in his cunning he holds our fate dearly. We thought at the time, he being such a noted liar, that if he was caught and named us, none would believe him."

"And who would believe him now?"

"Those who, when we were strong, would have weakly accepted our side of the story. Now, when we are weak, they'll strongly credit him with the truth. Francis Bacon for one."

"Then let's flush the rat from his hole and break his back," Skeres shouted and flourished his sword as if Morley was hiding behind the drapes.

"We've prepared the cheese," said Frizer, "and we'll offer him a nibble at Eleanor Bull's house in Deptford."

With impeccable timing, Walsingham pleaded fatigue and a slight distemper.

"One more or less is of no account," said Frizer smoothly. "I expect our company to be enlarged by another."

"Oh, who else is privy to this affair?" Walsingham asked peevishly. "Half of London and all of Kent before the week's out." He was less than pleased when told that the extra person was to be Robin Poley. "That soured cardinal and prime schemer. Was it not his lapdog Baines who betrayed Marlowe's hiding place to the Privy Council? Why must you recruit him to our business?"

"He is recruited by chance, having just returned from the Hague. He is resting in Deptford."

Walsingham stood up. "Finish this unpleasantry in whatever way you think fit," he said and stalked towards the door where he came face to face with Archer holding a flagon of wine. "How long have you been there?" The servant smirked. "Only this moment, sir."

When they were alone, Skeres muttered to Frizer, "I tell you, Ingram, Marlowe will have to die soon."

"In God's or the devil's good time but not here. Thomas would not look on us too kindly if we were the instruments of his dear friend's demise."

"Then where and when? While Marlowe lives – "

"Your envy is making you a rash fool, Nicholas."

"Don't mock me, Ingram. I'm jealous of my own life and wish for no impediment."

"Let us be rid of the first impediment in Deptford. Then we'll consider the how, where and when of clearing away the second."

Chapter forty-six

In the late afternoon of the 3rd of June, 1593, four men sat around a table in the anteroom of the long hall in Scadbury House. They nibbled at the food without much enthusiasm, drank the wine with a little more brio and talked in the desultory manner of people who wished for more pleasant company.

Poley was his usual dour self, Skeres fidgeted and crumbled bread between his fingers, Walsingham sighed with much heaving of his chest and Frizer growled and fingered the two fresh gashes on his forehead.

"If it pleases God – " said Walsingham for the umpteenth time.

"It didn't please me to be in such a public place," Skeres said, "and I thought to myself, this is folly of the first order – "

Frizer viciously jabbed at a thin slice of lamb. "But you gabbled along with the rest of us in happy compliance until – " He held up the meat skewered by his dagger. "And now I must face charges for a good deed done at a bad moment." He looked towards Poley. "And what do you say, Robin?"

"I'd say it's as good as one in the eye for all big mouths."

Walsingham dabbed his lips with a scented handkerchief. "If it pleases God that this then should be the twist to the tale, then it pleases us. And it is only proper Kit should know of all this."

He instructed Archer to take a set of clean clothes and a basin of washing water up to the invalid and to tell the cook to prepare a bowl of soup. "And when our unfortunate friend is fit and fresh, conduct him into our presence."

Archer barely hid his grimace. Outside he beckoned to the deaf and dumb lackey to follow him. "Fit and fresh, he says, but is it fitting for me to go up to that stink-hole? What if the raving madman scratches me and I'm infected with his fever?"

"To hear him cry aloud in his anguish would wrench a tear from the coldest of cold statues," said Walsingham piously to the others.

"I've heard of walking and talking statues," said Poley, "but none that would recognise the bawling of a diseased brawler."

Frizer was busy chopping the lamb slice into smaller and smaller portions. "But I have heard of statues that bleed and statues that weep and they all sing Papist hymns. How do you account for that?" He turned to Walsingham. "Thomas, let us neither weep nor bleed for Marlowe. You make too much of his ranting and raving."

"And what does he rant and rave?" Poley asked.

"In the paroxysms of his convulsions, he bellows rage against divinity, fate and fortune. These he blames for his malady but he spares his vilest curses for one Doctor Lopez of St Bartholomew's Hospital. He accuses him of poisoning him in vengeance for The Malta-Jew."

Poley appeared to be engrossed in an idea of his own. "So the declared Christian and acclaimed friend of Her Majesty is an undeclared Jew and a poisoner."

"What of it, Robin?" Frizer stabbed another sliver of meat."Do you intend to recruit the doctor to your ranks? I would have thought you had enough poisoners with Baines as your henchman. Where is he now?"

"Below in the kitchen, stuffing his gullet."

Christopher, supported by Archer, appeared in the doorway. Inured though he was to the ravages of battle-field and prison, even Poley was shocked at the sight of the ghastly face.

Walsingham solicitously guided him over to the fire. Coming from a dark, secluded room, the rare brightness tantalised Christopher's eyes. At the sight of Poley, he half-rose from the seat with what sounded like a cry of dread. "There's nothing to fear, Marlowe," said Frizer. "The dead do not live in terror."

"Dead? Living in terror? What cruel joke is this, Ingram Frizer?"

"I assure you, Kit Marlowe, it's not a jest."

"Lucifer would consider it so," said Skeres.

"Then, Nicholas," retorted Walsingham, "since you're on such good terms with the Prince of Darkness, I reckon you should take up abode in his quarters. Ingram, explain to Kit the true meaning of your remark."

Frizer and Skeres had gone to Deptford to greet Poley, who had just disembarked after a long journey.

"Scotland?" Christopher asked wearily. "I wanted to go there myself."

"For what purpose, Marlowe?" Poley asked sharply.

"For the purpose of a drama I had a fancy to prepare, one in which a Scottish lord had ambitions to be king – "

Frizer clattered his dagger on a dish. "Yesu, may I be allowed to continue? As I was saying, hardly had we ordered a meal when an old acquaintance by the name of Christopher Morley appeared and we invited him to join our party at supper for a game of backgammon."

"I also know a Christopher Morley."

"Morley is a common name enough name," Walsingham said quickly. "Did you not share a Cambridge chamber with a Christopher Morley who, it now appears, has turned Papist?"

"And there's Morley, the musician, who had at one time entertained the company in this very house," added Skeres.

Christopher intervened before any more Morleys could be produced. "The Christopher Morley I know is one who was employed by you to carry letters to Scotland." Frizer growled. "I told you at the time, Marlowe, that that weasel was an untrammelled liar."

Christopher took malicious delight in their discomfiture. "I had wondered then why a London punk with rancid breath should have been entrusted with such a mission."

Frizer sucked in his breath and then hurried through the rest of his narration. The backgammon was rather soured by Morley's increasingly irascible behaviour. He accused the other players of cheating, retired to a far corner in a sulk and then, when it came to the reckoning for the food, asserted that it was weighed against him. In an outburst of ill-temper, he attacked Frizer, who was wedged in between Poley and Skeres, and slashed Ingram across the forehead with a dagger. In the struggle to wrest the blade from the demented man, the point was turned and pierced Morley through the right eye.

The story was sufficiently plausible for the jury of sixteen men and the coroner William Danby to reach the verdict that the said Ingram Frizer, in the defence of his own life, had, by accident, slain the said Christopher Morley or Marley with a twelve-pence dagger. They recommended that the said Ingram Frizer and his two co-defendants be cleared of any charge. With documents to be written up and passed from one offical person to another, it would be some time before a pardon could be granted. Without a doubt, the good citizens were anxious to put a healthy distance between themselves and the fast-decomposing corpse; it was the first of June, very hot, and the plague was raging in nearby London.

"What is it to me that you've killed a thief, liar, spy and crawling maggot?" Christopher asked. "Should I weep?"

"Rather, you should laugh," Skeres said. "It's believed by some that the maggots now inhabiting Morley's pierced skull gorge on the brains of Christopher Marlowe."

"I don't understand. Whatever worms possess my body, none have invaded my mind."

"Then let this possess your mind and invade your brain," said Frizer. "In the confusion of the moment, while the stinkard lay dead on Mistress Bull's table, one asked who he was, another said Morley, a third, mishearing, pronounced it Marley, a fourth mumbled Marlar and William Danby cried, 'Is this Christopher Marlowe, scholar and poet? I know him well.' He puckered up his nose as he squinted at the blood-clotted and mutilated face half-masked by a swarm of insolent flies. 'This then is the body of Christopher Marlowe,' declared Coroner Danby and so it was recorded."

"You said or did nothing to disabuse him?"

"And make a liar of so eminent a gentleman?" Skeres sniggered.

Christopher trembled with rage. "Rather a whole kingdom be damned as liars than my existence be a lie. You've perjured me to an untimely grave. Was there not one among the jury who could say anything to the contrary?"

"On the contrary, neither the Chatham grocer, the Limehouse baker, the Lewisham farmer nor the rest of the honest tradesmen knew you or had even heard of the so-called scholar and poet."

"Then I'll go to Deptford and swear an oath I'm Christopher Marlowe. I'll gather witnesses and have them view this miserable Morley before Coroner Danby."

"How will they view one who was buried with great haste in St Nicholas's churchyard?

"He has a grave."

"It is unmarked."

"Mark this then, my birthplace and my baptismal lines are marked in Canterbury and my parents and sisters are not buried in an unmarked grave. They'll bear witness to my living presence." He tried to rise but Skeres and Frizer stood in front of him.

"Listen to reason, Kit," Walsingham said. "There's an intricate design in all this."

"There's only the design of a bird net in this. Do you think I'll wait for you to lime my tail and wring my neck?"

Poley pushed in between Skeres and Frizer and hovered over Christopher. "Do as Sir Thomas so kindly advises you, Marlowe. Hold your tongue and listen." There was a vicious edge to his voice. "I warn you now as I've done so before, there's many in this kingdom who'd see it as their Christian duty to stop your mouth. As it stands, only we, at present – " He glanced over to the doorway where the two manservants stood. "Sir Thomas, are they given to gossip?"

"Not so much as to betray my trust. Their loyalty is never in question."

The old lackey could neither hear or speak and Archer's features were impassive. "I'll see to it," declared Frizer and told him to fetch two stablemen to arrange the following day's hunt.

"As I was saying, Marlowe," Poley continued,"no one but us knows you live and another rots in your grave. Do you imagine the Privy Council are interested in calling upon a dead man to give an account of his presumed heresy? Or did you think that if you appeared to them as one risen from his grave, they'd remain content with gentle questioning?"

"Grasp fortune's gift, Kit," Walsingham pleaded. "Let this house be your covert for three months, six months, perhaps a year, until the politics of the day have taken a turn for the better. If the worst comes to the worst, we'll find you a safe haven in Holland. When you are revealed once again for all to see, we'll say to those who doubted your resurrection that Christopher Marlowe was so near death's door it was as if he had taken residence in a tomb. The reports of his demise confused the substance with the shade." Walsingham smiled benignly. "We'll give you pen, paper, ink and books. Surely there's some drama only asking for peace and quiet?"

Christopher's head was bowed as if he were studying the patterns in the tiles. The fire crackled and the spark of an incinerated insect shot across the floor.

A few seconds elapsed and then Frizer spoke. "We are settled in our agreement and for now and for the world outside these four walls, Christopher Marlowe is dead."

"Christopher Marlowe is not dead!" The sudden shout and his leap from the chair caught them unawares. "I'll tell the world outside that I, Christopher Marlowe, live and breathe." Frizer and Skeres grappled with him while Poley stood to one side and Walsingham fluttered about like a frightened hen.

The two stablemen appeared and Walsingham told them to escort Christopher to his room. "Sweet Yesu, I thought him cured. I must follow them to see he comes to no harm."

When he had gone and the sounds of scuffling had faded, the remaining three went into a huddled conference.

"Marlowe is officially dead," Skeres said. "Who is to gainsay us if we smothered that prattler tonight? He knows about our Scottish mission."

"But not here in Scadbury House," said Frizer. "Timorous Thomas would take it badly if we stopped Marlowe's gob under his roof; you see how fond he is of the blabberer. God knows it would be more comfort to us if he found some comfort in a woman's breast."

"What if Marlowe were to leave this house?" Poley speculated. "There are many cut-throats festering the Pilgrims' Way to Canterbury."

"They wouldn't bother with one who has nothing of value."

"They would if they were offered something of value."

"Let him escape. One of us shall pretend friendship, tell him we were in error and release the bolt."

"No, we'll act with more subtlety. Surely there's one among this gaggle of servants who'd welcome an extra coin in his purse. I never knew a household yet that had none fit to be bribed."

"I beg your pardon, sirs." Archer stood in the doorway. "May I be of service to you? If not, I'll clear away the dishes."

Poley went over to Archer and after a short conversation, returned to Frizer and Skeres.

"It's all arranged," he said. "We shall entertain Sir Thomas with far-fetched tales. Before then, I'll have a word with Baines – "

"I had forgotten him. He'll do the deed."

"No, not him. He shrives himself at night lest he dies in his sleep and must abstain from murder after dark. But his moon-lit sanctity will not spoil his willingness to make others do the deed. I'll send him to Cobham with instructions to one there who is indebted to me."

Skeres was not quite satisfied. "But what if Marlowe chooses a different route?"

"He knows no other route."

Chapter forty-seven

The bolt was slid gently back. A dark figure, holding a candle lantern aloft, stood in the doorway. "Marlowe. Marlowe."

Christopher scurried to crouch away from the light. "Who are you? What do you want? Leave me alone."

"Come, Marlowe, on your feet. I'm setting you free."

"Is that your name for murder."

The figure chuckled. "I'm not your Lightborn executioner nor your pitiful Edward, though while you lie in this sty, you're a pitiful Marlowe. I'm Archer. Perhaps when you dined at the long table, you may have noticed me as you raised your eyes from our grub."

"It was you who rode with me from Canterbury on my last visit to this cursed house."

"We've talked enough, Marlowe. I swear this stench would suffocate a cesspit farmer. Take this leather bottle. It's filled with wine which you'll need for your journey."

They went down several flights of a narrow stairway to a dank passageway. At the end was a small door. Archer removed the cross-beam. "Hurry," he urged.

Christopher was nearly overwhelmed by the heavy scent of damp grass and wet soil.

"Direct me to the Canterbury Road, Archer."

"Set your nose in a different direction. They've arranged to have you killed before you meet the Medway. They hired me to release you, believing you'd make for your parents' home. Go to The Bull Tavern in Bishopsgate Without and tell the landlord I sent you. He'll hide you till friends of Ralegh come to – collect you."

"But Ralegh's friends have pledged to kill me."

"That's in the past. I promise you, they'll welcome you now."

"Why are you helping me?"

Archer gave him a push. "Go to London."

Suddenly Skeres, with a lantern in one hand and a bared sword in the other, stood before them. "Run," Archer screeched. Christopher plunged into the thickets and tumbled into a ditch. Above him came the sounds of scuffling, curses, a half-scream, a gurgle and the thud of a falling body. "Show yourself, Marlowe," Skeres shouted. "I'm not finished with you."

Christopher crawled and wriggled like an eel through the slime of the trench till he had put a fair distance between himself and the small gathering standing over Archer's corpse.

Two servants were ordered to carry the body into the house. "He was a brave, loyal but foolish man," Frizer said loudly,"and I wish he had called for assistance instead of tackling the intruders on his own."

By noon the next day the dead Archer would be given the unlikely status of a hero in every village within a five-mile radius.

"We must see his widow and children do not want," Skeres said unctuously.

There were no pious platitudes uttered later in the anteroom.

Poley stomped up and down and indulged in a stream of profanities. He stopped at the table and leaned over so that he was nearly nose to nose with Skeres. "To London? But where in London? Didn't you even hear that?"

"Archer spoke of The Bull Tavern."

"Surely not Eleanor Bull?"

"No, no, that's Deptford. The Bull Tavern in London."

"Every third tavern in London is called The Bull. Where in London?"

"In my haste to put a stop to the traitor – "

"With you, Skeres, your haste is only equalled by your stupidity."

"It was you who hired a Ralegh spy. I was not fooled. That's why I confronted them –

"And killed the wrong man." Poley said. "We could have extracted information from the living Archer but now he's only fit meat for the dogs. We must search every sewer and gully for Marlowe."

"You're famliar with London's sewers and their rats," Skeres said sulkily. "You go."

"You compound your idiocy with insolence, Skeres. I've an

important mission in the Hague and must return today. Let it be you."

Skeres was most emphatic. "Let the plague take both you and Marlowe but it'll not take me."

"And you, Ingram? Are you less of a coward than Nicholas?"

"If you were less than a conniving fool, Poley, I'd challenge you to justify that slight. I dare not leave Sir Thomas alone to have another of his seizures. He's completely distraught that his dear, sweet Kit has spurned his hospitality."

"Then who can we send?"

"I'll go." They had forgotten the fourth man sitting in a dark corner.

"Don't you fear the pestilence, Baines?"

The fat man closed his piggy eyes. "I place myself in the hands of the Almighty and bow to his will."

"And when you find Marlowe? What will you do?"

"I have vowed before God, inasmuch as the sacred body and blood of Christ aids my temporal mission, to gather all such lost souls as Marlowe into the Lord's granary."

Chapter forty-eight

It was near dusk on the following day when Christopher reached the wooded hillock overlooking the scattered hamlet of Catford. He would have made a better journey of it by taking the well-trod paths but fear of pursuers forced him upon a more devious route. Tired, cold and hungry, with torn and filthy clothes, his only desire was to crawl into some secluded hole like a hunted animal. Perhaps when both cottagers and dogs slept, he could raid the vegetable patches for late spring carrots or turnips. Dodging from tree to tree, he lay down beneath a large flowering bramble, drank the final mouthful of wine and kept a watchful eye on the activities below.

The scene as he saw it was the stuff of a thousand idyllic poems. Swallows swooped through clouds of midges, a braggart thrush asserted his unique song, cattle lowed as they were driven in for milking, dogs barked, scratching fowls clucked, lambs gambolled, men made the first cutting in the drained water-meadows, children shouted in rough play and women washed clothes in the stream. Only one note jarred this pastoral rhapsody. Two drays were slewed across the north end of the road leading into the hamlet and the half-dozen youths standing by this barricade were armed with staves, clubs and pitchforks.

Suddenly the church bell began to ring with clangorous peals and every man, woman and child fit to run and carry a weapon swarmed towards the drays.

A procession of people, many pulling laden handcarts, appeared over the rise and trudged slowly down the road. Some sang hymns but the majority were silent until they were in shouting distance of the obstacles. "For Christ's sake, have mercy on us," they called out. "Milk and bread for the children, in the name of God." The villagers replied with a volley of stones and yells of, "Go back to stinking London. Take your plague with you." Undeterred by the rain of missiles, the plague-refugees pushed on and managed to turn the drays at an angle.

Immediately the villagers charged through the breach and smashed clubs, staves, brooms and other makeshift weapons down on the heads and shoulders of the strangers. The one-sided battle did not last long. Weakened by weariness and hunger, the refugees abandoned their pathetic belongings and scattered.

The villagers broke into separate hunting parties and, with yapping dogs to the fore, chased the fugitives over fields and into the woods. Shouts and screams preceded a ragged bundle of people who clambered up the slope where Christopher lay. In panic, he burrowed into the undergrowth like a frantic rabbit.

Two men, a boy and three dogs panted into view. "There's more of them than us and if they turn on us we'll be hard put to hold our ground."

The boy followed a sniffing cur around the bramble bush. "Here's one, Giles. Here's one, Ned."

"We'll learn him. Bringing his filth to our homes." The man raised his cudgel to strike but his companion grabbed his arm and called the dogs to heel.

"Are you blind, Ned? Can't you see he's a lazar? Look at his scabby face." With a mixture of dread and distaste, the men and boy retreated several paces. Giles suggested setting the dogs on the leper.

"No, we daren't," Ned said. "Old Harry the Smith had his brindle hound bite one of the lazars and next day she went raving mad and had to be put down. There's nothing for it but to burn him out. Let's fetch brands and warn the others there's a lazar on the loose."

When Christopher was sure they had gone, he staggered off in the opposite direction. It was now dark and after an age of aimless wandering and stumbling through briars he sank down on a small grassy embankment. "Is this then the dark wood?" he asked aloud.

"Who's there?" a man asked.

"Mother of divine Yesu," a woman moaned. "Have they found us?"

He recognised the nasal London accent. "Don't be afraid. I'm not a bully-boy." He could just about make out the shapes of several bodies nearby. Someone touched his shoulder. "Yesu, them turnip-eaters have torn your clothes to tatters," a woman said. "We're from Southwark. Weren't going to wait for the plague to cross the river. Where are you from?"

"They'll hear us," warned another woman.

"Let them," a man growled, "and I'll gut them straw-bellies as sure as I do the fish."

"Pity you weren't so quick with your blade when the curs were biting our arses." The woman placed a rough shawl round Christopher's shoulders. It stank of cod and flounders. The soft moan of a woman bewailing the loss of children and chattels was the last sound he heard as he drifted into sleep. When he awoke in the grey light of dawn the living had gone, leaving him in the sole company of a dead old man. A hunk of stale bread, either forgotten by the refugees or left as a kind gift by one of the women, lay by his head. He soaked it in a stream, slowly munched his meagre breakfast and stripped the corpse of its gabardine cloak.

Richard Baines' journey to London had been stalled when his horse went lame. It was an old nag grudgingly given to him from the Walsingham stables, well past its prime and more fit for the knacker's yard than a hard trot to the city. Baines had stayed overnight in a drovers' rest house – straw changed every Monday – two miles down the road from Catford and was now forced to continue his journey on foot.

The early-morning peace of the hamlet was hardly disturbed by the clucking hens and lowing cows and it seemed that the villagers and their dogs were having an extra hour's sleep to recover from their violent exertions of the day before. But not all were resting in their beds. Baines had passed the first cottage when two men brandishing cudgels confronted him. They demanded to know his business and their surly expressions did not alter one whit when he unctuously replied, "May the sacred peace of God be upon you, my sons. As our divine Lord said, I am about my Father's business."

The men appeared perplexed. "Your father's business is not ours. We're not having strangers here."

"Are you strangers to God's work then?"

"We're as good a Christian as you, but we're not having plague-carriers traipsing down our path."

"Truly it is written, do unto others."

"You've had your say, now show us the dust of your heels. We've fields to plough and no time for idle wanderers."

"As you sow, so shall you reap and I'm not one to hold the labourer from his holy toil with idle talk. I'll tell you, in repentance for man's vile sins, I've tramped the stony path along the Pilgrims' Way to Canterbury –

"You've walked all the way there?"

"And all the way back. And while I prayed on bended knees before the tomb of sainted Thomas, God commanded me to go to that Sodom and Gomorrah, that odious cesspit of sin known as London, now stricken for its abominations, where I am to preach among the afflicted and wrestle with the devil for their souls. My sons, Satan and his cohort rule the roost in that damned city."

"My very words, Ned." The men were now persuaded that the rotund person was either a holy fool or a saint. Mindful of their Christian beliefs, they offered him the refreshment of goat's milk, bread and cheese. Baines declined the milk – too strong for a stomach weakened by the rigours of fasting, he told them – and asked for ale as more suitable for his abstemious tastes.

"Do you have many strangers pass this way?" he asked them.

They laughed. "None from London so much as put their foot next nigh or near our homes," they said and gave him an account of yesterday's battle.

"My sons, it's your sacred duty as good Christians to ward off all evil from your children. And tell me, were there others taking the same road as myself?"

"There was that lazar Ned and me found skulking under the brambles. A young lad he was –

"But was he a lazar? He wasn't missing a nose, an ear or a hand. I think he was sickening – "

"Hold your gob, Ned. You said yourself he was one of them lepers. Anyway, he soon shifted himself when we said we were going to burn his arse. That was last night."

"Then Marlowe's not too far ahead," Baines muttered. The men accompanied him to the barricade. "God speed you, holy man," they said. A group of youths grinned, waved and returned to stoking up the burning piles of rags and broken handcarts.

Chapter forty-nine

The pitiful heads, spiked without pity above the arch of the first gateway, gazed with blank eyes towards the environs of St Margaret's Hill and the traffic leaving and entering the city. The dribs and drabs of people coming over London Bridge were not hindered in their departure; but those seeking to pass in the opposite direction were stopped by armed guards and many were turned back.

A string of empty death-carts trundled down from Long Southwark and Christopher, who had been lurking by St Saviour's, joined the party of scavengers walking at the rear. They glanced at him with suspicion but said nothing till they had reached Fish Street. "What's your game?" they demanded. Assuming a whining voice with a nasal accent and plucking at his disreputable clothes, he told them he was hoping to sell any trifles left unattended in deserted houses to buy food for his houseful of starving children. They agreed with each other that everybody must do the best they could for themselves in these hard times. Their only stricture was that he did not interfere with their rightful pickings.

Christopher and the scavengers parted by St Dionis Backchurch at the corner of Fenchurch Street. Though near exhaustion and very hungry – the hunk of soggy bread was his last meal – the nearness of The Bull Tavern in Bishopsgate Without ignited a final spark of energy. If Archer was to be believed, helpful friends might be there. Scorning to slink down alleys, he hurried towards his haven; every step he took lighter than the last.

For a full minute his whole being refused to believe the sight that met his eyes. The tavern's doors were barred and bolted and the black-tarred crosses smeared on the shuttered windows proclaimed that the great leveller, the plague, had paid an earlier visit. In the bleakness of his despair, he cried out an anguished "No! No!" Drained of hope and will, he turned from the bitter scene, blindly jostled against gawpers and, like a grievously wounded animal, staggered down a dark passageway to slump on a pile of rubble.

Someone gave him a kick in the ribs and said, "He's about alive but judging by the state of him, I'd say he's penniless."

Two men, their faces muffled with ragged scarves, stood over him.

"I reckon you're right, Dick," said the second man. "We'll leave him for the carts."

"Dick?" Christopher tried to raise his head and the first man swore as he bent down to have a closer look.

"Do you know him?" the second man asked.

"I did know someone who resembled this bag of skin and bones. He'd have been in better health if he listened to me and paid less heed to his own pride. He had hard words for me when he was cock of the walk but I'm not a man to bear a grudge. Help me to lift him to his feet, Jack."

"You're not taking him to your old place, are you?" Jack asked. "What's in it for us to lug him halfway across the city?"

"I'll carry him myself if you want to spend the day scrounging pennies from dead beggars' pockets, but I won't have a man like him mouldering in a pesthouse."

With their burly arms supporting Christopher, the trio stumbled through alleys and rubbish-filled passages till they came to a group of desolate tenements. They entered one, climbed the stairway to the top landing and went into a small room on the right.

"Who are you? What do you want?" A thin, dead-pale girl lying on a rag-strewn pallet screamed at them. "Go away. Leave me alone. I swear by Christ's bloody wounds, I haven't the plague."

"Shut your maggoty mouth, you raddled whore," Jack shouted at her, "or I'll give you such a kick in the crotch you'll never piss straight again without spattering your feet."

"Let her be," said Dick as he helped Christopher over to a corner by the slit window. "She's a sister, though she bawls to the contrary, and it's our bounden and peculiar duty, in the name of God's own strumpet, to help our own kind."

"He's less than our kind," Jack muttered.

"And it'd be less than kind to leave him for the dogs to lick his sores." The other man shrugged his shoulders and slouched out while Dick stood in the doorway. "I doubt we'll ever meet again, Kit. You could have been one of us but you chose your own path and it has led you here. God or the devil shall visit you but if either are tardy we'll send one after their time who'll offer you peace and comfort." He pulled the drape across the doorway and went down the stairs.

The girl's luminescent face made a startling white oval in the ill-lit room. She groaned and then spoke as if telling a mitigating tale to an unseen figure standing by her feet.

"Did you ever hear such a filthy liar as that Jack and him lower than a jerk-man. I wouldn't wonder if his own wife's a sluttish whore. As for me, God help me, I'm no trugging harlot, I swear by Christ's bleeding wounds I'm not, not in the same way as them big-teat trollops in the Cardinal's Cap or them bawdy-baskets who'd have you up the lane for a penny. Yesu and his holy mother help me, I only came to London to earn a crust for my widowed mother and her with six mouths to feed and I was taken into the Bankside stew to do the cleaning and if I did take a young man or two to my bed it was only to keep everything sweet and it's better than begging – " Her voice trailed away and she began to whimper. "Yesu, Yesu. Save me. Have mercy, Christ, have mercy." Suddenly she cried out, "I burn! Dear Holy Mother of God, I burn!"

There followed a silence in which Christopher held his breath the better to hear her breathing; but there was not a sound.

"God has been merciful, then, in ending your present torture and only God knows what's waiting for you. Should I mumble some Latin to give sanctified solemnity to your departure?"

"You over there, what did you say?" She sounded surprised and spoke in a normal tone. "What are you doing here? Have you brought any drink? Christ's sake, say something. I don't like the dark. What's your name? Mine's Helen, I come from near Chaldon, that's near the Downs. What did you say your name was?"

"I am Christopher Marlowe."

"You lie. He's dead." She shrieked, "Yesu, Yesu, save me, save me. I burn! I thirst! I burn!"

Chapter fifty

When challenged at London Bridge, Baines produced the warrant given to him five years previously in Canterbury by Poley. The bored guard glanced at the insignia, muttered, "On state business, are you?" and waved the holder on. Without looking to left or right, Baines marched across the bridge, up Fish Street into Cornhill, down an alley, turned right through a narrow passage into a backyard and thumped a closed door with his fists. A woman looked out of an upstairs window and called out, "What do you want?"

"A word with Dick Chomley."

"Never heard of him. Go away or I'll empty the pisspot on you."

He stepped back a few paces in case she carried out the threat. "You know Chomley as well as I do and I'll wait here till you give him a message to come out and speak to me."

"Then wait there till you rot. Who do you think you are, banging the arse of a respectable woman's house and telling her to do this and that?"

"Respectable woman's house, is it, Kate Quick? I'd say it's the hottest whorehouse this side of the river and a thieves' den into the bargain. Tell Sly Dick that Richard Baines wants a word with him."

"And what word is that, Baines?" He turned to face a small group of men standing in the mouth of the passage. Each one wore a scarf over his nose and chin.

"Marlowe is the word."

"That's a dead word," said the tallest.

Baines stared hard at the clumsy masks. "I'll try a few living ones. Chomley, for example. And I could recite a litany if asked by the law-officers of this parish."

"Let's take him," another man suggested. "Who's to know?"

"They that sent him, they'll know," said the tall man. "It's better to choose our enemies with more care than our friends. We may need them tomorrow and they'll need us the day afterwards. Baines, Kit Marlowe is beyond your ministration."

"Even so, where is he?"

"Where else than with Dick Chomley? Marlowe may have left before you reach him."

"Left? Where could he go?"

"Where you would also be welcome. Try the gates of Hell."

The drape across the doorway shivered. His limbs ached, the dried scabs itched, his throat felt as if it were lined with grit and the hard breath in his lungs made a rasping whistle. There were no other sounds in the house. Could it be that this tenement, like its recent residents, had been scourged by pestilence and its tired joints, beams and joists had quietly settled down to its final decay? Though the sparse daylight through the slit window had almost vanished and his eyelids seemed rimmed with sand, he could still make out the supine shape of the girl. Her face now had a blue-greenish glow. The drape shivered again.

"Marlowe. Marlowe." Was that the voice of he whom Chomley had promised to send? Or an emissary of God? Or Mephistophilis come to claim his soul?

[Ah, Faustus, now hast thou but one bare hour to live.]

Ah, proud Marlowe, have you but one bare hour, one half-hour, one minute? Fear and panic swelled within him as he tried to shout out to the unseen but his tongue clove to the roof of his mouth.

Yet where was the stench of sulphuric fire? Why was there no thunder clap? No lightning flash? No dreadful tremor as the earth gaped? He only heard his own harsh breathing, smelled the sour ordure of suppurating flesh and saw little beyond the pervading gloom. This surely was Hell and there was no call for a Satanic visitor with an entourage of limb-tearing demons to rend him apart.

He tried to speak but the words only formed in his mind. "If you are Mephistophilis, there's no need to lurk behind a curtain and question my existence. Are you not omniscient? Enter this small, dark room and let you and I, arch-devil and arch-scoffer, sift through our memories, talk of old times and damn the future."

As if accepting Christopher's unvoiced invitation, the drape was pulled to one side and a shape, made large and grotesque by the candle-lantern held aloft, stood just inside the door-frame.

After a moment's hesitation, the figure crossed the floor to swing the lantern over Christopher's face. "Yes, it's you, Marlowe." The voice was familar and yet, for one so close, sounded as though it came from a distant hollow. "Sweet judgement of Divinity, how ugly you've become, so scabbed and scarred, you and your fair features, who were so ready to jeer and jibe at my affliction. I tell you, it was the Almighty's way of testing me when those rats chewed my nose as I lay meditating in my monastic cell. But you, Marlowe, you chose to fly in the face of God with your bile and canker. Your countless contumacious sins are made manifest in those loathsome sores."

The feeble light was held over the girl.

"And who was she? A wasted whore you coaxed in for your last hour of lechery?"

The man put the lamp on the floor and stood outside the radius of its weak glow. Christopher tried to stare at him but the effort made him grimace with pain.

"There's no need to wince, Marlowe, I won't strike you. If you die as you've lived, there'll be enough and plenty torture awaiting your riven soul when it tumbles down that ghastly pit. And you will tumble and tumble till you shriek for respite, but there's no respite in all eternity for the damned. And what about this wretched rancid harlot? Is she now standing, naked and unashamed, before her Maker, without a blemish, washed clean by God's infinite mercy? She will be if by one single act of grace she has brought a lost soul back to Christ. And I too shall stand before the throne of God, straight, upright, pure, this gross body dissolved, this deformed face made bright as the angels when I have wrenched your soul from the claws of Satan."

From somewhere in the city a church bell tolled and the man, intoning a prayer in Latin, measured his orison to the steady rhythm of the chimes. He loudly proclaimed the concluding line, "Pie Yesu Domine, dona eis requiem, Amen," as the final note of the distant bell seeped through the thin walls of the tenement.

"You didn't add your 'amen' to that, did you, Marlowe? But

then, those for whom the prayer is intended would not be expected to respond. Have you forgotten your vulgar Latin? O wrathful day, that day witnessed by David and the Sibyl when nations in ashes lay. What terror awaits us when judgement comes? Yes, Marlowe, think on. What terror awaits us?"

Christopher slowly and painfully shook his head in a vain attempt to banish the dull drumming which increasingly filled his skull.

"Wagging your pate is no reply. Why don't you speak?" The man raised his voice to a shout."Speak, Marlowe, speak. Why don't you answer me? Am I still beneath your contempt?"

A surge of hatred rose within Christopher and its power drove the ache from his limbs, the cold from his fingers and forced violent speech through his teeth.

"You've crawled from the charnel-house, you white stinking slug." Every word was a hot cinder rasping his throat. "You've come to spew your pious vomit over me, have you? Go poison wells with your spoiled-priest's prayers, go suck your meal of rotted flesh and keep company with blow-flies. I'll have none of you." He struggled to rise from his crouching position but his energy was spent and he collapsed.

Baines sniggered. "So proud Marlowe, scourge of God, dies with a curse on his lips. You who made an art of dying with roaring rhetorics spouted by your heroes can only bawl obscenities in your extremities. But then, what are you under the silken cloak of poetry and noble gestures? Nothing more than a street lout, a tavern brawler, a common swearer, an atheist and a playhouse bullyboy. What else can we expect from the rowdy son of a bankrupt shoemaker and a Dover fishwife?"

The coldness in Christopher's fingers and toes crept through his limbs and his lungs felt as if they were clogged with shoddy fibres.

"Has the great prater lost the power to flash and thunder a cannonade of mighty lines?" Baines bent down and placed a leather bottle near the lantern. "Wine, Marlowe, blood-red wine as carnadine as the blood of Christ. Would one drop, one half of a drop, save your soul? Even now while Satan prepares to welcome you to his infernal perch, if you but repent, merciful Christ will pluck you from the claws of eternal damnation. Repent. Here is my body, here is my blood. Repent. A word, Marlowe, a single word of heart-felt contrition, of true remorse and you'll be saved. Speak, Marlowe, speak before it is too late."

Baines waited for a minute for a reply but none came.

"In the past, Marlowe, you've treated me with contempt, vilified me to others, uttered slanders against my person and tried to injure me with your intemperate blade. You believed, and revelled in your error, that I was your enemy whose sole mission in life was to destroy you. How wrong you were. Before God, I am a humble man who in his heart finds room to forgive you for failing to see the true purpose of my endeavours. I have come, not to destroy you, but to save you from your self-created destruction. Yet, in your perversion, you've seen me as the lowest of the low, a spy, a conniver of evil schemes, a liar and one who reeks with the seven deadly sins. I will not deny that I am human, I am venal and, from time to time, I am what men said I am. But am I alone in that? Am I the only sinner?"

He bent down, picked up the leather bottle, removed the stopper and drank a swig. "Bless me, Father, for I have sinned, grievously and wantonly, and for all those transgressions I am truly sorry." He squatted on his haunches and the uncertain glimmer of the lantern gave him the appearance of an over-large toad. "Sweet all-seeing, all-forgiving Yesu, accept my contrite offerings and my own afflicted penances and grace my soul with the sight of your radiant countenance. When I've soiled myself with lechery, wallowed in sloth, been bloated with gluttony, I've lacerated this wilful flesh till I've bled sore and fainted. When I've smouldered with envy and burned with wrath, I've immersed this fevered body in tubs of freezing water. When I've cloaked my covetousness with a sanctified shawl, I've stripped to the elements and ran naked through the furze. Naked we came into this world and naked shall we leave. God, I've suffered greatly for my sins on this earth. What more can I do?"

He drank some more wine and held the bottle towards Christopher.

"One drop, Marlowe, one drop of Christ's blood will save your soul. Ask for his mercy and you'll never thirst." He replaced the stopper and put the bottle on the floor. "O wrathful day, day of ashes. What terror awaits us – and yet the blind fools refuse to recognise my purpose. Know you then that I am on my Father's business, our divine Father who art in heaven, hallowed be thy name, thy kingdom come, thy will be done on earth as it is in heaven. Yes, Marlowe, that's my mission, my sacred design, God's will be done on earth as it is in heaven, thy kingdom come." His voice rose in a ranting lilt. "And this I say unto you, pestilence will sweep the land, cities will burn and rivers run dry, the kine will lie in the fields and birds fall from the sky. Then there shall be weeping and lamentation, palaces and churches shall crumble, the proud and mighty shall wear sackcloth, a storm will arise from the East and man will drink wormwood and eat ashes."

His apocalyptic preaching stopped suddenly on a high note.

"And if I bring one lost soul back to Christ, heaven's vaults will ring with rejoicing. Your soul, Marlowe, is my quarry. Abjure your pact with proud Lucifer and scourge your soul of his most sinful of sins. In pride the dark angels defied God, in pride our first father ate the forbidden fruit and you, Marlowe, are glutted with pride. Yes, in your craven insolence and proud arrogance, you flew in the face of God. Abase yourself, I say, at the feet of Christ. Beg for mercy, beg for forgiveness. Say but one word."

He held the bottle against Christopher's lips.

"One drop, Marlowe, one drop of Christ's blood. Say you repent. Drink of this wine. Here is my blood." He tipped the vessel so that the liquid spilled into Christopher's opened mouth. It trickled out again.

"You refuse to repent! You spurn salvation!" He flung the bottle across the room and, producing a dagger, plunged the blade into Christopher's breast. "Then you are damned for ever more." Again and again he stabbed and with each thrust he cried, "Damned, damned for ever more."

The fury of his outrage possessed him for a full minute. When he was exhausted, he slowly stood up, his face covered with sweat and his limbs shaking uncontrollably. "I've killed him. I am a murderer. Cain, Cain, where is your brother? What have I done? The voice of your brother cries from the bleeding earth. Blood. Christ's blood flows from the firmament." He turned the blade towards the light. "But his blood does not stain this bloodless knife."

He shone the lantern on Christopher's face. The cheeks were drawn and pale, the eyes were wide open and the mouth twisted into a grinning grimace. The dried wine made a mauve stain on the lower lip and chin.

"The same sardonic, contemptuous, superficial smile, Marlowe, even to the last. Are you laughing in hell? Enjoying this final jest with your Satanic master? What a prank to turn Richard Baines from his God-given mission and force him to sin against the Holy Ghost. And I had punished my flesh to make my soul pure. Shall I wander the earth, shunned by man and beast, marked with the sign of Cain?"

He picked up the body in his arms. "How light you are. Was it you soul that weighed so heavy?"

With little effort, he carried his burden out of the room, down the stairs and into an alley. He was breaking the curfew hour and there were no other living people to be seen. He kept to the darkest streets, stopped at every junction and peered round each corner till he came to the river and the ferry steps. There were three boats secured by ropes to the stanchions, two occupied by their sleeping owners. The third was empty and half-beached on the steps. With his back pressed against the damp wall, he sidled crab-wise down the slippery slabs, dropped his load into the vacant craft and untied the hawser. "Who's there?" a sleeper called out as Baines pushed the boat fully into the water and climbed aboard. He put out the oars and rowed to the middle of the Thames. The tide was on the turn and carried on its fast surface current the upstream detritus of tree branches, broken barrels, driftwood, rags and the bloated bodies of drowned animals.

Baines shipped the oars and the boat wobbled as he cradled the dead man in his arms. "Should I say a prayer? I fear it is too late for you. God forbid it's not too late for me. Go then, Marlowe, go to your restless damnation. You'll never haunt me again." The body disappeared under the water for a few seconds after the splash. Then it reappeared further on, the pale face floating just above the ripples and turning as if taking a final look at Baines.

He watched until it had vanished in the quickening rush under London Bridge and then, dipping the oars in the river, rowed across to the Surrey side.